The Life and Times of Precious Meat

Miles Coleman

COLEMAN BOOKS

Coleman Books
4484 Jackam Ridge Court
Lithonia, Georgia 30038

First Edition: July 2017

Published in North America by Miles Coleman. For information, please contact Miles Coleman at 4484 Jackam Ridge Court, Lithonia, Georgia 30038.

This book is a work of fiction. Any resemblance to actual persons, living or dead, events, or locales is entirely coincidental.

Library of Congress Cataloguing-In-Publication Data
Miles Coleman
The Life and Times of Precious Meat/Miles Coleman– 1st ed
p. cm.
Library of Congress Control Number: 2017910567
ISBN – 978-1-941859-68-1

1. **FICTION** / Erotica / General. 2. **FICTION** / Erotica / Gay. 3. **FICTION** / Erotica / BDSM. 4. **FICTION** / LGBT / Gay.

10 9 8 7 6 5 4 3 2 1

Comments about *The Life and Times of Precious Meat* and requests for additional copies, book club rates and author speaking appearances may be addressed to Miles Coleman, or you can send your comments and requests via e-mail to longdistancerunner@comcast.net.

Also available as an eBook from Internet retailers

Printed in the United States of America

For Laura Bell Coleman

"The best mother ever"

This is the story of Precious Meat. After years of being sexually abused by his crackhead mom's boyfriends, he soon noticed how much the men admired his prodigious tool. Soon they started paying him for the pleasure of it. After a while he made enough money for breast surgery and became a transsexual that calls herself Precious Meat. After her popularity grew, she started blackmailing her clients, which gets her into hot water. So she leaves her hometown of Detroit to come to Atlanta, where she's soon involved in a blackmail that leads to murder.

THE LIFE AND TIMES OF PRECIOUS MEAT

The Life and Times of

PRECIOUS MEAT

Miles Coleman

Chapter 1
Lust at First Sight

The morning started out like many Saturday mornings in the Evans family household. Gwen was running around trying to get her two kids, John Jr. and Maya, ready for their soccer games, while her husband, John, was sleeping off a hangover. He has been drinking and smoking weed heavily for months now, and Gwen was very worried. Being a probation officer meant that he'd get drug tested every year, so she was worried he would lose his job. If John lost his job, then they would lose the beautiful home they'd been living in for the last three years.

How could he ever get another job if his urine was dirty? Gwen thought as she ran around the house, retrieving the kid's uniforms. Before leaving, she went to say goodbye to him. He was sound asleep, so she woke him up.

"Hey baby, we gettin ready to go. Just wanted to say goodbye."

"I don't givva fuck!," he snarled, angry. "You woke me up just for that? Jeez! Leave me the fuck alone when I'm sleeping!" He put the pillow over his head and commenced to snoring and farting.

Gwen recoiled at her husband's behavior and left the room with tears in her eyes. *How could this bastard talk to her that way? She was a good wife and a very good mother to their children.* But she cringed at the reflection as she passed by the full-length mirror in the hallway. At five-feet-two-inches and 220 pounds, she was definitely fat. Not thick and sexy—bordering on obese. *When did this happen?* she thought, viewing herself in disgust.

At 33 years old, she went from being a thick redbone who turned guys heads to becoming that fat chick that people laughed at under their breath. After dieting for months, Gwen was bewildered that she was gaining weight instead of losing it. Waddling downstairs, she told the kids to get in the car, while she grabbed the last two Krispy Kreme donuts from the fridge. Warming them in the microwave made them soft and juicy, with the sweet aroma of sugar wafting through the air. Feeling guilty and excited at the same time, she swallowed them down whole, barely chewing. With her appetite sated for the time being, she hurried out to the car, huffing and puffing all the way.

"Y'all put your seatbelts on."

The children obeyed, and off they went to Redan Park, which was about 20 minutes from their house. Gwen didn't want to stand out in the cold-ass, chilly Atlanta weather all morning. At the end of November, it would be a cold blistery morning. If John was any kind of father, he would have been there and she could have stayed home in the nice central-heat atmosphere.

The more she thought about him, the angrier she got, and the cold, windy weather exacerbated her anger. While the kids ran over to their respective teams, Gwen began gossiping and laughing with the other mothers, trying to forget about her miserable existence, if only for a few moments.

"How you doin, Mrs. Evans?" a voice behind her asked. It was one of her students, Tyrique. His little sister was on the same team as Maya.

"I'm doin fine. How about you?"

Gwen couldn't help but admire this young teen's slim, muscular body and broad shoulders. His smooth chocolate skin glistened against the bright sun and contrasted with his pretty white teeth. At 17, he was "a sexy young thang," and Gwen could feel her panties moisten, like a young girl head over heels in love.

"I'm studying for my SAT. Hope to get at least a 2100 on it. I plan on going to either Georgia Tech or Kennesaw State when I graduate."

"Oh, I'm so proud of you! As smart as you are, anything's possible."

Tyrique was one of her best students at Lithonia High School. She taught 12th grade Algebra as well as Physics, and having a student like Tyrique made her job so enjoyable.

"Thank you, ma'am," he whispered, staring at the ground. "Can I ask you a question?" Before she could answer he blurted out, "Can I take you to the prom?"

Gwen was startled by his question, yet at the same she was thrilled that this fine young boy wanted her sexually. She imagined him jerking his big dick, thinking about her.

"You know I can't be your prom date, Tyrique, but I'm flattered that you asked. Besides, I know a good-looking young man like you can have any girl he wants."

Pleased by her compliment Tyrique continued, "But they don't look like you, Mrs. Evans."

"I find that hard to believe. I'm 33, and I've put on a few pounds. Don't you want one of those cute little slim girls that I see flirting with you all the time?"

"Not really. I like big women like my mama," Tyrique insisted.

Since Tyrique's father left two years earlier, he had been the man of the family—which included providing sex for his mom, Ophelia. What started out as innocent wrestling one night turned into full-fledged lust, when mom spied him playing with his penis while watching porn on the computer.

Ophelia hadn't been touched by a man in over two years, so to say that she was horny was an understatement. Her son's cock was big—like his father's. She was amazed at how manly her baby boy had become, and she shamefully threw herself on him like a wanton whore. Ever since that night, Tyrique had a thing for older, chubby women, like his mom.

"Whoa! You like women with some meat on their bones, huh?" Gwen asked. "But like I said—I can't honey, but thanks for asking."

They hugged and she wished him good luck on the SAT exam.

Tyrique walked away feeling good about himself. He had asked his teacher to the prom. Even though the young flirt knew what the answer would be, he couldn't wait to see Mrs. Evans in class on Monday. He loved the way her thighs rubbed together when she walked and how sweet she smelled.

As Tyrique watched his mom talking with the others, his dick got hard, so he went back to their car to jerk-off. It was a thrill to jerk-off in public, and he came fast, imagining a threesome with his mom and Mrs. Evans. With a vision of fucking Mrs. Evans doggy-style while she ate his mom's pussy, he shot thick cum all over his shirt. After relaxing for a moment, he turned the radio to V-103 and fell asleep in the nice warm Honda, listening to Rhianna.

****

About an hour after the wife and kids left, John finally woke from his drunken sleep. He felt like there was a freight train running through his head, and his stomach boiled over with indigestion. He ran to the bathroom and took a nice, relaxing shit. It was good to relieve his body of all the poisonous, bile substances he consumed the night before.

After brushing the teeth and showering, he went out to the garage to retrieve his weed and secret computer that he kept hidden. Rolling a fat joint, he puffed until a nice buzz permeated through his skull and he begin to relax. Then he went to one of his favorite websites: *backpage.com*. The website marketed everything, from soap to prostitution, like Craigslist did. John went to the TS Escort section and began shopping for a big-black-dick transsexual.

Even though John carried himself as a masculine heterosexual, he had a thing for trannys or she-males that started five years earlier in New Orleans. While in the Big Easy, he met a beautiful, chocolate transsexual, named Kyla Longwood, and boy was her wood long, he remembered fondly! After nutting in "her" beautiful fat ass, she turned him over and savagely invaded his virgin anus with her big stick. John protested initially, but she knew he really wanted it, and she gave it to him.

Kyla liked it raw, so the bitch didn't bother putting on a condom, knowing that this down-low drunk faggot didn't care anyway. At first, John told her to stop and put a rubber on, but she kept stroking, and his protests got weaker as the pleasure increased. When she cummed in him, it was like he died and went to heaven.

He enjoyed the feeling of his ass being taken and fucked like a woman. Kyla made him feel like a nasty slut when she took her dick out of his asshole and made him lick it clean. She laughed and degraded him about his little penis while she stuffed his mouth with her 11 inches. He liked how filthy he felt, begging for her dick and licking her beautiful feet while she called him every despicable name under the sun. She left him in the Sheraton with wet cum in his ass and dried cum on his lips. Ever since that wonderful first experience, trannies had been his muse and inspiration! At 34, they were an addiction that couldn't be controlled or tamed.

John had gone to Pleasers, a strip club over on Cleveland Avenue the night before. The chocolate honeys there made him horny as hell. Instead of going home to get some pussy from his wife after leaving the club, he went on the stroll in Midtown, looking for tranny dick. Atlanta was home to the most beautiful black transsexuals in the world, and he felt lucky to be in their midst. Plenty of girls were on the stroll, but the police were riding hot and heavy.

One girl was especially fine, thick and dark, and he just knew she had a big dick, so he pulled up beside her to chat. But before he could talk to her, the police pulled up behind him, flashed his lights

and told him to move along. John did not want to be picked up for solicitation—especially with a fucking she-male. He could just hear the snickering in the courtroom when they saw who he was trying to pick-up—not to mention how embarrassed the family would be to see their loved one stoop so low as to buy sex from a man dressed like a woman.

After that, he directed his Toyota Corolla to Interstate 20 and drove home to Lithonia, dreading the thought of getting in bed with his gassy, snoring wife. The funk was so strong in their bedroom that some nights, he regretted not buying a gas mask. What the hell did she eat to make her farts smell like they came from the depths of hell?

The house was quiet when he got in at 1:00 am. He fixed himself a peanut butter and jelly sandwich and ate at the kitchen table. After washing the sandwich down with a glass of wine, he quietly went to bed, trying not to disturb Gwen. She woke briefly and said something to him before dozing off. John fell asleep as soon as his head hit the pillow, with visions of big black dicks dancing through the brain.

Looking through the numerous ads on Backpage, John couldn't believe how beautiful and sexy some of them were. Damn! A lot of them looked better than real women—much better-looking than his chubby wife. There were so many that he was having a hard time choosing one. Then he saw an ad from the chick he was going to pick up earlier before the police made him move along.

Her name was Precious Meat. She was 24 years old, 5 feet-ten-inches, 170 thick pounds, and she supposedly had a ten-inch cock. With her dark skin and strong jaw-line, she reminded him of Indie Arie—only better looking. Precious, like most trannies, wasn't passable, but she was still cute and described herself as being a dominant top. This meant that she does the fucking, while the guy bends over and takes it up the ass.

John went gaga when he saw her ad and immediately called to make a date for later that night. He imagined his ass being violated by this strong, big-dick bitch. He could feel his barely 4-inch-long dick getting hard just looking at her picture. At five-feet-four-inches and weighing 130 pounds, John wasn't exactly a woman's idea of masculinity, and he knew it. Maybe that's why he liked to be fucked, he surmised—because a small penis could make any normal man feel inadequate.

Ever since high school, he had been self-conscious about having a tiny dick. It's why he always hated gym class. More precisely, he hated showering after gym class. He couldn't believe how big some of his classmate's cocks were. One guy who was nicknamed Horse would proudly walk around with no towel in the locker room, displaying his huge, ebony manhood for all to see and admire. John and the others would steal envious glances at his prodigious dick, wishing they had one half as big. It's bad enough for a man to have a small penis, but *it was doubly-bad for a black man*, he thought. Urban myth says black men are supposed to be big, but not every black man was hung like a horse, and John was exhibit "A" for that fact.

After getting off the phone with Precious, John hid the computer and weed back in the garage and started dinner. He knew Gwen would be pissed at him about the previous night and for cursing at her that morning, but things would go a lot smoother if dinner was ready when she got home.. *Soothe the fat, angry beast with food and wine*, John thought. He marinated some short ribs and put them in the oven at 300 degrees, and he then cut up some ham hocks for the collard greens. After putting the collard greens on the stove, he watched TV and cleaned the house.

****

Standing between two soccer fields, Gwen simultaneously watched both of her kids' boring games at the same time. She tried to get her head into the games, but it was so damn cold. Like a lot of the other parents, she didn't care which team won. She just wanted it to be over quick.

She found herself thinking about Tyrique and how his invitation might affect their student-teacher relationship. She felt apprehensive about seeing the boy in class on Monday. Would he feel resentful toward her and make things difficult, or would he just turn his attention somewhere else and forget about her? *Probably the latter,* she thought, but Gwen felt a tinge of disappointment in her heart if that happened. Not that she wanted to sleep with the young boy, but it was nice to feel wanted for a change.

Gwen and John made love about twice a month, and the lovemaking seemed forced and hurried. As soon as he got his nut, which was always too fast, she was left feeling frustrated and unfulfilled most of the time. As small as her husband's penis was, the

least he could do was eat her out or something. It wasn't like she was asking for anything out of the ordinary. She had come to terms with John's mini-baby-maker in college.

What he didn't have in penis size he more than made up with his big heart. After growing up in a single-parent household, she was determined to find a decent man and not fall in love with thug after thug, like her mom did. That's how she felt when they were young and in love with each other. But now, after 12 years of marriage and two kids, the love seems to have faded.

Woman's' intuition told her John was seeing other women, but she couldn't bring herself to confront him about it. She was afraid to ask him because of what she might discover. Or maybe she didn't confront him because deep-down in her heart, the love was gone. Both thoughts scared her.

Gwen definitely didn't want to get a divorce, even if John was being unfaithful. *He was only doing what men have been doing for thousands of years. If screwing around makes him happy, then who was she to take that happiness away.* She couldn't believe she was taking such a defeatist attitude. It wasn't exactly Oprah-esque, but damn Oprah—she's got a billion dollars, and she still can't get a man!

Gwen decided that whatever it would take to save their marriage, she was going to do it. If that meant letting John have his fun, then so be it. The last thing she wanted was her kids growing up in a broken family like she did. But Gwen was getting tired of her trusty vibrator and John's infrequent quickies, like his little dick-ass was doing her a favor! If he was so disgusted with her body, maybe she should find someone who wasn't. Find a big-dick-BBW-lover who appreciated all her soft curves and big floppy tits. Why should John be the only one to have his cake and eat it too?

Before John, she had been with only one other man, and that man was her brother, Dale. He took her virginity when she was 14 and he was 16. While she was taking a shower one day, he came in took his clothes off and jumped in with her. Despite her protests, he started tickling her and playing with her long, hard nipples until they both got aroused to the point of no return. As his dick kept growing, her mouth dropped open, staring at how big it got. He put his finger up her vice grip tight vagina until it become wet enough for his monstrous cock to enter. Then he bent her over and inserted his throbbing penis in from behind.

It hurt bad, like a hot poker being rammed in her. He stroked his little traumatized sister long, hard and deep until blood started gushing down her legs. Dale knew that this meant that his little sis had been a virgin, and his excitement ramped up furiously. Gwen freaked when she saw the blood and told Dale to stop, but her begging only made him fuck her harder and harder. Gwen's forehead was banging on the shower wall as Dale pounded her like this was going to be his last fuck on earth.

Finally, he let out an animal like guttural sound and ejaculated a load of baby-making juice into his sister's deflowered womb. After finishing, the boy seemed ashamed of what he did and left quietly. Gwen felt both violated and aroused at the same time. After a week or so of feeling awkward around each other, they couldn't fight their lust any longer.

One night, while mom and one of her many boyfriends were asleep, Gwen sneaked into her brother's room and they fucked like rabbits. They had to make love on the floor because his bed was too noisy, Gwen remembered. The last time her and Dale made love was right before she met John 12 years earlier. Gwen wondered what she would do if she walked in and saw JJ banging his little sister. They were very close, hardly ever fought and sometimes slept together, but they were too young to be thinking about sex.

Maybe she would do what her mother did when she caught Dale banging her. She remembered Mama had a surprised look on her face when she came into his room and found her daughter riding her son's cock. She simply turned around and closed the door without saying a word. The next day, she took Gwen to the clinic to get birth control pills. Later, Gwen found out why her mom said nothing. It was because Dale was fucking Mama too, a fact Gwen didn't learn until Mama got drunk and told her the night of the junior prom. Instead of it tearing the family apart, they became closer than ever, like the Three Musketeers.

Finally, both of Gwen's children's games were finished, and not a moment too soon. She was hungry, horny, and Burger King was calling. *Ain't nothing like a Double Whopper with Cheese to ease the stress and chase the blues away!* Gwen drove to the nearest Burger King, which was on Panola Road, ordered a Triple Whopper with Cheese and a milkshake for her, and she ordered two kid's meals.

They ate in the car because the restaurant was crowded, with too many bad-ass kids running around. She was in a state of bliss, slowly

devouring the massive sandwich in silence, while her offspring chatted away. Looking at the kids through the rearview mirror, she noticed them holding hands and thought it was so sweet. *No one could say they weren't a beautiful family.*

After finishing lunch, Gwen called John and asked if he wanted anything, which he didn't. He asked her to hurry home because he was about to put the ribs in the oven for dinner . It was good news to Gwen. Even though she just got through eating a one-pound sandwich and a large milkshake, hunger was right around the corner.

In busy traffic, she put the minivan in gear heading home to Willowbrook Subdivision off Stephenson Road. She couldn't wait to take a shit and a nice, long bubble bath with a glass of wine and her vibrator. Gwen smiled, remembering her vibrator needed batteries, so she stopped at the Texaco to get two AAA-batteries.

****

John grimaced as his family pulled up in the driveway. Putting on a happy smile, he went out to greet them

"There's my two soccer stars! Did y'all win?" he shouted, grinning from ear to ear.

"Yeah, Daddy—we both won. My team won 2-1, and JJ's team won 3-0," Maya volunteered. She wanted her daddy to come watch them play, but he always seemed too busy.

John kissed and hugged his wife as they walked in the house. The smell of ribs wafted throughout, making Gwen hungry again though she had eaten less than an hour earlier. John could see that she anticipated the ribs without her saying a word. He went to the master bathroom and drew a bath for his wife, knowing that by acting right and playing the good husband, there wouldn't be any argument when he went to meet Precious later. He didn't care what Gwen would say anyway. John needed some dick, and his wife wasn't going to stop him from accomplishing that feat.

After drawing her bath, he got a bottle of wine from the pantry and poured Gwen a large glass, not only to relax her, but to make her drowsy after the large meal she would certainly eat. When she was stuffed and plastered, Gwen usually nodded off in front of the TV, snoring like a buzz saw. In that drunken state, a nuclear bomb could explode right outside the house, and it wouldn't wake her.

Sometimes, John could leave for hours, and she wouldn't even know, unless he told her.

"Gwen, baby, the water's ready," John called in a sweet, syrupy voice, designed to ease his wife's anger about his morning outburst.

When he went to help her with the kids, he arrived just in time to see his son's big tool swinging between his skinny young legs. JJ was laughing and playing, oblivious about how lucky he was to have a large third leg. Looking at his offspring's dick, John felt like he was back in gym class again. *Jesus!* he thought, *How can his 12-year-old son's dick be bigger than his dad's? Did Gwen notice it too?* She seemed to be looking at JJ with a mysterious smile on her face.

Gwen had told the kids to undress and take a bath while she waited for John to run hers. Neither Gwen nor John saw anything wrong with Maya and her brother taking a bath together. The children undressed and got in the soapy water, all the while giggling and tickling each other. The way they played with each other reminded Gwen of her relationship with Dale growing up.

And she couldn't help but notice how big John Jr.'s penis was! Even without an erection, it was bigger than her husband's when he was fully-hard. She wondered if John noticed how much she was staring at her son when he came to tell her that the bath was ready. She watched her husband's eyes lock onto JJ's penis like a laser beam as the youngster rubbed soap all over his nubile body.

As a father, he was jealous and felt emasculated, *or was he proud of his son*, she wondered. After telling the kids not to get water on the floor, she went to soak in her bubble bath and tune the rest of the world out. Taking a long sip of wine, she inserted the vibrator into her vagina and had disgusting carnal thoughts about her son. She felt ashamed of her thoughts, but she couldn't help herself. After a few orgasms, Gwen nodded off with the thoughts of sex and ribs running through her inebriated mind.

Meanwhile, John went to check on dinner and found himself having conflicting thoughts about what he had seen. Noticing his erection, John wondered if looking at his children's naked body turned him on. If JJ's penis was about 5-inches while soft, *how big it must be when he was hard!* John surmised. *God! It must be ten or eleven inches, and he's only a twelve-year-old kid!* And his testicles were already the size of golf balls, easily dwarfing Johns' pea size nuts.

Maya was also cute, with her tits starting to grow and blossom. Her dark nipples reminded John of chocolate chips, just waiting to be

mom and dad for dinner, both a little older and wiser than when they got up that morning to go to their soccer games.

****

Gwen dried herself off, put on one of her raggedy nightgowns sans panties, and she waddled downstairs in the direction of the kitchen, her tits and big ass jiggling like jello. John and the kids were already seated and eating when she sat. After saying a silent blessing, she heaped her plate full of ribs and collard greens and began munching, like she hadn't eaten in days. The triple Whopper with cheese and large chocolate milkshake she had earlier were long-forgotten memories as Gwen tore the meat off the ribs like a hyena.

JJ giggled, watching his mom scarf down her food so fast. She paid him no mind and continued to eat until getting her fill, which meant eating a whole slab of ribs by herself. She could see the disgusted look on John's face. How she hated these judgmental stares he gave her, like she was a bad little girl! Why did he care how much she ate? He hardly ever touched her lately anyway.

Gwen found herself missing John's little penis. They hadn't made love in over a month, and she was getting hornier by the day. Her husband might have been small and only lasted 15 minutes tops, but he was better than a damn vibrator!

She noticed the kids were silent and wondered what they were up to. Gwen though she heard strange noises coming from Mayas room when she was taking her bath. It almost sounded like sex. Could her two little ones have been doing the dirty deed? *No, they're too young*, she thought to herself while sucking on a rib bone.

After eating, she helped clear the table, put the dirty dishes in the dishwasher, poured herself a glass of wine and plopped down in front of the big screen TV with John and the kids. It was 8 p.m., and yet by 9, she was snoring like a pregnant horse. When she was drunk and full of food, Gwen was oblivious to the world.

John's plan had worked to perfection: *get his wife drunk and feed her, and she'll be out like a light.* While the kids watched TV, John went to get dressed for his date with Precious. First, he took a nice long shit, because he didn't want a mess when Precious stuck her ten-inch pipe in him. He didn't want her dick to get shitty while she fucked him, which would have been awfully embarrassing.

After shitting, John gave himself an enema to make sure his rectum was completely free of any excrement. The shower felt good, as John could feel his body slowly begin to relax under the pulsating warm, soapy water. It had been a long, boring day, and now he was ready to have some fun. With Gwen snoring in front of the TV, he knew she would be too tired to argue about him leaving.

Standing naked in front of the mirror, John rubbed baby oil all over his body, while cursing his small penis. Then he splashed himself with some *Aramis* cologne and got dressed. After putting on a blue polo shirt and beige cargo slacks, he decided to wear penny loafers instead of sneakers, because the loafers made him look more mature. He hated older mature guys like himself who always dressed in sneakers, like they were teenagers.

He finally finished grooming, grabbed his keys off the dresser and headed downstairs to say goodbye before leaving. Entering the living room, the kids were on the floor playing Metal Gear Solid, while Gwen was stretched out on the couch, asleep. He told the kids he would be back soon and not to let anyone inside. Then he made sure all the doors were locked before leaving.

While in the garage, the down-low husband called Precious on the cell, telling her he was on the way. Backing out of the driveway, John had no idea how much that night would affect the rest of his life. He drove, annoyed by all the traffic and slow drivers on Panola Road. *Where did all this traffic come from?* he wondered while pulling into Bank of America to get Precious's $300 fee.

Chapter 2
Precious Meat

Tavarious Wilson, aka "Precious Meat," was born January 6, 1988 at Detroit Medical Center in downtown Detroit. He was born to a crack-head mother and a father who was killed in prison before Tavarious turned two years old. They lived in the Charles Terrace housing projects where his mom, Marsha, turned tricks to pay the bills. By the time he turned 10, Tavarious was used to seeing his mom getting fucked by numerous men at all times of the day and night. It's not like she tried very hard to hide it.

Some of the men walked around naked in front of him with their dicks swaying from side to side while he pretended not to look. They seemed oblivious to his presence or didn't care one way or the other. He would hear the constant creaking of his mom's bedsprings while she worked to feed her sons. But some of the men were nice, especially Larry, who would always pat Tavarious on the butt and tell him how cute he was. Tavarious would just smile and blush, not knowing what else to do but grateful for the attention.

Marsha had three sons, but her favorite by far was Tavarious. By the time he was eight, it was apparent that he was gay, but Marsha didn't care. As a matter of fact, she encouraged his feminine behavior. She let his hair grow like a girl's, and she even showed him how to put on makeup. When Tavarious turned fourteen, he carried himself full-time as a girl, and Marsha saw nothing wrong with it. He went to school and stayed out of trouble with the law, after all.

Her other two sons were doing time in the penitentiary. The oldest, Tommy, was sentenced to 20 years for rape and armed robbery, serving his sentence in Jackson. He robbed a Korean grocery store and would have gotten away with it if he hadn't bound the family with duct tape before raping their 15-year-old virgin daughter until her vagina bled so much that she almost died. Tommy didn't know the damage a big black penis could do to a little Korean girl. If he had known, he wouldn't have done it. But he was high as hell on crack and wasn't thinking straight. And not only did Tommy rape the little girl, but he did it in front of her mother and father.

When the facts emerged at the trial, the courtroom was noticeably shaken. The fact that he only got 20 years was testament to a sympathetic, all-black jury who probably didn't like "chinks." When Tommy walked through the prison gates at 22 years old, he

had no way of knowing that he wouldn't reach his 23rd birthday. Three months later, a riot broke out and Tommy was stabbed over fifty times with a filed toothbrush, sharpened like a knife. He bled out before they got him to the infirmary. At 22 years old, he was just another statistic—a dead black man who died at the hands of another black man.

Tavarious' other brother, Juquan, was doing time at the Huron Valley Correctional Complex in Ypsilanti for second-degree murder. He killed his girlfriend when he caught her fucking another dude. Juquan let the guy go before pumping three bullets in the woman's head as she begged for her life. Then he turned himself in to the police and pled guilty when the DA reduced the charges from first to second-degree murder. The judge sentenced him to 25 years, which meant Juquan would be 44 when he got out—if he served the entire sentence.

Juquan cried like a baby after hearing how long his "paid state vacation" would be. When he was 19, he was scared about his life's prospects, but he knew not to show any fear. Upon hearing about Tommys' death, he promised himself to survive no matter what. With "good time" behavior, his lawyer calculated that he would only have to serve 18 years. Not that 18 years wasn't a lot of time, but it was better than 25. At only five-feet-five-inches and 140 pounds, he had to fight off numerous rape attempts until he was befriended by a big bad guard named Willie.

Willie was about six-feet-five and must have weighed over 300 pounds. He used to play college football for Michigan State and played a few years in the NFL. Even the baddest of the bad didn't fuck with this big black nigga. Juquan was grateful for Willie's kindness and asked what he wanted in return. After about six months, Willie confronted him in the library.

"Yo dude, why we gotta play these games? I'm gonna come right out and say it: I wanna fuck your little cute ass." "But I've never been with a dude before, and I aint no faggot," Juquan protested.

"I didn't say you was, did I? I just wanna be more than friends. Nobody will know."

Willie took Juquans' right hand and placed it on his dick until it reached its full nine inches of hardness.

"You like this big dick?" he asked in a low husky voice.

Juquan didn't say anything at first since he was so taken aback by what was happening. He wasn't a fag, but he knew that without

Willie, he would've been raped and sold for cigarettes a long time earlier. Realizing what had to be done to survive, he answered.

"Yeah, I like it," Juquan said as he caressed Willie's meat through his uniform. Willie then threw his arm around Juquan, and they walked to the storage room, locking the door behind them.

Unzipping his pants, Willie told Juquan to get on his knees and then pulled out his dick and moaned softly while putting it in Juquan's mouth. This was his first-time sucking dick, but a man knows how to please another man. He tried to suck on Willie like his dead girl used to suck him, and apparently, it felt pretty good, judging by all the moaning coming from the big nigga. After ten minutes, Willie started fucking him in the mouth, like it was a pussy. The faster he stroked, the more excited he became until finally his dick exploded in Juquan's mouth. There was so much cum than it was running down both sides of his chin. Willie made him swallow all of it before zipping his pants up to go back to guard duty, leaving Juquan crying on his knees, with cum all over his face.

Before leaving, Willie said, "Tomorrow, I'm gonna get that pussy! You hear me, boy? Stop that damn crying. I'm the best friend you got in here."

Feeling relaxed after his nut, Willie smiled and left. Juquan realized that this was going to be his life at least for the next 18 years and the weight of it hit like a sledge hammer. After a few minutes, he gathered himself then went to the bathroom to wash his mouth out. Wiping the dried cum from his face, Juquan thought about what would happen if he refused Willie's advances. He would have probably ended up with AIDS, with all these niggas clamoring after his young virgin ass, he deduced. And if he was gonna have a boyfriend, it was better that the boyfriend was a guard who was feared by the baddest motherfuckers in the place.

What he didn't realize was that Willie was not only going to use him for sex, but also as a means to make money off his plump, chocolate butt. Young cute guys in prison were the equivalent of a Playboy model, and Willie knew he had a goldmine in Juquan. Of course, Juquan didn't know it at the moment. He was concerned with the present. *Fuck the future!* For the present, he had to do what Willie said or pay "God knows whatever" price for refusing it.

That night at home Willie couldn't keep his perverted mind off Juquan. He was so horny that he nutted in his wife, Gina's, asshole twice, imagining that it was his cute young boy-toy. Willie screwed

Gina in the ass more than in her pussy. He convinced her that it was better that way, because there was no chance of pregnancy. What she didn't know was that her husband was down-low and had been since college. After playing two injury-filled seasons in the NFL, Willie decided to take advantage of his Criminal Justice degree and got a job in the real world.

Injuries had taken a toll on him, and he was tired of being hurt and in pain all the time. Being a seventh-round draft choice, he felt grateful for his playing career, though it ended much too soon. Law enforcement was his second love, and to have a well-paying job as a prison guard was a dream come true. Having control over hundreds of black men kept his dick hard as a brick. Watching them shower and walk around naked was enough to make a man go insane with lust.

Sometimes to satisfy his lust, Willie took a prisoner out of his cell, handcuffed his hands behind his back and fucked the hell out of him. The shocked, surprised and frightened look on the unsuspecting prisoner heightened the intensity of the experience. He wasn't the only guard doing it. The prison staff had so much control over the prisoners that an inmate who complained would be found dead, usually beaten to death by other prisoners. The guards simply put a contract on the would-be snitch, and sooner or later, the contract was fulfilled.

For a carton of cigarettes, those crazy motherfuckers would do anything, least of all kill a nigga. Life inside a state prison was cheap, and the guards knew how to take advantage of that fact. Unlike the movies where the inmates supposedly ran the prison, guards controlled everything in real life. They controlled the dope coming in, the gambling and even the sex trade. If someone smuggling dope to an inmate was caught, that inmate was severely beaten as a warning to the others who might try it. But contraband was still smuggled in. After all, they were dealing with a bunch of murderers, rapists and assorted scum of the earth who had problems obeying authority. That is precisely why they wound up at Huron Valley in the first place. Willie went to bed with a smile on his face, thinking about Juquan's juicy booty. Before drifting off to sleep, he realized that he had the best job in the world, a job where he could look at big asses and big dicks all day. *God sure is good!* he thought.

Willie awoke the next morning feeling relaxed and eager to get to work. Dressing, he was gone before Gina rose from her deep

sleep. Thinking about Juquan, he could hardly contain the hard-on in his pants. Instead of jerking-off like he usually did, he wanted to save the first nut of the day for his boy-toy. Before leaving the house, he made a big lunch, because the prison cafeteria food, even though it was free, tasted horrible. Besides he didn't like inmates fixing his food, because they probably spit in it.

The most important items that he took with him were the extra-large condoms that he carried for protection. The condoms provided by the prison were of lower quality, and they had a tendency to tear and were less sensitive than the Trojans that he used.

Pulling into the parking lot at work, Willie damn near ran to clock in and then went straight to Juquan's cell. The inmates had finished breakfast and were back in their bunks before being let out in the yard. When Juquan heard the footsteps coming toward his cell, he knew by the cadence that it was Willie coming to fuck him. The keys rattled as the door opened and two guards appeared in the doorway. One of the guards was an old redneck named Otis, and the other was Willie. Otis told Juquan's cellmate to turn around, cuffing him and leading him out into the yard, while Willie closed and locked the door behind them.

Eyeing his cutie like a wolf eyes a small doe, Willie grabbed Juquan in a bear hug and planted a kiss on his soft, scared lips. Juquan was taken aback but didn't dare resist. Willie tore off the prisoner's clothes and laid him on his back with legs spread out, his virgin ass puckered, ready to be poked. Willie unzipped his pants, put the condom over his massive meat and got on top of Juquan, savoring every lustful moment. He wanted to get naked, but only had 15 minutes before he would be missed.

He took the KY jelly out and instructed Juquan to lubricate his big tool with it. Juquan obeyed, squeezing the lubricant on his hands then a running his hands over every inch of Willie's black dick as the big guard moaned in ecstasy. When it was lubricated to Willie's satisfaction, he spread Juquan's legs as wide as they would spread and slammed his dick in hard and rough. Even though it only went in a couple of inches, Juquan let out a yelp when the dick tore through his insides.

Juquan felt like a woman as this man on top of him repeatedly slammed his once virgin ass with stroke after lustful stroke. Juquan told him to go slow, but he may as well have been talking to a tree, because Willie wasn't listening at all. The harder he fucked, the more

Juquan screamed in pain, from the serious beating his anus was enduring. He screamed so loud that inmates in the next cell could hear the familiar cries and pleas for help, but he knew nobody would come to help.

Willie was grunting like a wild animal as he penetrated deeper and deeper into the crevices of Juquan's booty. Finally, he reached the deepest he could go as his testicles slapped against Juquan's now bloody butt cheeks. The rhythmic slapping of his balls against Juquan's fat blood-stained butt excited Willie beyond comprehension. Why did the pain and humiliation of others turn him on so much?

With Juquan crying and tears running down his face, Willie's strokes got slower and slower. He wanted to savor the sight of Juquan's cute ass, squirming and pleading for him to stop. He loved raping virgins, especially cute chocolate ones. When he could stand it no more, Willie's body tensed up and let out a loud guttural sound as he came like he never came before.

He lay on top of Juquan for a few minutes to gather himself and rest. Juquan was relieved that it was over with and wanted this big nigga off him pronto. Finally, Willie pulled his semi hard dick out, took the condom off, which by that time was covered with blood and shit. After flushing it down the toilet, he left without saying a word, with a satisfied look on his face. Juquan just lay in bed in the fetal position while blood and shit oozed out of his ass. This had by far been the worse eleven minutes of Juquan's life.

He remained Willie's jailhouse bitch for about a year, with Willie fucking him at least once a week, but suddenly the big guard stopped coming around. Juquan was right when he suspected that Willie had found another young boy to rape. In the library one day, he saw his former lover with a young, light-skinned teen, who was in for murdering his grandparents. Willie was "all up" on the boy, gazing with lust into his eyes. Then he took the boy and marched him into the same storage room where he and Juquan had been a year earlier.

When Juquan saw them, he grew jealous and angry. He had grown to love getting fucked and used by Willie, and being Willie's main piece of ass had its benefits. One of those was his job in the kitchen, the most coveted job in any prison. Food, like currency, was a tradable commodity in prison, and food could be traded for drugs or cigarettes.

Another benefit in the kitchen was being able to make hooch or rotgut alcohol. By combining fruit and vegetables in a plastic bag and

letting it ferment for about a week, the result was alcohol—not exactly a top-shelf spirit, but it got people drunk nonetheless.

Yet the main advantage that Juquan received from his relationship with Willie was protection from the other inmates. Nobody dared mess with him, because they knew he was Willie's bitch. However, he soon found out he had nothing to worry about. He had been incarcerated for two years by that time, so knew his way around the prison politics. As time went on, he got a new cellmate and they became lovers.

Although he went to prison 100% heterosexual, the loneliness and boredom made him lust after other men. He figured, *why deny myself the love and comfort of a companion, even if that companion happened to have a dick like me.* Juquan ceased thinking about pussy because it only made him bitter. *Why think about something that I can't get for at least 20 years?* After a while, a man's asshole feels just like pussy—even if it did stink sometimes.

****

At 17 years old, Tavarious quit school and put an ad in Backpage, advertising his services as a transsexual escort. He thought of numerous names to call his new persona, and he finally settled on "Precious Meat." The name seemed appropriate because his meat was indeed tasty and precious. Marsha encouraged his new enterprise and let him use their house for his dates for safety sake. Being a transsexual prostitute was dangerous work, so she didn't want anything to happen to her baby.

Meeting the men at their house served another purpose for Marsha, allowing her to make sure Precious got paid. Soon, Precious became popular, especially with older black men. She charged $200 an hour, depending on what the guy wanted. Usually they wanted to suck her dick and get fucked, but sometimes they wanted to be pissed on, humiliated and whipped. For these extra services, the price went up to $300 or more.

Marsha was amazed at how much money her "new daughter" was making. One month, Precious made over $3000, which was a hell of a lot more her mother made "selling pussy." After talking to some of her she-male friends, they convinced Precious to launch her own website. After putting a webcam in her room, she was able to make and put X-rated mini-movies on the site. Each movie was 20

minutes long, usually consisting of her screwing the daylights out of some nigga, who wore a ski mask to hide his identity.

Customers could watch by subscribing to her website for a monthly fee, which was paid through PayPal. This venture proved profitable, and after a year, she made enough to have breast-enhancement surgery.

Precious didn't go overboard like a lot of the girls. Instead, she settled for a 34B cup—not too small or too big, but just right. With her new breasts, her confidence went through the roof. She had been thinking about moving to her own place, but she didn't want to leave her mom. Yet life has a way of making up a person's mind.

One day, Precious caught Marsha stealing money from her secret hiding place. She didn't confront her mom, whose crack habit was out of control. Precious was also tired of paying damn near all the bills, while her mama blew her welfare check on liquor, cigarettes and crack.

When Precious shared her plans, Marsha tried to talk her out of it, but it was no use. She assured her mother that she would come see her every day, but both knew she was lying, as Precious wanted to be free from that scheming junkie.

A few weeks after telling Marsha her intentions, Precious moved into the Windsor Tower apartments on Antietam Ave in downtown Detroit. While admiring the view from her 6th-story bedroom window, she hatched a plan to make some real money. Having her own apartment meant that she could attract a more upscale clientele instead of the same old niggas that ask for discounts and shit.

She decided to deal strictly with white men in future business. Crackers were scared to come to the hood to see her, but they wouldn't be afraid to visit the new place. She also decided that she was going to put hidden cameras throughout the apartment to blackmail her clients. She was going to film them from the moment they walked in the door until they left and everything in between.

But she had to be careful to pick the right sucker. The guy she chose had to have something to lose by being exposed.. Ideally, he would have a family and a stable job—in other words, someone who would do anything to prevent his secret craving for black dick from getting out. If Precious played it right, she hoped to make at least a five-figure income per customer.

After three days, she had her first client, a chubby white guy in his twenties, who called himself "Steve." Even though he wasn't the

ideal candidate, she figured to try her scheme out on him to see how it went. There were two cameras in the bedroom—one disguised as a clock and the other as a teddy bear— to capture every angle and every grunt of their wild sex. She watched the tape after Steve left, laughing out loud at how easy this shit was going to be.

She decided to wait a couple of days before she threatened Steve with the tape. She didn't want any mistakes, so she had to be careful and not be too hasty. One wrong move could land her in jail, or dead like her two brothers.

Precious had no idea how Steve or any of her clients would react to being blackmailed, but she figured he would pay, because the consequences would be too great if he didn't. Precious knew she was playing a dangerous game, but the lure of money drove her. She wanted to maximize her money quickly, because being a tranny prostitute wasn't a long-term career.

She didn't want to be walking the streets in her 30s like some of her friends did. Instead of saving money when they were young and cute, they blew it on drugs and clothes. Most of them now lived in cheap motels, tricking for 50 bucks a pop. Precious shuddered at the thought of living like that. Visions of being broke and homeless ran through her head, making her determined to take advantage of her youth and beauty.

These faggot crackers in love with her huge black dick would make it the best year of her life. A week later, she called Steve and told him she had something for him. When he asked what it was, Precious insisted for him to come by her apartment the next day at 5 p.m. so she could give it to him.

Steve was surprised to hear from the tranny and wondered what the hell she had for him. He hadn't left his wallet or cell phone at the apartment. He wondered if she was going to reveal that she has HIV. Worried, he didn't get a lick of sleep that night.

When morning came, he called in sick to his job, where he was the day-shift manager at Burger King. With three drug possession felonies on his record, he felt lucky to have any job. At 27 years old, he decided to settle down, stop smoking crack and get a job.

For the last 18 months, he had been a faithful employee at one of the world's most popular burger joints, though it wasn't the life he or his parents envisioned for him. Feeling the need to measure up to two successful older siblings, he succumbed to the pressure and sought to relieve that stress by using drugs.

After getting a scholarship to Western Michigan, he was kicked out after the first semester for smoking crack in the dorm. He promised his family he'd go back to school, but all he did was sleep all day and party all night. After a while, it became apparent to his parents that their son was a junkie. After weighing their options, they had him admitted to Narconon Freedom Center, a rehab facility in Albion, about 100 miles west of Detroit.

Narconon was the first of four rehab centers that he would endure before finally caging the demon of addiction. When Steve got out of the Freedom Center, he didn't last a week before he was back sucking the glass dick. One night, after coming home high as hell, his parents confronted him about $400 he had stolen from them earlier. It wasn't the first time that money came up missing, so they were tired of Steve's thievery. After a bitter argument, they told him to pack his bags and leave.

Initially, he thought they were bluffing, but he discovered they weren't when his mom called the police. Weeping, his parents shut the door in his face. It was challenging to be homeless in Detroit, especially since it was winter. He wandered about until he found a homeless shelter for the night.

After a couple of weeks on the streets, Steve started prostituting to survive. His parents cut him off financially, so the only way to make any money was sucking dick or getting fucked. Being young, he was a favorite of the older white fags, who would take him to get drugs and then fuck the shit out of him while he smoked the mood-altering crack cocaine. After three months, he was so strung out that sleeping under cars or in rat infested alley ways became the norm.

Steve didn't care where he laid his head at night, because no matter where he slept, the first thing he thought of was where was he going to get crack that day. A junkie might start the day off broke as hell, but he'll know that he's going to get some dope, someway somehow, before the day is over. . Finally, after being on the streets for five months, weak and strung out, Steve decided to go home.

While struggling up the stone steps, he rang the doorbell and collapsed from exhaustion. He awoke a week later in Sinai Grace Hospital with three tubes stuck in his arms. His parents were at his bedside. After hugging him, they told him that they made plans for him to go back to rehab. He agreed and he went back to the Freedom Center for 90 days. However, it required two additional

stints at the Freedom Center before Steve finally straightened himself out.

While preparing to go see Precious, he thought about how far he had come in the last five years. Holding down a job and apartment was unimaginable just a few years before. The former junkie was proud of how far he had come, even if the apartment was raggedy and the job only paid ten bucks an hour, with no overtime.

He had to start somewhere, even if it meant flipping burgers. While his two brothers had advanced college degrees and made six-figure salaries with bonuses and paid vacations, he had made a little over $20,000, according to his last tax return.

After getting dressed, he locked his apartment and went down to the corner to catch the bus. When the bus arrived, it was so crowded that he had to stand in the aisle. The ride to Carmen's was slow and noisy as the bus snaked its way through rush-hour traffic. At exactly 4:43, the bus let Steve out in front of his destination. Nervous, he walked slowly to Carmen's apartment. He knocked three times.

"Who is it?" a voice from inside asked.

"It's me… Steve."

The door opened after a moment, but only as far as the chain lock would allow. Carmen noticed how disheveled and pitiful Steve looked and faked a smile to put him at ease.

"Here. I have something you need to see," she said, handing him a disk through the opening.

"What is it?" Steve asked.

"You'll see when you get home," she said, shutting the door in his face.

He felt even more bewildered than before, and so turning, he left, anxious to get home and view the disk. He thought it was a present, or a reward for letting Carmen cum in his mouth. She did say he was the best dick-sucker she ever had. Not to brag, but he drained every dick his lips touched, and he was proud of it.

After watching the disk, he realized Carmen was trying to blackmail him. The bitch actually demanded that he pay her ten thousand dollars… or she would show the disk to his family and coworkers on YouTube. Steve couldn't believe this nigger-bitch was trying to set up his broke ass! After calming down and drinking a beer he, called the devious ho.

"Hello?" Precious answered, trying to sound innocent.

"You black ape! You got some fucking nerve! I don't have any money! And if I did, I wouldn't give none of it to you!" he shouted at the top of his lungs.

She was stunned by his angry reaction.

"Well, if you don't pay muthafucka, it's yo ass. The whole world gonna know you a cock-sucking faggot."

"Listen, you nigger ape—I work at motherfucking Burger King and don't have no goddamn ten grand, you silly bitch! And I don't care who you tell because my parents and coworkers know I'm gay. Now go fuck yourself, you disease-carrying monkey. And by the way, I'm going to put an ad in Backpage, telling everybody about your scheme!"

Before she had a chance to respond, he hung up, feeling satisfied. After making a ham sandwich, he watched the disk over and over, jerking-off numerous times, until his gonads were empty. He was angry about what Precious tried to do, but he still desired her. Now he had to look through Backpage and find another big-dick sista to worship.

Precious didn't know what to do when the faggot hung up on her. At first, she thought about calling back, but what good would that do? He was calling her all kind of racist names, so he probably couldn't be reasoned with while he was angry. She realized how foolish she was to run her game on broke-ass Steve.

Reflecting on their first encounter, she realized the cheap blue slacks he was wearing looked like part of a fast food workers uniform. And right before Precious made him gag on her penis, the punk mentioned that he had taken the bus to come see her. *Jesus, how could she have been so blind?* Yet there was a silver lining in the experience: next time, she wouldn't make the same foolish mistake. Stunned by the incident, she didn't take any clients for a few days.

After feeling more comfortable about things, Precious put the unfortunate episode behind her and busied herself with being the best tranny prostitute in Detroit. A month later, she put her wicked scheme in action again after meeting Walter Finster.

Walter was a white down-lo fag from Pontiac. He was 56, married for 31 years, with three kids and seven grandchildren. Precious immediately liked the sucker the minute she opened the door to let him in. He had a pleasantness that made anyone in his presence feel relaxed.

He wasn't a bad fellow to look at either, considering his age. At five-feet-six, he was slightly paunchy, but he had few wrinkles and didn't wear a damn toupee like a lot of her other clients. There is nothing worse than a fag sucking your dick and his wig falls off, due to sweat. Precious liked men who weren't afraid to show their bald heads to the world.

During their first encounter, he only wanted her to cum in his mouth, for which he paid $500 for the privilege. After gargling with mouthwash that he brought with him, they talked roughly 15 minutes—about everything from sports to President Obama. Being an experienced businesswoman had taught Precious that the best way to get repeat business was good customer service. That's why she didn't rush Walter and let him stay and talk.

Sometimes she felt like a cross between a ho and a psychiatrist. But weren't they basically the same thing? Both were people who strangers give money to in exchange for making themselves feel better. And if said service is good, they're more than willing to come back and spend their money. When Walter got up to leave, she escorted him to the door and did something she hardly ever did. She gave him a deep French kiss, sticking her tongue deep inside the fag's mouth, surprising him with her passion. He made an appointment for the next day and thanked her for the wonderful evening.

Precious thought he could be the one to make her dreams come true if she played her cards right… or it could be a nightmare, depending on which side of the fence you're on. Watching him suck her dick on the hidden camera, she realized how much he enjoyed the endeavor. She was going to get to know her prey before she struck this time. Time was precious and not to be wasted.

****

Walter dreaded going home to his wife and hoped she was asleep. After three decades of marriage, he was tired of the old bat. Not that he didn't have love any for her, it's just that life has a way of beating you down, and the weariness of familiarity makes one cold. They hadn't had sex in over five years because of Walters's prostate cancer, which rendered him unable to get an erection. It was a perfect excuse for his lack of affection, but sometimes he wondered if she thought he wasn't a man anymore.

As he pulled into the driveway, the house was dark, except for the porch lights. He gathered himself for a few minutes before he entered. Suddenly, guilt racked his mind as he considered what would happen if Edith his wife found out about his fondness for chocolate men. First, there would be a divorce, wherein he would lose the house and all his savings. His kids would look at him with shame and disgust. But after ten years of sucking black dick, he still couldn't resist the lure of "nigger meat," but besides his family, he also had coworkers who could never find out. As vice president of one of the most prestigious accounting firms in Michigan, his reputation would be mud if his perverted lifestyle was revealed. He cursed himself for leading a reckless double life.

Edith was sleeping soundly with a half empty bottle of Jameson's whisky on the nightstand. It was obvious what she'd been doing all night, which was drinking her depression away. He took a quiet shower and brushed his teeth to wash away the taste of Carmen's salty cum from his mouth. Kissing Edith on the forehead, he closed his eyes and soon fell asleep.

Walter woke up the next morning well-rested and horny as hell. After a hot shower, he put on a charcoal gray suit with a light blue shirt and gray neck tie. After Edith shouted that breakfast was ready, he sauntered downstairs in a very good mood. They ate silently, and Walter downed a plate of pancakes and eggs, while Edith, hung over from the night before, had black coffee.

Sitting across from his wife, he couldn't help but notice how old and ugly she had become. God, she used to be so damn pretty! and now she looked like a bag of wrinkles. He wondered if she was getting any dick. Even though it was farfetched, it wasn't implausible. If anyone told his friends that he liked black transsexuals, they would say that that was unbelievable. But unbelievable doesn't mean it's not true.

He wished his wife was getting some dick, because life is too short to be unhappy. After finishing off his plate, he kissed her wrinkled cheek and practically ran down to the garage. After starting the black BMW, he called his secretary to tell her he would be a little late that morning. Then he pointed the car south and headed straight for Detroit.

He arrived at Precious' place 9:30 a.m., eager to get fucked. Anxious and nervous, he counted out five crisp 100-dollar bills and handed them to the new love of his life. Precious directed him to the

bedroom and undressed him, putting his clothes on a hanger and hanging them in the closet so they wouldn't get wrinkled.

"You ready for this black meat, baby?" She loved to exert her power over puny white men.

"I been thinking about you all night," Walter replied, his voice dripping with lust.

Precious, eyeing him like a cat eyes a mouse, put on an extra-large Trojan condom and turned the fag over on his stomach. She was too horny for foreplay, she just wanted some ass. Licking his lips with anticipation, Walter winced as her meat penetrated his old asshole. Finally, he loosened up and enjoyed the slow rhythmic motion of her glorious penis. She stroked him nice and slow, like they were lovers rather than john and prostitute.

He moaned in delight with each long stroke of her massive dick. The tranny had complete control over the old fag, and that's how she liked it. She also instinctively knew how Walter wanted it too. As her balls slapped against Walter's skinny butt, they slowly filled up with baby-making juice. After about 30 minutes, she couldn't hold back any longer. When she asked if he wanted her to cum in his butt or his mouth, he chose his mouth. She turned him over, pulled her condom off and made him suck before shooting a huge sticky load down his throat.

After swallowing every drop, he laid his head on her silicone breast and nodded off. She let him sleep in her arms, confident of her power over him. This fool was love-struck and practically begging to be taken advantage off.

When Walter awoke, he was surprised to find the tranny's arms wrapped around him, like she cared.

"How long have I been sleeping?" he asked.

"Oh, about an hour. You feelin better now, boo?" she inquired in a low sultry voice while stroking his bald head.

"With you, I always feel good. I love being dominated by your big manly dick. Damn, I wished I didn't have to go to the office!"

Precious called a suggestion as he put on his clothes.

"Well, you don't have to go, baby. You can relax here as long as you want."

A look of serenity overtook Walter as he dropped his pants on the floor and enthusiastically jumped back in bed, wrinkles be damned.

Precious let Walter talk for over an hour, learning more than she needed to blackmail him. It seemed like these faggot johns felt comfortable sharing with prostitutes because they knew prostitutes wouldn't judge them harshly. He poured his heart out, and it must have been cathartic because he revealed secrets about himself that he never told anyone else.

She learned that he always had a yearning for black men since college, but he was afraid to act on it until about ten years earlier. The old fag even told her that he belonged to Grace Lutheran Church, and the pastor was probably gay. From there, Walter told the big-dick-bitch that prostate cancer left him with a permanent limp dick and how it affected his marriage. He revealed how guilty he felt screwing around on Edith and the shame of what would happen if family found out about his alternative lifestyle.

Finally, after seeming to run out of words, he got dressed and left for the office. It was one o'clock and time to get to work. Being with Precious made him feel on top of the world, and he was hooked like a schoolboy who had a crush on the hot teacher.

After the old freak left, Precious was very pleased when she viewed the fuck session on camera. She downloaded the content onto the computer, burned it onto a compact disk and hid it with the other two, under the rug in the corner of the room. With people coming in and out so much, she wasn't taking any chances on it being stolen. Soon, another depressed old fag would be ringing the doorbell, so she took a quick shower and oiled her body with lotion from head to toe until she was glistening.

White men loved seeing her dark ebony body, all shiny and sweaty. Their mouths would pant like Pavlov's dog in anticipation of her bone. She decided to see Walter two more times before threatening him with the disks. When the doorbell rang, she turned her attention to her next client. Sauntering to the door butt-naked, dick swinging from side, she peered through the peephole and opened the door with a smile on her face. The john's jaw dropped as Precious stood there, glistening like the sun, her big shiny dick standing at attention. Her penis was so hard that he could have done chin-ups on it if he wasn't so fat.

She ushered the trick in and immediately made the sucker get on his knees and lick her feet. She couldn't believe how much these white men loved to get humiliated and fucked like bitches in heat. Looking down at the fool licking her toes, the big-dick-tranny

realized how much she loved her job. Another fag comes to drain her dick and give her money. Life was good.

After their fourth date, Precious decided to give Walter the downloaded disks from the hidden cameras. But instead of giving the disks to him at the crib, she told him to meet her at Regine's, a popular black gay club on the west side of Detroit. Reflecting on the blowout he had with Steve, she was cautious. This was her golden opportunity to cash in, and she didn't want to blow it.

She told the fag to meet her out front of the club at 11:00 p.m. the next day, which was on Thursday. She also mentioned that she had a present for him. The following day, she could hardly wait, thinking about all the money this down-low fool was going to fork over to her. The power of the dick is mightier than the sword, it seemed.

After taking a shower, she dressed in some tight-fitting jeans silk blue blouse and four-inch Joey Peep-Toe Pumps by Mark Fisher. She was looking fierce and damn well knew it. Heads turned when she walked in the front door of the club 9:30. At 6' 2" with heels on, she was hard to miss. The beautiful tranny stationed herself at the bar and ordered a mojito to relax her nerves.

The club was crowded, with mostly male sissies and a scattering of dykes, but to her surprise, there were no trannies. Precious rarely went to gay clubs, because she really didn't like being around a bunch of drama-loving faggots. And in the gay community it was a well-known fact that gays and transsexuals didn't get along. In the eyes of many gays, she-males and transsexuals were almost seen as "freaks." This bothered Precious, but she knew jealousy was driving the fags to hate. They were mad that they couldn't pull men like a fine tranny could. After a second drink, she began to wonder if Walter was going to show up. It was almost 11:00, and he hadn't called.

Walter was wondering what kind of present his big-dick-bitch had for him. Earlier, at dinner with the family, all he thought about was the present. Even though they had become very tight, he thought, *why would the nigger-tranny give him a gift?* Maybe she had feelings for him, and this was her way of expressing them. It was his hope, because she was all he thought about. After lying to Edith about where he was going, he drove to Detroit as fast as he could. When he reached the club, he parked in the near empty parking lot in the back and called Precious to tell her he had arrived. After five minutes, she came out, strutting like a proud peacock. Upon seeing

her, his eyes filled with lust. As she got nearer, he could see the imprint of her dick snaking down her thigh through the jeans. *Damn she didn't even tuck that big thing!*

"Hey baby, glad you could make it," Precious said as she entered the car. Then she gave him a big kiss on his thin lips.

"You know I can't resist you!" Walter said, trying to conceal his eagerness for her. "What is it that you wanted to give me?"

"Well, it's a big snake in my pants and it needs to be resuscitated baby. Look at it and see how limp it is. If you put your mouth on it, it may just come back to life." She unzipped her jeans and pushed Walter down on her throbbing chocolate penis. "You like this dick don't you baby" Precious whispered hoarsely, sounding like a man.

Walter said nothing, but how could he when she was pumping his mouth up and down her dick like a damn piston. After five minutes, Carmen shot off in his mouth as he gagged for dear life, almost choking on the sheer amount of her thick creamy load. They both laughed as he took out a silk handkerchief and wiped the cum off his face and lips.

"Wow, you taste so good! I wish I could have you every day."

"You just saying that. You know you don't really want me, but it is nice of you to say so."

"But I do want you! How can I prove it?"

Precious studied him and revealed the compact disks that she had gift-wrapped, giving them to Walter.

"Now don't open this until I leave," she told him.

"What's this?" he asked, seeming bewildered.

"That's your present, silly. You thought all I had for you was some dick?"

"Why can't I open it now?"

"Damn baby, because I said so. Why you gotta give a bitch a hard time? Look, I just didn't want to be getting all mushy and shit, so that's why I ask you to open it when I'm gone, that's all. Now give me some sugar. I gotta go, faggot."

They hugged and said their goodbye as Walter pushed $300 into her hand. She thanked him and returned to the club for another drink and to check out which sissy-boy she wanted to take back to the crib and fuck.

She had been eyeing a cute young boy who looked like a teenager before Walter showed up. Not only did he look young, but the boy seemed scared and out of place. And he had a backpack with

him—probably a sign that he was homeless or had no place to go. Yet he came in there, knowing those depressed faggots would buy him drinks in order to get his tender young ass in bed. It was either the club or the Detroit Rescue Mission, a rundown homeless shelter.

Having to fuck, suck or give up his booty was of little consequence to him, because the shelters were filthy and dangerous, especially for kids, and he would rather sleep with a strange faggot than in a lice infected bed at the Mission. He seemed to be doing well, sitting with two old bald queens, who were not trying to hide their lust for the cute boy. Everything he said seemed to elicit boisterous laughter from the chubby queens. And the kid was nodding in agreement with everything his new benefactors were saying, because he knew they knew he had no place to go, and he felt safe with them.

After being on the streets for three months, the boy had a sense of who was out to harm him and who just wanted to freak with him. Sensing that these two old dudes were okay, he let them buy him drinks.

Precious wanted to go talk to the boy, but she didn't want any drama with his fag friends. She thought he was too adorable to pass up, so she waited for the right moment, which came when the queens got up to go piss, leaving their prey alone. She walked right up to the youngster who seemed surprised and pleased by her approach.

"What's your name, sexy," Precious whispered in his ear over the loud hip-hop music, blasting from the sound system.

"Carlos Houston," he said in a drunken, sleepy voice.

Carlos was on his third drink and was feeling lightheaded. Being on the streets was tiresome, and it had taken its toll on him.

"You ever been with a transsexual before? Do you know what one is?"

"I ain't never been with one, but you like that Rupaul cat, right?" he laughed.

"Yeah, something like that. You wanna go home with me?"

"Well, I'm already going home with somebody."

"You mean them two fat freaks you sitting with? I know you not choosing them over me, are you? Let's go."

She must have been convincing, because after a moment of contemplation, Carlos agreed and off they went. Precious felt powerful that night—first, with Walter, and now luring this obviously underage boy back to the crib to fuck him until the cows came home.

She hoped his ass hadn't been deflowered, because *ain't nothing better than being the first dick to explore a virgin's rectum!* In her line of work virgins were kind of scarce.

When Carlos's companions came back to the table, they were surprised to find out their young meat left them for an ugly-ass tranny. Damn, they were only gone for about five minutes! These bitches be scandalous!

When Precious and Carlos got in the car, she suddenly realized how young he really looked, and he also smelled like shit.

"Okay, how old are you, now? Tell me the truth and don't lie."

Precious wanted some tight booty, but she was realizing the price might be too high… or was it because she abruptly sobered up. Going to jail for some ass didn't seem worth it. She contemplated putting the boy out and throwing him back to the hungry faggots like in the club.

"I'm almost 17," Carlos blurted.

"Almost 17? You mean you're only 16 years old," Precious protested.

"Yeah, my birthday is next month. If you don't wanna take me to your crib, I'll just go back in the club and go home with some old dude like I been doing. But sometimes I get tired of being used for sex by these mofos, just so they'll let me stay the night."

Tears welled up in the boy's eyes as he spoke about his life on the streets of Detroit. He had sucked so many dicks after running away from home three months earlier that he'd lost count. She felt sorry for the boy and wanted to help him. The least she could do was take him home and let the nigga take a bath. He smelled like some old collard greens.

"When the last time you had a bath? Cuz you funky!" she commented while cracking the back windows of the green Honda to let the funk out.

"Well, it's been three days, cuz I been staying in the streets and not going home with these niggas. I went home with this old dude last Monday. He musta been bout 45 or something. Anyway, his roommate was there and them two gray-headed muthafuckas fucked me all day and night long. They didn't use a condom either, and I bet they busted in my pussy about five times."

Being feminine, Carlos like a lot of gay males, referred to his asshole as a pussy.

"Why you out here in these streets? Did your parents throw you out?"

"Well, my mama did. I don't know my daddy. She got mad cuz I got kicked outta school for sucking another boy's dick in the locker room. It's not like I went that much anyway. And I didn't like her lazy-ass boyfriend staying with us. When I would walk around in my underwear, I could just see him staring at my fat butt. When I would tell Cookie about it, she would get mad and say I was lying. She always took up for her ugly-ass boyfriend. One day, I got out of the shower and wrapped a towel around me and went to the refrigerator. Well, he came up behind me and took the towel off and started trying to kiss me. At first, I tried to stop him, but his touch made me real hot. So, I just bent over the kitchen table and let him screw me until I felt hot cum shoot up my ass. I gave him my virginity and he started treating me real nice and stuff—so nice that Cookie became jealous."

"Is Cookie yo mama?"

Carlos nodded and continued with his story.

"When Cookie would leave for work in the morning, James, her boyfriend, would come in my room to fuck me. Damn he had some good dick too! Anyway, one morning Cookie came back to the house because she forgot something, and guess what she found? She walked in on us while I was riding his dick! I had the nigga about to cum to before this heffa showed up. She ran out the room, screaming and crying. Finally, when she came home from work, she told me that she was tired and since I didn't abide by her rules, I had to go. I mean she packed my clothes and threw me out while James was on the couch drinking a beer—like he did nothing."

"Damn," was all Precious could muster after hearing Carlos' story.

Precious thought her mother was bad, but Marsha would never throw her son out in the street for no nigga. She may have been a fucked-up mama, but she wasn't that fucked up. They drove together in silence as Carlos, feeling safe and secure, nodded off into a peaceful sleep. Precious thought he looked so angelic that she decided not to take advantage of him. She wanted to fuck him so bad, but he's been used enough and he needed a friend rather than her aching dick.

When they got to the apartment, she took his clothes and threw them in the washer while Carlos took a much-needed shower and brushed his teeth. While he washed his funky ass, Precious fixed him

something to eat. She put two frozen hamburger patties in a skillet with hot oil and made a double cheeseburger and fries. The meal was on the table when he came out the shower.

She gave him a pair of shorts to wear as he sat down to eat, grateful for the food he was about to devour. After he finished the hot, nutritious meal in a few minutes, she fixed him a place to sleep on the sofa. She could tell he was glad that he didn't have to give up his ass. When he was situated on the couch, she turned out the light and wished him a goodnight.

"Carlos, tomorrow we need to call your mother and get you home." He didn't respond, but she was concerned and demanded and answer. "You hear me boy?" "But my mama not around here," he mumbled, sounding irritated.

"But you said she threw you out, so what side of town you stay on?"

"Oh, I'm not from here. I'm from Kalamazoo."

"Damn! All this time I assumed you was from here. Well, in the morning we gonna call your mama, cuz you need to get off these streets and go home. Now goodnight and sleep tight."

The bed felt like heaven to Precious. Her eyelids grew heavy as soon as her head touched the pillow. Feeling horny, she thought about Carlos' young, nubile body, sleeping only a few feet away. All she had to do was go take his sweet young ass, and who would know? But she felt responsible for him. Damn she picked a fine time to be a Good Samaritan!

While contemplating whether to rape the boy or not, she oiled her thick, long penis with lotion and thought about Carlos' soft lips around her dick before shooting cum a foot in the air. She felt relaxed and quickly fell asleep, wondering if Walter had already viewed the disks. Though she left a typed note inside for him with specific instructions not to call until a certain time, she was sure he would call her, cursing and screaming. *Naw*, she surmised. If he'd viewed them, *the fag would have called by now.*

****

After Walter received his gift from Precious, he was eager to see what it was, so he pulled into the nearest parking lot and opened the package. He was surprised by its contents and shocked by the typed note which read:

I want $200,000 in seven days, or I'm going to put these videos on YouTube. Do not contact me until you have the money. When the money is ready, I will give you an account number where you will transfer the money to.

Utter shock consumed Walters's frail body as he read the note. Just a few minutes earlier, he was tasting Precious's sweet black meat. Now that nigger-freak was trying to blackmail him. He raced home, wondering if his sessions with the nigger were secretly filmed.

The drive seemed longer than usual—no doubt resulting from his anxiousness and worry about on the content on the disks. He thought about calling the ape, but heeded the note and decided not to. All this time, the old fag thought they had a special connection, but the bitch was just setting him up for a big payday. She made him so comfortable that he poured out his heart. Now, it was all coming back to haunt him.

He would be ruined if their lovemaking sessions became public. Edith would want a divorce and his kids would lose respect for him. His employer would fire him because he would be a laughing stock to their colleagues. When he pulled into the garage, he waited ten minutes, pulling himself together before entering the huge mansion. The house was quiet except for the TV coming from the bedroom.

He went to check on Edith, who was nodding in front of the idiot box high on her usual medicine of whisky and sleeping pills. After turning off the TV, he made a drink and went downstairs to the home office and watched the disk. After viewing them, he felt a mixture of anger, betrayal and lust, realizing that the nigger had him over a barrel and that he had no choice but to pay. Calling the police would be the equivalent of releasing the disks to the public.

Who knew how many copies the tranny had made? Going to the police was definitely out of the question, as it would still end in him being ruined and publicly humiliated. Before going to bed, he hid the disks for future viewing, deciding he had no choice but to pay. But Precious probably made dozens of copies and could blackmail him indefinitely. Damn, his life as he knew it was over all because he loved nigger dick!

In any event, he had a week to deliver the money, or the ape was going to make an otherwise idyllic life a living hell. With over seven figures in the bank, getting the money was no problem. Keeping it from Edith, however, was the problem. He had to find a way to explain it, or she might find out his secret life. Maybe he could blame

it on gambling debts or something along those lines. But it didn't matter because the immediate goal was delivering the money. Once that was done, he could think of a better explanation. Tired and worried with fright, Walter trudged slowly up to the bedroom, feeling thoroughly defeated. He kissed his wife on the forehead and fell asleep.

****

Morning couldn't come quick enough for Precious. Carlos was still sleeping when she got up at eight, eager to start the day. First, she checked her messages to see if Walter had called, and she confirmed two appointments for the day, both regulars. Both guys were cool, and they paid well to be pissed on. Even though she didn't particularly like pissing on folks, she always gave the customers what they wanted and didn't judge their perversions or idiosyncrasies.

Since Walter hadn't called, she concluded that he was going to follow the note to the letter and deliver the money to her account in seven days. But if he didn't deliver on time or didn't have all the money, she wasn't going to release the disks on YouTube. If she did, then Walter had no reason to pay her, because his secret would be out in the open. Besides, Precious figured, if he didn't give her the whole amount at one time, they could set up a payment plan.

But a man of Walter's stature had to pay. If not, his whole world would come tumbling down. He was a man of wealth and was respected in the community. He had no choice. At least that's what Precious hung her hat on, that the specter of being exposed greatly outweighed concerns about money. The wimpy faggot was so rich that he'd pay. And if her plans with Walter fell through for any reason, she had plenty of more clients to blackmail. Her personal porn library had become quite extensive, she filmed every session with her clients. *Always have a plan "B,"* was her motto.

"Wake up. Wake up, sleepyhead," Precious shouted to a snoring Carlos, "time to start the new day off right. You want some breakfast?"

Without waiting for an answer, she started breakfast as Carlos arose and went to take a piss.

When he finished in the bathroom, a breakfast of toast, scrambled eggs and sausages awaited him at the kitchen table. Precious watched as he ate, feeling pleased to see the thin little boy

eat his fill. After he finished, she rolled a joint and asked him for his home phone number. At first Carlos was hesitant, but he relented after Precious shot over an angry look from Precious.

She took a few puffs of the weed, dialed the number and listened as a pleasant woman's voice answered.

"Is this Mrs. Houston? Carlos' mom?"

"Yes, it is. Oh my God! Has something happened to my baby?"

"No ma'am, he's here in Detroit with me. My name is Precious, and your son spent the night with me last night."

"Detroit?" Mrs. Houston shouted. "How the hell he get to Detroit?"

"I don't know, but he needs to get off these streets and go home. I'm gonna put him on the bus this morning if you want him back."

"What the hell you mean *if* I want him back? Of course I want him back! What kind of mother do you think I am?"

"Well, he told me you threw him out when you caught him having sex with your boyfriend. Is that true?" Precious asked, bracing for an answer.

"Yes, I did catch them fucking," Mrs. Houston managed to say out loud. "But that was just the last straw. The boy was kicked outta school for having sex with another boy, and he would stay out all times of night. I just got tired of him running over me. That's why I sent him to stay with his grandparents on the other side of town. But then one day he just left, and we didn't know where he was. We had no idea he was in Detroit."

"Okay, I'll be putting him on the 12 o'clock bus, so he should be home by this evening."

"Oh, thank you so much, sir. Could I speak to Carlos?"

Perturbed at being called "sir," she gave the phone to Carlos, and after about ten minutes of crying and apologizing, he gave the phone back to Precious.

"Well, I just want to thank you for what you've done for my son. And by the way, I didn't get your name…"

"My name is Precious Meat."

Apparently, Mrs. Houston didn't hear her say it the first time, or maybe she thought her masculine voice didn't match up with a feminine name like "Precious."

"Oh, my bad! I thought you were a male," Mrs. Houston said, seeming embarrassed.

"No need to feel bad. I'm a transsexual, and sometimes my man voice comes out," Precious explained. "Anyway ma'am, we'll be going to the bus station soon. Anything else before I go?"

"Give me your address so I can repay you for the ticket."

"No need, Mrs. Houston. I'm just glad that I could help. Goodbye"

After they hung up, she drove her overnight guest to the Greyhound station on Howard Street, and they waited together. The bus finally arrived, after being an hour behind schedule. Carlos gave Precious a tight hug before boarding the nearly empty bus, waving as it drove off. Tears welled in Precious's eyes as she watched the massive vehicle disappear in the distance. She only knew the boy for a few hours, and she already missed him! Finally, after regaining composure, she went home to wait on the two white fags who were going to pay her to piss on them.

****

Four hours later, the bus pulled into the Kalamazoo station, where Carlos could see James and Cookie waiting for him. After he exited the bus, both rushed to greet and welcome the boy home. Carlos cried like a little baby at the sight of mom and her cute boyfriend, with the "oh so good lovemaking skills." The teen didn't know which one he was happy to see more. The boy had one thing to be glad about though, which was to be off the mean streets of Detroit.

When they got home, he called Precious and thanked her for her help. Cookie, meanwhile, asked a thousand questions and fussed and fretted over him like she hadn't in years. After Carlos got settled into his small, cramped bedroom, Cookie fixed his favorite dinner of fried chicken, French fries and grape Kool-Aid. They ate and talked about the future, as James couldn't keep his eyes off Carlos.

Cookie seemed to encourage the obvious eye fucking of her son and joked about how her two men had some catching up to do. Both James and Carlos laughed and nodded in agreement. Cookie realized that James loved to fuck young boys, and the only way to keep him was to let him do his thang. And since her son was gayer than Rupaul, why not kill two birds with one stone and keep James home at night. With young booty in the house, he wouldn't have to go out—it was right here at home for the taking.

With the scarcity of good black men, Cookie was going to do everything she could to hang on to James. He just started working a good job, and everything seemed to be coming together with Carlos back at home. She was determined to make the relationship with James work, even if it meant her son had to give him some ass every now and then.

And it wasn't that Carlos didn't want to the same. She remembered catching her son riding James' cock, months earlier. James seemed to have enjoyed her son riding him way more than when she rode him. Cookie threw her son out because she was jealous of him, but not because he was gay. She hated the way James' eyes lit up when Carlos came around, shaking his fat ass. She hated how James eased out of their bed and snuck into Carlos room to make love to him and not her. She hated hearing the bedsprings creaking when James and Carlos made love.

But that was part of the past. She just wanted her family together, no matter how fucked-up it was. Family was family. That night, James officially welcomed Carlos back home by fucking him for hours. As Cookie listened to their loud guttural moans of lust, the steady squeaking of the bedsprings was the last sound she heard before nodding off to sleep. Her family was together, and that's all that mattered.

****

Precious was finishing up with her second client of the day when she got the call from Carlos, saying that he made it home. It warmed her otherwise cold heart to hear the happiness in the youngster's voice. That day had been a good day for the big-dick-tranny, because she made $600 off the two fags who wanted golden showers. Sometimes, Precious was amazed at how easy she made money. But she was tired of this chump-change and wanted to make some real money. Being in the escort business was dangerous. She needed a nest egg to put away for the proverbial rainy days that were sure to come up.

Even though she was young and fine, she knew one day her looks would fade and the clients would cease to come. No longer would men pay to suck her toes or grovel at the sight of her dick, so the time to strike it rich was right then, when she had the power of youth on her side. Before going to bed, she reviewed the golden

showers on the webcam and downloaded the content onto her computer and burned it onto a disk.

After months, her library consisted of more than three dozen disks of down-low freaks, doing all kinds of unimaginable things they would never want the public to know. These disks were her insurance policy, and in a couple of days, she would cash one of them in.

The week went by too fast for Walter as he scrambled to get the money together without Edith knowing about it. He sold some stock and cashed out part of his 401k until he had a total of $200,000. When he called Precious for further instructions, she gave him a routing number and bank account number where the money should be transferred. After she checked the account online to verify the funds had been sent, she told the faggot to meet her at Regine's that night, and she would give him the rest of the disks.

Walter agreed and hung the phone up, still in fear of being exposed. He was torn, since he was still in love with Precious, worrying the mere sight of the beautiful tranny would cause him to lust after her like a forlorn teen. He thought he might be too weak to resist her charms and the sexual spell that she had over him. He promised himself that when he met her that night, it was only going to be business and nothing else. He was going to get the disks and "never see that nigger again!"

When Precious saw the money had been transferred to her account, she jumped for joy, letting out a shout so loud that the next-door neighbor came to check on her, thinking she was in danger. After a few minutes of ecstasy, her only regret was that she didn't ask for more money. Maybe when she met Walter later, she could convince the fool to give her even more loot.

But then, again maybe she wouldn't meet him—maybe she would cut her ties with him altogether, in case the police or some other agency got involved. A clean cut would be better for all parties involved. Later that evening after shopping all day at Great Lakes Crossing, an upscale mall in Auburn Hills, she called Walter. She was feeling good too, still on cloud nine high from shopping. It was good to have money.

"Hi Walt, how ya doing?" speaking to the fag as if her blackmailing him was normal.

"How do you think I'm doing, bitch? You evil whore! I just want the rest of the disks back, and then I won't ever see your ass again."

He couldn't believe how nonchalant the bitch sounded on the phone. *Arrogant black slut!*

"That's what I called to tell you about, you limp-dick fag. We won't be meeting tonight, and don't ever call me again!"

She was feeling good, but she wasn't about to take any shit from a freak who she fucked so many times that his asshole was shaped like her cock.

"Bu... ba... but what about the disks?" Walter angrily stammered.

"What about the disks? What about the disks?" she repeated. "I'm keepin the disks for insurance. And like I said—don't call me anymore—you stupid freak. After this phone call, we will never see each other again. And if you try to contact me, Edith will see how much you loved to get fucked by my big black meat! Buh bye, bitch!" After that retort, she hung up, never to hear from him again.

Walter realized he would never get the disks and would have to live the rest of his life in fear of being exposed. When Precious hung up, he felt a mixture of fear and anger: fear that one day Edith would find out, and anger that a nigger-tranny-prostitute had so much power over him for the rest of his or her life. The nigger could decide to blackmail him again anytime if she needed money.

After a few months, life had returned to normal for Walter. He didn't frequent any tranny prostitutes and he occasionally went to church on Sundays. Even though it was boring as hell, celibacy was the only way he could assure himself that he would stay out of trouble. He spent the evenings with Edith, drinking and playing solitaire, instead of out chasing black cock.

The only pleasure he had was watching the disk of Precious assaulting his asshole with her ten inches of prime dick. Every evening, after a couple of drinks, he would steal away to his home office and watch the disks for hours, wishing he could taste Precious's chocolate dick just one more time. One night, after too many gin and tonics, the old fag got careless and left the disk out on the desk, instead of hiding them like he usually did.

The next day, Edith, who was curious about what Walter did in the office at night, started snooping around and came upon the disk. When she saw what was on them, she was shocked but not surprised. After being in a sexless marriage for a decade, she had suspected Walter may be in the closet, but obviously she didn't know it was to

such an extent. Her first call after the initial shock was to a good divorce lawyer. The second was to Walter.

"I watched the filthy disk you been hiding! How could you do this to your family?" Edith shouted failing miserably to hold back her tears.

Walter's world came tumbling down at that instant. "Let me explain, honey, just let me explain!" Was all that he could manage to say.

"Explain what? Explain that you like to let niggers who dress up as women fuck you? There is no explanation, except that you're gay, and anything else is a lie!"

"Honey, please let me come home and explain! I was just going through a phase, that's all! I'm okay now."

"Walter, letting a big-dick-nigger cum in your mouth is not a phase! It's a fucking sickness! I've called a divorce lawyer and have a meeting set up for this afternoon. When he sees the disks, he'll have a field day in court. By the way, don't come home, you sick bastard! These last few years, you've ignored me and looked at me with disgust on your face, like you were too good for me. Now, I see you weren't man enough for a woman like me, you sick, twisted freak! Goodbye, Walter. Maybe Precious will take you in!" Edith shouted as she hung up and fixed a stiff drink to calm her nerves.

After she hung up Walter tried repeatedly to call her back, but he got no answer. His worst fears were being realized. He would be financially ruined and humiliated if his peers found out about his double life. Knowing his secret life would be made public sickened him He could just see the lawyers laughing at him as they watched the disks while discussing the divorce settlement with Edith. All that he'd work for would be wiped away.

After pulling himself together, he left work early and went to the nearest bar to drink his worries away. The more he drank, the clearer the solution to his problem became. He knew what had to be done. After falling off the barstool, the down-low fag stumbled out to his BMW to complete his mission. He drove to Interstate 75, weaving in and out of traffic, narrowly avoiding collisions several times.

He called Edith and left her a message, telling her he loved her and he was sorry. Then he drove until he found the perfect target; a fuel truck that he hoped was full of fuel. He accelerated until the speedometer reached 140 mph and crashed headlong into the backend of the truck, causing an explosion that shut the highway

down for hours. Walter knew none of this, because he died instantly. Now no one could hurt him.

Precious was getting her dick sucked when she first heard about the crash and paid no attention to it until the anchorwoman mentioned the name of the driver in the BMW. She was shocked. Looking down at the puny white fag on his knees, slobbering on her dick made her think of Walter. That limp dick muthafucka could sho suck some dick! Watching the news coverage of the terrible wreck aroused her as her testicles filled with sperm. Imagining it was Walter sucking on her right then, she shot a huge load on the clients' face until cum was dripping down his chin. Without hesitation, he gratefully licked it up and swallowed as much as he could.

After the client left, Precious wondered if she had anything to do with Walter deliberately crashing his car into a damn fuel tanker. Luckily, the tank was empty and the only victim was Walter. But why would he do it to himself? Did somebody find the disks and threatened to expose him? Precious tried to feel some empathy, but she was angry at herself for not getting more money from Walter. Now his dumb ass was dead, so she couldn't blackmail him again like she had intended to do. A few days later, she got a surprise call.

"Is this Precious Meat?" the drunken, slurred voice of a white woman asked.

"Yes, who is this?" Precious asked.

"I think you and I have a mutual acquaintance." Edith took a drink and continued. "His name is Walter Finster. He was my husband and I buried him today. I saw the disks of you and him making love, although I would hesitate to call what you two did as love."

"Oh yeah, I knew Walter. Sorry for your loss." Precious tried to sound sympathetic, but her act wasn't fooling the grieving widow.

"Well, that's an understatement to only say that you knew him. You were screwing him for months, so yeah, I think you did know him."

"What can I do for you, Edith?"

"Oh, you even know my name? How sweet," Edith said in the most sarcastic voice she could muster. "How can a person like you live with yourself? Looking through our records, I know Walter gave you $200,000, and I'm certain I know why. I think you secretly filmed you and my husband doing whatever you were doing. Then you threatened to go public unless he forked over some money."

"Edith, it was Walter's idea to film our lovemaking—not mine. He did it so he could watch himself getting fucked anytime he felt horny and lonely. By the way, do you want the rest of the disks?"

"You have some more disks? And I bet you want some money in exchange, right?"

Not wanting to incriminate herself in case someone on the other end was listening, Precious declined to answer the part about the money. Instead, she invited Edith to come and get the disks herself.

"I'm not coming to your neighborhood," Edith haughtily proclaimed. But then she relented after learning where Precious lived. She didn't want those other disks getting out, because it could be very embarrassing to the family. She agreed to come to the apartment the next day and pick up the disks.

At 3 pm the next day, Edith knocked on Precious's apartment door. When the tranny opened the door, a sullen, half-drunk white woman was on the other side. Precious handed the disks to her and braced for the questions the old bitch was sure to ask.

"So, you're the big-dick-whore who made my husband wreck his car," Edith shouted from the hallway. "I'm going to tell the manager and every tenant in the building that you're a prostitute and have HIV/AIDS, you filthy nigger faggot whore! Then I'm going to the police and tell them how you're using your website to blackmail people."

With that, Edith stomped away, mad that her husband went to this nigger for love and comfort instead of coming to her.

Precious didn't respond because she was sure nothing could be gained by arguing with the widow of the guy she blackmailed for $200,000. Better to let the old bat vent her frustrations than to escalate the bitch's rage. Besides, she doubted the white hag would go to the manager once her anger cooled down. And Edith's threat of going to the police would bring attention to Walter's alternative lifestyle, which she wanted kept secret. Just in case something unforeseen happened Precious realized she needed to make plans to leave town if things got too hot.

After a few days, she got a letter from the manager saying they got complaints of her running a prostitution ring out of the apartment, but she got really scared when a police detective came by to ask about the relationship she had with Walter. She thought the pig would never leave as she stuttered and stumbled for answers to his questions. She had nothing to do with the fag killing himself, and

the detective had no proof of blackmail. When he finally left, Precious broke out in a cold sweat, terrified she might go to prison like her two brothers.

With her lease up in less than a month, she looked online for houses in the Atlanta area, because she didn't want to be around when shit hit the fan. She had no way of knowing that the detective who came to see her was really just an out-of-work actor Edith hired to scare her away.

The manager waived the remaining weeks on her lease as she made plans to move down south. Online, she found a nice home in Decatur, a small town east of Atlanta. It was reasonably-priced, with an option to buy. Precious invited Marsha to come with her, but her mother declined outright.

The thought of her favorite child leaving made Marsha sad and angry. Even though she wanted to be with her daughter, Marsha couldn't leave the hood where she grew up. As awful as Detroit was, it was her home. Motown was in her blood, and she planned to die there—not in country-ass Atlanta. As long as Precious sent her money every month, she would be okay.

Chapter 3
Decatur, Georgia

After having been questioned about Walters's suicide, Precious couldn't leave Detroit fast enough. She hated leaving—especially after making so much money, but the thought of prison outweighed profit incentives. The past year had been very rewarding. Her website was popular, and she had a long list of faithful clients who paid well. She figured if she could make it in Detroit, then Georgia should be a piece of cake. Fine big-dick-transsexuals didn't grow on trees, so Precious knew the power she wielded, swinging between her legs. She had the dick that drove a man to kill himself! Now she was going to do the same thing in Atlanta—make a muthafucka go crazy over her cock—so crazy he'd worship the ground she walked on—crazy enough to go broke paying for her dick.

It took Precious 15 hours to drive the 700 some odd miles to Decatur, a beautiful little bedroom-community in the shadow Atlanta. She pulled into Walden Springs subdivision off Wesley Chapel road, tired as hell. Retrieving the key from under the flower pot where the real estate agent left it, she opened the door to a beautiful three-bedroom, two-bath house. She inspected every room and marveled at the spaciousness.

After taking a shit and unpacking, she called Marsha to let her know she made it safely. Surveying the neighborhood from the front yard, Precious appreciated the quiet and admired the manicured lawns. The only sounds in the air were crickets and an occasional barking dog. The house was hot inside, so she turned on the air conditioner to cool it down. She rolled a blunt and sat on the front porch for over an hour, waiting for the house to get nice and frosty. Since the house had no furniture, she made a pallet on the thick carpet and fell asleep, excited to start a new life.

The next days and weeks were filled with shopping and getting acclimated to her new surroundings. She liked the Decatur area and loved staying in a middle-class black community. A few of her neighbors came over to say hello, but when some of them saw that she was a transsexual, they didn't seem pleased to have her in the neighborhood. Precious was used to such reactions, so it didn't bother her. In her profession, the one thing she hated most was nosy-ass neighbors.

She didn't care if the neighbors hated her guts, as long as they didn't get in her business. It took about a month to get the house fully-furnished and livable enough to start accepting clients. From her experience in the business, she knew that a nice comfortable place made the clients relax and willing to spend money. She wanted to wow a client when he or she came to see her.

She learned in Detroit that *if you are going to do something, then do it top notch*. That's why she hired a website designer to re-launch her new and improved website. She had the old site shut down right after Walters's drunken-ass wife threatened to expose her. After the site was up for two hours, she got her first client, a chubby, professional black man, with a penchant for wearing women's underwear. She was surprised when the guy pulled off his conservative brown suit, revealing a red bra and a red silk thong. She smiled at the spectacle as she pushed him down face-first on the bed and inserted her cock easily into his plump ass from behind.

"Damn, baby, I see you just a slut ain't cha? As big as my dick is, you didn't even flinch, you ho!"

Precious loved talking dirty to her tricks. The dirtier she talked, the manlier her voice seemed to get. She didn't sound like Barry White, but her voice was kind of deep. The client seemed to enjoy her throaty raspy shit-talking while she pounded his asshole unmercifully.

"Yeah, baby. I'm a ho! I'm a ho! Damn, your big black dick fills me up! I love them titties on my back! Fuck me like the slut I am! Fuck me, ooohhhh!"

The client was silenced by the pleasurable long strokes of Precious's cock. For over 30 minutes, he was in heaven as the tranny fucked him doggy-style, like the bitch he was.

Right before she was about to cum, Precious pulled her dick out.

"Where you want this nut, bitch? In your mouth or yo ass?"

Personally, she liked cumming in a nigga's mouth rather than cumming in his ass. The clients couldn't really feel her nut through the condom. Besides, it gave her a thrill to see a mofo gagging on her heavy load of thick cum. The client pointed to his mouth and Precious obliged him by fucking his mouth like it was a pussy. After a few strokes, cum came gushing from her cock, like a fire hose. The head of her dick was touching the back of his throat as she ejaculated in his mouth, gagging him on her sticky juice. Like a good little boy, he swallowed all of it. After cleaning up, the client gave her a hug and

promised to be a regular. Precious pinched him on the ass and whistled as he walked to his blue Lexus.

"Shake that sexy fat ass, ho," she giggled as the client tried his best not to walk too feminine.

But after getting pounded by a big dick for the last half hour, it was hard for him not to feel like a woman. While getting in the car, he blew a kiss at Precious and disappeared into the night. As soon as he left, she watched her magnificent performance on the hidden cameras in the bedroom. This gave her a feeling of immense power, while it was also a way to critique her lovemaking skills. She was amazed at how big her dick looked on camera. After admiring herself, she hid the disks in the attic for safekeeping and future blackmailing.

Precious soon recognized that her clientele in Decatur would be different than in Detroit. It took six months to get her first white client, but she didn't mind because black fags in Georgia had money—unlike the tired, broke niggas up in Detroit who always asked for a damn discount or a freebie. She wanted another big payday, but hadn't come across anyone suitable yet. She realized that what happened with Walter was probably a once in a lifetime situation. She got lucky and hit pay dirt, but could she do it again?

Blackmailing a nigga may not go as smoothly as blackmailing a rich, white man, she wouldn't know for sure unless she tried. So, one night after smoking a blunt, she decided to study the disks and see who would be a good candidate for blackmail. This time, instead of asking for a large lump sum, she was gonna ask for weekly or monthly payments. Because they weren't as rich as Walter, she'd bleed these niggas slowly. Doing it that way, they wouldn't be likely to react violently.

She selected the two down-low fags to be blackmailed and decided on them after Googling both their names on the Internet. Precious had discovered with so much info on the net, you could find out a lot about a person if you had their phone number and full name. Since she didn't accept blocked or private calls, she knew all her customers' names from caller ID. The first unsuspecting freak she called was David Morris.

"Hello."

"Is this David?" she asked. "This is Precious Meat. How you doin, baby?"

"Damn, how did you get my number?" David was startled that his tranny lover called just when he was about to sit down to dinner with the wife and kids.

"What do you mean 'how did I get your number?' I have caller ID, and why can't I call you?" Precious was just fucking with him; she knew her clients never wanted their she-male prostitute lover calling them unexpectedly. What if he was in the shower and the wife answered his cell?

"So exactly why are you calling me?"

"Well, I have a present for you, and I'm not talking about my tootsie roll that you like to slob on." Precious felt her dick getting hard.

"Listen, I don't want no present and please don't call me again. I have to go," David whispered. With his house full of family and friends, he had to keep his voice down.

"No, you need to listen faggot! I been filming our fuck sessions, so you need to hear what the fuck I'm about to say!"

"I can't believe you did this, you fuckin pervert!" David said as his wife called him to say the blessing at dinner.

"Okay, baby. I'll be right there, I'm talking to a student right now," he lied.

"Is that the little wifey I hear in the background? It would be a shame if she found out about your addiction to big black dicks, now, wouldn't it?" There was silence on the other end. "Hello! Hello! Hello!" Precious shouted. "David, are you still there?"

"Yeah, I'm here. Right now, I'm going to sit down to dinner. I'll call you back later to discuss the details."

"Well, here's the details, fag! I want $300 a week, nonnegotiable, or I'll send the disks I downloaded of me cummin in you to everyone you know. Every Tom, Dick and Harry will know how good you suck dick. I bet your wife will be surprised, wont she? But then again, maybe she already knows you on the down-low. While you think you fooling her, she may already suspect you got some sugar in you."

"Listen, I can't talk right now, so I will definitely give you a call tomorrow. Good-bye."

Before she could respond, David hung up. However, she knew she had him on the hook.

The next morning, David called and they arranged to meet at Redan Park to discuss their new arrangement. The park was empty, except for a few kids and an old woman walking her Labrador

Retriever. David arrived first with an angry look on his face, watching as Precious drove up and parked next to him. She rolled the window down.

"Good morning, David," she said.

"Good morning? That's all you got to say? How is this a *good* morning?" David felt himself getting angrier by the millisecond.

"Well, here's the video I downloaded." She handed the disk to David and tried to gauge his reactions by the look on his face.

David took the disk and inserted it into the computer that Precious told him to bring. Still, he thought the bitch was lying... until he loaded the disk. After a few seconds of watching, he realized the bitch was right. If that video got out, he would be ruined and disgraced.

"Do you like what you see? Nobody give up that ass like you do, boy! Hell, I'm getting hard now just thinking about your sexy fat ass, riding this black cock! Damn boy, you got some good tight pussy! As long as you pay, we can keep your dick riding skills a secret, but that's totally up to you," she said, trying to sound reasonable.

"Please stop doing that. I'm disgusted with myself, and here you come blackmailing me! I'm not rich goddammit bitch!" David sobbed as he watched the video of Precious cumming in his mouth.

"Baby, I know you not rich. That's why I only want $300 a week. Now, I know you can afford that. You're a college professor, after all, with two kids and a wife."

"How the hell you know that," he asked, startled. "Who told you I teach college?" he demanded.

"I googled your name, baby," she responded. "As long as you have a computer, you can find out anything about a person. I found out that you're 39 years old and you graduated from Georgia State with a degree in Sociology in 2002. I know you've been teaching at Clark Atlanta since 2004. See David, I did my homework on you. I didn't just put this shit together all willy-nilly. Now when it comes to my paper—I'm serious bitch, and right now, I want my first payment. I really don't care how mad or upset you get, because it don't faze me one fucking bit. Now did you bring my money, because this conversation is getting boring?"

Precious admired her calmness in stressful situations. She had to make this whiney fag realize she was dead serious and not to be trifled with. Otherwise, he'd try to weasel out and give her some sad-ass sob story about his family and shit. But if this cock-sucking nigga

loved his family so much, he wouldn't be slobbering on her dick like a dog slob on a bone.

"Yeah, I brought your damn money," David mumbled through tears. Then he handed the tranny an envelope with fifteen $20 bills stuffed in it. "How can you do this to me?" David pleaded. "I have a wife and kids to support."

After counting the money, Precious answered, "I do it for the fucking money! Why else do you think I do it? And you weren't thinking about your ugly-ass wife or your kids when you was sucking on my cock, were you? So don't bring them up to me now, you freaking bitch! Now, today is Friday, and I want my money every fucking Friday—not Saturday, not Sunday or Monday—but Friday, until I give you further notice. You hear me? And I don't wanna meet here no more because it's to isolated. You know that Wendy's on Covington and Panola Rd?" David nodded. "Meet me there every Friday at 7 p.m. in the parking lot to make your payment. You got that?"

"Yes, I got it—meet you every Friday at Wendy's on Panola and Covington at 7 p.m.," he repeated.

Precious smiled. "Good, see you next Friday, faggot." She drove away, leaving David angry and confused about his future.

It was hard for Precious to feel sorry for these down-low fags who slobbered on her dick behind closed doors, but shunned her in public. Guys like David were all lovey-dovey in private, but they would never take her out for dinner or to the movies. The stigma of being ostracized for being gay is too much for the average guy to handle.

Men who fuck exclusively with transsexuals see themselves as being straight, not gay. But at the same time, they know deep-down that they like trannies because trannies have dicks. So, instead of fucking around with a regular homosexual, they get a homosexual who dresses and acts like a woman in order to justify their wanton lust for cock. In their warped minds, it's okay as long as the cock that's fucking them is wearing a dress, high heels and mascara.

That way, the illusion of them being heterosexual is enforced in theory, if not in practice. Even though its 100% wrong in theory, it's what keeps a lot of men from admitting that they're gay as hell. They think just because they fuck with a guy who thinks he's a woman, that that absolves them from being homosexual somehow. Such warped thinking is what leads to the high rate of social diseases.

In the black community, a lot of males experience their first homosexual experience in jail or prison. And with the high incarceration rate of black males, you can believe that a large proportion of them are engaging in sex with each other. It's only natural that, being locked up in a small cell with someone, eventually feelings of loneliness get the best of them, and sooner or later, they have sex. They figure it's okay, because they're only fucking each other because they're locked up together. But after a while, they stop fucking and start making love to each other. Soon they have feeling for one another that was once reserved for the opposite sex.

Thoughts of love and other emotions get in the way as they try to keep their feelings for each other on the down-low. Then once a guy who's been in a prison relationship gets released from jail, he may have had numerous homosexual affairs, but in his mind, he's still heterosexual. These are the type of men who seek the comfort of transsexuals—even though they have girlfriends and get plenty of pussy. They miss the comfort of a man, but they can't see themselves being a fag, so they seek out a fag who dresses like a woman.

Precious had been dealing with these self-delusional men since she was 16. She knew how they thought, and she used her knowledge to get over on them. After all, she was both man and woman—a dangerous combination.

The second trick she decided to blackmail was a short, chubby, light-skinned down-low fag by the name of James Green. He was an insurance salesman with a receding gray hairline who was 54 years young. Precious chose this old fool because she figured he wouldn't be any trouble to shakedown. At his age, the last thing he wanted was drama from a ruthless transsexual, hell-bent on making money. So after getting home from her appointment with whiney ass David, she called James. He answered on the second ring.

"Hello."

"Hey, how you doin, James? This is Precious Meat," the tranny said trying to sound sweet as syrup.

"Surprised to hear from you," James announced. "What can I do for you Ms. Meat?" He got a thrill out of calling her that.

"Well, it's more 'what I can do for you?' When you gonna come over here and get some more of this big black meat that you like slurping on? I'm horny and I got a big gob of goo I wanna shoot in your mouth!" Precious loved talking filthy to these cum sluts, almost as much they did.

"You really put it out there, don't you, Precious? I won't be able to come until tomorrow morning. This evening, I have bible study at my church, and then I'm taking my grandkids out to eat. But, like I said, we can get together tomorrow morning if you like." James truly liked Precious and was glad she called, but that day was reserved for family and the good Lord.

"Damn, you doing all that and you can't come see me baby? I was gonna throw this cock on you real good too." She tried her best to convince him to come over, but saw that his mind was made up.

"Baby you know how much I love going to church and being one with Jesus," James told her. "You know I love the Lawd."

"Yeah," Precious retorted, "I know you love the Lawd, cuz when I be fucking you, you yell out his name! 'Jesus! Jesus! Lawd, that dick sho is good!' is what you be shouting when I got this dick up your fat ass!"

James laughed at her impression of him while being fucked. "I don't sound like that, do I? That's a testament of God's gift to you. He gave you that big piece of meat for a reason. It was His will that we meet."

"Oh, that's what you think? That it was His will that I fuck you?" Precious asked trying to hold back her laughter. "You mean I'm doing the good Lawd's work every time I stick my dick in you?"

"Well, you don't have to be crass about it, but yes. When my wife died of cancer, I was lonely as could be. At this stage in my life, it's difficult to meet females, and most of the women my age are ugly and dried up on the inside. And another thing—I didn't want to have to hide my bisexuality from someone who probably wouldn't understand my need for a man. Nora—bless her heart—Nora knew about it, but married me anyway, and that's why I miss my baby and loved her to death. She kept my secret all the way to the grave." After his testimony, James blubbered like a child.

"Damn, boo! Why you crying? Everything gonna be alright. I know you miss your wife, but she wouldn't want you feeling all sad and shit now, would she?"

Precious tried her best to feign concern, but James' sad trick was getting on her already frayed nerves. To her, he was just another confused old fool who was afraid to be what he really was, a flaming homo.

"Like I said, I will see you tomorrow, Ms. Precious Meat. To be more precise, how about I come over at 9 a.m.? Sounds good?"

"You comin early to get this dick ain't cha, old man," Precious kidded.

"They say the early bird catches the worm, so I hope your worm will be good and hard tomorrow mornin. May God bless you. I have to go now, honey."

"Okay, baby, you better not be late. See ya."

After hanging up, Precious rolled a fat blunt and played with her cock she shot a load of cum into some tissue. Cumming always relaxed her, and after such a stressful day, she needed it. Maybe it was hearing James cry, but she felt lonely and sad.

To kick the blues, she decided to go to Club 708, in Midtown Atlanta. It was a place where black gays and transsexuals hung out. Unlike Regine's in Detroit, where the jealous fags sometimes made girls like her feel unwelcome, at Club 708, half the club-goers were trannies and their admirers.

Precious had gotten quite a few clients from this club and had to use "nigga repellant" to keep muthafuckas off her cock. Far from being arrogant, the bitch knew she was fine as hell. It was a club where the most beautiful black transsexuals in Atlanta came to compare themselves to each other and gossip amongst themselves, so she had to be on top of her game when she stepped through the door.

Despite it being a Friday night, the club was boring and half-empty due to all the construction on Spring Street. After speaking with the bartender, she was astonished to learn that she was there on the last night the club would be open, because a developer bought the property and planned to raze the one-story structure to put up condos. She spent the night gossiping with two of her tranny friends, Stacey Biggs and Dominique Michelle. Both were popular and almost as beautiful as Precious was!

"So, how has Atlanta been treating you, boo?" the short, plump dark-skinned Dominique asked.

"Girl, you know how it is—these niggas always trying to run game no matter where you at," Precious replied, feeling tipsy from a vodka and cranberry juice. "But I'm keeping these faggots in check, though."

Stacey chimed in, "Are you a 'top' or a 'bottom' or 'both?'"

In the homosexual community, tops are the ones that do the fucking, bottoms are the ones that get fucked.

"I'm strictly a top. Why you think my name is Precious *Meat*? In bed, I'm all man, baby. Nobody sticking they dick in me. I do the sticking, but if a guy's cute, I might suck his dick, but that's it. My pretty asshole is a virgin and gonna stay that way."

"Well, maybe you ain't met the right one," Stacey, the tall, light-skinned girl said. "As good as you make them guys feel when you fucking them, don't *you* wanna get fucked and feel what they feel? When my boyfriend's balls be slapping against my ass, then I know he fuckin me real good, cuz it makes me feel like I'm all woman."

"Damn, girl, calm down. You about to make me wet my panties!" Dominique screamed. "I know what you sayin, cuz I like to fuck too, but sometimes I just need a man to take this pussy like a man supposed to. I want a nigga to pull my hair while he fuckin me facedown, doggy style."

They laughed and ordered another round of drinks, enjoying each other's company as they swapped tales about their lives as transsexual prostitutes. Precious liked both women and enjoyed talking to them because they were about ten years older than she was and had been through the trials and tribulations that only a transsexual could understand. After finishing her fourth drink, Precious got up to go.

"You leavin already? You just got here!" Dominique shouted over the music.

"Yeah, it's getting late and it's a long drive to Decatur, especially when I'm drunk." Precious hugged both women and walked out into the hot, muggy Georgia night.

She felt a little guilty talking to Dominique after fucking her boyfriend, Lee, so hard that he had to get surgery for his rectum. Precious wanted to express her condolences, but since Nique didn't bring the subject up, why should she? She wanted to tell her they had been smoking crack that night, and things got out of hand because that shit made her dick harder than Mongolian arithmetic, but less sensitive to the touch.

When she put her dick in Lee's loose asshole, she could hardly feel anything, which made her pound him harder and harder, unaware that the drug dulled her cock's sensitivity so much that the loud protests from Lee for her to stop went unnoticed—until she nutted in him, through the torn condom. It wasn't until after finishing that Precious realized he was bleeding profusely and was crying from the intense pain her big dick inflicted on him. But dude

seemed okay when he left the crib, even if the fag did walk a little funny. That was months earlier, and Dominique seemed to have gotten over it.

"I can't stand that ugly, man-lookin bitch," Dominique said to Stacey after Precious left.

"What did she do to you?" Stacey asked, astonished.

"A couple a months ago, when I first met her here, I was with Lee. Don't you know that trifling bitch couldn't keep her hands off him! Kissing him on the cheek and whisperin in his ear and shit and disrespectin me right to my face."

"Whoa, hold up. You say she was disrespectin you? But she didn't even *know* you. It was your nigga that disrespected you, not her. You know good and well that Lee was just a two-faced whore, usin you for your money. You went with him for over a year, and his lazy ass never got a fuckin job."

"Damn, Stacey, why you gotta take her side? You weren't there, were you? You don't know how sneaky and conniving that ugly-ass donkey-face bitch is."

"You exactly right. I wasn't there, but she didn't do anything to Lee that he didn't want her to do. Don't get all mad at your sista over a trifling negro like Lee."

"That monkey-looking ho ain't my fuckin sista," Dominique snapped back. "That ho is the reason Lee had to get an operation to sew his rectum back up after she drugged and raped him. My baby coulda died fucking around with that big-shoulder bitch. She fucked him so hard that his asshole was bleeding and had to be stitched up!"

Stacey was shocked to hear that Precious put Lee in the hospital because she fucked him too hard. But in way, it was kind of funny—thinking about that nigga crying like a little girl, begging Precious to take her big black dick out.

"Aw, girl, you know good and well she didn't rape him. That nigga wanted that dick, and boy did she give it go him." Stacey tried, but she couldn't hold back her laughter.

"I fail to see why this is so amusing to you."

"It's funny, because you obviously loved Lee, but he didn't give a damn about you. Right now, he's stayin with another transsexual with low self-esteem who's lettin him use her like you did. You let the nigga use your car and everything, but what did he do for you besides giving you some dick?"

"But I loved him," was all Dominique could muster after hearing the truth from her friend.

"See, that's the problem right there. I think you loved him more than you loved yourself. I know how hard it is being a transsexual and the daily battles we have ta fight ta hold on to our dignity. Just like you, I've spent many lonely nights, afraid that no one in the world would ever love me for who I am. And you know what—these men can sense our desperation and use it against us. That's what Lee did to you, baby. He seen how madly in love you were with him and took advantage of it."

"I hear what you sayin, Stacey, believe me, I do. And from now, on I'm gonna let my head make the decision for me and not my heart, because I'm ready to settle down."

"Well, I hate to break this gabfest up, but I gotta go," a slightly drunk Stacey said as she stood to leave. "You take care of yourself and be strong." They hugged and promised to talk the next day. Precious was feeling pretty high as she walked to her car, oblivious to crisp, windy air on that cold Georgia night. There were a lot of tranny and gay prostitutes strolling along Spring and Peachtree Street. She was glad she never had to walk the damn streets and get in and outta cars all night for 30 bucks a trick. Right before she made it to the car, a Toyota Corolla pulled up beside her, and the driver asked her name. But before she could reply, the police pulled up behind his vehicle and told him to move on. Precious thought nothing of it and drove home, drunk as hell and feeling good. She wanted to get a good night's sleep before fat-ass James came over in the morning.

****

The next morning, James awoke feeling refreshed and eager to get the day started. After fixing a hearty breakfast of grits with cheese, scrambled eggs and sausage, he sat down to eat enjoying every bite, like it would be the last. To say he was a big eater would be the equivalent of saying ice is cold. That morning's fare consisted of a dozen of the eggs, along with eight Jimmy Dean sausage patties to go with a huge bowl of hot, steamy grits, topped with seven pieces of American cheese to give it that ooey-gooey deliciousness. All that cholesterol was washed down with four cups of black coffee.

When he was done consuming that huge feast, James took a nice long shit while reading the Bible. As lengthy as Precious' dick was, he

didn't want her dick to be painted with his shit as she fucked him. He loved to read the Good Book in the bathroom, because it usually took him about an hour to shit, so he got a lot of reading done. Now that he lived alone, there was nobody to nag him about his bathroom time or about his unhealthy eating habits.

The night before, at Fairfield Baptist Church, he prayed that God would give him strength to do the right thing and stop his lust for dicks. But the more he prayed, the more he lusted for the very thing he prayed to forgo. While listening to the reverend rail against fornication and homosexuality, all James could think of was having Precious' dick in his mouth—even with his grandkids sitting right beside him in the pews.

It was like he was addicted to black cock and needed an intervention from God to make him stop. After reading a few chapters of Revelation, he showered and got dressed, making sure to douche his fat, stinking asshole, which was definitely going to be abused. James called Precious at 8 a.m. to let her know he was on the way.

James' call woke her up from a drunken sleep, so the first thing she did was run to the bathroom to purge herself of all the poisons from the night before. After stinking up the bathroom, Precious took a quick cold shower and waited for her lover on the couch, completely nude, except for a towel around her waist. Why get dressed when she was going to be fucking in a few minutes?

At 9:25, James rang the doorbell, and he was excited as Michael Jackson at an all-boys orphanage when Precious opened the door with her big dick swaying from side to side, looking all sexy and shit.

"Good mornin, Ms. Lady," was all James could say as he gawked at the beauty of Precious.

"Sorry I'm late, but there was an accident on Covington Highway."

"C'mon in, honey. I'm doing fine. How was church last night? Did you pray for me?" Precious closed the door behind him and dropped the towel, revealing a semi-hard cock, pointing right at James.

"Baby, I pray for everybody—especially sinners like you." And saying that, he dropped down on his knees and eagerly gobbled Precious' meat in his mouth.

"Damn, baby, I love how you pray," Precious moaned as James massaged the head of her dick with his old, talented tongue. He was a

veteran dick-sucker and loved every minute of it. Even though she had called his fat ass over to blackmail him, she thought they may as well have some fun.

"God musta put you on earth to suck dick, baby, cuz nobody does it like you do!"

Precious stood over her prey, violently shoving her massive meat down his throat until her balls filled with cum. After a few minutes, she exploded in his mouth, like a fire hose putting out a fire. From the time James came over to the time she nutted in his mouth, only eight minutes had elapsed.

"Damn, I needed that nut! Swallow every bit of it, you fat ho," Precious said, sneering at James while he gagged on her thick milky cum.

Then she collapsed on the couch, feeling content after draining her cock in this faggot's mouth. James, still on his knees, crawled over to Precious and began slurping on her now limp dick to suck the remaining drops of sweet and salty cum from her gorgeous thick meat. Satisfied that he had extracted every drop of juice from her elegant over-flowing cock, he got up from his knees and sat down beside her, panting from exhaustion.

"Can I get some water, please," the fag said, trying to catch his breathe. His breathing was abnormal, and for a moment, both thought he may be having a heart attack.

Precious ran and retrieved a bottle of water, worried that this muthafucka might die in her living room! After giving him the water, James took two nitroglycerin pills for his angina and sat back on the couch, loosening his shirt to breath better.

"Damn, baby, you gave me a fuckin scare! Shit! I thought you was gonna die or somethin. I didn't know you had a heart condition. You need to slow your old ass down."

James smiled at the tranny's phony concern for his health and well-being.

"Young girl, when you get my age, everything starts messing up. I don't know what I'd do if I didn't have the Good Lawd watching out for me. I had my first heart attack three years ago, and the doctors thought I'd be dead right now, but God had other plans for me."

"Well, maybe if you lost some weight, you wouldn't have these heart attacks. Like how much do you weigh right now?"

"About 335 pounds last time I checked," James answered, embarrassed.

"You know good and well that's too much weight to be carryin around. And it's not that you're that old. You're only 54, but you need to stop eating so damn much. Instead of prayin so much, you need to take responsibility for your actions and eat a healthy diet. What's the use in praying when you killin yourself with food?"

"I know I have a weakness to overeat, and that's why I put it in the hands of Jesus, to help me with my addiction. All things are possible through Him."

"I think you have too much faith in God and not enough in yourself. You say all this bullshit about faith and God, but if your faith was that strong you wouldn't be here now, wheezin like you're about to keel over and die. Your faith is weaker than your love for food though, ain't it? Hell, you can barely walk 100 feet without losin your breath and stopping to rest."

James tried to speak, but the palpitations in his already overstressed heart made it difficult. He wanted to tell this sinful tranny that she was wrong about his relationship with God. He wanted to tell her that, while he'd spend eternity in the paradise of heaven, her cock-selling ass would burn with Lucifer in the fires of Hell.

She will burn because she uses her glorious penis that God blessed with her with for evil purposes. She enticed weak men into her temple of filthy, vile lust and made them worship her cock, like she was a god. God would make this whore pay for her arrogant and wanton ways. The events of the last few minutes had exhausted James to the extent that he had to unbuckle his belt and asked the host if it was okay to lie down on the couch until he could catch his breath.

Precious agreed, reluctant. "Sure, baby. Relax, take your shoes off and stay as long as it takes you to get yourself together. I don't want you dying over here. It would be very bad for business." She quit talking when she realized James had nodded off in the middle of her sentence.

After listening to James snore like a fucking rhinoceros for over five minutes, she checked the obese dick-sucker's wallet and commandeered all its contents, which consisted of $407.00 and numerous pictures of his wife. No wonder he liked dick, cuz the bitch he married looked like a damn man herself!

She inspected his credit cards but decided not to take them because it would only bring trouble, which was the last thing a tranny prostitute needed. After taking the money, she put the wallet back in his coat pocket. She was rethinking her decision to black mail James. At the rate his fat ass was going, he probably won't make it to Christmas. Hell, he may not make it off her couch!

After realizing fatty may be out for hours, she made herself a vodka with cranberry juice and puffed on a blunt while playing internet poker. She also fielded calls from potential clients, but of the three who called, only one had an unblocked number—a guy named John Evans. So she called him back and they made a date for later on that night. She figured he was just another down-low depressed fag who wanted to be punished by a big dick, because he loved big dicks. In other words, another fool with identity issues but hey, these fags paid her bills, so who was she to complain.

At 2 p.m., James finally woke up, glancing around the room, confused and disoriented. After remembering where he was, his fat ass relaxed a little and he lay back down.

"About time you wakin up, sleepyhead. You gotta go. I have company coming over," Precious announced in a loud voice to make sure he stayed awake. "I hope you feel better, sugar," she said while retrieving his shoes in order to hasten the fat fag's exit.

"How long was I asleep?" he asked as Precious put his shoes on for him.

"For about four hours. I should charge you by the hour," she kidded. "Can I have my $300 now?" She knew he didn't have any money on him because she stole it, but she was prepared to play it off if he accused her of taking the money.

"I got your money right here, baby," James assured her while reaching his wallet. "At least I thought I did. I had over $400 dollars in here."

"You sure about that, boo? Cuz when you came in, you looked kind of winded and excited. Maybe you forgot to get some money before you came over, or maybe you left it at home. I think you was so eager to get this dick that you probably forgot. Anyway, I can follow you to the ATM," the scheming tranny assured him.

Even though James didn't believe the lying bitch, he knew he was at a disadvantage, so he told her to follow him to the Wells Fargo on Wesley Chapel. Besides, after almost having a heart attack, he didn't have the energy or desire to argue with a muscular man,

dressed like a woman, over a couple of hundred dollars, and who was half his age. If the ho took his money, either she was a very good liar or he was gullible.

After much help from the host, James managed to pry his lazy ass off the couch. Precious went to get her purse while James huffed and puffed to his Ford Expedition. He started the air conditioner and waited for Precious to get in her car to follow him to the bank. He felt ashamed by his perverse lifestyle and said a silent prayer for God to give him strength to resist temptation as he watched sexy-ass Precious walk to her Honda, like she owned the world.

She wore a simple sundress, down to her knees, and sandals to showcase her beautiful, feminine feet. James cursed her beauty and hated the power she seemed to possess over him. He wondered if the tranny wore any panties, or were her giant testicles and cock swinging from side to side free from the restraints of the undergarment. After the transaction at the bank, they said their goodbyes and went their separate ways.

Precious went back home to rest up before John came over, and James to Burger King, where he ordered three Double Whoppers, large fries and a large, chocolate frosty. While scarfing his food down like a starving refugee, James had a massive heart attack and died in the parking lot of the establishment. At least he died doing what he loved the best: eating.

Meanwhile, Precious was getting ready for John Evans to come over and worship her ebony meat, like the pathetic fag she was sure he was. Over the phone, his voice sounded soft and nervous, just the type that longed to be dominated and humiliated by a real woman with a large pussy stick.

Looking at herself after taking a shower, Precious couldn't help but feel proud of the fine woman staring back in the full-length mirror. She was the epitome of a black womanhood and the proof was her bank account. While biological women whore around for free, a fine-ass tranny like Precious stacked paper because she had the one thing these down-low fags wanted in a woman: a dick.

Precious rubbed every square inch of her body with lotion and baby oil, because guys liked her to be glistening when they licked her from head to toe. After grooming, she slipped on a sexy blue nightgown, with no panties. Then to relax, she lay down on the couch, sipping a gin and juice and puffing on a blunt, eagerly awaiting the next fag to be mounted and conquered by her massive meat.

When she heard a car pull into the driveway at 10 p.m., she knew it must be John. Looking out the window as he exited the car, Precious thought he looked like a little boy. He was short and skinny, like a teenager. *Yeah, this was gonna be fun! This lil ho was gonna get the fucking of his life!* Before answering the door, she put on five-inch high heels, which made her six-foot-three. When she opened the door, she could see the lust in John's curious eyes.

"Hi, John. Nice to meet you. Come on in."

Precious liked that he was short and skinny, because she could easily dominate him.

"Nice to meet you, too," John said in a voice filled with nervousness and a lust. "I saw you last night on Spring Street, but the cop pulled up behind me, remember?"

"Oh, that was you? Come on into my bedroom, sugar." She could feel his eyes on her as he followed her into the den of sexual perversions. Precious sat down on the bed and then motioned for John to join her. As he sat beside her, she tongued kissed him to let him know who was in charge.

"You have my money, bitch," she said in her best pimp voice.

"Yeah, yeah I got it." John was nervous as he pulled out his wallet and gave the tranny her fee. Precious didn't even count the money. She just threw it in the nightstand beside the bed.

"Will you calm down John! Just relax. I'm not gonna hurt you," Precious said as she pulled her nightgown over her head, revealing her gorgeous body to the anxious fag. She lay down as John undressed, amused by his small cute dick. *Damn this nigga's dick was hard as hell, even then it was only about three inches!* No wonder he sounded like a bitch, he didn't have a dick, or at least one that a woman could feel.

John got naked and immediately started sucking on Precious' dick like a pro. Thoughts of Gwen, Maya and John Jr. went through his mind momentarily, making him feel pangs of guilt, but the taste of juicy black cock brought him back to his senses. The tiny-dick nigga couldn't believe he was lucky enough to be with a tranny this beautiful and hung like a horse. This was every tranny chaser's dream, and he was going to make the most of it.

After a while, Precious slapped him on the ass and told him to get ready for her meat. While on his back, she cocked the fag's legs behind his head like a bitch and inserted all ten inches into his loose rectum. Precious sometimes liked this position better than doggy-

style, because she liked to see the facial expressions of the guys while she pounded them with her thick cock. And she was pleasantly surprised that John knew how to throw his ass back and take her dick like a man. Her stroke felt so good that his little cock ejaculated cum all the way up to his chin.

"Damn, baby! This dick must be good," Precious laughed as she wiped the cum off John's face, all the while not missing a stroke. After about 20 minutes, it got even freakier when John told her to take the condom off and fuck him raw.

"Take the rubber off, baby. I want to feel you cum deep inside my boy pussy! I want you to make me pregnant," John said in a passionate girly voice that made Precious fuck him harder and harder.

Even though she usually practiced safe sex, raw always felt better, so she obliged him. After taking the condom off she made John get on top and ride her dick. Precious couldn't believe how good this faggot's asshole felt. He rode her dick like a stripper, his booty bouncing rhythmically up and down her long pole until she couldn't hold back any longer. John could see this big-dick-bitch was about to cum so he braced for the magnificent sweet liquid that made him feel like a woman.

"Damn, baby! Here it come, here it come, here it come, goddamn it!" Precious yelled as cum exploded from her dick into John's eagerly awaiting rectum.

She marveled as he took every inch of her thick cock like a champion dick rider. He continued to slowly ride the tranny's massive meat until it became soft and couldn't be ridden anymore. The ass was feeling so good to Precious that she didn't want to take her dick out, so they lay in each other's arms, both pleased and content that their lust had been sated.

"Damn, baby! You got some good dick! I love for a big dick ho to make a woman of me," John whispered with his head on Precious' breast.

"The way you throw that fat ass, boo, I couldn't help but put it on you like that," she said while gently slapping his cum-soaked ass. "You got a booty like a woman, and damn, you know how to throw that thang."

John didn't answer. He reluctantly reached for his underwear so he could get dressed and back home before Gwen's drunken-ass woke up. Precious offered to let him wash up, but he declined, saying he liked the feeling of cum in his rectum "because it made him feel

like a lady." He thought of his asshole as a pussy. With sticky cum running down the crack of his butt, John didn't notice that the wallet dropped outta his pants as he dressed. Somehow, it had rolled under the bed. Precious damn sure noticed, and the scheming, conniving bitch said nothing.

"Well, thank you. I do my best. I know I might not have the biggest ass, but what little I got, I can damn sho throw it," John assured her.

"You don't have to tell me that, boo. I know firsthand now the way you drained this dick. Not too many muthafuckas can tame this monster, but you sho did."

Precious sat up on the bed rubbing her dick, hoping to distract John from noticing that he dropped the wallet.

"You ready to go, boo?" Precious asked while leading him toward the door.

John followed her, not once taking his eyes off her beautiful naked body, oblivious to anything else at the moment. Like she did with all her tricks, she gave him a passionate kiss and sent him on his way, happy and content. When John's car exited the driveway, she was confident that he wouldn't come back for his wallet that night, but she didn't care. It was hers now, and if he wanted it back, he was going to have to pay for it.

John was on cloud nine driving back home. Hell, he was feeling so good that he might even fuck the old ball-and-chain tonight, but she was probably still asleep on the sofa where he left her two hours earlier. Feeling lucky, he stopped at the BP on Rockbridge Road and bought a Fantasy 5 lottery ticket. While there, he realized his wallet was gone. After paying a buck for the ticket, he called Precious and asked her if he had seen his wallet since he remembered taking it out to pay her.

The phone went right to voicemail, which seemed suspicious, since he was just over there less than 20 minutes earlier. The good feeling he had after leaving Precious' house now felt like gloom and doom. What if the bitch had his wallet and wouldn't give it back? She had his social security card, driver license, work I.D. card and his ATM card—in other words the ho had his freaking life in her hands. But maybe he was jumping to conclusions. Maybe Precious didn't answer the phone because she's seeing another client or she was in the bathroom.

He decided to go home and call her in the morning. Things always seemed better in the morning after a good night's sleep, he reasoned. Right then, all he wanted was a cold beer and a joint to ease his troubled mind.

Precious didn't answer the phone when John called, because she knew what it was about. He wasn't going to get the wallet back unless he made it worthwhile, which meant at least $2,500. Hell, not only did she have his social security card, she had his driver's license and work I.D as well. Discovering that the fag was a probation officer intrigued Precious.

She hated all law enforcement—even fuck-ass probation officers, because she remembered the way they screwed around her brothers by violating them and sending them back to jail if they failed a drug test.

The capitalistic tranny didn't want to appear anxious, so she decided to wait seven days before calling the little-prick ho back. A week gave her enough time to look at all the pros and cons, which minimize mistakes. Acting too hastily caused errors and mishaps, which could lead to prison or even worse—death.

Watching the video of her session with John made her wish the lil nigga would do videos for her website. Since coming to the Atlanta area, she had to shut the website down, because it was hard getting guys who wanted to be fucked on camera. And the ones who agreed to do it wanted to wear ski masks to hide their faces. Finally, if a fag did agree to fuck on camera sans mask, he was a damn crack-head who was more interesting in sucking on the glass dick instead of her dick.

And not only that—but her dick always got shitty after fucking them because the nasty muthafuckas wouldn't clean themselves out before getting fucked. A lot of guys underestimate the damage that a 10x5 dick can inflict on an unsuspecting rectum. She would fuck the niggas so hard with her mini baseball bat that sometimes they would shit on themselves.

Maybe she could work out something with John. He definitely enjoyed riding her big cock. Maybe he would agree to be her video lover in exchange for the wallet. But whether he agreed or not, it was getting late and time to go to bed. It had been another profitable day for the big-dick tranny. With just two clients that day, James and John, she made approximately $1,007. *Not bad not bad at all!* she

thought while lying in bed, sipping on a gin and orange juice and puffing on a blunt.

Now, if she could capitalize on the lost wallet, she could turn John's mistake into her gain. Precious only hoped he wasn't dangerous, and above else, broke. At least he got a steady paycheck working for the state. In the morning, she would look online to see how much probation officers made yearly. Then she would call James and tell him to come over, but since it would be Sunday she was sure his praying cock-sucking ass would be in church all day.

****

It was 1 a.m. when John got home, and the house was quiet, except for the TV in the living room. It incensed him to no end to waste electricity! After turning the big screen off, he made a drink and rolled a joint, which he smoked outside on the patio, enjoying the quiet and the night air.

His asshole was nice and sore, just the way he liked it after being abused by a big cock. He could still feel Precious' sticky cum lubricating his rectum, like a fine oiled engine. Damn that was the best dick he ever had! Even though he'd said the same thing before, this time he really meant it! She had him riding her dick like it was manna from heaven.

The liquor and weed made him sleepy, so he slogged upstairs to his bedroom and was surprised to see Maya asleep in the bed by herself. Then he went to JJ's room and found him asleep in his mother's arms. It wasn't a strange sight, but it was weird that with the cover down by their ankles, John could see they were both butt-naked and a used condom was on the floor.

He didn't know whether to feel disgust or shame: disgust at the way his wife raped their son, or shamed that his son could please his wife sexually, but he couldn't. After staring at them sleeping in each other's arms, he pulled the covers up over them and went to bed.

He undressed and lay down beside his daughter with an ass full of dried cum to keep him happy. John loved the feeling of another man's seed drying in his rectum. It made him feel so feminine. With the wife sleeping with their son, he surmised that she wanted him to fuck Maya. Damn and he thought he was the pervert! but it seems Gwen was the freak.

He pulled Maya's sleeping body close to him and realized she had no panties on, so he spread her legs to feel her young tender pussy. She awoke while he fingered her and let out a sleepy low moan of pleasure. Feeling ashamed, John quickly stopped and told her to go back to sleep. She climbed on top of her daddy's naked body and nodded back off into dreamland.

When John woke up the next morning the house was quiet because Gwen and the kids were in church. At first, he thought last night had been a weird dream, until he remembered the used condom, and thoughts of his son fucking Gwen brought him back to reality.

After jerking-off, he called Precious to see if she had his wallet. Again, he got no fucking answer from the arrogant long-cock tranny. While taking a shower, John decided to surprise the bitch by going over her house unexpected, because he really needed his identification. Washing her baby making juice out of his asshole made the fag realize how much he wanted more of her seed inside him. Fine black trannies were a dime a dozen in Atlanta, but she was something special. She wasn't the prettiest or most passable, but she possessed a certain sexiness that made a nigga want to worship her. On his way out the door, he called and left a message saying he was on the way.

Precious heard the message and didn't bulge from her soft bed. She had a wicked hangover, and at 11 a.m., it was much too early to get up, let alone talk to this fool about his damn wallet. When his car pulled into the driveway, she thought about going to the door but instead just lit a blunt and ignored the ringing doorbell. When she didn't answer the doorbell, the fool started knocking on the door, as if that would make her answer. Finally, he left after five minutes of knocking on the door like he was the police. Precious quickly fell back asleep.

Gwen loved going to church, it was her version of "clubbing." The Evans family had been going to Big Miller Grove Church for seven years. She believed going to church kept the family strong and loving to each other. Sitting between her two precious children, Gwen had never felt closer to them. On the previous night, she caught Maya sucking John Jr.'s big dick. But instead of stopping her, she watched and played with herself until her fingers got sticky from cum. Then she walked in on them like she hadn't seen anything, and feigning shock, explained the birds and bees to the tykes.

To her surprise, they knew a lot more than she thought they did. When Maya fell asleep, Gwen put the child in the master bedroom while she slept with her big-cock son. JJ watched her as she took her nightgown off, and he instantly got hard watching her big saggy tits flop up and down. She kissed him on the lips and then gave him a masterful blow job as she worshipped all ten inches of her son's beautiful man meat.

Then they sixty-nined, with her on top, sucking his dick while he ate her pussy out, like a hungry refugee from Sudan. When she couldn't take no more, she put a condom on JJ's eager dick and inserted it into her wet, aching pussy. He filled her up with a cock three times as big as her husband's pencil dick. Since it was his first time, he only lasted about four minutes before he filled the condom up with cum. JJ then cuddled in his mom's arms and fell asleep, like a good little boy. She put his mouth on her nipple, and that's how John found them when he got home later that night.

Gwen didn't care what John thought, because she was a woman who had needs, and one of those was dick. And since her weak-ass husband wasn't man enough for her, maybe her son was. *Scratch that, her son was now her man, fuck what society thought.* Why go out in the street to get some dick, when she had a big cock right under her roof? So what if it belonged to her son, cock was cock. It was better than screwing around in the street, like she knew John's was doing. What was more precious than a mother loving her son? He came out of her vagina, after all. Why not let him cum in her vagina?

When she heard John come into the room later in the night, she feigned sleep. She would have loved to have seen his face when he laid eyes on them, cuddled up like lovers. And when he pulled the covers over them, she knew he was a punk and was afraid to compete with his son for his wife's pussy. But after seeing how big JJ's dick was, he must have felt completely emasculated.

It served him right, because this shit never would have happened if he had stayed home. Since John was tired of her, she thought he wanted to fuck Maya, but when she asked her daughter did they do anything, she said "no." Hell, it seemed like he was scared of pussy, or maybe he was fucking around with fags, or maybe he thought Maya was too much woman for his little dick to handle.

That morning, before getting ready for church, she let JJ make love to her without a condom. It felt wonderful. His dick made her toes curl. When he nutted in her, she let out a loud yell that woke

both John and Maya from their sleep. She wished John could have made her feel that way. But some women got no dick at all, so why complain? The Good Lord had blessed her with a big-dick son, and she was grateful to Him for that.

Looking around the church, she wondered how many more mothers were screwing their sons… and how many of these fine Christian gentlemen were sneaking into their daughters' rooms at night, bloodying up the sheets. Tonight, she wanted Maya to feel the pleasure of a big, juicy dick in her virgin pussy. Sitting in church, the only thing she could think of was riding dick like a common slut. Damn, if these parishioners only knew what was on her mind, they'd banish her from the church for life. Finally, at 2 p.m., church was over, and she couldn't wait to get home. Hopefully, John cooked one of his great Sunday meals. The nigga couldn't fuck, but he sho could cook.

When John came back from Precious' house, he was beyond angry. First, he called Bank America to report that he'd lost his ATM card. He knew that bitch had his wallet and was purposely avoiding him. If he didn't get his wallet back by the next day, then he would have to report to his supervisor that his state ID was lost. He couldn't very well tell the bank that a tranny prostitute stole it. Like every Sunday, he made dinner, which consisted of Cornish game hens, mashed potatoes and gravy, and cornbread. Smoking a joint to relax, he reflected on what a wild weekend he had.

Friday night, he went to Pleasers to see some booty-shaking, and then he met Precious that same night in Midtown. And last night, he got fucked by Precious and lost his damn wallet. Then he came home and found Maya in his bed and his wife sleeping butt-naked with JJ, and a used condom on the floor. And to top it all off, this morning, he was awakened by his wife's screams of pleasure while getting fucked by big-dick JJ Damn, he couldn't wait for this weekend to be over!

Fucking with ex-cons was less stressful than the bullshit he was going through. Every time he thought of Gwen spreading her thighs for JJ, he felt impotent and weak. Damn, how could he have let that happen? He cursed God for giving him such a small penis while giving his son one the size of a large cucumber. Even while soft, his dick was still bigger than his father's tiny cock when erect.

At 2:30, he heard the garage door open and knew it was Gwen and the kids. Hurriedly, he set the table for their Sunday dinner.

"Mmmm, mmm! That smells good, baby," Gwen shouted as soon as she walked into the kitchen. Then she gave John a kiss on the lips. "Let me go take these clothes off and pee, and then I'll be ready to eat, sugar."

"Baby, I need to talk to you about what's been happenin between us and the kids."

"Later, baby, we can talk later, but right now let's just have a nice dinner, okay?" John nodded and said nothing. "You kids go take your clothes off and wash up for dinner."

After ten minutes, everyone was at the dinner table, heads bowed, while John said grace. They small-talked about everything, except for the one thing they were all thinking about, which was sex. In fact, if one didn't know any better, they might have been impressed with the family, who seemed like they were were the damn Huxtables or some other ordinary American family where incest wasn't the norm. When they finished dinner, the kids went to do their homework, while Gwen and John went to their bedroom to talk.

John spoke first. "How do you think I feel knowin you fuckin our son, JJ??"

"Well, how do you think I feel when you out whorin around at all hours of the night, comin home smellin like another woman's perfume? Hell, you ain't fucked me in over a month now, so don't get mad because I need some dick! I have desires and needs, just like you do. Don't be judgin me—like your shit don't stink. If you were doin your job, I wouldn't have to go to JJ for some dick. But since you givin your little cock to everybody except your wife, I have no choice."

"You do have a choice, bitch! You can fuck any man you want to, as long as it's not our son," John pleaded.

"Why I got to be a bitch? It's not my fault if your son is more of a man than you. And I don't want any man—I got my man, and he's my son—a beautiful big-dick son who fills me up like you never could."

Gwen could see the hurt in John's eyes, but she no longer cared.

"Oh, so I can't fill you up? Didn't I give you two kids? So I must have filled you up somethin!"

John turned around and left the room with his head hanging low, looking defeated. Gwen followed him downstairs.

"Baby, let me tell you somethin. Incest can keep a family together, believe me. There's nothin wrong with a family physically expressin their love for each other."

"Damn, you sound like a real pervert now. Fuckin your family is wrong, no matter how you try to spin it!"

"Well, like they say–if lovin my son is wrong, then I don't want to be right. And if you want me to stop fuckin my son, then you need to stay your ass home and stop fuckin them nasty-ass strippers. Them ho's gonna give you AIDS!"

Needing a smoke, John fixed a drink and went to the garage to roll a joint, while Gwen, feeling hungry as usual, grabbed some Ben & Jerry's ice cream from the freezer. After eating the whole pint of Chunky Monkey, she waddled up to their bedroom and fell asleep. Feeling a little guilty about what John said, she decided to sleep with her little-dick no-fucking husband that night.

Precious didn't get out of bed on that beautiful Sunday until after three o'clock. She tried to call James, but she got no answer. *Old fatty must be in church*, she surmised. Then she looked up the salaries of probation officers to gauge how much she would charge John to get the wallet back. Even though they didn't make much, John was still going to have to pay her about $2,500. If he didn't pay up, she would threaten to tell his wife or job or both.

Finally, James called her back—or at least she thought it was him. A lady on the other end informed her that James had died of an apparent heart attack on Saturday in the parking lot of Burger King on Panola Road. Precious expressed her condolences and hung up. Damn! It seemed that death followed her from Detroit to Decatur. She felt little sympathy for the obese fag.

The only thing the tranny was sorry about was that she didn't get more money from him. The death of James made her think about how fleeting life is, so she decided to give John a call Monday while he was at work and let him know she found his wallet. Hell, if she waited too long, he could have a heart attack, get shot, or any number of terrible things could befall him before she got her money.

It was 11 p.m. on Sunday night, and John was finishing off his second scotch and soda while watching the news. When they showed the winning numbers for the Fantasy 5, he looked at his ticket and did a double-take. With all the drama he was going through, he couldn't believe this stroke of luck! His ticket matched all the numbers, which meant he won $151,000.

John jumped up and down and let out a silent yell, cognizant not to wake up the family. It was definitely the best weekend in his entire life. At first, he contemplated whether to tell fat, lazy-ass Gwen. But it would be hard to keep something like this a secret, with the tax implications and all. *Damn!* he fantasized about buying a new car, but he knew Gwen wouldn't let him splurge like that once he told her about their windfall. The money would be going straight to the bank for things like the kids' college tuition, savings and other non-glamorous items. Finally, after rechecking the numbers over and over to make sure he really won, John went to bed, feeling giddy, oblivious to Gwen's lion-like snoring.

When morning came, John told her the good news. Gwen immediately got down on her knees and said a prayer to the Almighty, for blessing them with the money. After discussing what to do with the cash, they decided to bank at least 90% of it for the kid's future and splurge the remaining $15,100 on the family.

Driving to work, John remembered the look of respect Gwen gave him while she was on her knees, praying to God. But he couldn't help but wonder if she was thinking about him or JJ while she was down there praying. At work, he told the supervisor that he'd lost his I.D., which got him a stern warning not to let it happen again.

He decided not to tell the coworkers about his lottery windfall, because Negros would be trying to borrow money. Other than that, the day went like most days, wherein he talked to ex-cons who were just out of prison and trying to facilitate themselves back into society, which he knew most would fail to do. But he didn't give a fuck about these niggas anyway. They depressed the shit out of him, listening to their sad, hard-luck stories.

The fools didn't realize that they brought that shit on themselves by making fucked-up choices in life. Nobody told these illiterate, smart-aleck motherfuckers to rob a liquor store or sell crack or do the hundreds of other fucked-up things that land someone in prison. Then they get in front of him like they know everything, and they too dumb to listen to reason. He pitied these fools because most were hopeless. Their mammy should have aborted them and saved the world a lot of heartache and misery.

Based on the records of his probationers, most had engaged in homosexual acts while in prison, some voluntarily, and some involuntarily. John wondered if they acted so tough while they were being raped, or did they squeal like little girls while secretly yearning

for the dick. And did they tell their girlfriends about all the homo sex they got in prison. He hoped they used condoms on the unsuspecting women, but then again, he didn't really give a shit one way or the other. It was their lives, and he had enough problems of his own. He got a call from Precious around lunchtime.

"Hello—Officer Evans speaking," he said in an official voice.

"Hey John, this is Precious Meat. How you doin? I found your wallet this mornin under the bed. Do you want me to bring it to you?" The tranny was just fucking with him, keenly-aware that he didn't want to be seen with her in public.

"No, that's alright. I can swing by after work and pick it up." John felt a little nervous at the thought of Precious coming to his workplace.

"What time will you be here, baby?"

"Around six o'clock."

"Okay, but I'm gonna have to charge you a finder's fee."

"What do you mean by a finder's fee?" John suddenly realized this hustling tranny was trying to shake him down.

"If you want your wallet, it's gonna cost $2,500."

"You connivin bitch! What makes you think I'm gonna give you all that money to get my wallet back? I can get another social security card and driver's license."

"Well, after runnin your social security number on the Internet, I see that you're married and have two lovely kids. And I even have your address. Unless you want your wife to know how much you love tastin my dick, I suggest you pay up. What you don't know is that I have hidden cameras in my bedroom, and I'm sure your wife would love to see you ridin my dick raw. What do you think she would say about that?"

John was speechless and for a moment as he contemplated what to do. This bitch repeated his address to let him know she wasn't kidding. She knew his wife's name as well as the kid's names. This bitch had done her research—which meant she's done this type of thing before. Damn! Just when his luck was about to turn this shit pops up!

"Listen, I gotta call you back, but don't call here again, okay," was all John could muster.

"First of all, muthafucka, you don't give the orders—I do. And I can call any damn place I please—like your home phone number. Now I want my damn money in two days, faggot, or everybody

gonna know how big of a freak you are. Today's Monday.   By Wednesday, I better have $2,500, or your boss will see everything in living color. Remember when you told me to make you pregnant? They gonna get a big kick outta that shit!"

"I'll pay! I'll pay! Please don't do that!" John pleaded, careful not to raise his voice in the crowded office. "I'll call you Wednesday with the money. I gotta go now. I have a client."

After hanging up, he went to the bathroom and sat for half an hour, thinking over the few options available to him. But there was only one option, and that was to pay the tranny or risk exposure. What started out as a good day turned shitty really quick. Luckily, he hit the jackpot, so paying wouldn't be a problem; but the thought of being blackmailed that galled him to no end.

Since the big-dick bitch had all his ID, Gwen would have to go claim the lottery winnings herself, which they planned on doing the next day. When work was over, he rushed home and was greeted with hugs and kisses from his loving but incestuous family. After fighting through rush hour traffic on I-20 East, he was exhausted while pulling into the garage and was surprised when the family came out to greet him.

Gwen had dinner ready, and they all sat down to a meal of spaghetti and meatballs. Nobody would ever imagine they were about to get over $150,000 in a few hours, judging by as calm as they were. Both were careful not to tell anyone about the money, because they knew niggas would be begging bad. Things hadn't changed that much, because Gwen slept with JJ that night, leaving John in bed alone with his thoughts. The only thing the down-low fag thought about was Precious and her glistening cock, sliding in and out of his ass. After jerking his small cute dick, he dozed off and had a nightmare, dreaming that Gwen was about to have JJ's baby!

****

When Precious got off the phone with John, she was feeling as giddy as a fag in prison. She had John by the balls, and in two days, the fool was gonna put $2,500 in her hands, and all because of his clumsiness. In order for the fool him to drop his wallet and not notice it missing, he either had to be high or just plain in awe of her beauty. The bitch knew her dick was powerful, but damn! Sometimes she was surprised herself by its prowess.

Maybe it had magical powers that made niggas go gaga when they saw it. And speaking of fags and money—since it was Monday, she had to meet David at Wendy's on Covington Highway to get her weekly $300 shakedown payment from him. Even though he had just paid her two days before, Precious decided to tax him again. After calling and threatening his fat ass, he agreed to meet her, since to do otherwise would be professional suicide. Damn, extortion sure was fun—unless you're the one getting extorted.

Precious was pulling in about $1,500 a week tax-free, and she wanted more much more. She was one of the top black trannies in the Atlanta area, and guys liked coming to her because she stayed in a nice neighborhood and didn't live in a cheap motel like a lot of she-males did. When clients saw her house, it automatically put them at ease, which caused them to drop their guards and relax. Their state of relaxation made them open up more and talk about their lives, revealing secrets they shouldn't have.

Precious used the information she got from these fags to probe for weaknesses, in case she decided to blackmail them. That's how David fell into her web, and now he had to pay until she said otherwise. When she got to Wendy's, he was already waiting in the parking lot, eating a burger. She pulled up beside his car, and David got out and handed her an envelope containing three one-hundred dollar bills. Without saying a word, he got back in his car and drove off. The whole payoff lasted ten seconds.

She was surprised at how sexy David looked, with his fat juicy ass wiggling like a hooker on the stroll. Since she hadn't eaten all day and had the munchies from smoking too much, she ordered a Double Cheese with a large Coke then drove to Mainstreet Park on S. Hairston to eat and people-watch.

As she sat on a bench, eating and feeding the ducks, she could feel the eyes on her from both men and women. The women looked at her with a mixture of curiosity and envy. Even though she wasn't passable, she was still fine, with a fat ass and nice natural looking tits. Her hair and makeup was impeccable, as well as her manicured nails and pedicured feet.

The men looked at her with a mixture of lust and disgust. Some stared at her so hard she thought they were going to burn a hole right through her. She could tell a few guys wanted to holler at her but were afraid to do so in public, for fear of being labeled a fag. After

about an hour, she walked back to the car, and right before driving off, a couple approached her.

The man was about six-feet-tall with a salt and pepper beard, which looked sexy with his smooth bald head. He was slim but broad-shouldered, and he had a nice sensual smile that revealed his boyish charm. The woman was about five-feet-four and built like a brick house, 36-24-40. The guy looked to be in his late 40s, while the woman looked to be in her early 20s. Both were redbones. The lady spoke first.

"Hi, my name is Lois, and this is my husband Phillip. Are you Precious Meat," she asked.

"Yes. How do you know my name?"

Phillip chimed in, "We seen your add on Backpage, and it was really nice. We think you're a beautiful young lady and would like to get together with you."

"Well, I'm free tonight. Why don't you call me later?"

"First, let me ask you a question," Lois responded. "Do you fuck women?"

"Of course I do, baby—especially someone as fine as you. Goddamn that ass is fat! What time can y'all come over?" She could see Lois blush after the compliment.

"First, we have to go home and wash this funk off us, and then we'll give you a call," Phillip assured her. "Can I get your number?" Precious gave him the number and he entered it in his phone.

"So, what all do you want sexually? I charge extra for threesomes."

"All we want is for you to fuck me while my husband watches."

"Okay, that sounds cool. I'll charge y'all $400. Is that okay?" The couple nodded simultaneously.

Before leaving, they agreed to call later that night to make arrangements. After saying good-bye, Precious watched them walk hand in hand to a black Corvette and drive away, waving to her as they drove past. This was going to be her first time fucking a woman in over a year, so she was glad the woman was fine and sexy.

The last chick she fucked was a big, ugly white bitch up in Detroit. It was disgusting, but her cock was up to the challenge, because she put a hurting on that old pale pussy. When she got home, Precious took a shit and a hot bath in anticipation of her rendezvous with Lois and Phillip. They called about an hour later, and Precious texted them the directions to her house.

After checking to see that the cameras were in working order, she rolled a blunt and relaxed in bed, watching her past sexual conquests on the computer. Soon, Lois and Phillip would be another notch in her belt. In a little while, the female would feel the wrath of a huge Detroit cock, invading her sweet stinking pussy.

Chapter 4
Phillip & Lois

Phillip Hart was a 49-year-old businessman who loved young pussy. His wife of over two years was a former stripper who went by the stage name of "Honeybake"—as in the ham. Her real name was Lois Westbrook, and she hailed from Memphis. She started stripping at 13 to make money for her junkie parents. Her dad invited guys over and made his daughter dance butt-naked for them, and they would throw money at her feet, which went directly to the local crack dealer.

At first, she hated it, but after a while, she liked the power her naked sexy body wielded over the drunken niggas who lusted after it. At 15, she started organizing stripper parties with some of her friends, and sometimes they made over $200 a night, which was a lot to a girl growing up in raggedy-ass Lamar Terraces. Before turning 16, she moved in with an older woman who taught her the tricks of being a good prostitute.

Being a fine young redbone was good for business, so by the time she was 18, she had over $15,000 saved up. On her 18th birthday, she did two things: first she got her own apartment, and second, her stripper license. She went to work at Pure Passions, a ghetto strip joint where girls not only danced, but they turned tricks in the dressing room.

After a year, she grew tired of Memphis and thought about leaving for more lucrative pastures. One night, while sucking a niggas dick in the VIP room, the police busted through the door and scared the shit outta her. To make matters worse, the guy had just cummed all over her face. While the police held a gun on her, cuffed her and made her do a perp walk in front of the cameras, with sticky cum all over her mouth. It was a raid, complete with police dogs sniffing for drugs and the local news team filming everything. After spending the night in a nasty-ass, crowded holding cell, the self-righteous redneck judge charged her with one count of prostitution and fined $500. As soon as she got home, she packed her bags and drove to Atlanta.

After checking out numerous clubs, she decided to start dancing at Pleasers. Like most strippers, she moved from club to club, depending on the day of the week. Pleasers was her main employer, where she worked at least four nights a week, even though the

owners were white the girls and clientele was black. This spot wasn't as famous as Magic City or The Blue Flame, but Lois felt it was just right for her. She liked that the customers were mostly older guys in their 30s and 40s, who liked to show love to a young redbone with a cute face and fat ass.

And she enjoyed working here for another reason: she was one of if not the finest dancer in the joint. At the popular strip clubs, the competition would be greater, which equated to less tips. At Pleasers, she was always one of the top earners and could feel the envy of the other bitches when niggas made it rain while she danced. To make money in Memphis, a bitch had to fuck to get paid, but at Pleasers, it was definitely forbidden.

Lois didn't care, because she was making double of what she made in Tennessee. Why fuck in the club when you can fuck these niggas in the privacy of your own home? On some nights, she counted six or seven guys in the club who had been to her house to buy some of that good Memphis redbone twat. Lois was looking for a sugar daddy to take care of her.

She didn't want to turn out like her junkie mama, who used to strip back in the 90s. Instead of saving her money, she blew it on clothes cars and crack. Then she hooked up with a low-life drug dealer and became pregnant with Lois. Soon the drugs took its toll and then took her beauty. She became a nigga junkie whore, turning tricks for crack. Lois was determined not to make it her fate. On a slow Wednesday night, her dreams were answered when Phillip entered.

Phillip's lust for young pussy ruined a 20-year marriage to his high school sweetheart, Patricia. He had always been a dog, but it became obsessive when their two kids went off to college. Hell, after a while, he stopped trying to hide it, and some nights, didn't bother to come home. One evening, Patricia secretly followed him to some apartments off Glenwood and pleaded for him to come home.

Instead, he cursed her out and told his loving devoted wife to take her old pot-belly ass back to the house. She started crying when he slammed the door in her face as some half-naked girl laughed in the background. After banging on the door and pleading for him to come out, she took a baseball bat that was lying on the ground and smashed out all the windows on his BMW. Phillip came out cursing like a sailor, but it was too late. He started to call the police, but he

thought better of it. Besides, she was still his wife, and he didn't want her to get into any kind of legal trouble.

In the end, he was glad it happened, because he wanted to make Patricia hate him so much that she would want a separation—and the wish came true. Feeling hurt and bitter, she filed for divorce the next day. To her surprise, Phillip didn't contest it. A couple of weeks after she informed him, he bought another house and hardly saw anything of Patricia, unless it was a family function or something related to the children. When it was time to go sign the divorce papers he was noticeably happy and upbeat. Finally, he could be rid of the wife and free to do his own thing.

That night, he celebrated the divorce by having a threesome with a new chick he'd just met named Lois, aka Honeybake, and her friend, Diamond—two lovely, dick-sucking Memphis freaks, who loved eating each other's pussy—an old man's dream come true. After a while, he, and Lois fell in love, and they got married at city hall in downtown Decatur. That was two and a half years earlier, and he'd been on a wild ride ever since.

He thought he was a freak, but Lois made him look like an altar boy. She was addicted to sex, and it wore him out. His old ass couldn't keep up with this young fine stallion of a wife. So to please her, Phillip let the bitch have male lovers to compensate for his lack of virility. Even though it was an affront to his ego, this was the only way to keep her.

One evening when he came home early from the office, he was shocked at what he saw. She was having a threesome with two big-cock trannies. While she was on top of one of the trannies, riding his dick, the other tranny was behind, fucking her in the asshole. When they saw him standing in the bedroom doorway, Lois didn't even acknowledge his existence and just kept on begging for more cock while the trannies kept right on fucking. Without saying a word, Phillip just turned around and slinked away, like a dutiful husband.

He fixed himself a drink and then sat down on the floor outside their bedroom, listening to the moans of pleasure and pain coming out of his wife's sweet gutter-mouth. After wrecking his wife's pussy and rectum with a combined 21 inches of dick, they drowned her insides with their thick, sticky cum, nutting like a fire hose putting out a three-alarm fire. Then they collapsed in a sweaty, funky heap, exhausted from the intensity of their fucking.

After resting for a few minutes, Lois rolled a blunt and they chatted and laughed, while she hollered for Phillip to fix them a drink. Obeying like he always did, Phillip quickly whipped up three cranberry vodkas and brought them to his guests while they lounged, naked on his bed, with their cocks still glistening with cum. Phillip felt less emasculated by these trannies than he did when she fucked regular guys. Even with their obvious big dicks, they still looked pretty much like women from the waist up.

From that day on, every other one of their threesomes had a tranny in it. Phillip liked their combination of femininity and masculinity. He loved seeing a beautiful tranny fuck the shit out of his whorish slut-of-a-wife. The lines of what he would or won't do sexually were blurred with every tranny they experienced. At first, he only wanted to jerk-off, watching his wife, but then he started getting sloppy seconds or getting his dick sucked while the tranny fucked her.

One day, when an overly-aggressive tranny cummed in Lois, the big-dick bitch made him lick it out, and then unexpectedly, she started rubbing her still-hard cock between his butt cheeks. Before he could make her stop, she rammed all eight thick inches of dick into his virgin asshole. As he cursed in pain, Lois wrapped her legs around his bald head and made him suck her on clit harder and harder. Phillip never felt such excitement before, especially when the tranny slapped him on the ass and shot a load of hot cum up his previously virgin rectum.

As he lay there, sandwiched between his wife and the tranny, with cum dripping down the crack of his ass, Phillip felt on top of the world. The feeling of getting fucked almost rivaled getting some pussy. He didn't realize the power of the dick until getting some cock shoved up his virgin ass. At almost 50 years old, a damn tranny made him feel more like a man by fucking him like a woman.

That happened about six months before they met Precious, and he'd been addicted to tranny cock ever since. Not that he didn't want pussy anymore—to the contrary, getting fucked made him want to go out and prove his manhood by throwing his long dick in the first fine bitch he saw. He wanted the bitch to feel what he felt when a tranny was riding his fat ass. In other words, a tranny made him a more sensitive and considerate lover. The power of the dick is undeniable.

"You know where you goin?" Lois asked Phillip as they drove to Precious' house.

"Baby, why do you always ask these asinine questions? You know I grew up here," he said, feigning annoyance and rubbing her thigh.

Lois smiled, sat back and replied, "I know you do, because you want that dick more than me, don't cha biatch?" She then grabbed his hard cock and laughed out loud.

"Well, duh! Why you think I'm speeding? The quicker we get there the quicker I get the dick, bitch!"

Then he reached over and gave her a kiss on the cheek. Lois lit a joint, looking forward to a night of hot, nasty sex. Even though Phillip rarely smoked, he enjoyed seeing Lois smoke, because it loosened her up even more than she already was. She implored him to take a puff, and he took a long slow drag off the illegal but powerful substance. The shit must have been good, because he immediately felt the effects of the happy weed. Yep, tonight was definitely gonna to be freaky and wild.

"Whew! Goddamn! That shit strong!" Phillip said between coughs. "Where you get that shit from?"

"Over in Techwood. Its good, ain't it? Baby, you better slow down you goin too fast." Phillip was driving almost a hundred miles an hour down I-20.

"I'm not drivin that fast, and besides I thought you wanted to get there fast, so relax."

"Baby, the dick gonna be there when we get there. Now slow down, please."

Phillip slowed the Corvette to the speed limit and thought about their last threesome with a tranny. Lois had instructed him to fuck her, while the tranny fucked him at the same time. The sensation of getting fucked made him fuck Lois even harder and more sensual. It was as if the tranny dick turned him into a woman, and he could feel what Lois was feeling like only a woman could.

"Here—hit the joint again, baby, so you can relax."

Phillip took the joint and puffed some more, while getting off the interstate onto Wesley Chapel Road. As usual, the street was busy, and folks were driving crazy as bat shit. While trying to beat a red-light, Phillip mistakenly went through the intersection just as an 18-wheeler came speeding through, T-boning their car on the driver's side.

Phillip died immediately as the monstrous truck rolled on top of the car and crushed his head like a watermelon being dropped from a

ten-story building. Lois fared better, but not too much, as she was paralyzed from the waist down. Three months later, while recovering at Shepherd Spinal Center, she suddenly realized the gravity of being confined to a wheelchair for the rest of her life. One day, feeling more depressed than usual, she took a knife from the cafeteria and slit her wrists., To speed things along, she slit her throat, severing the carotid artery, and bled to death.

The day before the suicide, her friends from the club came by to visit. While they were laughing and talking, Lois let out a loud, stinking fart and shitted on herself. Feeling humiliated and embarrassed, she cried uncontrollably as her friends stared at the floor, trying not to look embarrassed for her. The beautiful girl couldn't handle a life of wearing a fucking diaper, because she couldn't control her bowels and sometimes shitted on herself. The former stripper couldn't handle not being fine and sexy like she used to be. Lois, aka Honeybake, died like she lived—on her own terms.

When the couple didn't show up, Precious called and called, but she didn't get an answer. She hated such inconsiderate muthafuckas who didn't have the courtesy to call and let her know they cancelled. Missing out on the $400 made her mad as hell, but it was okay, because she needed the rest anyway. Besides, John was going to give her $2,500 on Wednesday, so that soothed her anger.

Chapter 5
Big Money Tuesday

Tuesday morning couldn't have come soon enough for the Evans family. It was the day they were going to claim their lottery winnings. John woke up to a lonely bed and quickly jerked-off to memories of Precious, while his wife was getting a morning fuck from their son JJ. After her son cummed in her, Gwen got the kids ready for school, while John fixed a breakfast of pancakes, sausage and eggs.

He knew Gwen loved a big breakfast—especially after getting fucked. Hearing his wife and son making love was weird at first, but he was happy that JJ had taken over his coital duties, because making love to Gwen was truly disgusting. The sight of her body repulsed him to the point of revulsion. Most important, she didn't have the one thing he craved: a big black dick.

Other than that, she was a good mother and wife. The kids came down first and ate two bowls of Captain Crunch each before kissing their daddy and scurrying out the door to catch the school bus. Then Gwen huffed and puffed down the stairs and sat down to eat. She ate eight pancakes, six sausages and four eggs, washed down with a glass of orange juice.

John looked at her with a sense of shame and loathing. She didn't actually chew the food—she just swallowed, like a damn cow chewing cud. After fat ass finished stuffing her face, they drove to the district office of the Georgia Lottery Games in downtown Atlanta.

Since he didn't have any ID, Gwen had to claim the prize. She had to fill out numerous forms, and after taking an ill-advised picture, they walked out two hours later, $151,000 richer. They went to the nearest Bank of America and deposited the whole check. Driving back home in silence, both thanked God for their good fortune as they listened to gospel music on MyPraise 102.5 radio.

Before going home, Gwen stopped at their favorite pizza restaurant, Papa Johns, and ordered four large pizzas to celebrate the special occasion. They got home right before the kids' bus pulled up in front of the house. Looking at their son getting off the bus, her night was already planned, which included eating a whole pepperoni

"I'm your, ho, baby! Make mommy your ho! Ain't nobody got no pussy like mama's pussy!" Gwen couldn't stop cumming, delirious with pleasure.

Finally, JJ's body tensed up, signaling he was about to cum, so Gwen wrapped her thick legs around him so she could get every drop of baby-juice in her.

"Mama! Mama, mama it feels so good! Ahhh!" Those words were heard throughout the house as he shot a heavy load into his mother's womb. After finishing, he fell asleep with Gwen's nipple in his mouth as a pacifier.

Still feeling horny, she walked down the hall to John's room with JJ's cum running down her thighs and farting like a bullhorn. John pretended to be sleep, but he didn't fool Gwen.

"You know you ain't sleep so stop playing," she whispered standing over him, sweaty and naked.

"What you want woman? I'm tired!"

"I want some dick from my husband, if you don't mind."

She jumped on top of John and started tonguing him down all the way to his little dick.

"I knew this little thang could get hard," she said in between slurps of little cock. After choking on JJ's big piece of meat, Johns' dick fit perfectly in her mouth like a tootsie roll. Finally realizing that his dick was as big as it was going to get, she made him fuck her, but she could barely feel him inside her. Even though John was stroking with all his might, his 3½ inches just wasn't enough for her anymore. JJ had spoiled her.

"Damn, baby, you just too damn small!"

Gwen didn't want to hurt his feelings, but she had to be honest.

"Eat my pussy, bitch, since you can't fuck!"

She pushed John's head down between her thighs and made him suck on her clit.

"That's your son's cum inside me. It tastes good, don't it? Lick it, bitch, lick it!"

Strangely, it turned him on—licking his son's cum out of his wife's pussy. He loved the way Gwen treated him like a bitch, because he enjoyed being treated like a bitch. John just pretended Gwen was Precious and sucked on her stinky clit like it was a big juicy cock.

"That's right! Lick your son's sperm outta me like you mean it, ho! You ain't got no dick, but you got some good tongue action."

Gwen wrapped her big legs around his face and almost choked him while getting her last nut.

"Damn, damn, damn! That felt good! You made me nut three times with that magic tongue. That felt good, baby. Just because I'm fucking JJ don't mean you not my man. I love you, boo."

After they kissed and said goodnight, Gwen rolled over and let out a long, stinky fart, burped and fell asleep.

The next morning, John was awakened by JJ, crawling in bed between him and Gwen. Pretending to be asleep, he heard Gwen moan as JJ stuffed her pussy with all ten inches. Soon, the bed was rocking with JJ as its maestro, stroking his mother with lustful abandon, oblivious to his little-dick father who was lying inches away from them.

John tried not to get turned-on, but his little pecker got hard, listening to the sound of incest lust. He didn't know why he was turned on so much. Was it listening to his wife being manhandled like he couldn't do it, or was it thinking about JJ's big beautiful cock? To him, only one cock was more beautiful than JJ's dick, and that was the dick belonging to Precious. After listening to them fucking, he couldn't hold back any longer, so he turned over to watch. In the morning sunlight, he saw Gwen with her legs cocked up over her head and JJ stroking her, hard and slow. When Gwen saw him watching, she was amused and smiled.

"Your son got a big dick, don't he, baby," she said between moans and grunts. "Doesn't it look good, doesn't it look powerful— like a Mandingo!"

John nodded and proceeded to jerk-off.

"Show your daddy your dick, boo."

JJ pulled his cock out of Gwen's dripping pussy and put it next to John's face.

"Look how good that thang look," she bragged.

John couldn't believe how gorgeous his son's dick was. And it was right in his face, glistening with cum. First, he looked at Gwen to gauge her reaction, and since she seemed to encourage it, he hungrily put the head of the dick in his mouth.

JJ seemed afraid at first, but one look at mom eased the anxiety. Father lovingly licked son's penis, like it was the most natural thing on earth. To JJ, it seemed Dad was a better dick-sucker than Mommy. After a couple of minutes of watching him slurp on her man's dick, Gwen pulled JJ back on top of her until he lubricated her

downstairs to breakfast. Then he turned his thoughts to more important things, like the math test in Mr. Callaway's class.

****

As soon as she got up that morning, which was at 10 a.m., Precious called John and asked what time he was going to bring the money. He said that he couldn't meet until after work, which made her angry, because she wanted to get the transaction completed at lunch time. Since he was persistent, she told him to meet her at the Wendy's on Covington and Panola Roads at 6:00 that evening. To make sure he'd be there, she threatened to expose him if he was a no-show.

Right after she hung up on John, the doorbell rang, which was surprising because she didn't have any clients lined up for the day, and clients knew not to come over without calling. Peeking out the curtain, she saw that it was Marcus, her next door neighbor's 16-year-old son. What the fuck did he want? After eight months of living there, it was his first time knocking on her door. She was curious and apprehensive opening the door. Standing there, in just a nightgown, with her long cock barely peeking out from under the short nightie, she could tell he was startled by her bold sexiness.

"Yes? What can I do for you," she asked with a smile on her face.

"I, I, I, just wanted to see what you were doing, that's all," he stammered, trying not to look at the cock-head, peeking out from under her gown.

"What do you mean you wanted to see what I was doing? Is yo momma home?"

Marcus shook his head.

"Then what can I do for you?"

"Duh, duh, duh—I just wanted to get to know you, if it's alright with you," he stammered.

"First of all, you're too young for me, and will you stop looking at my dick!"

"I'm sorry, Precious Meat, but I seen your ad on Backpage, and I think you're beautiful."

"Thank you, boo, but like I said—this wouldn't work out. Plus, yo mama would have a fit and call the police on me. How old are you anyway?"

"I'll be 17 next month, so I'm not that young. I'm a virgin, and I want someone like you to make love to me. I don't really like girls, even though I date them it's just to please my mama. I'm really attracted to boys, but I don't know if I'm ready to take that step yet. But transsexuals are like a cross between a man and a woman. You look like a woman, but have what I want between your legs."

Taken aback by his honesty, she told him that if he was serious, he should come over later so they could talk more. Then the boy, who was almost six-feet-tall and slim, reached over to kiss her on the mouth, but Precious turned her head so that the kiss landed on her cheek.

"You sho is bold, ain't cha,' she said, smiling at the cute youngster's awkwardness. "Be over here around 10 o'clock tonight, and don't come over in the daytime anymore, or folks'll start talkin."

"Ok, Precious. I love you," he said before turning and running away, smiling and giggling like a little girl at his good fortune.

Watching him skip away like a little female, it was apparent the boy was gay. If Precious could see it, why couldn't his mama see it? In truth, folks see what they want to see. It was easier for his mom to pretend her son was straight than face the horrible fact that he was going to be a dick-sucker. Or maybe his mom, Rosa Lee, thought that if she didn't mention his obvious homosexuality, it would somehow disappear from his DNA, like magic.

Since she was a church going Christian woman, maybe she thought she could pray away his gayness, but damn! Don't God have enough trouble dealing with wars, disease and famine? Why should he givva fuck whether Marcus liked dick or not? It's more than likely that she resigned herself to the fact and quietly accepted the situation, hoping against hope that it was just a stage he's going through.

Her own common sense should tell her that at 16, it's beyond a phase. Phases don't last that long. Still feeling sleepy, Precious puffed on a blunt and lay down again. To relax, she jerked-off, thinking about Marcus. After imagining cumming in his tight virgin ass, she fell asleep and didn't wake up until 4:45 p.m.

After showering, she headed to the Wendy's to wait on John. While there, she ordered a "Baconator with Cheese" and a large coke. She hadn't eaten all day, so she was famished. At 6:45, John still hadn't shown up. She was worried the fag might be a no-show, especially since he hadn't answered her calls. Just as she was about to leave, he pulled up beside her and rolled his window down.

"You have the disk?" he asked, looking about to see if anyone he knew was watching him.

"Yes, I have it on a flash drive right here. Do you wanna see what's on it? I brought my computer with me, so you know I'm telling the truth."

Precious put the flash drive into her computer then moved over to the car's passenger side so she could hand him the computer without getting out of the car.

As John watched the contents of the flash drive, he was astonished by how whorish he had become. He acted like a fucking woman, begging for more and more dick and slurping this tranny's dick dry. God, if this got out, he would be ruined! Her voice broke his concentration.

"Now, I hope you got my money."
John nodded and handed her an envelope, took the flash drive from the computer, and putting it in his pocket, he handed the PC back to her. After counting the money, she returned his wallet.

John checked the wallet's contents, and satisfied everything was there, he left without saying anything to the big-dick tranny. He had dodged a bullet and felt relieved that she didn't know about his lottery winnings. But what if the bitch found out about it somehow? Surely she had copied his social security number and home address, and since she's made extorting people her business, it would be within the realm of possibilities.

As John approached his street and house, he realized she could blackmail him over and over. Despite the fact that she gave him the flash drive, he was certain she didn't erase the files from her computer. That would be stupid—especially if your business is extorting down-low fags. Why would she give up her power by erasing the files? Without the files, she'd be any other tranny prostitute, trying to hustle anyway she could.

Just then, it dawned on him that she must have been blackmailing plenty of guys like him. He felt like a damn fool to fall into the clutches of such a demented psycho bitch. Her crazy ass could wreck his marriage if she exposed him as the dick-hungry whoremonger that he really was. John relaxed when he realized it was probably the last time he would ever see Precious Meat, especially since he could get the same thing at home for free.

Precious felt happy after leaving Wendy's $2,500 richer. As she watched the NBA game on her 40-inch flat screen TV while sipping

on a vodka and orange juice, she was on top of the world. Surveying her comfortable house, she was pleased with the progress she made since coming south.

It amazed her that after only eight months in Decatur, she had these niggas right where she wanted them—face-down/ass-up on her bed, getting the shit fucked out of them, while hidden cameras filmed all their sexual proclivities in living color. She fell asleep while watching the game, but the doorbell awakened her, and then she remembered Marcus was coming. Wearing only panties and a t-shirt, she answered the door, smiling at the youngster.

"C'mon in. I see you weren't kiddin, were you?" She let the boy in and offered him a drink.

"Can I get a beer or something," he asked.

"You ain't old enough to drank!"

"My mama let me drink beer all the time. Can I have one, please?"

Precious gave him a cold Budweiser, and they sat down to talk. She could see Marcus staring at the big dick-print in her panties, and it excited her, evidenced by the print getting larger. She could tell the boy was nervous as he chugged the beer down.

"So what exactly do you want from me, baby?" Precious asked in a voice with equal parts sweetness, innocence and lust.

"Well, I want you to do something for me that I'm scared to do," he replied, looking down at the floor. "I want you to tell mama that I'm gay." He braced for a "no" answer.

"Wow! That's something you should tell her, don't you think? You may be surprised by how she acts, if she don't already know."

"But I'm afraid of what she might say or do to me."

"Listen, child, and I say this with all sincerity: she already knows. She just hadn't said anything to you about it. I knew you was gay the first time I seen you. Remember when you came over with Rosa Lee to welcome me to the neighborhood?" Marcus nodded. "Hell! You was switching like a little girl then!"

"Dang! I didn't even think about that," Marcus said in a low-pitched voice. "Sometimes I wonder how other people pick up on my gay-vibe, but mama seems blind to it. Anyway, I want to dress like a female too; I just feel so much like a girl. So how will mama feel when I tell her I wanna be a woman? That's a lot of shit to handle all at once."

"As cute as you are, you'll make a beautiful, tall sexy young lady. The earlier you transition, the easier it will be for you to adapt physically and psychologically to the challenges that transsexuals face. And your mama is stronger than you think. Give her some credit. She loves you, no matter what."

"Can you teach me how to do that?" he asked. "I want to get my eyebrows arched, but I'm afraid to. I'm scared I might look weird or funny. And I wanna change my name to Monique Devereux, because I like French names."

"First, it would be helpful for you to tell Rosa Lee, and then I'll help you, because I don't want her calling the police on me for messing with her baby boy. Since I'm a transsexual, she may not want you hanging around here, thinking I may be turning you out. Where is she now, by the way?"

"Oh, she's working the graveyard shift at Grady. She won't get off until seven in the morning."

Precious thought of an idea for how the boy could break the news to his mama, and he wouldn't have to be there when she found out about his desire to be a transsexual woman. She told the future-tranny the plan.

"You can write a letter and leave it on the kitchen table for her to read while you're at school. That way, you can tell her your true feelings, and your mom will have time to think about it. It will give her time to contemplate what to say and how to handle it. Then Rosa Lee won't be so apt to fly off the handle and say something she may regret later."

"Is that how you broke the news to your mama?" Marcus asked thinking if it worked for Precious, it could work for him.

"Naw, child, I was wearing my mama's clothes at 14. Shit, I didn't have to tell her—when I'm trying on her high heels and tight dress for my Halloween costume in the 8th grade. I was looking good, too. A few male teachers was checking me out hard. From then on, I dressed like a girl almost every day." Precious smiled reminiscing about the good old days.

"But didn't your mama and daddy try to stop you?"

"My mama—bless her heart—was a hustlin ho with three sons by three different daddies. She was just glad I wasn't like my brothers, who were thugs and end up doin time in prison. My oldest brother, Tommy, got killed in a prison riot, and my other brother got 25 years for killing his girlfriend. With two brothers like that, Mama

was just grateful that the police didn't come knockin at the door, lookin for me. My brothers got in so much trouble that the po-po knew my mama by name. See, everybody's life is different. Yo mama may not be as understandin as mine was, but your mom is a good decent woman who loves you more than anything else on earth. And as for my daddy—the last time I seen him was when I was ten."

"Will you help me write the letter?" Marcus asked.

"Yeah, I'll help if you want me to," she assured him. "We can get started right now, because the quicker you do it, the better-off both of you will be. I bet this time next year—you'll be wearin high heels every day, and Rosa Lee won't be battin an eye. She just has to get used to it first."

They both laughed at the thought of him in heels and went to the bedroom, where both lay on the spacious, king-sized bed and typed out the letter to Rosa Lee. Before getting started, Precious rolled a blunt and let Marcus take a few puffs to relax his nervous ass. After wheezing and coughing from the smoke, Marcus started typing a heartfelt, nervous letter to his mom. With the help of drunken-ass Precious, he typed the manifesto in an hour and downloaded it off her copier. After reading it to himself, he seemed pleased with the contents. It was going to be his message to the person who loved him the most, so it had to be right.

"I sure hope this works," Marcus concluded, looking at Precious for encouragement.

"Listen young'un—once you decide to be who you really are, then you've already won the battle. Whether your mama accepts your lifestyle or not, you still have to be the person God made you to be. God made you gay, and ain't nothin anybody can do about it, includin you. You think I givva damn about what society says about me? Fuck society and its' hypocritical backward ass moralities! You have to be you. If not, then you're just a slave. Hell, I see bitches out with their man, looking at me like I'm a freak, while they nigga be trying to get my number on the low-low. Them hos don't know that I'll fuck them *and* their down-low dick-lustin boyfriend too."

"So you saying it don't really matter what my mom does, because my life is really up to me?"

"Ding! Ding! Ding! My God! I think he's got it," Precious said in the best British accent she could muster. "Once you have that attitude, anything is possible. Look at me—I grew up in some tough-ass projects in Detroit. Now, I own this beautiful, three-bedroom

crib. I did this all on my own. If I can do it, you can too. But unlike me, you don't have to quit school, like I did. You can still and should get your education, because this game ain't no joke. I'm an escort because that's the only way I knew how to make money. If I had better parents, they would have seen that I finished high school and went to college."

Listening to Precious opened Marcus' eyes to the many possibilities life as a transsexual offered. He could still achieve his dream, which was to become an actress. If he put limitations on himself, then that gave others license to do the same thing.

"I definitely don't wanna quit school. I'm on the honor roll, with a 3.4 GPA," the youngster proclaimed. "And I plan on going to Georgia State when I graduate."

"That's what I'm talkin bout! Do yo thang, child, cuz if you don't, you'll always be miserable. Don't be like the millions of people who get up in the morning and dread going to work. I love what I do. I fuck niggas for money, and they pay good too. I wish I had gone to college, but this is my career now, and besides—I make more than most college grads ever thought of making."

Precious went into the kitchen to fix a double Scotch, came back and flopped on the bed. After taking a swig of the liquor, she pulled off her panties and started playing with her beautiful, erect ten-inch monster right in front of an astonished Marcus.

Without saying a word, she took the young faggot's head and roughly pushed his mouth down on her throbbing penis that was already oozing with pre-cum. By palming the back of his head like a basketball player palms a ball, she steadily increased the rhythm of his mouth, gyrating up and down her long cock. Precious took delight in watching the youngster gag and slob on her monster meat.

Seeing that he couldn't take it any longer, she paused to let him catch his breathe. Marcus rolled over on his back gasping for air after having his mouth violently raped by the drunken tranny. He had tears rolling down his face and snot coming out of his nose. Precious gave him some tissue to blow his nose and wipe away the tears.

Then she stood, drinking the rest of the scotch, and told Marcus to get on his knees in front of her. After obeying like an eager pup, Precious slammed her cock in the boy's mouth and preceded to give him a vicious face-fuck. Luckily for both of them, the dick-sucker had a wide mouth and small teeth to accommodate such a large piece of meat. Marcus' soft lips were driving her crazy with each stroke,

bringing her closer and closer to ejaculation. After less than five minutes, she exploded in his mouth dumping so much cum down his throat that he gagged and vomited on her feet.

"Damn! I didn't mean to hurt you. You alright, baby?" She reached down and helped him to the bed. "Sometimes, I get carried away and can't help myself."

Marcus just looked at her. "You just surprised me, that's all, and that was my first time sucking a dick."

Precious gave the boy a damp towel to wipe the vomit and cum from his mouth then she wiped her feet.

"Damn, baby! I didn't know that. You shoulda told me," Precious said, trying to seem apologetic, even though it wouldn't have done any good, because *what the dick wants, the dick gets.* With her cock thoroughly drained, she sent the little fag home.

"Now, remember to leave the letter on your mom's bed or some other place where she can easily find it."

As Marcus was about to leave, Precious kissed him on the mouth and wished him luck. He thanked her for helping him write the note and then walked across the yard to his house, feeling faint due to an enormous headache from getting gagged and choked by a big cock. Inside, he went straight to the medicine cabinet, took three Anacins to relieve the throbbing in his head, and after reading the letter again, he fell asleep with the taste of Precious' cum still in his mouth.

****

At 7:30, John made it home to the arms of his loving family. After meeting with sleazy-ass Precious, he felt thankful to have a beautiful-if-flawed family waiting for him. Strangely, he felt sorry for the blackmailing tranny, who must have been lonely as hell. The kids were doing homework and Gwen was grading papers. After looking in on the kids, he took a hot bath to wash away the funk of a stressful day.

After putting on a pair of comfortable old boxers, he made himself a drink and escaped to the basement to smoke a joint, chill and watch ESPN. After spending the day on pins and needles, worrying if his secret life would be exposed, he stopped worrying about it for the moment. What if the truth did come out? What would happen to him anyway? The job couldn't fire him—that would

"Yeah, I wonder who he gets it from? It sure ain't you, with your little pencil-dick." Gwen delighted in emasculating John in front of JJ, especially since she believed he was screwing other women.

"Why you gotta go there and try to be hateful?" John asked, obviously hurt by his wife's remarks.

"It's not as hateful as you going out fuckin other women, now, is it? If you can get some pussy on the side, can't I get some dick? Just because I chose my son as my lover doesn't make me a bad person. Who can love a mother more than her own flesh and blood? But the way you sucked on JJ's dick the other night, I'm beginnin to think you on the down-low."

"What's down-low, Mama?"

"It's a man who secretly likes other men."

"You mean like when daddy kissed my dick?"

"Yeah, something like that," she answered. "Shit! Get off my back. I'm tired," Gwen said to JJ as she got up and plopped her drunken ass in bed beside her husband, with JJ in the middle. Minutes later, she was snoring and farting as usual. John and JJ soon joined her in dreamland.

Chapter 6
A letter To Rosa Lee

The next morning, Marcus placed the letter on his mom's bed, like Precious suggested, and he prayed that she would understand his plight. Before leaving for school, the boy wondered if he would be welcome back home when mom read the letter. Some of his gay friends were kicked out of the house when they told their parents of their homosexuality. Or maybe mom would take him to talk to their pastor and ask God to "pray away the gay," like it was some sort of disease.

Either way, the youngster knew he would remember that day for the rest of his life, because it's the day he finally "came out" to his mother. On one hand, he was worried about her rejecting him, while on the other, he felt a sense of freedom and relief—like an intense weight had been lifted off his frail shoulders. Being a teen was hard, being a black teen harder, and being a gay black teen still exponentially harder.

Homophobia was rampant in the African American community. Many black parents threw their children out in the street rather than be stigmatized by their neighbors or church for raising a faggot. Marcus knew the stakes, but talking to Precious gave him the confidence he needed to face the trying days ahead.

After Mom read the letter, everything would be out in the open, and he wouldn't have to hide his sexuality anymore. The teen was lonely and longed for a boyfriend so that he could have someone to hold hands with or cuddle with on a cold rainy night. After eating two bowls of Honey Nut Cheerios, Marcus grabbed his bookbag and went outside to wait on the school bus. When the bus arrived, he marched back to the very last seat and stared out the window at his house, wondering if he would be able to stay in it when mom found out the big secret.

Rosa Lee was a RN and had been working in the emergency room at Grady Hospital for the last 12 years. For the past year and a half, she worked the 11-to-7 graveyard shift because it paid more. She enjoyed the work—not only because it paid almost $100,000 a year, but because she loved helping people. It gave her a sense of accomplishment to be a force for good in the community. What could be nobler than helping sick people, after all? To her, she was

doing God's work—just like the minister did on Sundays, only she helped people more directly. The patients may call on The Good Lawd, but it was the nurses and doctors who relieved their ailments. Religion worked very well, especially when it coincided with modern science.

Rosa Lee loved her colleagues and coworkers because most were like her: caring, dedicated professionals who did everything in their power to help patients. It had been a tough shift, with three patients suffering gunshot wounds, and she was grateful that none of the young black men had died—though she was saddened that one was paralyzed from the neck down.

While walking to her car, she thought about Marcus and how grateful she was that he didn't aspire to be a goddamn thug like those three hoodlums. Her son was into his books and was on his way to Georgia State to become a doctor, she hoped. Pulling out of the crowded hospital parking lot, she was relieved to be going home after so much blood and pain on her shift. The farther she drove down I-20 East, the better she felt about the day ahead.

It was Thursday, and she didn't have to be back at work until Sunday. After pulling into the driveway, she noticed the yard needed mowing and the hedges needed trimming and made a mental note to remind Marcus to do it this weekend. She smiled to herself anticipating the many protests he would bring up to avoid doing the chore.

As she walked into the kitchen she, was pleasantly surprised that Marcus didn't leave the house a mess, like he usually did. This time, he actually put the dirty dishes into the dishwasher, and to top it off, he turned it on too. The day was getting better and better. Humming a church hymn, Rosa Lee went to her bedroom to undress and take a hot shower. While taking off her bra she noticed an envelope on the bed with the word, "MAMA," written on it.

Suddenly, a feeling of apprehension and dread overshadowed her formerly good mood. Why did Marcus have to write her a letter and leave it for her to read when he wasn't here? What was so big a secret that he didn't want to be around when she found out about it? At first, she thought about tearing the letter up and flushing it down the toilet. She could pretend to have read it while saying nothing to Marcus when he returned from school. But curiosity won out over avoidance, so Rosa Lee sat and read the letter.

Dear Mama

I love you, and I hope after you read this letter, you will still love me too. Ever since I can remember, I have felt like a woman, trapped inside a man's body. I know this is a shock to you, but there is nothing that you or anybody can do to make me feel otherwise. In my mind, I'm a girl, and want to start living my life as a female as soon as possible. As far as I'm concerned, God made a mistake by making me a boy instead of a girl, and I can correct that only by being who I really am, instead of who I'm supposed to be.

Living as a boy feels like a prison sentence, and I want to be free from these shackles that society imposes on me. I'm tired of lying to you by saying I have a girlfriend. Tameka and me have never even kissed. She knows I'm gay, but you don't. When we be up in my room, we on the Internet, looking at cute guys—not making out like you pretend we are.

Have you actually seen us kiss or ever caught us making love? You haven't caught us, not because we're careful, but because I hate the thought of having sex with a girl, especially because I'm a girl myself, but I'm not a lesbian. I want a boyfriend to take me to the movies and school dances and to dinner. I'm tired of going places with a bunch of girls, pretending to be straight. And I'm also tired of dressing like a boy. I want to buy some girl clothes, so I can start transitioning to transsexual as soon as possible!

You don't know what it's like to live, being trapped in another body. Sometimes, I think of killing myself, but knowing the pain it will cause you brings me back to my senses. And I want you to start calling me by my girl name, which is Monique Devereux. Well, that's all I have to say.

Your loving daughter,
Monique

After reading the letter, Rosa Lee sat down on the bed to collect her thoughts. She wasn't greatly surprised by the notion that Marcus may be a little gay, and she had wished against science that he would grow out of it. That's why she left him alone with girls in his room, hoping that something would spark and his dick would awaken to the pleasures of the female body.

The letter indicated it not only hadn't happened, but was never going to happen. It was bad enough for him to be gay but, he wanted to be a goddamn woman too! When she started reading the letter, she

braced herself for the worst, but the worst was much worse than she could ever imagine.

How could she explain to her family and friends that she was raising a boy who feels he's a woman? Beyond that, he wanted to start dressing like a girl and change his name to Monique. She could already see the look on the store clerk's face when she went with Marcus to pick out his dress for the senior prom. The embarrassment and shame would be unbearable to face. At such times, she missed Kenneth, Marcus' father who died in a car accident five years earlier. Even though they weren't married he was a good provider and a steady, strong hand who would know what to do.

Fortunately, Kenneth took out a $300,000-dollar life insurance policy on himself and made her the sole beneficiary six months before he died. Half of it would go to Marcus when he turned 21. But what would Kenneth have said or done in the situation? Their son was going to be a transsexual, no matter what she or anybody else said or did. Being in the medical profession, she understood that Marcus was born gay and that nobody turned him that way.

Trying to explain as much to the members of her church was another matter. They wouldn't be so apt to accept the medical profession's diagnosis of homosexuality. Instead, the sanctimonious assholes would blame the mother for her son's "ungodly perversion." What would happen if Marcus—dressed as Monique—still wanted to sing in the church choir? Those were just some of the thoughts running through her mind as she struggled to come to terms with the stressful situation.

She didn't have anyone to talk to who had any expertise on the matter other than the clinical psychologists at Grady, but their expert opinions were useless, since the letter was so conclusive. Marcus was not only a fag, but he wanted to dress like a woman—that was a double-whammy for any mother to confront.

Glancing out the window, it occurred to her that there was an expert living right next door to them. Precious was the last person on earth she wanted to talk to about her son, but since she was a transsexual, perhaps she could provide a few pointers on how to handle the situation. Feeling tired from the nightshift Rosa Lee stretched out on the bed, trying to figure out her next move, and fell asleep. She slept soundly and didn't wake up until she heard Marcus come home from school.

When Marcus turned the key to the front door, he expected Rosa Lee to come charging at him with a boatload of accusations and questions. But to his surprise, it didn't happen. Dropping the bookbag in the kitchen, he fixed a roast beef sandwich, poured a glass of orange juice and went to his room to chow down.

As he passed his mom's room, he peeked through the cracked door and saw that she was lying down, still tired from the night before, so he didn't say anything to wake her up. He figured that either she was okay with the letter, or she was probably thinking about what to say to him. He sat in front of the computer, checking his emails and eating, thinking about what would happen when mom woke up.

Suddenly, his phone rang, scaring the shit out of him. It was his "girlfriend," Tameka.

"Wassup, boy? Did Rosa Lee say anything to you yet?"

"Nope. When I came in, she was still sleepin, so I don't know how she gonna react. I wish you could come over and give me some support."

"Man, I don't wanna be around your mom when she get mad. Shit, I seen her go off on a Wal-Mart cashier, and it wasn't pretty."

"Tameka! You know my mom love you to death."

"Yeah, but that was when she thought we went together. But now, she knows that was just a fat lie, and I don't want her going off on me."

"I'm just worried about her going off on me," Marcus said, feeling a little better since Tameka called. "What if she throws me out like DeAngelo's parents threw him out?"

There was silence on the other end of the phone. DeAngelo was a classmate of theirs who told his parents he was gay. Shortly afterwards, they threw him out of the house "in the name of Jesus." Not only did his immediate family wash their hands of him, but so did his community and church. After crashing on numerous friends' couches here and there, he finally ended up in a downtown Atlanta homeless shelter. To make ends meet, he sold his body to the old nigga faggots that roam the streets of Atlanta at night like goddamn vampires.

When he asked his ultra-religious parents if he could come home, they told him "no," accusing him of being a spawn of Satan. No matter how much their 16-year-old child pleaded to come home, the only help they provided was an occasional stop by the homeless

shelter on Peachtree Street to bring him money, but was once in a blue moon. After a year, the streets had taken its toll on the teen. By then, he was a hustling prostitute with a reputation for giving good head and being able to ride a big dick.

DeAngelo practiced safe sex at first, but that went out the window when men made money offers to fuck him raw. Disillusioned, he stopped calling home and medicated his loneliness and shame with crack and liquor. He loved the immediate intense high that crack gave him. It made the boy feel like he was on top of the world. One day, after smoking the drug for hours, the teen got so depressed that he went to the 17th Street Bridge, took his clothes off and climbed out onto the protective barrier, threatening to jump.

Traffic came to a screeching halt as onlookers gawked and took pictures of the butt-naked, crazy suicidal nigger. After three hours, the police finally talked him down and took him to Grady for psychiatric treatment. The crowd of onlookers was disappointed that the fool didn't jump, because they were ready with their iPhones to record the incident to put it on YouTube. It did go viral, but it would have caused a bigger splash if he had jumped.

After two weeks, the troubled youngster was released from Grady back onto the mean streets of Atlanta. During his time in the hospital, the only visitors he had were Marcus and Rosa Lee. She came to see him after her shift was over, asking how he was doing or if he needed anything. DeAngelo needed love and a place to stay, but no one ever offered. His pious parents called a few times, but they never came to see him, fearing his homosexuality would rub-off on their younger two sons.

With no alternative other than the hustle, he began selling his body again in order to get something to eat. Hustling accomplished two things: it put money in his pocket and sustenance in the belly. The downside of hustling was the danger involved with dealing with strangers. One evening at eight o'clock, an older black man, driving a white work van, picked him up on Mitchell Street. The sign on the van read "Cunningham Plumbing—Atlanta's Most Trusted Plumber Since 1978."

DeAngelo immediately liked the guy, because the old dude had some beer and weed to smoke on. He drove to Mozley Park off Martin Luther King Drive, and they proceeded to get high as a kite. After a while, he suggested they drive to a more private location, because he wanted DeAngelo to give him a blow job. The desperate

and hungry hustler agreed to suck the old guy's cock for the measly sum of ten dollars—beggars can't be choosy, especially a hungry one.

They drove down Hollywood Road and turned off onto Johnson Road, a ghetto in the northwest part of the city where there were a lot of crack-heads and abandoned houses. The driver, who seemed familiar with the area, pulled into a secluded driveway next to a yard that was overrun with weeds and garbage.

As soon as he parked, the old man pulled out his pissy-smelling dick and grinned as DeAngelo slowly started sucking on it. Trying not to gag on the smell, his magical mouth soon brought murmurs of pleasure from the drunk old fag. Since the guy had a small dick, it was easy to get him off. Being a veteran sucker, DeAngelo liked tiny cocks, because he could make his mouth feel like a pussy as he went up and down on it. That's exactly what he did there as the friction from his talented oral skills drove the drunk into a frenzy and he exploded in the youngster's mouth.

While they both recovered from the pleasurable ordeal, DeAngelo asked for his money and instead got a gun pulled in his face. Calmly, the old dude told him to take off his clothes. After complying, the scared teen started crying like a baby, begging the maniac not to shoot him. The next to last thing DeAngelo saw on earth was the stranger, grinning, and the sparks from the business end of a .38 special, before three bullets ripped into his frail body.

The assailant retrieved a can of gasoline from the backseat and poured it inside the van. As DeAngelo begged for mercy, the old guy calmly lit a cigarette and, after taking a few drags, threw it into the van from the outside driver's window. The last image the young troubled boy saw was himself burned into a crisp. The police found his half-charred body the next day. Only the bottom portion of his body was incinerated, so it didn't take the authorities long to identify the victim once they took it to the coroner to discover the cause of death.

****

The murderer was a 54-year-old pervert named Harold Washington, who lived in the Dixie Hills community, near Westlake Train station in southwest Atlanta. He was a happily-married man, who had three teen girls. In fact, on the night that he killed DeAngelo, the family had just celebrated he and his wife's 23rd

wedding anniversary. His reputation as a good family man masked the monster that raged within. The burned teen was his 4th victim in the last year, and it seemed easier for him after every kill.

The van he used to pick up the boy was an old, beat-up piece of crap that he secretly bought without the wife's knowledge. He torched the vehicle because he was afraid of being connected to it, though he never registered it in his name. The van had a stolen license plate, no insurance or any paperwork, so burning it was a way of covering his tracks in case the police came snooping.

Between killings, he parked the van at Hightower train station, and left it there for weeks until he had an urge to hunt for human flesh again. As with all predators, most of his hunts were unsuccessful, but he loved the thrill of the chase. On some nights, he rode around downtown Atlanta for hours, looking for the perfect victim to butcher. With a large homeless black population, it was easy to get a desperate nigga to get into his van—sometimes too damn easy. All he had to do was offer a couple of dollars for a blow job, and just like that, he had a fresh victim. Of course, not every guy that got into the van was killed. Most of the time, Harold just wanted a blow job and someone to talk to, or was sizing the unsuspecting person up for later date.

As a budding serial killer, he had perfected the craft down to a science. His first victim was a homeless brotha who was walking through Washington Park after midnight. Harold was scared shitless and the murder was clumsily and hastily completed. That night, the emerging murderer was sitting in the park, nervous, but determined to whet his appetite for bloodlust. It was late, so the park was closed, except for those who stayed out of the lighted areas, where the police couldn't spot them. Harold knew that some fool would come through, looking for a handout, hungry and desperate for a friend, and anything else that was offered to brighten up their desperate lives.

On that particular night, Jerome Long, a 35-year-old alcoholic, was that fool. Pushing a grocery cart, the drunk stumbled through the park, looking through the garbage bins for soda cans, when he had the unfortunate fate of meeting Harold. The friendly killer offered his intended victim a drink of scotch, and they immediately became friends. Not only did his new "friend" have liquor, but he also pulled out a crack pipe.

Shit, to Jerome, it was "homeless niggas' heaven." Usually, a nigga had to let some fag suck his dick to get treated that good, but on that night, he was just walking through the park, and *voila!* an angel of mercy appeared with a glass dick, full of rocks. God must have been smiling down on him! After hitting the pipe, Jerome let the crack ooze through his inebriated brain, taking him away from reality and to a place where nothing or no one could harm him.

As they talked about nothing, Harold felt more relaxed as the scotch dulled the senses. Soon he knew what needed to be done and was determined to do it. When Jerome turned around to take a piss, Harold snuck up behind and hit him in the head with a hatchet, which split his head wide-open. After Jerome stumbled and fell to the ground, dazed and confused, he looked around to see Harold coming at him, with a crazed look in his eyes.

It was too late, and Jerome was too high to escape the murderous madman's bloody hatchet. Cowering on the ground like a scared rabbit, Jerome begged for mercy, but his pleas only emboldened the murderer. Standing over his wounded prey, Harold smirked as he swung the hatchet down on the victim until the body went into convulsions and died in a bloody heap. What seemed to take forever lasted less than three minutes from start to finish.

At first, Harold couldn't believe what just happened as he stared at the dead body, unable to comprehend the rage that came over him. Soon, a sense of satisfaction and power swept through his body. In fact, he pulled out his dick and jerked-off over the bloody body of Jerome Long. After pleasuring himself, he wiped the blood off his hands and walked to his car, which was parked at Ashy Street Train station, and drove home to his wife and kids, feeling content and happy.

The murder of DeAngelo was Harold's last kill, but not because he had a change of heart. Rather, he suffered from a diabetic stroke one month later, which resulted in paralysis affecting the entire left side of his body. His inability to move his left-side arms and legs put an abrupt end to his career in murder. Seeking to replace the thrill of killing was useless, so he retreated into the bottle.

Initially, he worried the police would come knocking at the door, but after a while, he knew that he got away with four perfect murders. No one cared about the homeless niggas he killed, so the police stopped looking. Less than a year later, he succumbed to illness brought on by his sedentary, alcoholic lifestyle, and died

peacefully in his sleep. At his funeral, the killer was praised as a loving and hardworking family man.

****

"Your mama not like DeAngelo's parents. She ain't no Jesus freak," Tameka assured Marcus, breaking the silence.

"I hope not, but you never can tell."

"If she was gonna throw you out, don't you think she would have said somethin when you came home? You said she was still sleepin, so she must not be too stressed about you being gay. If that was the case, she would be waitin for you as soon as you opened the door. I think you worryin about nothin, boy. Rosa Lee love her baby boy," Tameka said, trying to put her friend at ease.

"Maybe she's so upset that she's afraid what she might do. DeAngelo told me that his mom and pops just kicked him out with no warning or anything. I'm scared that might happen to me too."

"C'mon, man. Think positive. What happened to DeAngelo not gonna happen to you. You a straight "A" student going to college next year, so why would Rosa Lee kick her only son outta the house, when you'll be staying in the Georgia State dorms next year anyway? When you leave, she'll be all alone, so she not gonna kick you out, believe me."

"Well, we'll find out today, one way or the other."

A knock on the door startled Marcus, because he knew it was mom.

"I gotta go right now. Talk to you later."

Tameka made him promise to call her later with details.

"Yeah ma?" Marcus answered.

"Interesting letter you wrote me, to say the least. First of all, let me tell you that I have no trouble that you're gay, but I do have a problem with you wanting to be a transsexual."

Marcus was startled by his mom's calmness. He had braced himself for a knock-down, drag-out fight.

"You, you, you don't care that I like boys?" he stammered.

"To be honest, I do care, but I can't do anything about that. People are born gay, baby. Nobody can make a person gay. Listen, dearest son, I wanted you to get married so I could have grandkids in my old age, and your wife could be the daughter I never had. I kind

of suspected you were gay, so I can't say this comes as a complete surprise."

Marcus got up and hugged his mom so tight that she almost lost her breath.

"I feel like I'm a woman on the inside, and I wanna dress like I feel."

"But what about school and stuff? Your classmates gonna make fun of you. And not only that, but will the school district let you dress like a girl?"

"They let lesbians dress like boys," Marcus countered.

"But you know good and well that in this society, it's acceptable for a girl to dress like a boy, but not vice versa. All females dress in jeans, but not all boys wear makeup and dress in skirts."

"Mama, I don't care about society. I just wanna be me. Why should I be unhappy just to make society happy?"

"It's not about making society happy. It's about conforming to certain roles that society expects, so one can be successful in life. Don't you wanna be rich and successful when you graduate from college?"

"Being a transsexual won't stop me from being a success. Look at RuPaul," Marcus replied in argument.

"But you ain't RuPaul. You're Marcus, my only son, and I don't want you getting hurt."

"So what if I get hurt! That's part of life, and it will only make me stronger for the future. Not allowing me to be me is what's hurtful. As far as I'm concerned, I'm a girl, and I want you to start calling me Monique from now on."

"How the hell can I call you that, when you're still a boy? I didn't name you that, so I'm not gonna be calling you by a girl's name. I'm sorry, but that's the way I feel."

"See—you're just like the people who you say will hurt me! I tell you how I feel, and you don't take it seriously. I told you I want you to call me Monique, and the first thing you say is 'no.'"

"How dare you say I'm trying to hurt you! I'm the only one on this earth who loves you more than life itself. I carried you in here", Rosa Lee said, rubbing her stomach, "so it hurts to hear you say I'm trying to harm you in any way. I just don't want you getting your penis cut off then regretting it later."

"If you say you love me, then you should know that calling me by what I want to be called. That's part of love and understanding. I

don't expect to get it out in the street, but it would be nice to get it from the person I love the most. And I love my penis. I don't want it chopped off."

"Well that's a relief! Praise God!" she said mockingly.

Rosa Lee sighed, realizing that her son was telling the truth, though it was difficult to admit. His mind was made up, and if she resisted too much, she might have alienated him. She didn't want to lose him to the streets, like his friend DeAngelo. The thought of her sweet, precious son selling his body to old men repulsed her more than his homosexuality did. Marcus had a brilliant mind and could do anything he wanted to in life, as long as he was given the right guidance—and boy did he need guidance now more than ever!

She wondered what Kenneth would have said about their gay son. Would he have tried to blame it on her, like most fathers did to the mothers, or would he understand and embrace his son's lifestyle? It would probably be the former, as was the case for most overly macho black. Maybe it was better that Kenneth was dead, because the news would have broken his heart. Yet if she wasn't surprised that Marcus was gay, maybe he wouldn't have been either. Maybe he knew all along and kept it a secret. Father and son had spent plenty of time together, camping and hiking.

"Here's what we gonna do, son—tomorrow we gonna have a talk with our neighbor next door. If anybody knows about your situation, she does. We can't solve everything all at once. We can continue this discussion later, but right now, I'm hungry. What do you want for dinner, fried chicken or spaghetti?"

"Spaghetti," Marcus answered, "and please don't put any garlic in it."

"Okay. After dinner, I'm going over and have a talk with Precious, the 'RuPaul' of our neighborhood," she said. "Ain't no need in putting it off for tomorrow."

Marcus didn't tell Rosa Le that he already had a talk with Precious one night earlier. He also didn't mention that she helped write the "coming out" letter. Marcus was afraid to tell because his mother because she had open disdain for the friendly tranny and he was scared Precious would get blamed for his desire to be a woman. It seemed the letter worked—just like the tranny said it would, so the teen was grateful for her advice, though he didn't want Mom thinking he went behind her back.

After dinner, Rosa Lee decided it was best if she talked to Precious alone and told Marcus to do his homework while she went next door to seek advice on how to handle a son who wants to be a woman. Before going over, she waited until the strange car parked in Precious' driveway left. A hurried, older gentleman got in and sped away, like he had done something shameful, like was sneaking away from a crime scene. She wondered if the down-low faggot's wife knew what he was doing.

Rosa Lee knew of her neighbors' lifestyle, because she looked on the Internet and found the enormous-dick tranny's website. With a name like "Precious Meat," she couldn't resist. She was surprised to have one of the most popular transsexuals in the south move in next door. The size of Precious' beautiful dick was amazing, but at the same time, seeing men sucking and riding it made her sick to the stomach.

As a good Christian, she started a petition with the homeowner's association to have the prostitute removed, but they didn't seem to care. In a depressed economy, they were just glad the house was sold—even to a transsexual prostitute, because the sale translated to higher property values.

Even when she showed the website to board members, they were shocked but didn't care. They told her to keep an eye out for anything suspicious. but as long as Precious' business didn't disturb the tranquility of the community, they didn't care one way or the other. Precious paid all her HOA fees and kept the yard immaculate. As long as she did that, she could fuck as many faggots as she wanted. When the car disappeared into the twilight, the desperate mom walked over to her neighbor, fearing the very answers she sought.

When Precious heard the doorbell, she thought it was Thomas, the guy who just left, because his hat was still on the couch. She was surprised to look out the window and see Rosa Lee standing there. She opened the door after putting on a robe, expecting to get cursed out about Marcus.

"How you doin, Rosa Lee? What can I do for you?"

"It's about Marcus. Can we talk inside, please?"

Precious invited her in, and both sat on the sofa, nervous about the upcoming discussion. Precious offered her guest a drink of wine, which Rosa Lee accepted. After a few sips, she relaxed.

"I got a very interesting letter from my son. He wants to be a transsexual—just like you."

"And how do you feel about that?"

"I'm shocked! That's how I feel. To be honest, I've always had a feeling Marcus was a little feminine, possibly gay, but I didn't know it was to this extent. A mother can only take so much in one day." Rosa Lee sighed, taking a swig of wine and sitting back on the sofa. She studied Precious to gage her reaction.

"What can I do for you... exactly?" Precious asked, uncertain if Marcus told his mom who helped him write the letter.

"I need some advice on how to best handle the situation with my son. I don't want to alienate him and lose him to the streets."

"Just love him like you always have, that's all he needs. As long as you do that, he'll be okay. You're a strong, beautiful woman. You'll know what to do."

"Yeah, that sounds good, but it's embarrassing for me to have my son dressing like a goddamn girl! What will my family and friends say? He's in the church choir, for God's sake! How can he go to church dressed like a girl, wearing lipstick and eyeliner? Oh God, it's disgusting!" Rosa Lee blurted, weeping.

"If he sees you like acting like this, you just may lose him," Precious comforted while handing the woman a tissue box. "I know this is a hard pill to swallow, but you have no choice, and you know it. Now here's some practical advice: start the transition off slowly. Don't allow him to wear dress or skirt just yet, but let him experiment with makeup. That way, it won't be such a shock to people."

"Is that how you started, growing up?"

"I started dressin like a girl full-time at 14 years old. Everybody knew I was a girl. My mama was, and still is, a hustling, crack-head drunk, so she didn't care, and my father was nowhere around. I had two brothers: one died in prison, and the other is still in prison. See, my home life was very unstable compared to Marcus. At 15, I was prostitutin, with my mama's help. She was basically my pimp. For the majority of transsexuals—prostitutin is the only way to make any money. Marcus doesn't have to do any of that shit. He told me he was going to college next year." Precious realized a second after she said the last sentence that she let something slip that she shouldn't have.

"Yes, he is going to school next year and how did you hear about that," she asked drying her tears.

"Well, I'm going to come clean. He came over last night, and I helped him write that letter to you. And while he was here, he told me his plans for the future."

"Marcus didn't tell me that," Rosa Lee remarked while drying her tears. "Instead of coming to me first he comes talk to you!" she said, sounding annoyed and pissed at Precious for advising her son.

"Now, I know you angry but, the boy was scared of being thrown out into the streets when you found out about his homosexuality. I simply told him that he wasn't bein fair, because nobody will love him more than you do. I suggested the letter as a way to break the ice, because he was embarrassed to tell you face-to-face. Tellin a parent that you're a homosexual is probably the hardest thing a child can do. Even in the best of circumstances, the parents will feel sad and betrayed or blame themselves. Listen, your son came to me for help, and I extended a hand to a troubled teenager who was afraid to go to anybody else. If I overstepped my boundaries, then I'm glad I did, because now the big secret's out and guess what? It's not the end of the world."

Rosa Lee didn't know whether to thank Precious or curse her out, but she came over for some real world advice—not to argue and lay blame, because anger wouldn't do Marcus any good. He needed his mother to be as level-headed as possible in the future. She imagined the ridicule her son would face the first day he puts on a dress. Society would be hard enough on him. The least she could do was make sure her home was a safe, loving haven. In a moment of epiphany, she realized the tranny was right. No matter what happened in the future, she had to be there for her son, whatever the circumstances.

"You did overstep, but I'm glad you did," she said to Precious, who seemed surprised. "When you have a child, you have so many hopes and dreams for them, and then when they tell you something like this, it's like a kick in the gut. I had visions of my boy getting married and having a dozen grandkids to play with in my old age."

"Well, he can still get married and have kids. It'll just be to a guy and not a woman."

"But I don't want him to adopt. I want my grandchildren to have my blood in them, not some stranger's blood. Marcus' father is dead, so he's the only one that can carry on his father's bloodline."

"Maybe he can pay a surrogate to have his baby, or maybe he don't want kids, but I understand your concerns. You puttin the cart before the horse right now. The last thang on any teenager's mind is havin children. Besides, no matter what he chooses, you're gonna be a supportive mother anyway. I can feel the love you have for your son, and it permeates through every fiber of your body. I envy Marcus because he has a mother like you. My mama only calls me when she needs something, which is every week. See—you already have the answers, because of the love you have for Monique." Precious called him Monique on purpose—just to see what Rosa Lee would say.

"I see you already calling him by that girl name, huh," she said, shaking her head and taking another drink.

"If that's what he wants to be called, why not? In the future, he will need to change his name officially if he wants to be taken seriously and transition all the way. I didn't change my name, but I'm not going to college or have a 9 to 5. The new generation of transsexuals will be more mainstreamed into society, especially the educated ones. Who knows? One day he may be runnin for president."

Rosa Lee tried not to imagine her son running for office in a dress. It was a strange and disturbing thought to say the least. Who would be the campaign manager? RuPaul? Just the thought of calling her son Monique and thinking about his size-12 foot in high heels made her shudder with shame and embarrassment. It had become apparent that her life would be much different than what she imagined. Every time someone talked about their kids, she would have to explain how her son became her daughter.

"So you think I should let him wear makeup?"

"Yeah, and get his hair done. He has some nice, long cornrow braids and a cute face. I know all this is a shock to you but you'll get through it. But right now, I hate to be rude, but I have a client coming over so…"

Rosa Lee didn't wait for her to finish the sentence. She rose to leave and thanked Precious for the advice and encouragement. Awkward, they shook hands and said goodnight. Although the tranny sympathized with her neighbor's situation, she was tired and had enough of her own problems. There was no client coming over. She just lied to get rid of the sad, whiney half-drunken bitch. It wasn't like Rosa Lee made any effort to befriend or get to know her since she

moved in. So when she discovers her son is a peter-puffer, all of a
sudden, she wants to be best friends and shit. Precious was glad to
give her some practical advice, but she didn't want to get to involve
in another family's problems. In the end, people were going to do
what they wanted to do anyway. Precious had enough troubles of her
own. Fuck Marcus and his homophobic mammy!

Tired, the big-dick tranny took a shower and went to bed-butt
naked. Remembering the lottery tickets purchased a day earlier, she
checked the numbers for the Powerball game online. Angry because
her ticket lost, as usual, she looked at the pictures of past winners.
While there were very few big game winners, there were plenty of
winners in the smaller money games like Pick 3, Cash 4 and Fantasy
5.

Seeing those smiling faces of the winners made the tranny
envious, but one picture almost made her fall off the bed. It was a
picture of a short, ugly, fat lady and her skinny husband, grinning
from ear to ear holding a giant check that displayed a cash prize:
"$151,000. It wasn't the amount that startled her. The man in the
picture threw her for a loop. It was none other than John and Gwen
Evans.

It made her wonder if she was born under a lucky star. First
Walter, and now John, how lucky could a bitch be? She reached
under the bed and retrieved a shoe box full of memory sticks
containing sex acts with unsuspecting clients, used for blackmail.

When she came upon Johns' footage, she put it in the computer,
reminiscing about his juicy "pussy" and how he wanted to be
impregnated just last Saturday. She decided in that moment that if he
didn't want it on YouTube, he was going to have to fork over
$100,000. She couldn't wait to call John to tell him the good news!
She was going to call immediately, but she thought better of it. With
the experience of the successful extortion in Detroit, she knew it was
better to use caution and devise a plan first, so she rolled a blunt and
went to sleep thinking of the best way to take a faggot niggas' money.

Chapter 7
The Proposition

It had become a common occurrence: John woke up in JJ's bed, kicked out of his own bedroom by his wife. After jerking-off to a fantasy of getting raped by Precious and his son, he took a shower and met the family for breakfast. It was a beautiful December Friday morning, cold, but very sunny. As with all Fridays, the family was excited about the weekend—especially that weekend, because they were going to the Mall of Georgia for Christmas shopping.

In a scene played out all over America, the Evans were going to show their kids how much they loved them by spending an insane amount of money on them. And the kids wouldn't have it any other way. The two happy siblings laughed and ate their bowls of cereal, while Gwen couldn't take her eyes off JJ.

She attended to his every need, asking if he wanted more breakfast, while ignoring Maya. When he wanted toast, she buttered the bread for him. When Maya asked for toast, her mother just threw it on her plate, minus the butter.

The power of the dick made the perverted mom do things. It was overwhelming. She was only human, made of flesh and blood. As they proudly watched the kids get on the school bus, Gwen and John kissed each other on the cheek and headed to their jobs, content with their degenerate lives. Appearances can be deceiving. From the outside, nobody would ever have known how fucked up the family really was. If they did know, Gwen and John would be in jail.

When John got to work, there were several messages left for him from Precious. Recognizing the number, he reluctantly called the bitch. This time he was going to curse the ho out and make it clear to her that he was the wrong nigga for her game. She answered on the third ring.

"Hello," she said in her husky man voice.

"You the one that left two messages for me, I thought I told you not to call me anymore."

"First of all, boo, you don't tell me any damn thang, okay? Precious do what the fuck Precious wanna do," she replied, referring to herself in the third person. "I'm tired of you down-low muthafuckin faggots trying to dictate to me after you been slobbing

on my dick! The reason why I called, muthafucka, was because I seen you and your fat, ugly wife on the AJC Georgia Lottery website, holdin yo big lottery check. But when I talked to you a few days ago, you didn't tell me anything about it. I'm guessing it slipped your mind, due to the brain damage caused by your addiction to dick." Precious was just beginning to have fun fucking with this cum drinker.

John was at a loss for words when the tranny mentioned the money. He knew they shouldn't have taken the picture, but the lottery commission loved to show a photo of the winners holding a big check for everybody to see. That way, the commission could entice others to play. What better advertisement than showing everyday people, hitting it big?

"I knew you didn't erase the damn files, bitch! What do you want?" John demanded, trying hard to sound confident and in control.

"Wow! Give that man a gold star! Of course I didn't erase my files, fool! Gee whiz, muthafucka! What the fuck do you think I want? Duh! It starts with an "m" and ends with a "y". Figure it out, freak."

"Listen—my wife won that money, not me," he pleaded.

"Oh, is that a fact? Okay, I'll just hang up and call Gwen, then."

"No! No! No, you can't do that!" John was beside himself with fear. "Please don't do that," he begged the cold, calculating tranny.

"So who should I talk to then? I don't like these little games you trying to play. This ain't my first rodeo, nigga, and you need to know that. Hell, I eat puny faggots like you for breakfast, so don't be trying to play fuckin games with me, you got that?"

"Yeah, I got it," John replied, like a meek church mouse.

"Good, now we can get somewhere. I want $100,000 in a week, or I'm gonna put your dick-riding ass on YouTube so the whole world can marvel at your unique skills. I dare say once the world sees what you can do with a dick, you'll be famous."

John went numb thinking about handing the tranny all that money. How could he even begin to explain it to Gwen? The family was being blackmailed, and his kid's future was being held hostage by a big-dick freak with ice in her veins. God, why the hell was he addicted to transsexuals anyway? Then he remembered Precious' beautiful body and knew why he was addicted to transsexuals. If all

that money suddenly disappeared from their account, Gwen would know right away.

"What if I gave you the money on installments, say like a thousand dollars a week or something like that," he said trying to appease the ho.

"Negro please! A thousand a week? I want my money upfront—not on muthafuckin lay-a-way. See—I knew you was gonna play these little ho games and try to stall me. I don't take shorts, fool. I want all the money at one time. In my experience, when someone say they can't pay it all, then that means they're stallin and don't plan to pay anything. They think I'll go away, like a bad-smellin fart or something. But let me tell you, boo—I'm not going anywhere. Believe that!"

"So how much can I give you then to make you go away," John asked, dreading the answer.

"Did I stutter, muthafucka? I said $100,000, and that's what I mean. You know, I woke this mornin feeling good, and you done pissed me off. Here you are, tryin to negotiate when the negotiatin is already done. In order to negotiate, you need some leverage, and you don't have any. So why the fuck should I listen to your goddamn counter-offer? I could ruin you by pushin the send button on my computer, and you'll be famous as hell. Matter fact, I'll be famous too, in much greater demand than I am now. Fags from all over the world will clamor for this beautiful meat between my legs. Damn! I almost wanna send it to YouTube right now."

"Please don't do that! I'll pay! Just give me till next Friday."

"Now that's what I like to hear—cooperation, especially when you have no other choice. Meet me at the Wendy's around 7 p.m. next Friday, you got that? And if you don't have the money, well let's just say you're going to be a YouTube star."

'Yeah, bitch, I got it."

Precious hung up the phone— so happy that she did a cart wheel in the living room floor. Taking money from these married fags was a very profitable business! That's why she liked fucking married guys—because they had more to lose and didn't want to bring attention to themselves, which meant they were easier to blackmail.

John was shaken after getting off the phone with the blackmailing transsexual. He felt ill and took a sick day to get his thoughts together. Instead of going home, he bought a double-deuce

Budweiser and went to Redan Park to contemplate his next move. How the fuck could he take $100,000 out of their account without Gwen finding out? That money belonged to their kids, and yet there he was, contemplating about giving it to a damn extortionist—an extortionist who already blackmailed him before and who would surely do it again and again if he didn't put a stop to it.

Why should he give his children's money away just so he could keep his homosexuality a secret? What's the worst that could happen anyway, besides being exposed as a fag to millions on the internet? Nothing whatsoever! That sobering thought revealed what clearly had to be done: either he had to break into Precious' house and steal her computer, which no doubt had numerous sex files of fools like him she was blackmailing, or kill the bitch.

As he took a swig of the beer, he became angrier. He wasn't about to let that trifling hustling bitch bring his family down. Even though JJ had the bigger dick and slept with his wife, John was still the man of the house, and therefore, its protector. And as the guardian of the kingdom, he was determined to do everything in his power to make sure no harm came to his loved ones—even if that meant killing someone.

John's own thoughts frightened him. He was never a violent person, let alone a killer. The last time he had even been in a fight was when he was 13 when got beaten up by two girls who called him sissy boy and took his book bag. His mom and dad had to go to the girls' house retrieve the bookbag. To think he was seriously considering murdering a bitch!

Was he so desperate to keep his sordid secret from being revealed to the world that he would resort to murder? Even if he did kill the tranny, he would still have to get rid of all the evidence from her house. What about her phone records? The police would definitely check those and eventually get around to interviewing him. Or maybe they wouldn't? Maybe they would just chalk it up as a prostituting freak that lived a dangerous lifestyle, and it caught up with her.

In small urban cities, most murders never get solved anyway. It wasn't like the Decatur police department was the best in the world, especially when it came to solving crimes where the victim was unsympathetic. Who would care about a tranny nigga prostitute anyway? White suburbanites wouldn't care and would see it as nigger killing nigger—no reason for alarm. Black folks would say the he-she

was an embarrassment to the race and had it coming to her, so good riddance!

Hell, most folks would say John did the world a favor by getting rid of that despicable tranny trash. A million thoughts ran through his mind on how best to go about his audacious endeavor. What would be the best way to kill the bitch? Strangling wouldn't work, because she was stronger than he was and would beat his ass. Besides, strangling would leave DNA that cops could trace back to him.

The only alternative that made sense was to shoot her down, like a dog. That way, he wouldn't have to touch her. Still, he had to devise a plan to get inside her house. If he did not get the computer files, then he along with the other blackmail victims would be prime suspects.

First he had to buy a gun, so he finished the beer and headed to Maddox Park off Donald Lee Hollowell Drive in northwest Atlanta.

Maddox Park was named after the 41st mayor of Atlanta, Robert Foster Maddox, who was born in 1870. He attended UGA and completed his studies at Harvard. After graduating from Harvard, he served on the board of the Atlanta National Bank, which was partly founded by his father. In 1908, he served as a Fulton County Commissioner, and he was elected mayor the next year. During his mayoral term, he issued the city's first large bond and raised three million dollars, which was used to build new schools and sewage disposal plants. He also built an addition to Grady Hospital and purchased the old post office, to be used as City Hall. During his term, Oakland City was annexed, almost doubling the size of Atlanta. When he was in his 80s, the brilliant Vernon E. Jordan Jr. served as his driver for a time to earn money for college.

Maddox would have rolled over in his grave if he knew the shy nigger chauffeur would grow up to be a "mover and shaker" in the world of politics and play golf with future presidents. He would also be appalled at the trashy ghetto that surrounded the once beautiful park. Like the rest of America, white flight left the inner cities in shambles as Caucasians moved out into the suburbs to get away from having to share their schools, churches, clubs etc. with the niggers who were moving into their neighborhood.

Atlanta wasn't immune to the effect as ofays left in droves for the whiter pastures in Cobb, Gwinnet and north Fulton counties, leaving the inner city for the niggers to destroy. Yet these problems were not on John's mind when he pulled into the park, which was

already packed, on that brisk December Friday. As usual, the park was crowded, with people selling everything from barbeque to crack, and everything in between.

You want a pit bull? You could buy it there. You need a gun? Well step right up and look at the merchandise. After asking around and convincing the thugs he wasn't an undercover officer, he found a guy named Rick who sold him a .38 snub nosed revolver for $400. After learning John wasn't able to handle the weapon, Rick gave him a 20-minute tutorial on how to load, unload and fire it.

Since gunshots in the park were a common occurrence, nobody batted an eye when John fired off three shots into the ground. A feeling of power and strength, like he never felt before, ran through his body after shooting the pistol. It was amazing what a hunk of metal could do for a faggot's fragile ego. The gun did for him what a big dick does for a young boy's ego—it made him feel like a man.

John left the park thinking he was John Shaft instead of John Evans. He didn't know if it was the gun that made him feel that way or the beer and weed he smoked, courtesy of Rick, but did it really matter? In seven days, he had to make a monumental decision: either pay-up, or get exposed and be the laughing stock of his world.

Getting this pistol meant that he chose to fight, which meant that in the minute he went to get the firearm, the $100,000 payment to the tranny was out of the question. Being embarrassed on YouTube wasn't about to happen either. There was no way that conniving tranny ho was going to break up his beautiful loving family.

If he let it happen, then what kind of man, husband, father would he be? Already perceived as being a feckless weakling in bed by Gwen, his failure to protect the family would only confirm her beliefs. She would seek a divorce, and he would have to pay child support for kids who would grow up hating their father. They would grow up as kids of divorced parents, with a whole host of other problems, especially when being ridiculed by their classmates for the sins of the father.

That was why Precious has to die. John couldn't stand the thought of Maya and JJ being teased at school because of his love for big black cock. And not only would the students know, but the teachers and faculty would find out too. How could he go to a teacher parent conference, knowing the teacher had seen him begging a tranny for more dick on YouTube.

John didn't *want* to murder Precious, but he had to, and that realization made the task much easier. Deep in thought, he turned his attention to the moment at hand, which was fighting Atlanta's bumper-to-bumper traffic on I-20 East. As usual, cars were backed up from Panola Road, all the way down to Candler Road. Instead of getting frustrated, he sighed and turned off the radio, praying under his breath for God to show him the right thing to do.

He rubbed on the gun and likened the feeling of the barrel to a hard prick, which reminded him of how he got into this situation in the first place. Yet no matter how much he prayed, the fag knew what had to be done, God be damned. If God was so good, how come he made being a fag so fucking hard in this world? Why can't a guy suck dick in peace without having to hide it, for fear of being ridiculed by family and friends? Fuck God and all his goddamn rules!—which no one followed anyway, unless it suited their agenda. The tranny was already as good as dead, and she didn't even know it.

Even then, the ho was probably banging some down-low nigga out, while secretly filming the whole thing. She not only received financial gain, but also a perverse pleasure from making a big nigga scream like a little girl, without realizing he was being filmed. Unaware of the camera, the trick would forgo all his inhibitions and act the way the good lord intended for him to be. In other words, he'd be a freaky bitch and worship the big black cock like it was a god—not *the God*, but a god nonetheless.

Even though John was incensed at Precious, he was getting a hard-on, thinking of all the filthy things she did to him and how much he wished she would do it again. But the ho had to go and put their lovemaking on camera, and now she had to die for that transgression.

John knew he was just another trick to her, but he rode her cock like he never rode a cock before. The fool even thought they might be able to have a secret relationship built on privacy and respect. Obviously, that wasn't going to happen. He missed the comfort of having a regular tranny girlfriend or a regular piece of dick he could call on when the craving to be treated like a woman overwhelmed him.

Before meeting Precious, he carried on a relationship with a tranny named Caramel, a thick redbone of about 5'2" and 170 pounds. She had a fat ass and a seven-inch dick that stayed hard and nice, natural breasts, with suckable nipples. Not only a sex fiend in

bed, but she also had a wonderful personality. After she up and moved to Miami over six months earlier, John went to see her twice a month for a year with no drama—nothing but a lot of dick and love.

When John first laid eyes on Precious, he thought he could be one of her "boyfriends" too, but she had other ideas. It was a shame that a beautiful creature had to die, because he knew she couldn't be reasoned with—not when the bitch was insisting on getting $100,000, not when she had already successfully blackmailed him earlier. That first little blackmail money seemed like pocket change now compared to the new demand. He wasn't going to be her big score—*hell fucking naw! That bitch ain't riding off into the sunset with his kid's future in her fucking Prada bag, bought with their fathers' shame.*

After crawling through rush hour traffic, he finally pulled of onto Panola Road, made a left and headed home to their peaceful subdivision, with its manicured lawns and seemingly happy families. With a new-found purpose in life, John felt more alive than he had in a long time. As he pulled into the driveway, he could see his wonderful family through the curtains, waiting for their daddy to get home. It was a brisk, windy night. A few hardy neighbors were walking their dogs, imploring their pets to hurry up and "do their business" so all could get out of the weather.

John parked in the garage hid the pistol in the ceiling—the same place he hid his weed. He was greeted by nobody. When he came in the house, he barely got a "hello" from the family he was going to kill to defend. Maya was in her room, experimenting with her mom's vibrator, JJ was playing video games on the big screen TV, and Gwen was at the kitchen table, drinking a glass of wine and grading papers.

John figured it wasn't exactly like the Huxtables, but then again, he wasn't exactly like Heathcliff either. Looking at his fat, slob of a wife—she definitely wasn't Claire—not with her proclivity to fuck their son almost every night and eat like a pregnant moose. He smiled and gave Gwen a sloppy kiss on her chubby cheek.

"Why you home so late? Its past 7 o'clock," Gwen commented while pouring more wine.

"All this damn traffic. It was two wrecks on I-20 and one on 285 south. You know how crazy folks be driving on Fridays, everybody trying to either get home or get away for the weekend."

John was right about the traffic, but he declined to tell her that he was coming from an illegal gun buy in downtown Atlanta. So he, like every other red-blooded Atlanta resident, blamed his lateness on

the god-awful traffic. And no one could argue, especially since they probably used traffic as a scapegoat as well. Anyone who didn't want to be somewhere just blamed traffic, which was enough to keep the doubters at bay most of the time. Of course, the excuse didn't work every time, but it worked enough, especially when the other party didn't give a fuck whether you showed up or not.

When John blamed his tardiness on the traffic, Gwen didn't really believe him, but she didn't give a fuck, so why argue? As long as he brought the checks home every two weeks, she didn't really care what John did or who he did it with. She didn't want a divorce. In fact, she wanted things to stay the way they were. It wasn't a perfect family or marriage by any means, but it was better than most. The kids were happy, healthy and doing well in school, and they had a lovely home in a nice community.

What more could a woman ask for? Her husband was gainfully employed and not a down-low homo, even if he did have a tiny cock. Hell, she knew that most black women would love to be in her position—having a husband instead of fucking every nigga who smiled at them and looking for love in all the wrong places. To her, they weren't exactly the Huxtables, but they were close enough.

"Well, I fried some chicken if you hungry. The kids and I have already ate," Gwen said, in order to relieve John's obvious stress. "Go take your clothes off and I'll fix you a plate."

John sighed and trudged upstairs, weary from the weight of the world resting on his narrow shoulders. The feeling of euphoria he had before coming home was gone, replaced by the reality of being JJ's bitch. Opening the chest of drawers, he could see his clothes were crammed together in the top two drawers, while JJ's were neatly-folded in the bottom two.

Gwen was replacing him, little by little, and there wasn't a damn thing that he could do about it. There he was, ready to commit a murder in less than a week, and his wife didn't even respect him enough to hide her affair with their son. Not only did she flaunt the affair, but it seemed like she wanted JJ to fuck his father too. John admitted to himself that sucking JJ's cock felt good, but he chalked it up to the heat of the moment. Even though the down-low fag liked being dominated by transsexuals, being fucked by his 12-year-old son was a different story.

John couldn't help but think about how sweet the youngster's cock tasted. *God, the boy was so lucky to have a big piece of meat that men and*

women would lust after, like it was manna from heaven! But like all youngsters, he didn't appreciate or understand the gifts that God had bestowed on him. The boy took it for granted that having a dick the size of a telephone pole was the rule instead of the exception. After brushing his teeth, John checked on Maya and found the door locked. Startled, she pretended like she was doing homework instead of pleasuring herself with Gwen's vibrator.

"How's my little queen?" John asked as soon as Maya opened the door. "What you doin in here baby with the door locked?"

"Just doing my math homework," she answered. Even though the door was locked, the little liar had her math book at the ready, in case anyone barged in on her. The vibrator was hidden under the pillow, still hot from Maya's use. "Daddy, we still goin Christmas shopping tomorrow, aren't we?" she asked, trying to sound nonchalant.

"I don't see why not. Of course we are," John said, excited to see her eyes light up like a Christmas tree. "Yeah, we gonna do all our shoppin tomorrow. If you can't find what you want at *The Mall of Georgia*, then they don't make it," he assured her. Like a proud papa, he delighted in making his little girl happy.

John didn't know it, but his little girl was pleased, not only because they were going shopping, but because her young vagina was wet with pussy juice. Now all the horny child wanted was for dad to get the fuck out so she could resume masturbation. After a moment talking about boys, school and other things, John smelled the fried chicken coming from downstairs and remembered he had the munchies, since he hadn't eaten all day.

After kissing Maya on the lips, he turned and left, locking the door behind him, but not before giving her a sly wink and a smile, as if to say he knew what she was doing and it was okay. After making sure the door was locked, Maya retrieved the vibrator from beneath the pillow and grinned at it like a Cheshire cat. She was amazed that this battery-powered device could give her so much pleasure. No wonder Mom used it so much. Maya turned out the lights, put the vibrator up to her clit, pressed a button, which took her to another dimension, a place so pleasurable that she stayed in her room until morning, exhausted from orgasm after orgasm.

"This chicken sho do smell good, baby! You should open a restaurant and put KFC outta business," John said, sitting at the kitchen table.

"Thanks, boo. When I knew you was gonna be late, I cooked, knowin you wouldn't feel like it when you got home," Gwen mentioned between swigs of California white wine. "What was Maya doing? She been up there since she finished eating," she asked, seeming worried.

"Her math homework," John lied. He knew she was doing something sexual, but he didn't bother to tell Gwen. It's not like she really cared anyway, because JJ was her pride and joy. He just hoped Maya didn't feel left out.

"That young lady sure do love math. Last year, she hated it. Now, it's her favorite subject. How do the chicken taste?"

"Fantastic," John said between bites.

"Good. Then after you finish, we can have a threesome, if you're up to it, of course. Why you lookin at me like that?" she asked with a mischievous grin.

John was taken aback by Gwen's sudden casual proposal. Now, he was the third wheel in their marriage, and he was being offered a pity-fuck by his wife and son. It was as if they lowered their standards and invited him along for the ride because they felt sorry for him. What arrogance that fat bitch had, and to use his son against him was lower than a snake belly.

He couldn't turn her down, however, because he wanted to suck on JJ's cock, and she knew it too. Not only did he want to demonstrate his tremendous dick-sucking skills on the boy, but John also wanted the lad to put that monster dick in him and make him scream like a bitch. Envisioning JJ long-stroking his fine fat ass with that ten-inch piece of meat made John's nipples hard.

He ate faster, anticipating dessert, which was going to be a big chocolate stick, with a white creamy filling.

"Sure, baby, you know I'm game," John said trying to hide his eagerness. "I'll be finished in a few, then I gotta go take a shit. I don't want the boys' dick getting any brown paint on it when he sticks it in." He couldn't believe he just said that.

"So, let me ask you something: are you down-low? If you are, just let me know. But the way you sucked your son's dick the other day, it looked like that wasn't your first rodeo. I mean, you know I'm obviously open-minded about sex, so you don't have to hide anything from me, boo." Gwen emptied her glass and stared at John.

John suddenly stopped eating, contemplating whether he should just come clean and tell her the whole sordid history of his numerous

transsexual "girlfriends." He could tell her about his first tranny experience with Kyla, the New Orleans she-male who made him feel like a 16-year-old school girl when she busted a nut inside his virgin asshole.

He still remembered how she overpowered and raped him until he begged for more. Gwen was right about him being down-low, but he only messed with transsexuals, and not mainstream gay guys. Usually, the thought of regular gay guys didn't really turn him on much. Even though he lived in metro Atlanta, the capital of black gay America, he never hooked up with another dude unless that dude dressed like a woman.

John also realized that if he started telling Gwen everything, then he would have to tell about Precious, and he really wasn't up to that. He didn't want to tell her he planned to murder the blackmailing ho, because it would make her an accessory to murder. The less she knew about that, the better. But Gwen wasn't stupid, especially after he just told her he wanted his asshole fresh and clean for JJ's eventual entry.

"Baby, I been fucking with transsexual for about five years now," the fag blurted out, as if he just asked her to pass the salt.

To his surprise, Gwen said nothing. She poured herself more wine took a long drink and smiled.

"So, you like them he-shes?" seeming more curious than surprised.

John looked down at his plate and nodded, ashamed to look at the reaction on Gwen's face. She gently rubbed his hands, reassuring him that her love was unconditional and unshakable. Then, like in a scene from a damn Lifetime movie, the down-low fool blubbered his heart out until he told almost everything. The fag told her about the first time being with a tranny down in the Crescent City during Mardi Gras.

"You mean to tell me that while I was stuck in the hotel, sick from food poisoning, you went on a dick hunt?" Gwen seemed pissed, but she regained her composure. "And how did you meet this drag queen?"

"Remember when I went down to get some Pepto-Bismol? Well, I met her in the elevator."

"What you really mean is that you met *him* not her on the elevator," Gwen corrected him.

"Baby, is it really important how I met her. That was almost five years ago."

"If I asked, then it's important to me. So, while I was throwing up in the room, almost dyin, you was out gettin your groove on with a drag queen, right? Was she staying in the hotel too?"

"C'mon now, you wasn't dyin. Let's not get all dramatic and shit. And yes, she was stayin in the hotel. Matter of fact, she had a room on the same floor as us. Look, I confessed. If you wanna get a divorce, let me know, but I'm through talkin."

"I was sick as fuck, and you was out getting fucked! My my, my! Naw, baby, I don't want a divorce. I just hope you used protection when you let them thangs fucks you."

"You know, I would never put my wife or myself in danger. Of course I used protection," John said so convincingly that even he believed the lie.

In reality, he only used protection about eight out of ten times. A beautiful woman like Precious was one-of-a-kind though. That's why he let her fuck him sans condom.

"And how do you know I'm not fuckin them?"

"Baby, with a cock as small as yours, I know when you pulled out that little pee-wee, they had to laugh. And besides, if you wanted some asshole you coulda fucked me or another woman. Be real with me now. You wanted them he-shes for their cocks, right? They had something that you lacked—a big dick."

"So what? I let them fuck me. You already knew the answer. You don't have to mock me because I have a small dick. All my life, muthafuckas laughed about my little penis, but I never expected my wife to. If you thought my dick was too little, why did you marry me?"

"I married you because I love you, and I still do, but the bigger question is 'why did you marry me' knowin you secretly liked dick?"

"The first time I had some dick was when we were at Mardi Gras, and even then I chalked that up to all the booze and weed I been smoking. I never thought I'd fall in love with transsexuals. Well, not in love, but in lust, I guess. Baby, you know I love you and the kids first and foremost, but sometimes to break the monotony, I need some outside recreation."

"To be honest, I was getting tired of your little manhood anyway, and without my trusty vibrator, I don't know what I woulda done. The only reason I didn't have an affair was because the vibrator kept me sane. I came to loath our lovemaking and only pretended to enjoy it. I became good at the art of faking orgasms.

But after a while, I wanted the real thing and started looking at other men wondering what they had between their legs. Luckily, before I stepped out and had an affair, I seen the big cock dangling between JJ's legs and it hit me: why not fuck my son? Boys love their mamas more than they'll love any woman in their lives, so it was only natural to let him make love to me. That way, I wouldn't have to worry about getting a disease and shit."

"So, let me get this straight, your solution to saving our marriage was incest?"

"Negro, don't get all smart with me! You the one out chasin dick. We hadn't fucked in months, and now you finally tell me the real reason—after making me think it was somehow my fault. I can't help it if you have been emasculated by your son. Take that up with God, not me."

"I remember gym class and how everybody made jokes about my small penis, so I guess I internalized those feelings and told myself that it didn't matter. But the older I got, the more it bothered me. Every guy I saw, I wondered if he had a big dick or a small one like me. Every girlfriend I ever had, startin in high school, seemed to break up with me after we had sex. And it soon became apparent why, after talking to my homeboys."

"Baby, all that is fine and dandy, but the reason you like dick is because you were born that way. Hell, you not the only nigga with a tiny cock, but just because a man has a tiny cock don't mean he wants to get fucked. You took psychology in college. You know what I'm talking about. Face it, boo, you were born bisexual. I think the fact that you had trouble pleasing women made it easier for you to explore the other side."

"But I still feel ashamed of myself. Please don't tell anyone—especially big-mouth Barbara."

"Me and Barbara may gossip, but believe it or not, I don't tell her everything—even if she is my best friend. By the way, since Joe left her, she's been worried sick because he's got a young, 20-year-old girlfriend now. And not only that, but she told me he wanted to have at least one child with that young girl. When Joe called her last week, she thought he wanted to get back together, but he told her he filed for divorce. Baby, I don't want that to happen to this family. Think about the kids. Joe's not thinkin about their four children, or the fact that he's 41 years old now. The man is out there trying to relive his

youth, and that young girl gonna take him to the cleaners. He already bought the bitch a brand-new car. Can you believe that shit?"

"Well, I may like to get fucked by she-males but I'm not abandonin my family for no one, baby, and you can believe that," John said rather proudly.

"See, you say that now, but we don't know what the future holds, do we? You might decide to leave us when one of them he-shes throw some good dick on you and get you hooked, like a fish on tranny cock."

"But that's the difference between me and Joe. I know where my priorities are. They're with my family, not a fuckin prostitute. When I married you, it was until death do us part, not until I get tired of you. Joe knows that young bitch is using him, but the ego won't let him think straight. The dude actin like he's 16 and this is his first piece of pussy."

"Speakin of pussy, mine's getting a little wet right now, I'm going to take a shower. Hurry up and finish so we can get this threesome going."

"You know what? I'm not up to it tonight. I had a long day at work and just wanna relax in front of the TV."

"But you was fine with it a few minutes ago," Gwen protested.

"And another thing—I want my bed back. You and JJ can fuck in his room from now on, okay."

It wasn't a question. It was a request. Gwen was taken aback by his request, but after thinking about Barbara and Joe's shaky marriage, she agreed to his demand.

"Okay, boo. We'll use JJ's room from now on."

She kissed him on the forehead and waddled upstairs to wash the sweat and funk from her soft ample body.

John wanted to join, but he had other things on his mind—like planning a murder. He had no idea how he would do it or if he even had the nerve. So, instead of sucking on JJ's dick that night, he was going to do reconnaissance on Precious' house. Maybe surveying the neighborhood would give him an idea or two about how best to go about doing the dastardly deed. After sitting at the table for a few minutes, he put his empty plate in the dishwasher and went to play video games with JJ

Gwen was pissed that John didn't want to have a threesome. She wanted to see him get fucked by his son. Then after fucking his dad, JJ would fuck her, and they would all be happy and content. But, for

some reason, John didn't want to go along with the program and suddenly backed out. Oh well, more cock for her, she surmised.

John's confession made her feel a little better, because he wasn't seeing a fine young skinny girl, which meant that he still probably thought she was fine and sexy. The only reason he hadn't fucked her was because of nature: he naturally wanted cock instead of pussy. She could live with that, knowing it was nothing she'd done to turn him off.

After taking a shower, she oiled every inch of her body with lotion and perfume. After changing the sheets on JJ's bed, she told him to take a shower and get ready for bed. As soon as he heard his mom's request, the boy immediately jumped from the couch and ran upstairs to wash up and get ready for some all-night fucking.

The youngster was surprised to learn that they would be using his bed, because he had gotten used to the king-sized bed in the master suite. On that bed, he could fuck Gwen from one end to the other and still have room for his little-prick father. In his little twin-sized bed, mama's fat ass took up most of the room. After taking a shower, the boy admired his body in the bathroom mirror, playing with his cock until it was hard and straight as an arrow. Then he pranced to the bedroom butt-naked with that big cock, swaying from side to side, ready to make Mommy scream with pleasure.

When the boy opened the bedroom door, Gwen was waiting with her legs wide open and wet with desire for her true love. On cue, he immediately positioned himself between her ample thighs and inserted all ten inches into her until she moaned like a common slut, begging for more. After a few minutes, they were lost in the throes of passion and oblivious to the world around them. They didn't hear John when he tip-toed up the stairs to listen to their lustful noises and grunts.

When satisfied that he wouldn't be missed, John rolled a joint and drank a cold beer to get up the nerve to check to see if he could find a way to kill Precious without getting caught—or better yet, steal her computer and files. That way, he wouldn't have to kill the bitch.

Arriving in the tranny's subdivision around 9:30, he noticed how quiet and serene it was. An older neighborhood built in the 1970s, it had the typical brick ranch-style houses of that era. All the homes had big lawns with mature trees, unlike the newer subdivisions that had tiny postage-stamp-sized yards. John noticed also that there were a lot of shrubs, flowers and fences for hiding.

The would-be murderer stopped in front of Precious's house to see any weaknesses in her security. There was an ADT security sign in the yard, but that didn't mean it was hooked up. Many people put those signs in their yards to make burglars think they had a security system. Hell, he and Gwen have been doing it for three years. They figured, "why pay a security company when all you need is a sign to ward off thieves?"

John noticed a car in her driveway—probably some unsuspecting trick's car. He wanted to bang on the door and tell that nigga to get the hell outta there, because he's "on Candid Camera." He sure wished somebody had warned him. If someone had, he wouldn't be planning a fucking murder right now. Driving around the subdivision, he noticed there was one way in and out. The neighborhood consisted of three streets that dead ended in a circular cul-de-sac. The back of the subdivision was fenced off and separated from the highway by a steep hill, with a chain-link fence and lots of trees.

John made a note to get on I-20 tomorrow so he could see if he could spot the bitch's house from the highway. If he could do that, he had a plan on how to get into her house. Feeling satisfied, he drove around the subdivision a couple more times to get familiar with it, and then he headed home, confident that he had the guts to do what had to be done.

Knowing what was waiting at home, he drove slowly, stopping at all the yellow lights instead of driving through them like a normal person. The house was eerily quiet when he entered, which was okay, because planning a murder was both mentally and physically exhausting. Seeing that it was past midnight, he went straight to bed, dreading the long day ahead, which would be spent at the mall, spending boatloads of money on the kids to prove how much he loved them. Grateful to be back in his king-sized bed, he dozed off with visions of Precious' dead body running through his brain.

****

Precious could have sworn she saw a car checking out the house. At first, she thought it may be a robbing crew, but then she remembered what kind of car John drove and put two and two together. That low-down fag was spying on her. *Who the fuck do he think he is? Jason Bourne?*

The big-cock tranny was amused that the fool was going through so much trouble to keep an eye on her. Now the bitch knew she had his undivided attention. *But this shit can't happen again*, she reasoned. A bitch had to let these-dick suckers know she was not to be trifled with. Next thang you know, the muthafucka would get bold and try to break in or worse—fuck her up.

Precious was angry and knew a message had to be sent to let the fag know she was definitely for real. The message had to be so strong that it would make a nigga think twice about fucking with her. The nerve this cocksucker had—thinking he was smarter than her. Hell, she invented this fucking game. Presently, she had five niggas on the hook, paying her $2000 a week in hush money alone. Secrets cost, and they knew it. The dudes may have grumbled about paying, but the alternative would be far worse, which made it easy to bleed them, little by little. The money they were giving her was just their fuck-around money or money they were gonna blow anyway. So why not blow it on her? Every Monday, like clockwork she went to Wendy's restaurant to collect her dough from the five pissed-off benefactors. Nice and simple, with no drama involved.

That's how she liked it, but now, *this damn John gotta be different and shit. He wanted to do his own thang, but she wasn't gonna allow it to happen.* Tomorrow, she would make the fag realize she's not to be fucked with, and the blackmailing tranny already had an idea on how best to accomplish that. If the fag was gonna spy on her, she figured "why not turn the tables and spy on him?"

With Siri, all she had to do was type in the address and get directions to his house. Before going to bed, she noticed the time was 12:34 am Saturday morning. The last thoughts on her mind before dozing off were money, money, money... and John riding her dick! To say the down-low dick rider was on her mind was an understatement, because she actually dreamed she impregnated the fool!

Chapter 8
At the Mall

The Evans family got up before seven a.m. on that cold Saturday morning to get ready for an American tradition—Christmas shopping. The brood didn't even bother eating breakfast to save time so they could get a plum parking space. Even though the parking lot was gigantic, it filled up quickly during the holiday season. JJ and Maya were especially excited because they knew Santa was going to be very generous that year.

Not that the fat cracker wasn't nice the year before, but they both figured he could have done a little better. Compared to most children in the world, these two were living very good. They wore the latest designer clothes, had a nice house, went to one of the best schools in the state, and had two stable, loving parents. But did they know this? Of course not.

Like every other human being on Earth, they just knew they wanted more. Living in a society that saw mass consumption as a basic human right, kids, along with their adult counterparts, eagerly participated in this rite of passage. Like pre-teens and teens all over America, they knew which buttons to push to get more from their guilt-ridden, overworked and overmedicated parents.

Most parents, already feeling guilty from working so much, tried to make up for ignoring their kids all year by going in debt to show them how much they were loved. Instead of offering love and understanding that the kids needed, parents found it easier to shower them with material things.

JJ wanted every video game under the sun, and he figured that as much dick he was putting in mama, she was *gonna give him everything his heart desired*. Resembling the cunning devil that he was becoming, the boy made love to mama all night, nutting in her four freaking times. He realized the more dick he gave her, the more obedient she was.

In the previous night, after they finished making love, he asked her to make some brownies, and she readily agreed. Before they started fucking, his request would have been met with a resounding "no." But his big cock had her baking and running around the kitchen like Martha Stewart. He also wanted Daddy to suck his dick again. As good as mama was, daddy seemed to be an expert cocksucker.

At twelve, the boy was keenly aware of the powerful male body and found himself looking at his nude schoolmates in gym class. He liked gym, because all the guys envied his fat cock and would watch from the corner of their eyes when he walked around naked. Even the teacher, Mr. Atkins, seemed to stare at him without trying to hide it, probably because JJ encouraged the long gazes and playful winks by rubbing that big piece of meat right in front of him. The youngster knew the power his big dick had over people. It was like a magic wand that could make mere mortals bend to his will. Yep he was gonna have a nice Christmas.

Maya wanted Santa to bring her a boyfriend like her daddy. After learning about the affair between brother and mama, she was jealous of the attention Gwen showered on JJ That morning at two a.m., she found Mom in the kitchen baking brownies for her lover. Who in the world did JJ think he was to have their mama cooking him brownies at two in the morning? There was no way she would have done that for Maya, no way.

But Daddy didn't even look at her like that, and she was angry about it. If JJ could be Mama's boyfriend, why couldn't she be Daddy's girlfriend? Did Daddy think she was ugly? Or maybe he didn't love her enough, like mama loved JJ. What did she have to do to make Daddy love her? They slept in the bed together, but other than hugging her, he didn't do anything. She wanted Daddy to make her make noises like Mama made when JJ stuck his big thing in her. Other than that, she wanted Santa to bring her lots and lots of clothes and jewelry.

Gwen was enjoying the ride to the mall in blissful silence. Other than an occasional fart, she was quiet as a church mouse, pissing on cotton. After a night of getting fucked in every position possible by her beautiful son, life was indeed looking rosy. JJ came in her so much she thought she might drown from the intense pleasure his big cock unleashed on her needy vagina. She wanted Santa to bring her a baby, preferably a boy.

The thought of having another baby didn't cross her mind until the first time JJ made love to her. He unleashed feelings in her that she thought were long forgotten. The boy made her feel like a complete woman, and she wanted to reward him by having his baby. Of course, she had to discuss it with Chief Little-Dick first and see what he said. He might have surprised her and said "yes," but that was a longshot. No real man would want his wife to have a baby by

their son. But then again, how many real men would let a son take his place in bed.

Hell, maybe she could just stop taking her birth control pills and let nature take its course. She closed her eyes and said a silent prayer asking God for guidance in making the right decision. If anyone could help her, it would be the Almighty. A baby would bring the family closer together and would forever seal the bond of love between her and JJ. Then again maybe she was just longing to have someone who loved and depended on her.

With the kids growing up so fast, they'd be out of the house and in college soon. At least they better be in college, because time was precious, and these days an education was essential for any type of career. Soon, JJ would be looking at girls and giving them what he gave her. When that happened, he wouldn't be able to fight them little hot bitches off with a stick.

She felt herself getting jealous thinking about JJ fucking another woman. It would be nice if she could keep Mr. Big all to herself, but she knew that wouldn't be possible. He was going to meet a cute, skinny thang in college, get married and bring the heffa back home to meet old fat mama. Suddenly, the future was beginning to look depressing, so Gwen listened to the radio to take her mind off such gloomy thoughts.

It was a beautiful day, and nothing could spoil it. What was better than going Christmas shopping with your family, especially when you have a lot of money to spend? All Gwen wanted for Christmas was to have her son's baby. With it being the season of miracles, anything was possible... at least that's what they said in the Bible so Gwen made a vow to pray extra hard in church tomorrow for her yet-to-be-born son.

John was still feeling high from the joint he smoked before leaving the house. All he thought about was the impending murder and how to get away with it. The fag figured he could sneak into Precious' house from the sloped hill behind the subdivision that separated her neighborhood from the busy highway below. With the trees and high-grass that the Georgia Department of Transportation hardly ever cut, he would be invisible from the noisy highway traffic below.

He could park at the Church's Chicken, which was right around the corner on Wesley Chapel Road, and walk to her subdivision. Then he could sneak into her backyard with no trouble at all. At least

that's the plan he came up with. It had been less than 24 hours since the bitch threatened to expose him, so his plan was the best he could do on such short notice.

He knew he couldn't just knock on the back door, because she would be too scared to open it at nighttime. How many people got strange knocks at their backdoor in the middle of the night? He definitely wasn't going to break the door down like the police and come in blasting. No, it had to be subtler. He had to get her to open the back door late at night.

The only way to do that was to lightly tap on the door to get her to come out and see what it was. But if she was too scared, she wouldn't come out. The trick was to make the ho curious enough to open the door without frightening her. John figured he could hide in some bushes, and when she opened the door, he would start shooting immediately. If he hesitated, she might get away, or it's possible the bitch may be packing and shoot his ass first.

That thought was sobering. He didn't want his gravestone reading: Here lies John Evans, killed by a transsexual prostitute. RIP! What a way to go, getting capped by a tranny! He could just imagine the blaring headlines on the local news stations, touting the shooting as a sensational sex scandal. Then they would trot out the psychologists who gleefully warn the world about the down-low epidemic in the black community. Naw, he definitely didn't want this blowing back on the family.

But if he were to die, the shame and guilt of what he did wouldn't fall on him, which was comforting in a weird sort of way. Being dead shields people from the worries and stress of the living world. John mused that if he committed suicide, all his troubles would go away. If he made it look like an accident, the family would still collect the life insurance money. He could drive the car into an 18-wheeler and be smashed to smithereens and not feel a thing. After a few seconds of this insane thinking, dude came to his senses. Suicide was out of the question, and it was a punk's way out. This was a mess, and he had to clean it up.

They got to the mall at 8 a.m. and barely found a parking spot. With over 5000 parking spaces, one would think there would be plenty available, especially so early in the morning. Because shopping was one of America's favorite pastimes, it wasn't surprising. And folks were eager to forget about the supposedly lousy economy and spend, spend, spend.

With over 200 stores, The Mall of Georgia was a cathedral, built to satisfy the customers' excess appetite to consume too much. With Madison Avenue telling Americans that it's okay to go into debt, people were shopping like there was no tomorrow. Who cares about the bills, as long as little Johnny and Mary had a happy holiday?

In the real world, a happy Christmas was one with a lot of goodies under the tree. Fuck peace on earth and goodwill towards man! A brand-new car or pearl necklace was what brought happiness and peace in the households across this great greedy land. We may pay a weak homage to Jesus, but in reality, humans like to get material things—something they can feel, touch and play with. The Evans family was a typical American household, who preached that money wasn't everything, but knew the consequences if the kids didn't have a big Christmas. They would be made out as the worse parents in the neighborhood.

After five hectic hours of shopping, Gwen's fat ass was tired and ready to go. They had walked from one end of the mall to the other on all three levels, and she was getting irritated from her sweaty thighs rubbing together. She dreaded the long walk to the van, because they had parked in the back corner of the cavernous lot, over two miles away.

All four were loaded down with bags of goodies. JJ gleefully carried three pairs of Air Jordans, five video games an X-box and an iPad. Maya was equally loaded down, with four pairs of shoes, including her first pair of three-inch heels. Gwen thought her daughter would look sexy in them, especially with that big butt sashaying from side to side. Along with the shoes, she got three purses and a couple of dresses to round out her wardrobe. John was weighed down by the flat screen TV he got to replace the old one in the bedroom. And Gwen was straggling along behind, trying to keep up, but the box of Cinnabons was too good to resist. It was hard to walk and eat at the same time for her; she liked to relax while eating and hated all the running around. She couldn't wait to get to the van so she could plop her big ass down.

After fighting through the crowd inside, they had to fight the parking lot traffic outside, maneuvering deftly through the mishmash of cars, and eager consumers hell-bent on having a merry Christmas. Tired as hell, Gwen wanted to wait at the main entrance while John got the van to come pick her up, but she realized that would have taken much too long. Vehicles were lined up by the dozens, waiting

to drop off or pick up tired, frustrated shoppers, loaded down with presents.

Gwen cursed under her breath as she followed Maya, who followed JJ, who followed John to the waiting mini-van. When they got to their vehicle, the family was glad they came, but they knew they didn't want to return until next year. After loading their gifts, they slinked in their seats tired but happy. John, wishing he had a joint to puff on, became the world's rudest driver, cutting in front of slow-moving cars and not letting anyone cut in front of him, even if they asked. It took the family 30 minutes to get out of the parking lot and another 15 to reach Interstate 85 South, the ribbon of asphalt that would take them home.

The brood let out a collective sigh of relief when John turned left off Buford Drive and headed home down the busy highway. While Gwen nodded off, JJ took his dick out and let Maya play with it. At first, the boy tried to hide what they were doing by putting one of the numerous bags on his knees to block the view. Yet the more that little sister stroked, the more uninhibited they became. When John realized what they were doing, he said nothing and pretended not to notice, stealing glances through the rear-view mirror all the while. The big-cock boy could see John staring enviously at his dick, and it made him feel proud to know that his father was jealous of his meat.

For the next 20 miles, Daddy watched Maya stroking JJ's engorged penis until it erupted all over her face. JJ tried to contain his excitement, but he still let out a yelp that woke Gwen. Oblivious to what was happening behind her, she farted and fell back asleep. The kids laughed and went back to doing what they were doing, JJ playing video games, while Maya texted her friends about boys and sex. Kids will be kids!

****

Saturday was turning out to be a pretty good day for Precious. On that day, she decided not to take any clients because she had a special errand to run. Monique came over, and Precious gave the fledging tranny tips on makeup and hair. The big-cock tranny felt like an older sister to the teen, giving her advice on practical matters, such as how to tuck her dick while out in public. Some tranny's tuck or

hide their dicks, while some don't mind showing the world their package.

Precious never hid her gigantic tool. She found out early on that men like to see her dick print when she wore jeans. She knew Monique looked up to her, and it felt good to be wanted and needed by someone. To her mom and brother, she was just an ATM machine, but to this youngster, she was a wealth of knowledge and information to be mined.

They smoked a blunt while Precious gave her a makeover. She applied eyeliner, false eyelashes, blush, ruby-red lipstick, and to top it off, a lace front wig to give her that extra sex appeal. Monique couldn't believe how she looked; it was as if a different person was staring back at her in the mirror. Finally, she saw her potential as a woman, and she had Precious to thank for that.

"Wow! I can't believe how pretty I am," Monique exclaimed. "Finally, I look how I've always felt." She gave her mentor a heartfelt hug and couldn't wait to show the world the new and improved Monique.

"You do look cute with them big soft lips."

Precious couldn't help but plant a kiss on her little "sister's" mouth. Then she unzipped the youngster's jeans got on her knees and started sucking her dick until it was hard as concrete. "Mmmmm, you taste so so good! I ain't tasted teenage dick in a long time," she murmured between slurps. After a few more minutes, she took Monique by the hand and led her into the bedroom where both hastily undressed and laid down on the bed.

Monique was astonished by the sudden passion that overcame Precious. Her six-inch cock looked small, compared to Precious' ten-by-five huge piece of meat. Since getting fucked in the mouth on Wednesday, it was hard to get the dick that wrecked her mouth off her mind. It reminded her of a magical black wand that had mystical powers. When Precious told her to lie down on her stomach, she knew what was coming next. Precious got on top of her, rubbing that big cock between her virgin butt cheeks. Feeling both excited and afraid, the teen waited for the inevitable violent invasion of her anus by a ten-inch alien.

To Precious, fucking a virgin was a rare unexpected opportunity, especially one this damn young! She was turning him into a girl in every way, except biologically. He came over, looking like a cute sissy. *He's gonna leave with his asshole, aka pussy pumped full of cum!* Rosa Lee will

be surprised when she sees her son looking and acting like the daughter she never had. Reaching for the K-Y jelly, she stuck the tube up Monique's' rectum and squeezed until she was satisfied enough had been applied to receive her huge, condom-covered cock. Without hesitation, she slammed her meat violently into the teen's once virgin rectum.

"I take it this is your first time getting fucked?"

The dick was so big that all Monique could do was nod weakly. It felt like an 18-wheeler had slammed into her anus.

"Well, you ain't no more," Precious bragged as she slammed harder and harder until her nuts were slapping against the 16-year-old's ass cheeks. Monique was writhing in pain, but the older tranny didn't care. It was the same way Precious was deflowered at the tender age of 13, by one of her "uncles." If it was good enough for her it was good enough for this bitch.

"Please go slow, please go slow," Monique whispered between violent stokes.

'Bitch, shaddup! This is my pussy now. I do what the fuck I want, you got that ho?" Even though she was her little pupil, she had to show the youngster who's the boss.

Like always, the more she fucked, the looser the teen's anus became. Soon she was long stroking nice and slow with no resistance as Monique started arching her ass, telling Precious not to stop. The more she begged for it, the harder Precious stroked, pulling all ten-inches out then slamming it back in with all the force she could muster. The teen moaned in ecstasy as Precious cursed and called her every vile derogatory name under the sun.

The older tranny's filthy words excited the youngster almost as much as the big meat pounding her insides did. This went on for about ten more minutes while her balls filled up with cum. Then, when she couldn't stand it anymore, Precious let out an animal like sound as she cummed so much it was leaking out the condom. Physically and emotionally spent, they just lay there, Precious on top Monique on the bottom, for over twenty minutes—double the time of their actual fucking. Her pussy felt so good that Precious didn't bother taking the dick out. She let it stay in until it got hard again.

Monique felt like a complete woman. Her pussy had been deflowered, and now she knew why she loved dick instead of pussy. She liked being manhandled and treated like a slut in bed. Precious fucked her so good that she cummed on herself without even

touching her dick. Feeling Precious' dick growing inside her again Monique just surrendered and let the big dick bitch have her way with her. Besides, there wasn't anything she could do to stop her anyway.

She had witnessed firsthand what Precious' dick wanted Precious' dick got. She knew it presently wanted some more of her 16-year-old boi pussy. The older tranny fucked the young pupil for hours, cumming in the teen four more times until her big cock was finally empty.

When she left, Monique had trouble walking because her ass, back and mouth were aching so much. But it was a pleasurable pain and it made her feel complete. Her body felt like it had run a marathon, and her asshole felt as if a ton of dynamite had exploded in it. When she got home, she went directly to bed and didn't wake up until the next day. The youngster didn't bother washing all the cum Precious had pumped in her mouth. Needless to say, she slept like a log. She fell asleep with big dicks on her mind and dried cum on her in her face. Yep, that bitch's dick is powerful.

Precious' cock was drained by Monique's cute tight apple-bottom booty. As usual, her big dick took over like it was Mr. Hyde and she couldn't control its rage. She didn't mean to go psycho on the young ass, but how many times does one get to fuck a 16-year-old virgin? After fucking middle-aged down-low niggas all the time, it was good to enjoy some young, tenderoni booty.

The savvy tranny wished she could have seen the look on Rosa Lee's face when the old bag saw her son with makeup and a wig on. That'll teach the bitch not to complain to the HOA about her anymore! Every time she nutted in Monique, she thought of ugly-ass Rosa Lee and how horrified the old lady would be if she could have seen how violently her former son was fucked. The old bitch would be saddened at the way her son begged to be humiliated and treated like a female slut.

He came over her house as Marcus, but from that day on, he'd be a woman named Monique. When Rosa Lee left for work, she had a son, but by the time she got back home, she'd have a daughter, courtesy of Precious. Precious smiled at her handiwork, but she had an important appointment to keep. After taking a quick shower and within minutes of Monique leaving, she was out the door, headed for John Evans house.

After what that muthafucka did to her, she was gonna show him two could play that game. She put the fag's address into her Hondas' navigation system and made a bee-line to his house. It took only 20 minutes to get there, and it seemed no one was at home, so she parked across the street from the house and waited. Hardly anybody was outside, which was probably due to the cold cloudy weather. The thermometer in her car displayed 35 degrees, and it definitely felt that frigid, too, especially with no sun in sight. It was as if the sun refused to come out that day.

Glancing at the gas gauge, she cursed for not getting any while she was at the store a day earlier. Hell, the tank was almost on "E." Being from Motown, the weather in Georgia didn't bother her too much, so she cut the heater off to preserve gas. The fool had to come home sooner or later, and when he did, she wanted to be the first thing the fag saw when he pulls up. Sitting in the cold car, Precious wondered how John would react when he saw her. Surely, he wouldn't act a fool and blow the coveted down-low status that he worked so hard to conceal. All the vengeful tranny wanted to do was scare the shit out of him and let the bitch know she means business. Just when she was about to abort the mission, a minivan turned into the Evan's driveway.

John almost shitted when he saw Precious' Honda Accord parked across the street from his house. What the fuck did she want? Was his gig up? Hurriedly, he parked inside the garage and told the kids to take the bags in while he went to the mailbox. At the mailbox, he asked her what she was doing there.

"I'm here, spyin on you, like ya were doin to me. Now you know how I feel."

"Okay I get your point. Now will you please go," John pleaded, trying not to look conspicuous, in case anyone was watching.

"So, you're not even gonna deny that you were spying on me last night?"

"Would it do any good if I did deny it?"

"Nope. Save your lies for your fat, ugly-ass wife, nigga. I came over here to let you know I'm not fuckin around! Now it would behoove you to have my money by Friday."

John nodded that he would, and hearing that, Precious drove off, leaving the foolish fag visibly nervous.

"I'm gon get my money! I'm gon get my money," Precious shouted to herself while driving away, happy and content. Now all

she wanted to do was go home, have a drink, smoke some bud, watch sports and relax. The big-dick bitch was confident she was going to get her money, especially after she saw how nervous John reacted by her mere presence. *If the fool was that shaken, then he has to pay up.*

Precious wondered what would have happened if she actually knocked on his door? She smiled, thinking about the explaining he would have to do to his fat wife if a tranny came asking for her husband. That would be funny, but it would also fuck her big-money scheme up. If his wife did find out, she might have gone ballistic on his ass, but then he wouldn't pay because the cat would have been out of the bag. John would figure that if his wife found out, that's the worst that could happen to him, so why pay up.

Blackmailing Walter was easier, because he was rich and successful; he would have paid double the amount if he had to. Being a big-time corporate muckety-muck meant he had a lot more to lose than a fucking probation officer did. Walter was a mover and shaker, a leader of men, a man that others respected. John, on the other hand, talked to fucking low-life criminals all day—hardly a position of respect, and the dude only made about $50,000 a year. Walter made that much in one month.

The money she got from Walter hardly dented his bank account, but she knew the Evans family needed every bit of their lottery winnings to maintain a comfortable life. They were a dual-income family, which meant both incomes were needed to sustain their standard of living. If either lost their job, the family might lose the house, or at the very least, have to take out a second mortgage. Being just one income away from losing their beautiful home was not exactly a ringing endorsement to fork over $100,000 to an extortionist, especially one that's already burnt him once.

She could threaten to expose his secret lifestyle to his job, but other than a few laughs, it wasn't like they could fire him for being a dick-sucker. Precious realized she had to turn up the heat on this faggot, because he may have had second-thoughts about paying up. She had to make the fool realize life would be much harder if he didn't pay than if he did. Before going to the crib, Precious stopped at Wendy's on Panola Road to get her favorite, a double with cheese and large fries. A girl had to keep her strength up, because all this blackmailing and scheming was mentally draining.

"Daddy, who were you talking to?" JJ asked.

"Just some woman who asked about buying Mr. Burns' house, that's all. Now y'all put them bags in the closet. Yo mama gonna wrap the presents tomorrow."

While the kids did as they were told, Gwen went to JJ's room to take a nap. Getting up at the break of day and walking around that goddamn big-ass mall had worn her out. Her thighs were irritating her, because they were chafing together and making it unpleasant to walk. She both loved and hated that time of year. It seemed the older one gets, the more it seemed the holidays were one big chore. There was so much pressure to have a big Christmas, whatever that is, that people seem to forget that it's Jesus' birthday.

Most of the people at the mall didn't seem happy; they looked tired and frazzled, frightened of not getting the hippest new toy for their spoiled loved one. Advertisers have duped the public that love equated to material wealth, while at the same time, Hollywood pushes out sappy movies where the heroes/heroines are poor but happy. The way she spoiled her children, Gwen knew she was just as guilty as anyone else. And that Christmas, she was definitely spoiling JJ. She planned on getting him some sexy lingerie and thongs to wear around the house to showoff mamas' meat, dangling betwixt his legs. Gwen smiled just thinking about her young lover prancing around proudly in his revealing thong.

In the week since she first started fucking her son, Mama had grown more and more possessive of him. She even got jealous when she heard Maya and him playing together. Either it was love or that big dick that made her jealous, or more appropriately, love of the big dick that made her that way, but Gwen didn't care. She knew she was going to hate on any bitch that put their hands on her precious son, including Maya. That dick was hers and nobody else's.

As his mother, she was determined to put his seed in her and have his baby. Gwen wanted to have another big-dick son to love and play with when JJ finally left the nest. She was determined to have another son by next Christmas. Big mama dozed off butt-naked on her stomach, with her fat ass spread, waiting on JJ to eventually come in and climb on top of her. Doggy-style was his favorite position, because he loved to long stroke his horny mama until the sheets got wet with her cum. Gwen dreamed she was already pregnant and that she and JJ got married!

John was thankful that Gwen didn't see that conniving tranny outside their house. The bitch had some fucking nerve, coming to his

home to threaten and lay down the goddamn law to him. Who the hell did she think she was? He's just an ugly-ass faggot that dressed like a woman, nothing more. Granted, she was sexy and all, but realistically, she was just a confused man who wanted to be a female.

At the moment that didn't matter, because she, he or it, was holding all the proverbial cards right, so John had to make the tranny play a new game, one where he at least had some cards to play. While the kids played video games, John smoked on a blunt in the cold garage, wracking his brain on how best to deal with Precious.

There was no way he was going to fork over all that money to the bitch. He was confident that no matter what happened, Gwen had his back. As for his job finding out—who would care? After a few stares and giggles, it would blow over like everything else does. Besides, he knew he wasn't the only down-low fag at work. Ever since he started there, there had always been rumors and stories about certain officers having sex with probationers, especially after the scandal involving one of his most respected colleagues.

One officer named Randall Moore, a big black dude, would threaten to violate a probationer for a failed drug test, unless the scared probationer dropped his pants and bent over Officer Moore's desk. As usual, the first reaction after being asked was a distinct "no," followed by an objection about being a "faggot." However, after Moore explained the consequences to them, which involved more jail time, they all relented.

Moore liked making these hard-headed thugs bend over while he fondled their asses and cocks right in his office. He would make them get on their knees, and he would fuck them in the mouth until he shot hot sticky juice down their throats. The sadistic fuck loved to make these cute-ass thugs gag on his thick cum. He delighted in making them swallow every drop of milky juice. For the grand finale, he would bend them over and rub his big penis between their quivering butt cheeks until the time was just right, then he would slowly but forcefully insert his horse-dick into the hardened thugs until they sounded like little girls begging for more.

The threat of jail must have been a very good motivator, because this went on for over 20 years with no one knowing about it. When Moore retired, he couldn't feed his appetite for young boys fast enough. One night, while cruising down Joseph Lowery Boulevard in ghetto Atlanta, he saw a young redbone walking and

offered to give him a ride. The boy looked to be about 17 or 18 and Moore couldn't take his eyes off the young tenderoni.

The boy obviously needed some money. Otherwise, he wouldn't have gotten in the car with a 52-year-old man. Moore offered the lad 20 bucks for the youngster to suck his old fat dick. The teen readily agreed, and they drove to Washington Park, which was dark and almost deserted at night. After parking behind some trees, Moore took his dick out and violently pushed the youngster's head down on it. To his surprise, the boy was an excellent dick-sucker—obviously, it wasn't his first rodeo. But more of a surprise was the blue lights that flashed in his rear-view mirror. Just as the pervert nutted in the boy's mouth, he saw the lights and almost had a heart attack.

Not only did he get arrested for indecent exposure, but also for aggravated sodomy and child molestation. The boy he picked up was only 13-years-old. It was plain to see he was very young, unless viewed by a lustful pervert like Moore. Lust had blinded this man to the extent that he thought this little boy was 18 years old, when it was obvious he wasn't. When word got back to the Decatur Probation center about the arrest, some of the probationers went to the supervisor and told how Moore would rape and sodomize them to buy his silence of a failed drug test or other violation that could send them back to jail.

Then they hired a lawyer and sued the state. After the local news picked up the story, it went national, courtesy of America's fascination with a tawdry sex scandal. Moore took a plea-deal and got sentenced to five years, to be served at the Atlanta transitional Center on Key Road in southeast Atlanta, a prison where he died of cardiac arrest while being raped. They found him slumped over a table in the cafeteria after he'd been savagely raped by about five or six horny inmates who fucked him until his anus started bleeding profusely.

He knew one of the rapists—a guy that failed a drug test and begged Moore not to violate him. When the officer told him to either suck his dick or go to prison, the guy chose prison. That was four years earlier, so there was Moore, getting his ass dug out by the same guy. Justice indeed was so funny. The last thing Moore saw before he died was a bunch of big-dick niggas cumming in his mouth and ass, like there was no tomorrow. Luckily, or unluckily for him, there were no more tomorrows. Other than being a rapist, Randall Moore was a swell guy.

John didn't know of Moore's extracurricular activities. It seemed the probationers liked and respected him. In hindsight, John did remember some probationers coming out of Moore's' office with tears in their eyes, but he thought they were crying because they might be violated and sent back to jail. Now he believed maybe they were crying because they'd just got fucked in the ass and didn't know how to process it. If they told someone, then they'd be labeled as a fag for letting a man bend them over and spread their asses like a woman.

These guys were young, black and tough, so it must have been very hard to think straight after going into his office a thug but after coming out a bitch. Once a guy bends another man over and has him squirming and begging for more cock, he's officially the guy's bitch. It didn't matter that some of these dudes were built like football players with broad shoulders, deep chests and six-pack abs. No one wanted their freedom taken away, especially hustling young niggas in their late teens and early twenties. They'd do anything to stay away from jail or prison. Hell, some of these guys were so "tough" that they'd bend over if they were facing as little as 30 days for some minor violation.

John wondered if any of his probationers had given up any ass to stay out of prison. Many probably would have or did under pressure. So, if his secret life did become public, John knew they wouldn't be able to fire him. To the chagrin of conservatives, being a gay dick-sucker m might have been morally wrong, but it was not legally wrong. If it were, a lot of closeted fags would have been locked up.

After his anger subsided, John realized it was cold as hell and went back into the house through the kitchen door, where he found the kids microwaving White Castle cheeseburgers. Looking at the beautiful children sitting at the kitchen table, laughing and giggling, John knew it was time to play offense and let that bitch know he was not to be trifled with when it came to his family. After grabbing a beer from the fridge, he called the trifling tranny on his cell from the living room.

"Hello, this is Precious," the tranny said in a voice sweeter than chocolate cake. She recognized the number and knew it was John. After scaring him silly earlier, she thought he was calling to beg her forgiveness for spying on her, but she was wrong.

"You know who this is! Why you playin like you don't?"

"Yes, what can I do for you, boo? You gonna give me my money sooner instead of waiting for Friday?"

"That's what I wanted to talk to you about. Here's my one and final offer, ho: I'm not giving you a goddamn cent, you ignorant, uncouth bitch!"

Unsure how she would take his new-found courage, John braced for her reaction. Surprisingly, Precious played it cool. She figured it was just the storm before the big payoff. There was no way he wasn't going to pay up. Dude was just feeling the pressure and wanted to blow off steam, so she tried reasoning with him.

"Now hold on, boo. You know the consequences if you *don't* pay, don't you?"

"No, fool! I know the consequences if I *do* pay. I'm not gonna turn over my kid's future to a hustling nigga with fake boobs and big feet. Like I said, you ain't getting a red cent of my money. I don't care what you do with the file. Put it on YouTube, for all I care, and let's see what happens."

"Yo muthafuckin ass think I'm bluffin, don't you?" Precious was getting very heated at this fag's uppity attitude. How dare this dick-sucker talk to her that way. And she was especially mad at John for calling her a man. Transsexuals hated that, and guys who messed with trannies knew it too, and they would say it to get under their skin.

"Bitch, I don't care if you're bluffin or not! Do what you gotta do, and I'm gonna do what I gotta do. Now remember, filming people secretly is against the law, and I will press charges on your sneaky ass. I know you don't want the police knocking on your door, do you? That would be very bad for your business, which is built on trust and secrecy for your clients. How would they feel if they knew you was secretly filmin them having sex?"

Precious was shocked at the sudden turn of events. Yesterday, she was confident the fool would pay up, but now, he was having not only second-thoughts, but third and fourth thoughts as well. In fact, the dick-sucker said he wasn't going to pay anything.

"Okay, Negro! You gonna be sorry, because if you don't have my money by Friday…"

John cut her off, "Bitch, please stop trying to scare me! You just a gay dude with tits and a bad weave, nothing more. Society looks at you like you a confused freak, so you take your anger out on anybody you can. I repeat: you ain't getting shit from me! *Comprende*, ho? Now git somewhere, and if you call my job or home again, I will call the

police on you. I will pass out flyers in your neighborhood, everybody that they have an evil, blackmailing tranny bitch in their community. You fucked with the wrong one this time, bitch." John had no intention of passing out flyers, he was just trying to scare her.

"Naw, muthafucka! I got the right one. I'm gonna show you better can I can tell you. Since you done pissed me off, I'm gonna put it on YouTube tonight if you don't watch out." Precious was beside herself with anger, but she was bluffing and John knew it.

"Yeah, and if you do, all your clientele would go somewhere else, and you know it. See, bitch—you not as smart as you think. Now I'm gonna hang up, and this will be the last time we ever talk to each other again... unless I see you in court. Goodbye and good riddance, you ugly-ass dude!"

John felt a burden had been lifted off his shoulders as he got off the phone he. Feeling a sense of relief, the tranny-lover said a silent prayer and promised to be more careful when he was out chasing dick. The down-low fag dodged a very dangerous bullet that time, the next time he might not be so lucky.

After John hung up the phone, Precious wanted to call back, but she thought it would make her look weak and indecisive. She knew she had to do something to make the fool realize it would be in his best interest to pay up. But what could she do? The one advantage she had hanging over the heads of her numerous blackmail victims was their fear and shame about being outed as faggots, so if they weren't afraid of being outed, she was powerless over them.

Their shame and fear made her more powerful. Without it, she was nothing but another big-dick hustling bitch. The angry tranny realized she made a mistake by going over to the house. She scared him so much that the fag wasn't afraid anymore. The down-low father of two knew that if he paid her again, she would be in his pockets for life, and he was right, because Precious had no intention of ever letting these niggas off the hook unless they died.

If her other blackmail victims realized what John did, they might stop paying too. Things were different in this situation, because of the absurd amount of money involved. The other guys paid because their reputations and good standing in the community was worth much more than the money they paid to keep their secret. What was a few hundred dollars a week, compared with keeping your sterling image intact? She realized her mistake with John was that for him, the money meant more than his reputation. He wasn't a leader in the

Being a tranny escort, the last thing a girl in her line of business needed to deal with was the law. Clicking off the TV, she listened to the silence of the quiet middle-class black neighborhood. Other than Mrs. Bryant's chocolate lab barking, there was nary a sound. Exhausted from all the scheming and planning, she fell asleep, not knowing what to do about the situation with John.

****

Sunday morning found the Evans family in church. Even John went this time, grateful that he'd gotten rid of the predatory tranny trying to hustle him. He half-expected Precious to call, but to his surprise, she never rang. Admiring his family, the patriarch couldn't believe how happy he felt, listening to the minister, and singing along with the choir at Big Miller Grove Baptist. Usually, he hated church, but after the epiphany yesterday, he decided somebody up there must be watching over the family.

The devil in the form of a big-dick transsexual tried to come between his loved ones, but God in His infinite wisdom, rebuked the interloper and saved the family from the clutches of evil. Thank God that Gwen never found out, or she may have shot that bitch for real. Gwen seemed happy with her arms around JJ, while he rubbed on Mom's ample thighs, right there in church. Of course, to the untrained eye it all seemed innocent, but to those versed in lustful incest, it was anything but. Even when lying the child's head on her soft breasts, it looked like nothing more than a loving mom, spoiling her child, and nothing sexual.

But John knew what was up and felt a tinge of jealousy toward Gwen. Last night had been one of the most incredible nights of his life, but he couldn't tell anyone about it, or he'd be in jail. But that's also what made it so special, the fact that it's considered immoral and outside the bounds of decency. That's why the next time would feel even better than the first time, because knowing the consequences heightens the fear of getting caught, which in turn intensifies the excitement factor. After overthinking the matter, he went to the bathroom to pass time and to jerk off.

It was past one o'clock, and *the preacher was still running his fucking mouth. Don't this muthafucka know its football season, and the Falcons are playing in the playoffs today?* Obviously not! *Besides, haven't we already heard what he's saying before?* John spent almost 30 minutes in the bathroom,

listening to his iPod and taking a nice relaxing shit in peace. Upon exiting, he was delighted to find the minister finishing up the long, drawn-out boring sermon.

Thank God for small favors! because black folks spent too much damn time in church already. These damn preachers needed to understand that it was football season and cut their sermons accordingly. After the service, Gwen, as usual, wanted to talk and chit-chat with the other ladies, so the family didn't get home until almost three o'clock.

John grabbed a beer and plopped down in front of the big screen, Maya went to do homework, while Gwen and JJ went to his room to make a baby. Gwen figured that, with all the praying she did in church, it was time to put action to words and start the procreation. She knew JJ would put a baby in her belly by the New Year. She had prayed and God always answers His children's prayers, after all.

****

Precious started to call John three times, but each time, she stopped herself, thinking he would call her and offer to negotiate, but he never did. She couldn't believe she let that fag get away. One minute, she had him by his little mini-balls, and the next, he grew a big pair. After a few days of anger and feeling the holiday blues, she deleted his number and never attempted to call him again.

That Saturday was the last time she saw or spoke with John Evans. With Christmas less than a week away, she did her best to put the episode behind her and concentrate on the future. With the holidays approaching, it seemed that her clientele was getting scarcer by the day. But in her business, that's was natural, because men wanted to be with their families during the holidays.

Being with a tranny prostitute on Christmas made men feel more guilty than usual. She figured that no man wanted to go home with dried cum on his lips or up his ass on Christmas day. Precious always hated Christmas. Growing up in the ghetto, holidays held certain sadness. It was like the day promised so much, but delivered so little. A feeling of sadness overcame the tranny as she thought about Christmas's with no tree or presents to put under, it there was even a tree. TV displayed happy families, gathered around the table, while

around her table growing up, there were a bunch of crack-heads, scheming on how to get their next fix.

Sometimes, her mom would sell her, then as a young son, to some horny old dude, if she was desperate for a hit. Marsha, being the good mother, reasoned that since Tavarious is already a sissy, he may as well start giving up the ass as soon as possible. And men loved her son's ten-year-old ass! With an upbringing like that, the holidays brought on a sense of fear and anger toward her mother in particular and families in general. Precious envied John and his beautiful family.

She imagined they had a big tall beautiful tree, with presents piled high all around it. Except for a call from Marsha to elicit money from her, she would spend the holidays alone, as usual. Her clients lusted and groveled over her behind closed doors, but they didn't want to be seen anywhere in public with her. While they were having parties and get-togethers, none would think about calling and wishing her a Merry Christmas. She was the part of themselves they kept hidden away, until the beast needed to be tamed again and appetite for humiliation sated.

Just once, she wished one of her clients would ask her to dinner or a movie. Precious knew it wouldn't happen because she wasn't passable as a woman. And the men wouldn't be able to handle the stares and whispers that came with being with a transsexual. To them, she was just an exotic piece of fruit that they desired on special occasion. Once they ate of the fruit, they didn't acknowledge her again until they wanted more. But the day after Jesus' birthday, the fags would start calling again and feigning concern, asking how her Christmas went, as if they really cared. She hated the obvious phoniness, but it still felt good to be asked, even if she knew the person asking didn't care.

It wasn't like she cared anything about her clients either, except learning how to separate them from their money. If one of them showed her any kindness, she would use it against him, as she did with Walter. As the year 2013 approached, Precious looked forward to a happy and more prosperous new year. She didn't know it at the time, but it would be one of the most difficult years of her young life—even more difficult than the nightmare she fled from in Detroit a year earlier.

Chapter 9
The Murder

The new year came in like it always did, loud and noisy as ever, with drunks all over the world making impossible resolutions that they knew wouldn't be kept. While watching the Peach Drop on WSB.TV, Precious found herself counting money as the new year rolled in. As she watched drunkards bring in the New Year at Underground Atlanta, the money-hungry tranny smiled at the $33,659 laid out on her bed in neat rows, saved from the previous year.

Since prostitution was illegal, she couldn't keep the illicit money in the bank so it was kept under the floorboard in the bedroom closet. As always, the only resolution the sexy transsexual made was to make more money than the year before. While superstitious niggas were cooking collard greens and black eye peas on New Year's Eve in hopes of having a prosperous year, she was counting real green—the kind of green that never lets you down. The only thing collard greens and black eye peas did was give a person gas and indigestion.

While the hoopla of the holidays died down, the cold gray winter months of January and February gripped the country and had everyone wishing for the warmth and rejuvenation of spring. Precious was no different, because wintertime always made her feel more depressed and lonelier than usual. Even though winters in Georgia were a lot more pleasant and shorter than those in Michigan, it increased her homesickness nonetheless.

Almost a year after Walter's death, she was still afraid of going back to Detroit. Since Marsha didn't like to travel outside the hood, and with Juquan in prison, the lonely tranny really had no family. The conversations over the phone she had with both always started and ended with talk about money and how or when she sent it. She didn't mind sending money every month—she just wished they didn't act so thirsty. To her, both were in their own kind of prison. Marsha imprisoned herself with crack and alcohol, while Juquan broke the law.

Mom seemed sadder than big brother, maybe because by imprisoning herself, it made her 100% responsible for the plight she was in. If she was wholly responsible, then it was up to her and nobody else to save herself. Maybe she seemed sadder because

nobody gave a fuck about her and what she'd been through. She birthed three sons, and they all abandoned her. One was murdered in prison, one had been turned into a fag while in prison, and the "good" one dressed like a woman.

Sometimes while talking to Juquan, Precious she could hear the "sugar" in his voice. The boy sounded more like a woman than she did. He almost seemed to like being locked up, or maybe he was just making the best of a fucked-up situation. It was hard to believe that the former gangsta thug was now spreading his legs like a woman and begging for dick. Precious still loved her mom and brother, but thinking about how fucked-up the family was exacerbated the winter blues even more.

When she imagined Juquan getting fucked, it sometimes amused and made her want to throw up at the same time. The tranny imagined him being like her numerous clients, who put on a masculine front until she took her cock out and then they went straight to acting like females in heat. She figured that by the time Juquan got out of prison, he'd be a full-fledged woman. She wondered if he became a fag naturally, or if prison had turned him out.

Since her brother spoke often about being lonely, it was probably his environment that made him into a faggot. Sometimes, while fucking, a client she would close her eyes and imagine it was Juquan underneath her, begging for more dick. Even though she knew incest was sick as hell, it turned her on to no end, thinking about her once big bad brother, squirming in pleasurable pain at the end of her thick, black, veiny ten-inch-cock. Remembering how he used to beat up on her to make her tough, she wanted to exact revenge on his faggot ass. They were just evil fantasies, and nothing more, something she thought about when she was all alone, with only her thoughts to keep her company.

Thankfully, the tranny had a growing clientele and a blackmailing business to get her through the chilly winter nights. After the holidays, clients started calling again glad so they could get back to their normal down-low selves and suck cock without feeling guiltier than usual, because of the holidays. By the end of March, she was extorting 12 fags for $3000 a week—not bad work if you can get it. Life was good for Precious, and she celebrated by picking up young homeless teenage boys in downtown Atlanta. After fucking so many

old ass niggas with worn out assholes, she started cruising the gay clubs and streets for young black virgin ass.

The lusty she-male wanted fresh-faced teens who could be easily turned out. Fucking the old dudes was business, but fucking these fine young boys was all about pleasure for her, and for them pain. The boys were eager to get into her car too. After being tired and hungry, they'd do anything to ride around and relax in a nice car. Sometimes, she took them back to her crib, and sometimes they would ride around while the youngster sucked her dick. Precious loved public sex and got an extra charge driving down Peachtree Street in broad daylight while getting her dick sucked.

Her business clients would never have done the same, because they were the epitome of on the down-low. But give these desperate youngsters $20, and they'd do anything. If the guy was really young and cute, she would take him home so he could take a nice hot shower get a good meal and spend the night getting his tight ass plowed for hours. Precious loved the innocent look on the teen's faces while they writhed in agony as their virginity and purity was taken by her unforgiving cock. She liked how they would beg her to stop at first, and then after a few minutes, they would ask for more. Their transformation from being a straight-male to begging for dick in a matter of hours was what made this especially exciting to Precious.

When the tranny turned these teens out, it was like a notch in her belt. She felt like a lone gunslinger in the Wild West—only this time, the "outlaws" were young black boys, whose only "crime" was having a fat virgin ass that need to be invaded by her thick chocolate stick. With so many cuties walking the streets, the big-dick bitch had her pick of dozens of fresh-faced eager youngsters. She felt it was her duty to fuck every last one of them. Sometimes, Precious felt sorry for the boys, but after a while, she started seeing them as nothing more than sex objects who were put on this Earth solely to pleasure her, and nothing else.

She was doing them a favor. All they had to do to make $20 was to suck her dick until she cummed in their mouths. That money they made fed them for another day or two. Precious knew, from a rough childhood, that a person could make better decisions on a full stomach. An empty stomach brought desperation, and desperation made a person do things they wouldn't normally do. To Precious, it never occurred to her that the boys she fucked were hungry and

desperate. If they weren't, then why would they get in a car with a masculine-looking tranny? But her lust overrode commonsense on the subject, so she thought the boys were happy to get in the car and be her sex slave.

Soon, the warmth of spring enveloped the country, and like everyone else, Precious had spring fever. By then it was May, and her lust was out of control as she cruised the streets of Atlanta, three or four days a week in her new BMW, hunting for virgin nigga assholes. By then, she had her routine down pat. She would take the boys off Johnson Road in NW Atlanta to an abandoned house and fuck him in the car, while parked in the driveway. She knew they wouldn't be bothered, because the area was the epitome of a rough neighborhood, with crack dealers, whores and hustlers everywhere.

Sometimes, they would walk up to peep inside to see what was happening. Often, they would walk away in shock after seeing Precious' cock, either in a boy's mouth or ass. Stunned, they would leave without saying a word. *Shit, like that wasn't anything unusual in slums and ghettos across America!* As long as it's kept hidden from mainstream America, a person can get away with anything in the hood. The tranny got away with it, not only at night, but in broad daylight too. She would lie the youngster's seat all the way back, take his pants off, spread the boys' legs and fuck him, missionary-style, in the front passenger seat.

By fucking him in that position, the tranny could keep a look out behind them to see if anybody was trying to be nosey or jack her car. She did this because the thrill of getting caught was an immense turn on. She loved it when someone would walk by and see the car shaking from her massive dick strokes.

One hot day at the end of May, Precious was cruising through the ghettos of Atlanta, stalking her prey like a cheetah stalks a gazelle on the Serengeti plains. Only, her prey was young black boys, preferably with virgin assholes that needed a good fucking. Riding by Washington High School just as the school day began, she noticed a young cutie with a bubble butt, walking alone instead of interacting with his classmates. The youngster had the unmistakable walk of a fag, switching from side to side to emphasize his juicy apple bottom. With a butt that big, it wasn't hard to do. She wondered how many down-low men in the hood had tried to tap that fresh fat ass. The boy's blonde hair made him standout among the rest of the students. How many times did anyone see a black male teen with blonde hair?

With his sagging jeans revealing a plump ass, Precious couldn't take her eyes off the boy. He looked to be about 13 or 14, was short, dark and chubby, with some very soft dick-sucking lips. Judging from his arched eyebrows, Precious knew the boy was gay possibly a future tranny. No wonder he was walking alone. There were not too many openly-gay fags in inner-city high schools. He probably didn't have many friends, because not many teenage black boys would befriend an openly-gay person, especially one of their peers. Precious smiled, thinking about how lonely and vulnerable the boy must have felt.

The perverted tranny pictured him being ostracized and ridiculed all day in school. If that was the case, then she could use his insecurities and loneliness to get him into the car. He probably longed for another gay person to talk to, who could tell him what it was like to grow up in America, black and homosexual. And once the youngster got into the car, Precious had already decided she was going to take him home and introduce his tight asshole to her ten-inch power drill. She was going to take her time and fuck the boy all day and night.

With those thoughts on her mind, she first had to see if the teen wanted a ride. When he turned down Joseph E. Lowery Street, Precious realized he was about to go into the Ashby Street Train station. If he did that, she may have never seen him again. Pulling the BMW up beside the boy as he walked, she offered him a ride. At first, he looked shocked that someone in a car so beautiful would offer him a ride. Then his reluctance turned to curiosity as he gave Precious a big bright smile and quickly got in. Plopping into the soft, Corinthian-leather seat, the boy was thankful that he accepted the tranny's offer. Besides, he had nothing to do anyway, but go home to a crowded, nasty apartment.

"My name's Precious. What's yours?"

"Deshawnte," the boy said nervously.

"That's a beautiful name for a little cutie like you," Precious kidded. "You just getting out of school?"

"Yeah, on my way home," the boy said. "But I don't have to go right now," he volunteered.

That was all the opening she needed.

"Well, you wanna go home with me? I stay out in Decatur?"

He agreed before she finished the last syllable.

"Won't your mom and dad worry where you're at?" she said, sincerely hoping they wouldn't.

"Naw, they don't care. I have no curfew."

It was like manna from heaven to the conniving tranny's ears. "How old are you, cutie?"

"Fourteen, I'll be fifteen in July."

"So, are you a Cancer or a Leo? I'm a Leo, born on the 24th of July." Sometimes, Precious wondered if her dominant personality was a result of being a Leo.

"I'm a Cancer. I was born July 16th."

"So, tell me a little about yourself. What grade are you in? How many brothers and sisters do you have?" Precious asked while getting on interstate I-20 East, heading to the crib.

At first, Deshawnte seemed a little nervous and mumbled his answers, but the tranny knew he was just anxious and tried to put the boy's mind at ease by turning up the radio. Before turning on the music, she found out he was the youngest of four kids and the only male child.

They all had different fathers who didn't give a shit about any of them, hardly ever coming around at all. His two oldest sisters, 18 and 19, both had children, while the younger was six months pregnant. He stayed at Overlook Atlanta, and there were eight people living in the tiny three-bedroom apartment off Hollywood Road, including his mom's boyfriend. The anxious teen said he was in the ninth grade and hated school, because guys were always picking on him. Precious knew exactly where he lived, because she's gotten plenty of young, thug-man pussy from there. Her dick got hard just thinking about all the sexy young niggas with swag who were turned out by her big meat. Precious had an evil look in her eyes while studying the little boy, trying to gauge how he would react the first time he saw her enormous cock.

"So, are you gay?" Precious asked abruptly.

Deshawnte smiled and said, inconvincibly, "I don't know. Are you?"

"Well, you do know that I'm a transsexual, don't you?" The boy nodded. "So I'm a man who dresses and carries himself as a woman, so yes, I am gay. Being a tranny is as gay as a nigga can get."

"How long have you been dressin like a girl?" he asked.

"Why? Do you wanna start dressin like a girl? I see you have your eyebrows arched. Did you do that?"

"Yes," he said proudly. "My sister, Marleena, taught me."

"Is she the oldest?" The boy nodded. "It looks like she taught you well." Precious could see he appreciated the compliment.

"Thanks! Now I do them better than her," the youngster said, smiling from ear to ear.

"So, do you have a girlfriend?" Precious already knew the feminine little boy didn't have a girlfriend, but she asked, curious to see what the answer would be.

"I have some friends who are females, but we don't do nothin but kiss." Deshawnte didn't tell her that those kisses were mostly friendly pecks on the cheek.

"So, what you're saying is that you really *don't* have a girlfriend, right? Be honest, do you like boys or girls, sexually?"

Deshawnte thought for a moment and admitted that he finds thugs sexy, and that in his apartment building, there was a certain sexy dreadlocked drug dealer he had a secret crush on. The dealer happened to be the baby-daddy of Marleena's child. The two siblings sometimes went down to the dealer's apartment to smoke weed while he watched TV. The dealer and Marleena would go to the bedroom to fuck. With a mischievous smile on his face, the boy admitted to spying on them while they were making a baby. He described how his sister would scream while the dealer fucked her with his huge sexy dick. And after they got through fucking, the dealer would walk around naked in front of him with that big dick, curvy like a banana, swinging from side to side. Deshawnte thought the thug liked him sexually, *or why else would he let him see his naked body?* The youngster told Precious that he wished the dealer, aka Mookie, would make love to him like he did to Marleena.

"Why don't you tell him that? Are you afraid of what he may do or say?" Precious asked.

"Yeah, I am afraid because I don't know if he likes guys or not," Deshawnte admitted. "What if I tell him how I feel, and he gets mad and beat my ass or something?"

"That could happen, or he might surprise you and take that big cock out for you to suck on," she told him with a smile on her face. "Let me tell you something little boy—you'd be surprised by all the hard thugs, walking around Atlanta, suckin dick and gettin fucked. Lookin at them, you would never think they were gay, because they look all hard and shit, but in private, they like getting bent over and fucked by another thug or a woman like me. That dealer you got a crush on is probably screwin and gettin screwed by his boys. I bet he

was testin you out, and once he feels comfortable enough, he'll make a pass at you. Mark my words: if he didn't wanna fuck you, he wouldn't be walkin around naked in front of your little gay ass. Any other dude would tell you to get lost while he fucked yo sis, but this guy let you stay. He knows you're gay, yet still struts around in front of you, like a proud bull, showin off his big cock. Maybe he uses your sister as an excuse to walk around in the nude. In other words, ta get you down to the apartment, he pretends to like your sister, to keep things on the down-low. I mean, if you went by yourself, neighbors would start talking, so the boy uses your sister as cover to get you down there. Well, that's what I think, but then again, I may be 100% wrong. Dude might not be gay, and you could get your ass whooped if you said the wrong thang."

After listening to Precious, Deshawnte realized she had to be right, or at least he desperately wanted her to be right. All the boy dreamt about was Mookie's dark, sexy body with the long dreads, broad muscular shoulders, six-pack abs and a bright sexy smile that made the fourteen-year-old's asshole tingle. He imagined lying on his back, with legs spread like Marleena, while Mookie buried his cock deep in his virgin anus until he screamed with a mixture of joy and pain.

"So, you sayin he'll make the first move if he's interested in me?"

"Yep, that's exactly what I'm sayin, boo. He's the man, and when the right time comes, he'll make his move. But you let *him* make the move. I don't want the nigga to beat your ass if he doesn't swing that way."

They drove in silence, listening to the radio; both contemplating what would happen when they got to the house. Precious couldn't wait to get home so she could introduce his tender ass to ten inches of Motown Meat. But it was the dreaded rush-hour and traffic was backed up at interstate I-285 and I-20, as usual. With two wrecks, it was business as usual along this busy portion of the highway, where people drove like lunatics while texting and talking on the phone, with little regard for the safety of others. Finally, after taking 30 minutes to crawl five miles, they reached the Wesley Chapel Road exit, where Precious let out a sigh of relief, glad to be out of the traffic and almost home.

The tranny couldn't help but notice a look of curiosity on her young passenger's face.

"You ever come out this way," she asked.

"Nope. I ain't never been out here before."

"You mean you were born in Atlanta, and never been to Decatur?"

"I been to Decatur before, but not this far out."

"We almost home now, hon. I can fix you something to eat when we get there if you like. You hungry?"

"Kinda," was all the boy said while taking in the scenery.

Precious made a left at the exit, and in a few minutes, pulled into her subdivision, and not a minute too soon, because nature called. After checking the mailbox, she pulled the BMW into the garage so that nosy neighbors wouldn't see her underage passenger, about to be defiled. As soon as the garage door closed, the tranny told her guest to make himself at home, while she kicked off her three-inch heels and ran to take a piss. It was such a relief, because she had been holding it in since they left Atlanta. After finishing, she took her jeans and blouse off and put on a big tee-shirt and flip flops to relax. Those tight jeans and high heels were sexy, but they were not the most comfortable attire to wear. She came out into the living room to find Deshawnte, sitting quietly, looking nervous and scared.

"Why didn't you turn the TV on?" she joked, pinching him on his fat cheeks. "I said to make yourself at home." Precious turned the big screen on and gave him the remote.

"You want a sandwich or something? I make a really good burger," she advised, while standing right in front of him. "Would you like a cheeseburger and fries?"

Looking up at his host, Deshawnte couldn't help but notice how beautiful she was. Even though she was a transsexual, she was still cute—not as cute as Mookie, but sexy in a different way. He knew he didn't like girls, but was certainly turned on by this man, dressed as a girl.

"Yeah," he said quietly. The boy was so in awe of his surroundings that speech became difficult, and Precious didn't make it any easier by staring at him so intently.

"Okay, would you like a soda?" The boy nodded. "Look Deshawnte, you have no reason to be afraid. We're not going to do anything you don't want to do, you understand? So stop acting all shy and shit. You smoke weed?"

"Sometimes, like almost every day."

Precious went to retrieve her illegal buds from under the bed and sat down beside Deshawnte to roll a fat blunt. The child molester

fucked that nigga Lee and put him in the hospital with a tore-up rectum. Looking at her young lover's face while making love to him was such a turn-on that she took her cock out of his ass and immediately shoved the bloody thing in his mouth. The perverted tranny loved watching muthafucka's gag on her big meat.

After a few minutes, she nutted in the boy's mouth, her third nut in an hour, and she wasn't finished yet. Deshawnte, on the other hand, was exhausted. After having his mouth and virgin asshole fucked by this big-dick bitch for over an hour, he couldn't take it anymore. With his rectum bleeding and mouth full of dried blood and cum, he looked like he'd been raped by a prison gang. The boy had begged the tranny to stop, but she was having none of that. Deshawnte was her bitch, and she was going to do with him whatever her evil warped mind desired.

Precious crushed the rest of crack-rock up until it was powder and rubbed it on her bloody dick. When the white cocaine mixed with the blood, her dick looked like a nasty, giant-ass peppermint stick. Then she grabbed Deshawnte's aching mouth and forcefully pushed it down on her meat, until his lips were touching her testicles. Using both her hands, she had his mouth going up and down her cock, like a yoyo on speed. The crack had her feeling sensations never achieved before. After watching the boy choke and gag, with snot running out of his nose, Precious put him back on his stomach for one final nut.

The boy seemed to be in no pain after sucking ten inches of crack-covered dick. He must have slurped $100 worth of crack off her long cock… or maybe the youngster was so high he didn't know whether or not he was in pain. Either way, the bitch didn't care as she snorted the rest of the crack down her nose in eager anticipation of climbing on top of the boy and wrecking his tender asshole.

As soon as she inserted her cock in the boy from behind, Deshawnte screamed with either pain or pleasure, but Precious didn't care which. She just rode his ass for over an hour as the boy writhed in pain under her, begging her to stop or at least to slow down. But the pervert was oblivious to his pleas, only thinking of her own selfish, vile pleasure. The crack had turned her into a fucking machine that couldn't be stopped until she got a nut.

She was so high that she didn't notice that Deshawnte had passed out after about forty minutes into her savage lovemaking. So for the last twenty minutes, she was fucking the boy while he was

unconscious. When the tranny got ready to cum, she let out a yell that would have made Tarzan proud. Then, high as a kite and exhausted, she fell asleep on top of her lover and didn't wake up until the next day, with her dick still impaled in Deshawnte's bloody butt.

Precious had a terrific headache and an aching cock when she finally woke up, still on top of her young lover. It was 12:30 in the afternoon, and she had slept like a log. Still groggy, she went to take a piss and shower the blood off her. After showering, she noticed Deshawnte wasn't moving and tried to wake him, but he seemed cold and stiff. When she turned him over, the tranny shrieked in horror, fell back and stumbled on the floor, bumping her head against the dresser.

Blood was all over the bed. The boy's eyes were open, but he looked dead. Precious kept looking for signs of life, but the lad just lay there; unblinking eyes open, starring into the abyss. She couldn't believe the boy was dead! How could it have happened? What the hell did they do last night? She surveyed the room and noticed the empty bag of crack cocaine on the floor. They had smoked a whole eight-ball of crack, along with a couple of blunts, chased by vodka. Damn! That was too much for her but for a 14-year-old who never tried crack—it was dangerous.

She tried to remember the night before. It was difficult, but she did recall making the boy smoke the crack until his eyes rolled up in his head. When he complained about his bleeding ass, she just shoved the crack pipe in his mouth to shut him up. Jesus Christ! What the fuck was she going to do now? Why didn't she listen to the boy and stop when his rectum first started bleeding? Just like with Lee, she let her animal lust take over, and this is the result of her savage bestial lovemaking!

With Lee, her big cock ruptured his asshole, and it had to be stitched up. With the amount of blood this young nigga's anus had leaked, it seemed like she had fucked the boy to death. And the drugs certainly didn't help. What the tranny didn't know was that Deshawnte had a heart murmur, and the crack caused him to have a heart attack. So her assessment was correct—the drugs certainly didn't help.

After sitting on the floor for what seemed like a long time—but had only been a couple of minutes—Precious realized she had to think about her future. First, she had to get rid of the body, so she got a sleeping bag out in the garage and put Deshante's stiffening

body in it. Before zipping it, she gently reached down with her hands and closed his beautiful eyes. Then she threw his body over the shoulder and put him in the trunk of her car. Before she did that, the tranny lined her trunk with plastic garbage bags, in case of any blood seeping through the sleeping bag. At moments like that, one was thankful for the things one took for granted, and the tranny was grateful right to have a garage which afforded her privacy.

After putting the boy in the trunk, she put all his clothes in a garbage bag, along with the sheets, pillowcases and her nice, expensive comforter. Precious noticed blood on her mattress and decided that had to go too along with the plate, silverware and glass the boy used the day before. Not only that, but she also threw the soap and bath towels the boy showered with into garbage bags as well. She didn't watch *CSI: Miami* for years without picking up a few tips.

Finally, after putting everything in garbage bags that might have Deshawnte's DNA on them, she sat on the couch in silence, waiting for the cloak of darkness so she could get rid of the body. She decided to dump the body in Redan Park. It would be deserted late night, and there were enough woods to hide a corpse. The murdering rapist not only had to hide the body, but she also had to burn it to get rid of all her DNA on the boy.

Precious sat in the house for hours, not answering the phone or turning on the TV. The bitch was too nervous to eat. At 11 p.m., she figured it was time to do the dastardly deed. Not only did she murder the boy, but now she was going to burn his body. When he was eventually found and identified, the family would not get back a body, but for a few burnt bones to bury. She was disgusted with herself, but she didn't want to spend the rest of her life in prison. If caught, she knew they would give her the death penalty.

An evil transsexual stalker picked up an innocent 14-year-old, drugged him, raped and murdered him. She could see the headlines! Everyone and their mama would be calling for her head on a platter, and who could blame them? Not even Jesse or Al would come to her defense, let alone anyone else!

Precious started the BMW and sat in the closed garage for a few minutes, too nervous and scared to open the door. Finally, after gathering her nerves, she opened the garage door and backed out into the warm, dark night. In her head, she had memorized the shortest and quickest route to the park. The tranny drove to Wesley Chapel

Road, made a right and then a left onto I-20 East. Two exits down, she got off on Evans Mill Road, made a left up to Covington Highway, drove down about two miles then made a right on Phillips Road. From there, it took only a few minutes to reach the park, which sat on the left side of the road. Instead of dumping the body right away, she did quick surveillance to make sure no one was around.

Satisfied that the park was empty, she drove to the side parking lot, which was surrounded by woods, and immediately jumped out and retrieved Deshawnte's corpse, now smelly and stiffened, from the trunk. She threw him over her shoulder and walked 20 yards to the wood line and dumped the body behind one of the baseball dugouts. Then she drenched the body with a 64 oz. bottle of Kingsford lighter fluid until it was empty. After baptizing the corpse in flammable liquid, she lit a book of matches and threw it on the dead boy, and he went up in flames.

At first, Precious was mesmerized by the fire, but after a few minutes, self-preservation shook her out of the malaise, and she ran back to the car, which was still running. She jumped in and high-tailed it out of there, like a black man running from the KKK. Making a left on Phillips Road, she didn't notice the police coming toward her until they passed each other. In her rearview mirror, she noticed the cop saw the fire and turned into the park to investigate.

By then, she could imagine him calling in and reporting that a person driving a black BMW had dumped a body in the park. The murderer made a right onto Stone Mountain Industrial, drove down to Evans Mill Road and got back on the highway, heading home. Careful not to speed, she drove 65 mph and tried her best to relax by turning on the radio.

When Precious finally parked the car in the garage, she let out a big sigh of relief and promptly threw up on herself while still sitting inside the vehicle. After vomiting her guts out, she cried like a baby at the thought of what her future might bring. The scared tranny could just see the police and news reporters, banging on the door and her being lead out in handcuffs, doing the perp walk, while reporters asked stupid, asinine questions.

Precious sat in the car all night, too afraid to do anything else. She woke up the next morning with her head pressed against the steering wheel and dried vomit everywhere. After clearing the cobwebs from her head, she peeked out the garage door, and

everything seemed normal. A couple of neighbors were walking their dogs, and others were doing their daily yard work. There was not a cop or reporter in sight. Maybe she'd gotten away with it. It's not like every murderer was ever caught.

If Deshawnte's body wasn't burned completely, investigators might be able to get DNA off it. What if the cop put the fire out? But why would he? He wasn't a fireman. The officer probably called the fire department instead of risking burning himself for a dead nigga. Or better yet, maybe he let the body burn until it went out by itself. In a few days, she, along with the rest of the public, would know whether or not they were able to get any DNA off the body. For the moment, she had to get rid of her blood-stained mattress.

Since the blood couldn't be scrubbed out of the mattress, she decided to burn the section that was stained. That way, if anyone questioned what happened, the tranny could blame it on falling asleep in bed while smoking. After getting rid of the bloody evidence, she called and ordered another mattress from Wal-Mart, and then she showered and waited for the twelve o'clock news, to see if they had identified Deshawnte's burnt remains. Exhausted by the whole ordeal, the scared murderer lay down on the sofa, but she couldn't get any rest because her heart was racing a mile a minute.

She was sure the Decatur police would be knocking on the door at any moment, asking questions for which she had no answer. Minutes seemed like hours as she waited impatiently for the midday news to air. The grisly murder of her young former lover indeed was the top story of the day. Every one of the local Atlanta news crews were broadcasting from the park and reporting the horror and tragedy of the murder. Yet the broadcasts said something that made Precious rejoice—the body was burned beyond comprehension and couldn't be identified until further investigation.

The tranny was glad to have had the foresight to unzip the sleeping bag and pour the lighter fluid directly onto the body to make sure it burned quickly and thoroughly. If not, the bag may have prevented the body from burning completely. While this was a small victory, she knew she wasn't out of the woods yet. There was still a possibility that the authorities could find her DNA somewhere in the burnt remains. Scared and tense, she sat on the sofa all day, waiting for a knock on the door that never came. After watching the news numerous times to see if the police had found any new evidence, sleep overtook her, and by midnight she was out like a light.

She slept in one of the guest bedrooms, since obviously her mattress wasn't available. As soon as her head hit the pillow, she was out like a new-born baby. If the tranny was worried about anything, it didn't affect her ability to get a good night's sleep—or it could have been because the bitch was an unfeeling psychopath, incapable of feeling remorse or empathy.

****

Days, weeks and finally a month had passed since the homicide, and Precious was growing confident she had gotten away with murder. It has been two weeks since they showed Deshawnte's mother crying crocodile tears after being informed that the naked, burnt body was her son. She lied and said he was a good boy who loved school and wanted to be a doctor when he grew up.

When the tranny heard that, she almost choked on her vodka and orange juice, from laughing so hard. The tranny wished she could set the record straight and tell the world the truth about the boy. In the end, nobody cared about another dead nigga, even if he was only 14 years old. And after the next sensational murder, he would be forgotten—like everything else in today's fast-food news-cycle.

Still, not wanting to push her luck, she laid low, going out only at night and to collect the extortion money from her clients at the Wendy's on Covington and Panola Roads. The cruising for young boys stopped, and for a month, the tranny was completely celibate. Other than Monique Devereux, formerly Marcus, she didn't have any other visitors. Precious was pleasantly surprised at Monique's transition to full-fledged transsexual, and she couldn't help but feel pride, because she was the girl's mentor.

Being celibate and staying in the house was growing tedious and boring, but it kept her out of trouble. After having been fortunate enough to get away with murder, she didn't want to tempt fate again by doing something stupid—like picking up underage boys to rape and murder—even if it was fun. From then on, she promised herself not to fuck any underage nigga, no matter how cute and sexy he was. It was going to be hard, because the tranny had gotten addicted to young 16-year-old boy pussy. She loved the look on their faces after plunging her cock deep into the recesses of their virgin assholes. After the Deshawnte fiasco, no ass was worth going to jail over, even if it was fat and juicy.

Just when things were getting back to normal, or as normal as could be after committing such a horrific crime, she got an unsuspected call from one of the tricks she was extorting. It was David, the college professor, with the fat, dick-sucking lips, who definitely hated her.

"Hello?" the tranny answered in her girlie voice.

"Hey, this is David, and I'm not going to be able to make my payment today."

"And why not, nigga? Today's Tuesday, which means it's payday. If you gonna be late, that's cool but I need my muthafuckin money! You know I don't like these fucking games." Precious hated when these tricks try to play her, like she was Willie-Lump-Lump.

"And if I don't pay your blackmail money, what will happen? Are you going to ruin me and my family by exposing my sex life?"

"Nigga, by the time I finish with you, the whole university will know how good you suck dick," Precious said, with extra vigor in her voice.

"Let me tell you something, you freak! I was in Redan Park that night."

When the tranny heard those words, she panicked, but she tried to play it nonchalantly. "What are you talking about?"

"You evil slut! You know what I'm talking about. I saw you burn that boy's body, like he was a piece of trash! And guess what? There's going to be a new arrangement from now on. I want $500 a week, you disease-carryin ho, or I'm going to drop a dime to the police."

"But if you knew all that, why have you been paying me every week?"

"Because I wanted to give your dumb ass a false sense of security. Just when you thought you'd gotten away with it, BAM!—here comes the monkey wrench, or the fly in the ointment!"

Precious couldn't believe what she was hearing and denied the accusations.

"I don't know where you're getting your information from, but you're wrong about that. I didn't kill anybody, and if you think I did, then you would have gone to the police right away."

"I thought about going to the police, but I figured I may as well profit from my information. Now you need to wrap your head around that fact and pay my money, or the Decatur police will soon be searching your house from top to bottom. And I know you got

plenty of money hidden away, not to mention the computer files you use to blackmail innocent guys like myself."

"Nigga, if you had any fucking proof, you'd show me, but you don't, so don't be calling here with that monkey shit," Precious yelled into the phone, forgetting to use her girlie voice. By then, her voice had deepened as she tried to figure out if this nigga was lying or not.

"Okay, okay" David said calmly. "Here's my proposal: I'm going to hang up now, and if you don't call me back in five minutes, agreeing to my terms, I'm going to call authorities and tell them I saw a ugly ass tranny pour lighter fluid on the dead body then speed away in a black BMW. Oh yeah, and my terms have changed: I want a $1,000 a week. And I want my first payment today! I figure you must be blackmailing about ten or eleven guys, so the money shouldn't be a problem. Goodbye, ho! The next time I see you will either be in person, with you handing me some money, or on TV, bein led away in handcuffs. The ball is in your court."

After the phone went dead, Precious couldn't believe what had just happened. The scared tranny thought she had gotten away with the murder, but now she realized that was a false premise. Somehow, someway—that faggot David happened to be in the park at the same time that she dumped the body. What were the chances of that happening? What were the chances that the one person that sees her is the nigga that she'd been blackmailing? God, what the fuck was she going do?

The fag threatened to ruin her, and if he told the police what he knew, then it was one-way ticket to the electric chair. Precious frantically weighed her pathetic options. If she didn't pay, it was prison for sure, if she did pay, David would lord it over her head for the rest of his or her life. As an experienced extortionist, Precious knew that once the payments started, the nigga would never let her off the hook. She could potentially give the angry fag hundreds of thousands of dollars over a lifetime, and still there would be no guarantee of him not going to the cops. The guy might just wake up mad one day and decide to drop a dime, just because he can.

She didn't exactly endear herself to him by talking shit when she went to collect at Wendy's. Suddenly, the tranny regretted needling David so much and complimenting him on his fat ass. Why couldn't she have kept it more businesslike instead of being so arrogant and haughty? It wasn't like dude was such an asshole. He was just rightfully angry about being secretly-filmed and blackmailed. But all

that was water under the proverbial bridge, and couldn't be taken back. Precious knew there was only one option, so she picked up the phone and dialed David's number. Now the murderer was going to find out what it was like to be blackmailed.

Chapter 10
Why David Was in the Park That Night?

The night Precious burned Deshawnte's body just happened to be a night that David and his wife, Tammy, were visiting their old friends in the subdivision adjacent to the park. They got together almost every week for dinner, to gossip and talk about old times. Derrick, the husband, had been David's roommate in college, and they'd remained best friends ever since. In fact, they had been each other's "best man" at their respective weddings. Not only did the guys get along, but their wives adored each other too.

Yet behind this seemingly-perfect façade lay a very deep secret; Derrick was in love with David, and vice versa. They loved each other so much that both named their sons after each other, instead of themselves. At first, the wives thought it was strange, but they agreed it was a sincere gesture of friendship. Both men were professionals, with Ph.D.s in Sociology, and both taught at local universities, so they kept their gay lifestyle a deep secret.

For the last three years, they'd been fucking once a week and assumed nobody else knew. But like a fool, David was attracted to transsexuals and wanted to try something different, which angered Derrick, who tried to talk his secret lover out of it. Hindsight being 20/20, David wished he had listened, because the second tranny he met was a big-dick bitch named Precious Meat. Every week since then, his wallet had been $300 lighter.

With their wives gossiping and on their second bottle of wine, the husbands excused themselves for a walk around the park, like always. At first, they looked like two regular heterosexual friends, taking a walk, but as soon as they got out of sight, they drew closer and held hands. After they reached the other side of the huge park, they nonchalantly strolled into one of the baseball dugouts and made love, like mad dogs in heat.

Derrick, who was 6' 5" and weighed almost 300 muscular pounds, bent David over and fucked him like he was his wife, nice, slow and hard. Then, after nutting in David's mouth or ass or both, they pulled their pants back up and walked back to the house, as if nothing happened. They relished their erotic secret and loved that they were doing it right under their wives' noses. It was their inside joke, and they enjoyed it to the hilt. David loved tonguing his wife

after Derrick nutted in his mouth. It turned both on immensely and heightened the sexual taboo of their lovemaking.

On that particular night after making love, they were shocked to see a transsexual drive up, take a dead body out of the trunk and set it on fire. For a minute, David couldn't believe his eyes! It was Precious, and she looked as beautiful as ever. After she sped off, they quickly pulled their trousers up and took a short-cut through the park just as the police showed up, with lights flashing. The gay lovers decided to say nothing about the incident to their wives.

David didn't even bother to mention to Derrick that he knew the tranny. Whatever happened had already happened, and nothing could change the dirty deed now. When they got back to Derrick's house, they cuddled with their wives and talked about what all couples talk about: their kids and the future. David couldn't keep his cum-soaked tongue out of his wife's mouth and let her unknowingly taste Derrick's baby making juice. Derrick dick got hard watching Tammy passionately kissing her husband. He wanted to ask what her husband's mouth tasted like!

After finishing a third bottle of wine, the couples said their goodbyes and made a date to meet at David and Tammy's house the next week. As David drove by the park, it was teeming with police and ambulances. He slowed the car down to gawk, but an officer told him to move along.

"I wonder what happened over there," Tammy remarked, sounding concerned. "You and Derrick didn't see anything on you all's walk around the park?"

"Nope. Hopefully nobody got hurt, but by the look of it, something big must have happened," he surmised.

With the kids asleep in the backseat, they drove in silence, consumed with the thoughts of a very pleasurable evening. David couldn't believe how good Derrick's rough manly lovemaking made him feel, and wished he could get that feeling from his wife. What the down low-fag didn't know was that, while he was getting fucked by Derrick, Tammy was getting fucked by his wife, Joanne. The women had been lovers for the last year and a half, and the men had no idea.

Tammy's pussy was still wet from all the cum induced by her friend's long, thick tongue and double vibrator. The wives were professionals like their husbands, and they knew how to keep their sex lives a secret. To the women, their lesbian affair just added a layer of excitement to their sometimes staid and boring lives. What their

husbands didn't know wouldn't bother them. It's wasn't like they were messing around with other men.

It was past 1 a.m. when they got home, and after putting the kids to bed, they made love, and as always, David was finished in less than ten minutes. Luckily, Tammy had Joanne and her double-vibrating dildo to pick up the slack! She couldn't wait until next week when the couple visited her home.

The top story on the news the next morning was about a dead body that had been burnt. Police found it in Redan Park. David listened as the investigators explained that they had no clues or motives to go on, and "if anyone knew anything, they were to contact the Decatur Police Department."

While sitting in his office at Clark Atlanta University, David considered his next move. If he went to the police, they would surely ask what was he doing in the park that night, and in the dugout no less. Then Derrick would be questioned, and he too, would have to lie to cover up their illicit secret. No, too many things could go wrong, and the police asked too many damn questions. The professor surmised that the only way he would come forward was if a reward was offered, and it would have to be substantial.

He had a career family and house to consider, and he didn't want to bring any embarrassment upon them. As for Precious, he decided to play her game a few more weeks, continuing to pay her, as if nothing had happened, before springing the news on the conniving bitch. The down-low fag wanted to have all his ducks in a row and as much information as possible before approaching the murdering tranny with this knowledge.

Precious was a career hustler, and he couldn't be underestimated, especially after seeing her burn a freaking body, like it was trash. If he didn't play his cards right, he could be next. David propped his big feet up on his cluttered desk and decided to be cautious when dealing with this trifling tranny. Knowing that soon the tables would be turned on his blackmailer brought a big smile to the fag's face. It was a turn on to be the only one in the city to have knowledge about who committed one of the most heinous crimes of the year in Georgia. Yep, that bitch was going to pay, and pay big time. No more would he be under her perverse control or have to listen to her snide, crude sexual remarks when paying the bitch his hard-earned money!

After a month, David decided it was time to spring his trap. Like all sensational tragedies, the news of the murder had died

considerably. In the current 24-hour news cycle, the public was inundated with mass school shootings and other high-profile crimes. To the professor, it seemed the fine fellows at Decatur Police Department had hit a dead-end in the case. He figured Precious was probably over-confident, thinking she'd gotten away with murder. If that was the case, it could work to his advantage, because the last thing the she-male expected was a phone call from one of her blackmail victims… who was an eyewitness to the crime cover-up.

But what was the crime exactly? He saw her burn the body, but he couldn't prove she actually committed the murder. Maybe the tranny had an accomplice or two, and by exposing himself to Precious, it also meant exposure to them, which could be dangerous. David considered many scenarios in his head before calling Precious. He tried to anticipate every possible angle in which things could go wrong.

What if the bitch threatened him and his family? She knew where he stayed, and God knows what else. Or what if she threatened to tell Tammy about his down-low lifestyle? All that was a distinct possibility, but there was no doubt who had the ace in the hole. If she revealed his lifestyle, the worst that could happen would be a divorce, if that. As for her blabbing to the university administrators that he was gay—so what? They couldn't fire him for it.

But if Precious' secret got out, her best-case scenario was a lifetime behind bars rotting away in a filthy prison, if she was lucky. Surely, the arrogant bitch wouldn't risk that, even to spite him, would she? Because of her dominant personality, overall arrogant attitude of superiority and disdain for fellow human beings, David figured the bitch would yell and scream in order to bluff him. However, after all was said and done, the tranny didn't have a choice, because all her leverage was gone unless of course she chose prison, which would be okay with him.

If she didn't agree to the terms, then no problem: a quick, anonymous call to the police would be her reward for being a stubborn, hard-headed bitch. Since it was Tuesday, or what she sarcastically referred to as "extortion day," he was supposed to meet the big-dick bitch at Wendy's to pay his hush money. Today though, would be different, and after calling and telling her what he saw in the park that night, Precious knew the gig was up.

Through the cell phone, David could hear her voice go from authoritative arrogance to outright humbleness and humility in a matter of minutes. She had been used to giving orders, but now the tables had turned. Just as he predicted, she tried yelling and backing him down, but when the slick tranny saw that wasn't working, she acted like they were best friends and the blackmailing was just a slight misunderstanding.

David couldn't believe the nerve the bitch had to try and say her extorting him had been in error. *Damn right, bitch! It was a big fucking error and you're going to pay for it!* When David told her his blackmail demands, he hung up and gave her five minutes to make a decision. After the whore called back, agreeing to his demands, David told her to meet him in Redan Park at 8 p.m. that evening and to have the $1000 waiting for him. When he hung up, a sense of power overcame him like never before. It felt good, turning the tables on Precious, and the tax-free money didn't hurt either. If he played his hand right, he could have her on the hook for years. This murdering bitch could end up paying for his kids' college education.

That night at dinner, David savored the pork chops, mashed potatoes, topped with gravy, and the buttery cornbread, like it was the Last Supper. When Tammy felt like cooking, no one was better. Looking at his wife and two kids, seated around the dinner table, the magnitude about what he was about to do hit him, like the proverbial ton of bricks. All he ever worked for could be lost if the meeting went wrong. What if the murdering tranny tried to get violent? There were so many variables and things that could go awry. No matter how much planning and preparation he did, there was always the distinct possibility that something unexpected would happen and mess everything up. Having a rational mind helped, because he thought of every minute detail and how best to handle it.

After finishing off a big slice of sweet potato pie, he lied and said he left something at the office. Tammy didn't believe him, but she'd been married long enough to know that sometimes a man just needed some space. David was a good and decent man, so it did not matter if he wanted to get away for a while to recharge his batteries? Before leaving, he retrieved the Glock 19 from the master bedroom closet and hid it under his shirt.

Looking in the mirror, the professor realized he wasn't exactly the poster boy of "black masculinity." At 5'7" and 250 chubby pounds, with man boobs and a fat ass that would make a black

woman jealous, he didn't exactly look like a bad motherfucker to be feared. He had dark skin, with a fat head and receding hairline, causing some to say he looked like Faizon Love.

He did, however, have a steady rational mind. Having watched many detective shows, he realized the reason why most perpetrators got caught involved panic, which had led to a mistake. David was too smart for that. He had, after all, a Ph.D. in sociology, while Precious was just a two-bit prostitute. Surely his mental capacity far outweighed her shallow, greedy little mind. After kissing Tammy goodbye, he backed out the driveway, not knowing if this would be his last time seeing it. The night was hot and muggy, with no wind blowing—a typical July night in the south.

From where David lived off Gresham Road in east Atlanta, it took about 25 minutes to get to the park. Taking his time, he arrived at 8:45 and saw the black BMW, waiting near the dugouts, backed into the parking space. He was purposely late to make the tranny wait and to heighten her fear and anxiety. The park was filled with Little Leaguers and their proud parents, cheering every pitch and hit ball, like it was the World Series. On instructions from David, the murderer parked in the rear where she burned the body over a month earlier. He made the tranny park there to remind her of the magnitude of what was at stake. If anything went wrong and he didn't get the money they negotiated over the phone, then she would go to jail for murder. Bringing Precious back to the scene of the crime made the bitch realize that she didn't get away with it, and that he, not her, was in charge of her destiny. Before pulling up beside her, the nervous professor put the Glock between his knees, just in case of trouble, and he left the engine running. As they both let their windows down David spoke first in a dry, efficient manner.

"You have what I asked for?" If she didn't, he was prepared to make a phone call to the police.

Without saying a word, Precious handed him an envelope with ten $100 bills inside. After counting it, David nodded ensuring that everything was okay.

"Now we're going to meet here, every Tuesday, like we did at Wendy's. Only, now you'll be paying me. Any questions?"

"David, boo—it ain't gotta be like this! Why don't you come over my place and we can talk about it," the frustrated she-male pleaded.

"There's nothing to talk about, except what I just said."

"Baby, you come over my crib and, I'll throw this fat juicy dick on you like I used too." Precious knew her long thick cock was these faggots' Achilles heel, but would it save her this time? "Nigga you know you want this cock! Why fight it?" she begged in the sweetest voice ever.

For a moment David could feel his resolve weakening, but the logical side of his brain overrode the emotional side. As good and juicy as her penis was, he thought that if he stepped inside her house, she would probably kill him. Besides, with all these fine black men in Atlanta, it wasn't like she had the only good meat to suck on.

The difficulty with trannies was that guys had to sneak and hide so they would not be seen with a tranny the public. To be seen with one meant everybody would know you were a homosexual. But if you were with a down-low guy like Derrick, then no one was the wiser. He would never go to the movies or the sports bars with a transsexual, but he'd done it numerous times with down-low buddies. Being with a tranny, especially a murdering one, wasn't healthy, physically or mentally.

"Nope, I don't trust you. You're a damn murderer. Why did you kill that boy?" Initially, he wasn't going to ask about any details because of legal concerns, but curiosity got the best of him.

Before answering, Precious drew a deep breath and wondered how best to address the question. Should she lie and say it was an accident? Or maybe she could say that someone else killed the boy, while her only crime was getting rid of the body? Or would she tell him the whole sordid truth—that she drugged a 14-year-old boy and fucked him to death?

Either way, he wasn't going to believe it was an accident—that's the lame excuse every murderer used when caught. If she didn't believe their lies, why would anyone believe her lies? This faggot saw her take a body from her car and burn it. He was the least likely person to be convinced that it was an accident.

"If you wanna know all that, you'll have to come to my place. I'm not discussing anything with you out here in public." Precious hoped the thirst for knowledge and lust for her would override the fag's fear.

"On second thought, I don't really need to know that badly," he assured her.

"Why you acting like this, David? Let's go to my place so I can fuck you and have you screaming my name, like you used to," she

pleaded, trying to sound as innocent as possible. "I'm not gonna do anything to you, baby. You don't have to be afraid of me. Damn! It's not like I'm some kind of monster."

"Oh, you're not? After seeing what I saw, I don't know about that. I suspect Deshawnte would have a different opinion too. Anyway, next Tuesday, eight o'clock. Be here with my money or be in jail." David backed out and disappeared into the night, leaving Precious lonely and afraid.

She waited for ten minutes before heading back home, frustrated that David didn't take her up on the invitation. Somehow, someway—she had to get him to come to her house. But once there, she wouldn't know what to do. Would she kill him, or would she try to convince him to leave her alone and stop the extortion? The thought of killing him sounded terrible, but what else could she do? At any time, he could ruin her life, and she wasn't going to take that chance. To live with extortion over one's head was almost like a death sentence, because sooner or later, he was going to tell, and she couldn't sit idly by and wait for that to happen.

Her only chance was to get David to trust her, but how, after having been blackmailing him for a year. No way would the fag step foot in her crib, because not only was he afraid of her, but the trust factor was gone. Precious figured the best way to lure a reluctant fish was to use her big black worm. She had to make David want her again, but how could she do that if they were never alone together?

The troubled tranny figured he would get tired of only getting a $1000 a week and would up the price after a few more payoffs—at least that's how she always played it. Get them comfortable and used to paying, and then after a while hit the faggots up for more money. At first they'd argue, but she'd remind them that losing a few extra dollars a week wasn't worth losing your wife, job or reputation over. Invariably, they always listened to reason and ponied up the extra dough.

Well, most listened to reason, except that goddamn faggot, John Evans. She still cursed herself for letting all that damn money slip through her crafty fingers. But this time, the shoe was on the other foot, since now, she was the one being blackmailed, and it didn't feel good. Someone else was pulling the strings, which meant he had control of her destiny. The only way to take back control was to neutralize the adversary, which was a polite way of saying she had to "kill the nigga." Not only did she have to kill him, but she had to do

it soon or she might be facing the electric chair, or lethal injection, or whatever hideous method they used in Georgia to kill prisoners who have forfeited their right to live.

Precious pulled into her garage, feeling depressed and defeated. After putting the herbie-curbie out by the mailbox, she took a long shower to wash the day's funk off her gorgeous, chocolate body. Fondling her testicles, she couldn't believe David could resist her forever. It wasn't like beautiful, big-dick trannies grew on trees in Atlanta. There were quite a few nice-looking girls, but few had her combination of femininity, size and sexual, take-charge aggressiveness. The button-downed fags she dealt with liked nothing better than to be rode hard and fucked, like a ghetto hoodrat. Her aggressiveness was what made them come back for more. When she fucked the unsuspecting fags, she owned their boy pussies, like they were hers and no one else's. They loved the manly way she fucked and how much she made them feel like dirty whores.

After being with so many trannies that couldn't get it up or lied about their dick-size, many men were pleasantly surprised when she took off her panties, and a baseball bat, replete with balls, fell out! And she knew good and damn well that David ain't had no bitch as fine as her fucking him. Yet that nigga was trying to ignore her, like she was some fuckin groupie, jockin his fat, ugly black ass!

While drying off, she heard the doorbell ring, For a minute, she was afraid to answer it. Was it the police or David? She ran naked to the living room window, peered through the blinds and was relieved to see no cop cars in the drive way. Looking through the peephole, she was relieved to see Monique standing on the other side. For a moment, a feeling of relief came over her, but that was quickly replaced by annoyance.

With so much on her plate, the last thing the tired tranny wanted to hear was Monique, talking about her problems with Rosa Lee. Precious pretended not to be at home and didn't answer the door. Satisfied that no one was at home—or at least no one who wanted to be bothered, the young girl finally left. Precious finished drying off, fixed a vodka cranberry and curled up on the couch in front of the big-screen to watch NBA TV. Within the hour, the tranny nodded off, with visions of tall, naked, sexy niggas running through her head.

Chapter 11
Monique, Marcus & Rosa Lee

Marcus's transition to Monique had been rough and heartbreaking for her mother. The more he changed, the more Rosa Lee tried in vain to be supportive, but it was hard as hell. She cringed when his girl friends came over and he acted more girlie than they did. When they went to his room, she could hear them giggling as they talked about boys and makeup. Rosa Lee was disgusted.

While most mothers worried about their son getting a girl pregnant, she worried about hers getting fucked by some diseased pervert. When they went anyplace together, she could feel the stares of the other parents burning a hole through her, as if to say she was the worst mother in the world. She stopped going to church, because she didn't want Monique to go with her or be subject to judgmental gawks from the sanctimonious Christians.

Watching her son get off the school bus wearing lipstick and a lace front wig was very embarrassing. Luckily, he didn't start transition until the last few months of school, but still the principal called her in for a long talk about Marcus. He asked Rosa if the boy needed psychological help and offered to set up an appointment with the school counselor. It all came to a head on graduation night.

When she got home from work that morning, she surprised the boy with some new clothes. Rosa Lee wanted the boy to wear the brand-new suit she bought so he could look like a handsome young man. The suit was blue, with gray stripes, and she imagined her fine son would look like President Obama when he put it on.

But Monique had other ideas. She wanted to go fully-dressed as a woman. Up to that time, Marcus had only been wearing wigs and makeup, but he still wore boy's clothes. So mom was surprised when he pulled a cute Ann Taylor dress from his closet, along with pumps and a fierce handbag to match.

"I know good and damn well you not going to your senior graduation dressed like a damn girl! Now I think I've been more than patient, and have supported you in your transition, but you have to meet me halfway too," Rosa Lee yelled while inspecting the dress and secretly admiring her son's good taste in style. Then she made herself a cup of coffee and stared at Monique from across the kitchen table, mad as hell.

"But Mama—I *am* a girl and you're supposed to support me. It's not like I've done anything wrong. I'm only doing what comes natural for me, nothing more. God made me like this, so if you're going to be mad, be mad at Him."

"But son," Rosa Lee pleaded, "think about me—don't you think I'm tired of all the stares and whispers from everybody? Remember—you're not the *only* one that has to deal with your changing from male to female."

"If I can't go the way I wanna go, then I'm not going. What's the point of being who I am if I'm not allowed to be who I am when I want to? You can't blame me because the world is ignorant. And I'm sorry if you're ashamed of me," Monique said, with tears welling in her eyes.

When she saw the tears, Rosa Lee's heart broke. She wanted to hug the troubled, confused boy and take away the pain. But how? How could she provide any comfort, when she was embarrassed and ashamed of him? She was tired of pretending everything was going to be okay, because dealing with the realities of the ordeal was taxing her last nerves.

The thought of her son getting his diploma in a wig and three-inch sling-back pumps reviled her. He would be the "star" of the graduation, and everybody would wonder who the freak's parents were, and then all eyes would be on her. The men in attendance would blame his father, Kenneth, thinking he wasn't hard enough on the boy and probably babied him. The mothers would blame Rosa Lee, thinking she was too mothering or did some weird shit to make her son turn into a freak.

Why would her son want to subject his mother to this mental torture? She wasn't the best mom in the world, but damn! She didn't deserve the bullshit. After 18 years of making sacrifices for him, surely he could wear a suit to graduation if she asked.

"C'mere, baby… Don't cry," the loving mother implored as they hugged for a minute, both sobbing, albeit for different reasons. Monique thought her mom's hug was a sign of acceptance, but Rosa Lee was really sobbing, knowing that if her son decided to wear a dress to graduation, then she was not going. She hoped the child will do the right thing, but if he didn't, she was prepared to miss one of the greatest joys of parenting, an important milestone in her son's life. She felt a twinge of guilt, but she was too embarrassed and worn-

out to face a throng of thousands, with their accusatory stares and whispers directed at mother and son/daughter.

"Marcus, baby—Monique, or whatever your name is," she said while caressing his face with her soft palm, "if you wear that dress, then I'm not going. Case closed. I love you. You know that, but I will not be ridiculed in front of my family and friends. I'm tired of answering all the questions and listening to the ignorant-ass comments from people about you. When you decided to dress as a woman, it not only affected you. It affected me too, because you're a reflection of me. If you want me to go, then you'll wear the suit. If not, then wear the damn dress. Now, you got eight hours to decide what to do. I'm going to go lie down. Let me know what your plans are."

Without saying another word, she went to her room and read the Bible until she fell asleep. The last sound she heard was Marcus, or Monique, leaving for school.

Monique couldn't believe the ultimatum that Rosa Lee had put forth. Would she really miss graduation because she was ashamed to be seen with her soon-to-be-daughter? Didn't she know how much the night meant? To Monique, it meant that her son was graduating from boyhood into womanhood. The night meant that he would be a "she" from that night until eternity.

If Mom didn't come, then she would miss out on everything. What was supposed to be one of the happiest days of a young person's life was starting off very bad for Monique. First a fight with Mom, and now, whatever "she" decided to wear would guarantee that one of them would be unhappy. As much as "she" loved her mother, she couldn't believe Mom wouldn't show up to see her only child graduate.

Unwilling to let her mom miss graduation, and knowing no one had loved a child more than Rosa Lee did, she decided to go as Marcus and wear the ugly-ass suit. Maybe being so wrapped up in doing "her" own thing, she had ignored the trials and tribulations her mom went through and the battles she fought on a daily basis on behalf of her child.

Monique realized why Mom stopped going to church—it was because of her child's choice to be a woman. Mom couldn't endure the whispering and phony smiles from self-righteous assholes. Marcus promised himself that graduation day would be his last dressing like a man. From that day on, he would dress like the sexy

bitch that he was. Graduation night would be a gift to his beautiful mother, but come tomorrow, watch out, world!—Monique Devereux would be born.

Despite what he was sacrificing for Mom, he was angry at her for making him choose between her and the dress. He wanted to pick up his diploma at Southwest DeKalb High School dressed as Monique, but to satisfy Mom, he compromised and wore the suit.

Southwest DeKalb High (SWD) was located in Decatur, on Kelly Chapel Road, between Wesley Chapel to the east and Candler Road to the west. It student body consisted of over 1,800 pupils in grades 9-12, and was 100% black. Since the white flight of the early 60s, the school had been virtually all-black. The school was nestled in a quiet, black middle-class community, where the lawns were perfectly-manicured, and there was not a single liquor store in sight. There were no thugs or prostitutes hanging out on corners, and kids played in their yards, oblivious to the troubles of the ghetto or the inner-city. There was no fear of drive-by shootings or home-invasion perpetrators kicking in doors, robbing people.

The household median incomes averaged well above $100,000, and home ownership is over 90%. Most of the households were headed by married couples—unlike many other black-dominated communities in America. As a further distinction, almost all of the residents in the community boasted at least a Master's Degree in their field of study

To think that a school in a community like this would be one of the top schools in the state or country would be wrong. Like most of black America, SWD suffered from "Ignorant Nigga Syndrome." Ignorant kids, bussed in from Gresham Road projects, and their uncouth counterparts from the Flat Shoals ghetto community, make up a 50% of the student body. These students came from the single-parent homes on welfare, and they caused most of the problems. These were the children of mothers who had numerous kids by different men and did drugs around their kids.

The boys from these relationships usually grew up to be thugs, in and out of jail—or, if lucky, good enough in football or basketball to get a scholarship to college. The girls grew up too fast and were sexually active by 13 years old, with two or three babies before they turned 18. Dropout rates at SWD are 35%, with black males leaving school at a rate of over 45%.

The figures were astonishing, considering the school was in a ghetto hood or in inner-city Atlanta. The school was located in a thriving, upwardly-mobile black community. Like most predominately black high schools, they have given up the impossible goal of being a great academic institution and instead concentrated on being the best in sports.

With notable alumni like former NFL quarterback Quincy Carter and Olympians like Angelo Taylor, it was safe to say that sports didn't take a backseat to academia. The reverse was true. Why spend money on chemistry equipment, when the football team needed new practice jerseys? Why buy new textbooks for Spanish class, when that money could finance a trip for the basketball team to play in some national tournament? The only rankings the school cared about were those for their successful sports teams.

Instead of buckling down and challenging the students, the administration gave up and dumbed-down the curriculum so that every student could feel good and pass. Yet even with this downward adjustment, nearly four out of ten students still dropped out. The high attrition rates actually helped the school, because most of the dropouts were troublemaking kids, with the welfare mentality, who came from the housing projects outside the neighborhood.

Teachers and administrators were content to let the thugs and thug-ettes go. *They weren't learning anything so, good riddance!* It seemed most only came to school to get a free meal twice a day, which was true, because often their mom's food stamps didn't stretch the whole month, especially mothers traded them some for weed, crack or liquor. Many of these students came to school angry and hungry, which was why hardly any fights happened until after lunch. *Why fight before you got something to eat? Wait until after lunch before busting somebody upside the head—that way, when the police came, at least you'll go to juvenile with a full stomach.* In addition to inherent problems, the Southern Association of Colleges and Schools placed SWD on probation and warned the school system that they were in danger of losing their accreditation.

So from the outside, the school seemed to be one of those high-achieving, white suburban schools in Gwinnet, Cobb County or North Fulton. However, a school's success was dependent on its students as opposed to the aesthetics of the neighborhood. Though many students at the school did well, they were in the minority. While the sports stars were lauded and cheered as big men on campus and

feted with banquets and cheers, the Dean's List students were barely mentioned and played second-fiddle to the instant gratification that sports brought.

The male athletes were the most popular, and they usually got preferential treatment from students, teachers, and even administrators. Any teacher who had the audacity to fail one of the prized athletes had to answer to principal Mary Lee Collis, who preached about the joys of academia publicly, but privately let the students who played sports get a pass, which kept them eligible to compete. She knew how much the community's pride was tied to sports, which also brought in the dollars.

Every boys' football and basketball game was sold out, and with the concession money from the food and retail sales, they turned a small profit. On top of that, the football coach, William "Billy" Wilkins, was a living legend. He became the school's first black head football coach at the age of 26 in 1971. And since then, the team won over 300 games and seven state titles.

Not only did the teachers fear him, but the principal did too. They didn't want to suffer the wrath of Coach Wilkins, because it could literally mean their jobs. In the previous year, when Rashard Jordan, the All-State running back, was caught stealing a laptop and beating another student, nothing was done about it. In both incidents, the matter was turned over to Coach Wilkins, on instructions from Principal Collis.

It was Mr. Lawrence, the Algebra teacher, who saw Rashard stealing the computer, and he inquired to find out if the school would bring charges. When he found out the thief wouldn't have to go before a disciplinary review board, like the other students, he fired off an angry email to the superintendent of DeKalb County schools. It was regrettable for Lawrence that he didn't know that the superintendent was a big fan of football, and even bigger fan of the legendary coach. When word got back to Principal Collis, she informed coach of the email, and in a later meeting they decided that, "with the shortage of good Algebra teachers around the county, Mr. Lawrence's expertise could best be utilized elsewhere." So the school administrators threw a good, dedicated teacher under the bus because he tried to discipline an unruly student. Coach Wilkins was the de facto leader at SWD, and whoever dared challenge him would have to play hardball.

Monique hated sports, and the only reason she went to the games was to see the band and watch the cheerleaders. She wanted to be a cheerleader, but she didn't want the publicity and drama that would accompany a transsexual trying out for the cheerleading squad. Being openly gay and an academic nerd insulated her from a lot of the hullabaloo and drama at the school, and she shied away from bringing attention to herself.

There were other gays and lesbians who went to SWD, but they were very few in number. At least the lesbian girls weren't scoffed at and berated as much as their gay male counterparts. That was partly because the girls' basketball team was made up of predominantly lesbian studs, and another reason involved society refusing to value females as much as men. In other words, if a woman is a lesbian, who really cares? It was okay for a girl to be a tomboy, but it was not okay for a boy to act too feminine or like a sissy.

Monique mostly kept to herself and concentrated on getting good grades so that she could get an academic scholarship. She and the other gay/lesbian students usually ate lunch together and even had their own special table. It was "special," because no other students, especially male, dared sit with them for fear of being labeled a fag. After four years of the bullshit, she was thankful to be graduating and off to college, where she would encounter enlightened adults rather than being subjected to sophomoric homophobes and their crude jokes.

Monique had been called "sissy" and "faggot" so many times that she stopped reporting it, because the teachers didn't do anything. Further, they made her feel like the harassment was her fault or that she was imagining it. After a while, she just withdrew and kept quiet about the aggravation, not wanting to cause any unnecessary drama. Thank God it would all end soon!

Rosa Lee was proud to see her handsome son walk across the stage to receive his diploma. She marveled at how handsome Marcus was, only wishing he had a manlier gait. She was pleased, nonetheless, since his preference had been to wear a dress. Not only was he on the Dean's List, but he got a partial scholarship to Georgia State University.

The partial scholarship took a financial load off her mind, since it provided half of his tuition. Rosa Lee she could easily afford the rest without having to touch her 401k. In four years, Marcus wouldn't graduate with a load of student debt weighing him down.

Three hundred seniors graduated that night, but Rosa Lee wanted everybody in the auditorium to know how proud she was of her son, who was the only male receiving an academic scholarship.

Three other males received sports scholarships, for football and basketball, which meant they got standing ovations. Rosa Lee and a few of the other parents were pissed off that the athletes were favored, but they knew sports had a powerful sway over the black community. After the ceremonies, she chatted with the other proud parents, all bragging about their children and how bright their futures would be. When they got home that night, Marcus was surprised to discover a brand-new, shiny-black Toyota Corolla in the driveway, causing him to scream in girlie excitement.

Rosa Lee knew she made the right decision in buying the car, but she knew it meant Marcus would be leaving the nest soon, even if Georgia State was only a few minutes away in Atlanta. She also knew that he would become a fulltime "she," and there was nothing she could do about it but pray. A couple of weeks after graduation, Marcus was indeed gone forever, replaced by a very proud Monique.

With money from savings the considerate teen donated all her male clothing to a homeless shelter and bought an entirely new female wardrobe. Her mom's worse fear was realized: she had birthed a son, but now she had a daughter. Instead of wearing only a wig and a little bit of lipstick, Monique began to ask Rosa Lee for makeup tips. Rosa cringed, watching her son defile his body with perfume, rouge and lip gloss, only to walk out the house in a blouse and skirt, like all that shit was normal. To make matters worse, her new "daughter" insisted on going to the hair dresser with her mom.

As much as Rosa Lee loved Monique, she couldn't wait for school to start, because then she wouldn't have to look at her faggot son every day and blame herself for his perverted lifestyle. Like most people in such a situation, she tried to keep an open mind, but that was easier said than done. It was easy to be open-minded and liberal when it was someone else's child, but when it was your own, then things weren't so simple.

As Rosa Lee looked at Marcus' baby pictures, she cried and cursed God for making her son a tranny faggot. Then she would tell the Almighty that *if he had to be gay, the least You could have done was make him a regular homosexual, instead of a goddamn transsexual!* Regular gays were more tolerable, unless they were the flamboyant kind, but even those were better than being fucking trannies.

As the long, hot summer wore on, the worried mom almost forgot she had a son as the Monique persona took over her child's body. Sometimes she wished Marcus had been a thug and gotten in trouble with the law—nothing too serious, but at least he'd look and act like a man, instead of acting like a goddamn woman, shaking his ass when he walked. As his mother, she felt ashamed to think of him in that way, but she couldn't help herself. Every mom wanted a strong, masculine son rather than the opposite, which was what her son had become. Rosa Lee came to the understanding that she had witnessed two graduations that night: one from high school student to college student, and the other from man to woman.

Monique was so excited about the car that she cried tears of joy. She knew Mama was going to buy her one before she went off to college, but was expecting a used vehicle, not a brand-new car. With three free months ahead and a new car, the teen planned on making this the best summer ever. She and the few friends she had rode around, getting high and having more fun than the law allowed. As a full-time woman, the young transsexual never felt better or more comfortable in her own skin. The world was hers for the taking and she planned on grabbing as much as possible. With high school over, she could really spread her wings and explore opportunities, and one of those involved finding a fine ass-boyfriend. Being a tranny wasn't the best way to get one, because most guys didn't mess with transsexuals in public.

Free from the pressures of school and having no curfew, the bored teen began going out to gay clubs, even though she was underage. Her height made her seem older, because she never had a problem at the door. Or maybe it was the nice car or professional makeup that did the trick, but she never once got carded. Her favorite joint was Traxxx, a new club on Buford Highway that catered to black gays and transsexuals.

She went the first time with her friends: Princess, a wild tranny two years her senior, and a buttoned down fem-boy named Jason, who graduated the year before from SWD. He was a sophomore at Clayton State University, majoring Business. Monique looked to Jason as a role model, even if he was only 5'4" and looked like Kevin Hart—only with a bigger booty.

She had an okay time at the club, but many of the guys were either too old or fat and out of shape. Monique wasn't the pickiest bitch in the world, but she did have standards. Her only sexual

experience was with Precious, but she wanted a young, sexy, bald-headed man—not another woman—to fuck her. She certainly did not want the old, down-low, snaggle toothed, bad-breath fools who were in the club that night!

She wasn't rude. She let the old tranny-chasers buy her a few drinks, and in return, she gave a few of them her number, knowing it would never lead anywhere. Monique learned that by being nice, one could save money on drinks. There were a few sexy, masculine guys in the club, but none approached her.

However, after a few drinks, she did work up the nerve to approach a caramel-colored guy named Eric, who seemed to be in his early 20s. His sexy smile revealed teeth white as snow, along with a smooth, bald head. At 5' 9", he wasn't as tall as she liked, but his thick chest and muscular arms more than made up for the lack of height. He was wearing a gray Nike tank-top, khaki cargo shorts and Nike sandals to show off his gorgeous feet and suckable toes. The hunk looked like a muscular Chris Brown, without the tattoos, and she wanted to be his Rihanna.

Nervous, Monique asked the cutie his name, and from there they seem to hit it off. They sat and chatted for twenty minutes despite the loud music, and they exchanged numbers before he got up to leave. The attractive hunk had a previous engagement and told her to call the next day so they could get together. As he rose to leave, he kissed the smitten tranny on the cheek and bade her goodbye. Disappointed, but head over heels in lust, she watched as he swaggered confidently to the door and disappeared into the parking lot, driving off in a gray Dodge Charger.

More than being smitten; the young bitch fell instantly in love with the handsome stranger. Over the protests of her two companions, she was ready to leave the club, and since they came with her, they had no choice. Princess, however, decided to stay, knowing that as long as she had a talented tongue, a big dick and a fat ass—getting a ride home would be no problem.

After dropping off Jason at the crib, she got home at three in the morning, drunk and horny. As soon as she got inside, she flicked off her heels and headed to the refrigerator for something to eat. Surveying the contents of the fridge the inebriated tranny decided on leftover pizza from Papa Johns. Instead of microwaving, she ate three pepperoni slices cold and washed the meal down with a ginger ale.

Before going to bed she took a nice, slow shit that felt like utopia. After wiping her ass, Monique took her clothes off and left them on the bathroom floor for Rosa Lee to pick up. With her dick on hard, she laid awake in bed, staring up at the ceiling fan, thinking about Eric making slow sweet passionate love to her. Stroking her cock furiously, the horny youngster shot a load of cum up in the air and fell asleep with visions of Eric in her confused little head.

She slept like a baby that night, unaware that in her drunken state, she left both the garage and kitchen doors open, enabling anyone to stroll into the house, right up to her bedroom! But luckily God watched out for fools, and sometimes even drunk ones.

The gorgeous hunk she met that night was named Eric Owens, a 25-year-old who was employed as a store manager at Burger King. He was born in Augusta, and had moved with his mom, Iris, to Decatur when he was 14. His mother was fleeing a sexually-abusive husband who also abused Eric. After being married to Roger for only six months, Iris came home early from an appointment one night and found her husband with his dick in Eric's mouth. The 11-year-old boy was sitting on his bed, with tears rolling down his face, while Roger stood over him, moaning in ecstasy as his long cock slid in and out like a well-oiled machine.

When the shocked mother saw what he was doing, she screamed for him to stop, but she didn't want to anger him too much, because his backhand left bruises. Instead of stopping, Roger smiled and enjoyed the look of horror, disgust and shame on her face. After watching for a moment in tortuous silence, she ran to the bathroom and vomited, struggling to erase the sight of her innocent son, crying and pleading for Mommy to help him.

Then she could hear Roger smacking the boy telling him to shut up and suck his dick right, or else he was going to get a real ass-whipping. Slowly, Eric's 'cries of protestation were drowned out by Roger's pleasurable moans. And after a few minutes, Iris heard her husband moan and grunt in the universal language that every human makes before cumming. When he finished, she went in to comfort Eric and with a warm, wet towel, wiping the cum from his lips, and then she took the traumatized boy to the bathroom to brush his teeth and gargle. She knew Roger was fucking around on her and didn't want Eric catching anything. That was Eric's stepfather's first time abusing him, but it wouldn't be the last.

goodbye and told Eric to behave in school and even gave him a couple of dollars before going to work. Left alone with her son, neither mentioned the horror of the night before.

When Eric left for school, she immediately went to his bedroom and couldn't believe how much blood and shit was on the sheets. She cried out, like a wounded animal, cursing her husband and his fondness for little boys. Instead of washing the soiled linen, she put it in trash bags and took it out to the herbie-curbie so the garbage men could take it away.

For the next three years, her husband made love to her less and less and to Eric more and more. At first, she didn't care, but after a while, jealousy got the best of her. Almost every night, like clockwork, he eased out of bed and got under the covers with his stepson. Then Iris would hear the familiar sounds of the bed squeaking as Roger made love to the child, while she lay unloved and untouched.

Slowly her hatred of Roger turned into jealousy of Eric. How could she blame the boy, when he couldn't stop Roger from raping him? She noticed that, after a while, her son had resigned himself to getting raped, and later seemed to welcome it by wearing biker shorts and dancing in front of Roger, like a girl. On some weekends, the husband and son would go camping in the mountains and leave her behind, like a fifth wheel. Being so lonely, she did what any woman would do: she got a lover.

He was a garbage man on her route, and some mornings she waited to hear his truck before taking the trash out, just so they could meet. If her husband didn't appreciate her fine fat self, then someone else would. At 5' 3" and 200 pounds, she still had some curves left, even if they were flabby. She was starved for the love and attention of a man—a real man, not some bisexual faggot, like Roger. She had no one to talk to about the shit she was going through. Neither family nor the preacher would understand and would probably blame her for letting it happen.

Iris threw herself into the arms of Alfonzo, a dark-skinned, chubby sanitation worker who was just as foolish as she was desperate. He wasn't as handsome as Roger, but at least the nigga liked pussy. After a month, the relationship ended, because Iris was quickly bored and wanted more than what a broke-ass garbage man could give.

At 1 a.m., Roger quietly got out of bed and went to his stepson's room, where he found the boy eagerly awaiting him. Already on hard, he pounced on the boy and tongue kissed him. Then, rolling Eric onto his stomach, Roger pulled the teen's panties down to reveal the soft, fat ass that was the object of his desire. He first ran his tongue between his stepson's ass cheeks for a few minutes before Eric begged for the big black dick. Roger acquiesced and slammed his penis in as Eric yelped, like a little girl, in the throes of ecstasy. They were in their favorite position, which was doggy-style. Roger was in heaven, watching his son's plump ass ride his swollen cock better than any woman could, certainly better than Iris. Noting how cute the boy looked in the negligee and how sweet he smelled, Roger wondered why the hell he even bothered sleeping with his ugly, gas-filled wife.

The bed rocked to their lovemaking as they lost themselves in each other's desires. Roger stopped and rolled Eric over on his back before cocking the boys' flexible legs all the way back behind his head. He couldn't believe how beautiful the boy looked, with his legs spread and asshole puckered, waiting for Daddy's love-stick. Roger got on top of Eric and plunged his chocolate cock in until he felt his swollen testicles slapping against the youngster's tender cheeks.

For over an hour, he made love to his son, nutting in him twice as his cock explored the inner sanctum of Eric's sweet ass. After the third nut, he collapsed on top of Eric, both exhausted and satisfied. When Roger took his cock out, cum gushed from the boy's ass, staining the already sweaty sheets. There they lay, tenderly stroking each other and whispering sweet nothings until falling asleep, oblivious to the world around them.

From the doorway, Iris had watched as her son and husband were making love,. Since the hallway was dark, they couldn't see her peeking in, enjoying the show. She was turned on watching her two men make love to each other. She imagined it was her rather than Eric getting pummeled by Rogers' prodigious tool. Her pussy was moist and nipples hard from witnessing the illicit taboo lovemaking.

Yet she knew what needed to be done, which was to stop her husband from infecting the world with AIDS. The reason why she chose that moment to do it—in her son's bed, Roger was at his most vulnerable. She crept into the bedroom, gun cocked, when she heard Roger snoring, and she aimed the gun. When Eric saw she had a gun, he screamed, waking Daddy, who was startled awake.

Roger tried to reason with his wife and begged her not to shoot, but his anger got the best of him. He called her vile, degrading names and threatened to hurt her. Emboldened Roger rose and surged at her, tried taking the pistol, but that's when Iris got off two shots, hitting him in the stomach and chest. He collapsed onto the bed, gasping for air, while Eric ran out the room, screaming at the top of his lungs. Iris watched as life slowly seeped from her husband, enjoying every second of his last painful moments on Earth. The last thing the pedophile saw was Iris' smiling face, looking down at him. She called the authorities only after he stopped breathing.

Eric backed up the story she told the police: that she killed her husband who was raping her son. The investigation was over after a few days, ruled as a justifiable homicide. Eric was diagnosed with HIV, and, after selling the house, they moved to Atlanta to start a new life.

Moving didn't help the mother/son relationship, since Eric blamed his mom for him contracting AIDS, for not protecting him from Roger. He frequently ran away from home and was often kicked out of school. Finally, after years of intense family counseling, he forgave Mom and even graduated from high school in the top ten percent of his class, but that wasn't anything to brag about, since it was Washington High—a school that was not rated high for academics.

After graduating, the teen knew college wasn't for him, so he took a job at one of the many Burger Kings that dotted the city's landscape, like modern day cattle feeds. He started off as a cashier and, working hard, quickly moved up through the ranks. After two years, he became shift supervisor. When he turned 21, the owner of the franchise made him store manager—one of the youngest employees in south to earn that title.

Yet even after getting his life on track, Eric still had to deal with HIV and his confused sexuality. Even though he liked girls, he still fantasized about Roger and big cocks. So like most guys, he screwed plenty of girls, but he had several secret male lovers on the side. He rarely used condoms, so he spread the disease to sexual partners without remorse. His rape at such a tender, early age left him unsympathetic for others. He even enjoyed infecting people, which was an outlet for his anger, toward Iris, toward Roger and unfairness in life.

Over time, the biological girls gave way to transsexuals, because in his mind girls were too insecure and needy—unlike trannies and male lovers. The women in his life wanted much more than he was capable of giving, while the guys just wanted to fuck and bust a nut. Yet the transsexuals were the best of both worlds: they looked like women, but they were men, biologically. That's why he frequented clubs like Traxxx—many trannies hung out there, running the gamut from butt-ugly to Beyonce-like gorgeousness.

The chick, Monique, who he just met, wasn't the prettiest, but she was young and eager. As a tranny-chaser, it was rare to find a teen tranny, and rarer to fuck one. Most transsexuals made their transition in their 20s—after leaving home, where there was pressure from parents, and because they lacked money. Eric couldn't wait to fuck this bitch and bust an HIV nut in her young, silly ass.

It was too bad the unsuspecting Monique didn't know anything about the handsome stranger other than *he was fine as hell!* After waking from a terrible hangover and silently promising never to drink again, she couldn't wait to call Eric. But first she had to take a shit to relieve her stomach of the nausea from consuming too many Sex on the Beach cocktails.

The bartender at Traxxx sure made strong drinks, evidenced by Monique sitting on the toilet for 30 minutes and regretting every sip of alcohol she consumed. Her farts were so funky that she could barely stand the smell, and she vomited on herself while still on the toilet. Vomiting seemed to relieve her nausea, so she slinked back to bed and fell asleep until Rosa Lee came in, fussing that Monique had left the garage and kitchen doors open all night.

"Wake up! Wake up, Monique—you need to stop bein so irresponsible," Rosa Lee shouted at the sleeping teen. "Girl, don't you know you left my house wide open? Any damn body could have come in and did *Lord knows what* to you or me! You need to cut out all this partyin and drinkin."

Monique just turned over and tried to ignore her mother, but Rosa Lee turned the lights on and opened the curtains, making the teen recoil like a vampire does when exposed to sunlight. When Monique tried pulling the covers over her face, Rosa Lee snatched them off and threw them on the floor.

"Mama! Mama—can you please leave me alone? I'm not feeling too good right now!" the girl pleaded.

"You're not feeling well because you been out all night gettin drunk and smokin weed. Don't you know you left the garage and kitchen doors open? Any fuckin body could have come in here and killed you or me," she repeated at the top of her lungs.

"I did? I'm sorry," Monique said meekly, still half-asleep. Trying to get back to sleep though was impossible, because Mom was madder than a broke crack-head.

"You left both the garage and kitchen doors open," she repeated a third time. "Did you hear me, Monique? I said this house was wide-open, and you was up here, dead to the world!"

"I heard you the first and second time, Mama, but what good is yellin about it gonna do? I said I was sorry! Now can I get back to sleep now," the teen protested while reaching down and picking up the covers and pulling them over her head.

"Girl, you are some piece of work! If you're gonna be a woman, at least be a lady, and not some drunk ho, and I hope if you havin sex that the guy is wearing a condom. Don't trust anybody who says *there's no need* to use protection. That person could be giving you AIDS on purpose. You'd be surprised at how many people set out to spread that disease out of spite or ignorance."

"Okay, Mama. Okay, I will, you tell me that stuff all the time," she insisted.

"Well, I hope you're telling me the truth, because I see so many young black men at Grady who become HIV infected."

Rosa Lee always tried to scare her child into having safe sex. Being a nurse helped because Monique knew her mom wasn't bullshitting her.

"I know, Ma. You tell me that almost every day now. Can you get out so I can get some sleep?"

"As long as you're listening, because you're my baby. I just want to protect you from the monsters in this world. Okay, we'll talk later. I'll let you get some sleep, because you're obviously still drunk from whatever you were drinking last night." She leaned over and kissed her beautiful child on the forehead, closed the curtain, turned the lights off and left the room.

Rosa Lee had been horrified when she got home that morning, and she had thought the worse and ran up to Monique's room to make sure she was okay. Only after making sure her child was safe did she get mad as hell at the girl's irresponsibility. She was grateful that school would start in a couple of weeks and hoped partying

would stop when the time came to buckle down and concentrate on academics.

Rosa Lee didn't approve of most of Monique's new friends— especially Princess, an ugly, foulmouthed tranny who was illiterate and uncouth. Rosa Lee knew the bitch didn't practice safe sex, while probably encouraging her child to do the same. She hated that Monique hung with low-life, trashy fags who had no family values or morals. Many, who were abused and ostracized growing up, took their anger and resentment out on society.

They saw an innocent, like Monique, and would try to turn the girl into a whore, like they were, out of spite and jealousy. Like all mothers, Rosa Lee wanted the girl to enjoy life, but she discouraged trusting other people. Unfortunately, her daughter would have to learn through pain and experience? Unlike 99% of other mothers, Rosa Lee was raising a transsexual rather than a "regular" child.

Yet she wanted to protect the child from as much hurt as possible. After making sure the doors were locked and nothing was missing, Rosa Lee went to bed and had a fitful sleep, tossing and turning, after having a nightmare that an intruder was hiding in the house and chasing her with a hammer.

Monique didn't wake again until late afternoon, feeling relieved her terrible hangover was gone. After pulling herself together, she checked her phone for any messages and saw Eric had been calling all day. She called him back at once.

"Hello," the deep voice answered.

"Hi, this is Monique, the girl you met at the club last night," she said, trying not to seem too anxious.

"I know who this is. Whassup, tall n sexy?" Eric kidded her in his most masculine.

"Nothing I was just returning your calls. What are you doing today?"

"You wanna get together today? I'm free and don't have to work? I was thinking you could come over to my crib, since I stay by myself. We could kick it."

"That sounds okay. Where do you stay?"

"Over off Memorial Drive in the Kensington Apartments. You know where that is? I can come pick you up if you like. Do you have a car?"

"I have a car. What time do you want me to come over?" Monique was beyond excited and tried not to reveal to Eric how much she wanted him to take her virginity.

"It's 4:30 now. How about you be here round about six o'clock," Eric said, cool and collected.

"Okay, then. I can do that. I'll call you back to get your apartment number before I leave."

"Baby, I hope you ready to get fucked, because I've been thinking about your fine ass all night!" he lied. "I got eight inches of fat dick, just itching to make your acquaintance!"

When he told her of his intentions, she blushed. She wanted a man to take control and sweep her off her size ten feet before making passionate love to her until they collapsed into each other's arms, sweaty and exhausted. Then she remembered what Mama said about safe sex and HIV.

"You do practice safe sex, right? I mean, you wear condoms all the time?" she inquired nervously. If he said no, would she be able to resist the temptation?

"Well I don't have AIDS, and I do wear a condom most of the time. I get tested every six months," he asserted.

The nigga lied so good, he even believed his bullshit! He's been living with HIV for the last ten years, so it was just a normal part of his life. Sometimes the fear people had about the disease amused. He had lived a normal, productive life in spite of being infected, and so could others.

"This is my first time, so I want you to use a condom, okay?" Monique insisted in a voice that let him know she was serious.

"Sure, baby—anythang for a sexy tenderoni like you," he assured her in a deep baritone voice that would put Billy Dee Williams to shame.

He always told his future lovers the same thing, but when push came to shove, he usually could convince them to let him fuck condom-free. It also helped that he was 200 pounds of muscle and was very aggressive. Aggressiveness was a handy tactic he learned from Roger, and to many, he was so gorgeous that he didn't look like a person with a disease.

"Let me get dressed, and I'll see you in a little bit, boo," Monique told him, trying to sound sexy.

Eric couldn't wait for the bitch to come over. He lifted weights and worked out, like he always did before a good fuck. Dude liked to

greet the guest at the door with nothing on but a speedo to show off his deep chest and sinewy arms and legs. The look on the face of the unsuspecting visitor when encountering his magnificent body drove him wild with excitement.

Monique took a shower, washing the sluggishness from the night before down the drain. Then she bathed herself from head to toe in Burberry lotion and Vera Wang's *Lovestruck* perfume. Because it was her first time with a real man, she wanted to smell like the Garden of Eden. Looking through her messy closet, she picked out a dark blue spaghetti-strapped dress that went down to her knees and highlighted her long-bowed legs. Surveying more than 20 pairs of shoes thrown about the room, she settled on a pair of Rosie Flat sandals, made by American Rag, to complete her girl-next-door look.

After applying Lancôme Rouge to her lips, she fixed her hair in a ponytail while silently thanking Mom for never cutting it. She didn't have to wear a wig or get an expensive-ass weave sown in to look natural, like a lot of trannies did. Looking in the mirror, she liked who stared back at her. She was beautiful. Before leaving, she called Eric and got his apartment number and to confirm the date. Since Mom was downstairs in the kitchen, Monique knew she had to run a gauntlet of questions and suspicious looks.

"What are you cookin?" Monique asked, nonchalantly.

"Just some baked chicken and mashed some potatoes," Rosa Lee answered, eying the girl up and down. "Where are you goin, smelling all good and sweet?"

"Just over to Princess' house," she lied, kissing mom on the cheek.

"Well, whatever you do, be careful, honey—and remember what I said this morning about AIDS."

Rosa Lee didn't believe her daughter was going to Princess's house. She wished she could make her stay home, but that would have been impossible.

"Okay, Mama, but I'm just going over to Princess', that's all," she retorted, trying to sound convincing. "I love you."

"I love you too, hon. Now be careful," mom said, watching her leave.

As soon as Monique left, Rosa Lee wept, thinking about what might have been if her son was a normal child. She wanted him to marry a nice girl and have grandkids for her to spoil. Instead, he dressed like a damn girl and wore makeup! Why had God chosen to

punish her? What evil had she done to be cursed with raising a transsexual? What had Marcus done to deserve a life of ridicule and shame? Depressed, the woman reached to the upper cabinet and pulled out a bottle of Dewar's Scotch, pouring herself a shot, and sat at the kitchen table, reading the Bible until dinner was ready.

****

Monique was nervous as could be as she stood before Eric's door, ready to knock. She waited a few seconds and rang the doorbell, only to be greeted by a handsome stud who was wearing nothing but an orange speedo, revealing a large bulge between his legs. He had a big smile on his face and evil in his heart.

"I see you made it! Come on in," Eric said looking oh so sexy.

After Monique walked in, he gave her a kiss on the lips, sticking his tongue deep into her mouth, startling the girl.

"You get right to the point, don't you, baby?"

"As fine as you lookin, I couldn't help it," he said while standing back to get a full view of the sexy tranny he was about to fuck. "Yes, indeed, you fine as fuck, with a nice bubble ass, begging for some dick. C'mon, have a seat so we can get to know each other."

As Monique sat on the sofa, she couldn't take her eyes of her gorgeous host. With his broad shoulders and six-pack abs, he looked like a model in a magazine.

"So you smoke?" he asked while pulling out a shoe box, filled with weed.

"Yeah, I love blunts!" Monique volunteered.

She watched him expertly roll a fat spliff, put it between his sexy lips and light it. After a few puffs, he handed it to Monique. When both were sufficiently high, Eric suggested they would be more comfortable in the bedroom.

As soon as they got in the bedroom Eric jumped on the bed and watched Monique nervously take her clothes off. As she did, he took off the speedo, revealing an eight-by-five-inch thick cock that curved to the left like a banana! She couldn't believe how beautiful it was, and she responded by removing her silk panties to show him her hard, slim seven inches.

He pulled her head down on his engorged dick and groaned in delight as her magical tongue did its job. After a few minutes, Eric changed positions and sucked her dick until she came in his mouth.

It was only the second time anyone had given her head, and his expert tongue drove her to passions she never thought possible. Watching this sexy bald head going up and down on her dick like a piston drove her wild. Even sexier and kinkier, he swallowed every drop of her love juice.

Next, he turned her onto her stomach and started licking her asshole until it was ready to be entered. Monique was glad she took extra care to wash and douche her anus like Precious had told her. *Ain't nothing worse than a smelly ass during lovemaking,* her mentor had warned. Eric put his cock between her cheeks before entering, savoring the view of a beautiful virgin-ass he was about to defile. Reaching for the KY-jelly, he squirted a hug gob in and around her anus, and without warning, he plunged his cock in—to the dismay of Monique. She screamed and let out an animal-like noise as the big pole slammed into her ass.

She protested and told him to put on a condom, but he ignored her and kept stroking until he was all the way in and his balls were slapping her butt cheeks. By that time, the tranny was in too much pain and pleasure to protest, so she just lay there with her ass arched, inviting her lover to do what he did best, which was fucking. At that point, resistance was futile, because Eric was much stronger and outweighed her by 50 pounds.

He nutted in the sweet young booty after ten passionate minutes, and then he rested on top of her with his dick still in until he was ready to go again. The second fuck was more like a couple making love, as he stroked her nice and slow while nibbling on her ear. Monique never knew she could feel so good and was glad he was the first real man to bust her cherry. She knew what it felt to be a real woman, and to be made love to by a real man, who knew how to hit the right spots.

Eric made love to the unsuspecting Monique for three hours, cumming in her four times, or until his nut-sack was dry as a bone. Dude didn't care if he gave the bitch HIV or not, he only thought of his own selfish pleasure. After getting dressed, Monique sauntered to the door, escorted by naked Eric, with his semi-hard dick caked with dry cum. They kissed and promised to see each other again, but Eric knew it would be his last time seeing her. He was strictly stick and move—not one to have relationships or fall in love.

Walking to the car was a little difficult, because Monique's ass ached from getting pounded for hours. Yet it was a "good" ache,

because she had been taken to heights of desire she never knew existed. After the euphoria of the intense lovemaking subsided, Monique suddenly remembered what mom told her about safe sex and began worrying about AIDS. *There was no way that good-looking guy had AIDS*, she thought. *People with HIV look old and sickly, not young and buffed, like a sexy weightlifter. Mom was just like all mothers; they worry too much.* She figured the chance of catching the disease during the first sexual encounter sans condom was slim to none.

She couldn't wait to tell Precious about Eric and the incredible lovemaking skills he possessed. The young tranny already could see herself falling for the handsome hunk and wondered if the feeling was reciprocated. It seemed reciprocal to her, judging by the way he passionately and savagely fucked her for hours on end. When she got home, Rosa Lee was asleep on the sofa with the TV still on, which was good, because the teen didn't want to face her mom's third-degree grilling about where she'd been and with who. Before going to bed Monique called Eric to let him know she made it home okay, but for the phone operator said the number was disconnected. The tired young tranny thought she had dialed the wrong number and decided to call again in the morning.

She could hardly sleep, thinking about how life would be with a cute guy like Eric on her arm. She was not the other trannies, who had plenty of down-low lovers, and yet not one lover would take them out to dinner or be seen with them in public. She knew that wasn't the life for her. Any man who was ashamed to be seen with her wasn't going to get the time of day, let alone some ass!

She fell asleep, feeling like a real woman as her lovers HIV-infected semen dried in her now-loose anus. His seed felt good inside her and she knew she would be going back for more. With visions of Eric's nude, sweaty body running through her head, she enjoyed a peaceful sleep, dreaming of herself in a long, white wedding dress, being walked down the aisle by Rosa Lee. There, waiting at the altar, is a butt-naked, with his big cock hard as concrete pointing directly at her. It seemed everyone, but her, was oblivious to his nudity.

While the minister directs the vows, Eric makes her kneel in front of him and puts his cock in her mouth, while Rosa Lee smiles and nods in approval. The minister then unzips his pants and puts his enormous cock in Rosa Lee's mouth, causing everyone at the church to say "Amen" in unison! The only sounds to be heard are of Monique and mom slurping dicks as the preacher mumbled the

wedding vows between moans of ecstasy, with Rosa Lee sucking his fat dick like a professional.

Unable to take it anymore, the reverend lets out a whooping, "Lawd Jesus!" and nuts all over a grateful Rosa Lee's face. The congregation applauds as she licks the cum off her face with a tongue that must be over a foot long. Then she crawls over to Eric, like a dog in heat, and pants, with her tongue hanging out, dripping with thick salty cum. Rosa Lee knocks the bride out of the way and begins slurping on her future son-in-law's cock like a good mother-in-law should.

Eric is startled at first, but he is soon under the spell of Rosa Lee's giant tongue and cums all over her face, just like the good reverend did. Seeing her groom enjoy himself with her mother makes Monique angry, and she attacks Rosa Lee. They fight viciously, rolling on the floor and tearing each other's clothes. When the church sees that Monique is really a man, they start booing her and beating the young confused tranny with bibles and calling her a spawn of Satan.

While getting beat like a mule, Monique sees Rosa Lee put on the wedding dress and smiling at her, like a deranged whore. Then Eric takes her mother's hand and the minister pronounces them man and wife. The whole church cheers as the brand-new couple walk down the aisle, stepping over bloody and bruised Monique. As the happy couple saunters down the aisle and disappears out the door, the congregation follows, and Monique is left alone, lying on the floor, crying uncontrollably.

She notices the reverend was gathering his things in the pulpit and calls out for his assistance. He comes over and smiles, pulls out his dick and pisses all over her! After finishing, he zips back up and goes to see the happy couple off. Then Monique woke up.

Wow! What a fucked-up dream! Monique thought as she awoke from the nightmare. Looking at the clock, she noticed it was 10 a.m. and reached for the cell to call Eric. Again, the operator said the number was not in service. Bewildered, the young tranny rechecked the number and dialed three more times, only to get the same result. How come the number worked yesterday, but not today?

Hoping against hope, the girl thought maybe Eric's' phone was damaged, and once it gets fixed, the number would work. After getting dressed, she went over to talk to Precious, who she had hardly seen that long hot summer. In fact, the youngster only saw her next-

door neighbor four times since graduation. It was like Precious was a vampire—rarely coming out during the day. Monique knocked on the thick mahogany door, but there was no answer, though Monique knew the horse-dick bitch was at home.

She thought someone was peeking through the curtains, but she couldn't be sure. The youngster knocked a few more times and slowly walked away, sad that Precious didn't want to be bothered by a love-struck, confused teen. Of course, the teen had no way of knowing that her neighbor had committed the most-talked-about murder of the summer and thought she might be the police at the door... or that she was being blackmailed by a down-low fag who saw her dump the body. No, Monique had no idea what was going on, and for her sake, ignorance was healthier than knowledge. To get on the wrong side of Precious was dangerous, and could be fatal.

After eating three bowls of Lucky Charms and redialing Eric's number 15 more times, Monique thought it would be a bright idea to surprise him. There had to be a reasonable explanation for why the number didn't work, and she figured he could fuck her brains out again if she showed up. *Maybe not!* Milk gave her gas, and she didn't want to be farting too much in his presence.

The teen took a quick shower and dashed over to her future boyfriend's apartment as fast as the speed limit would allow. Feeling confident yet nervous, she knocked on the door and was greeted by an angry Eric.

"What the fuck you want," he asked in a low deep voice.

"Why you talking to me like this?" Monique asked, startled. "I just came over to get your number, because it's not working or something," she explained.

"Look, what happened yesterday was cool, but don't come knockin on my fuckin door again! We fucked—that's it! I'm not in love with you, and don't wanna see your ass again. You got that?"

Before she could answer, he slammed the door in her face. She felt tears welling in her eyes and ran back to the car, so nobody would see her sobbing over this nigga, who apparently didn't give a fuck about her. Unable to calm down, she sat in the car for 30 minutes, listening to MyPraise Gospel on 102.5 to find some serenity. Before driving off, she noticed a cab pull up in front of Eric's apartment, and to her utter, dumbfounded surprise, her supposed best-friend Princess exited.

After she walked up to his door, the ho didn't even have to knock, as Eric greeted her with a big smile, wearing only a G-string. Monique became furious and left the apartment complex, feeling sick to her stomach, like she was about to vomit. She felt like a total idiot to think some stranger she met in a bar was going to be the love of her life! While driving around for hours, the hurt and anger subsided, and she felt lucky to have seen Eric for what he really was—just another big-dick whore and nothing else.

Guys like him were a dime a dozen. Precious told her that! Soon however, she began to worry if Eric ever practiced safe sex. If he didn't use a condom on her, why would he use one with anyone else? Suddenly, the hardheaded girl wished she had listened to Mom. In an effort to put this incident behind her, Monique changed her cell number and deleted Princess's number, determined not to see the trifling whore again.

The only reason she ever befriended the bitch in the first place was because she was a young transsexual, like herself—but their personalities and goals in life were completely different. She would soon be off to college, while Princess's only goal was to be a prostitute and have her own sex website. The only thing the two had in common was that they were born males and wanted to be females—hardly a basis for a long-lasting friendship.

After the incident with Eric, Monique became scared shitless that she might have been infected with HIV, so she stopped going out to the clubs. She became a homebody choosing the comfort and familiarity of home over partying with friends. The young tranny stopped smoking weed and drinking, because it impaired judgment by lowering inhibitions. It was why she didn't insist on Eric wearing a condom—because the blunt they smoked made her feel so good and loose that the thought of HIV never entered her mind.

She wanted to tell Rosa Lee, but she didn't want to alarm her mom for no reason. It was not likely that she had contracted the disease anyway, being fucked without a condom for a first and only time. How many people who had AIDS contracted the disease during their initial sexual encounter? Probably less than 1%, she imagined.

The day she left for college was a mixture of joy and sorrow, for both mother and daughter. While helping her daughter unpack in the dorm, Rosa Lee was proud the moment had come, while at the same time she felt a twinge of sadness, realizing her child had become an adult. Not only had she become an adult, but she had become a

confident, competent woman. After making the dorm room livable, they sat and chatted on the bed for a while before finally saying their goodbyes through tears and many hugs.

When Rosa Lee finally left, the dedicated nurse went straight to work. The hospital was only about a mile from her daughter's dorm room. Being in such proximity would make it convenient for a nosy mom to show up unannounced to check on her child, and she planned on doing just that. Rosa Lee could walk to the dorm during her lunch break, but she knew not to be too conspicuous with visitation.

After mom left, Monique stared out the window at the teeming traffic below, both human and automobile. The excited girl couldn't believe it had actually happened: she was now a college student. She jumped for joy, looking around the beautiful private suite, which would be her home for the next four years. Now she could have complete privacy, without worrying about a mom or a roommate.

Nervous about how people would react to a transsexual, the freshman explored the campus, and to her surprise, she saw no one staring back in angry judgment. Nor had anyone heckled her with ignorant, crude language. She chanced upon the student activities center, where different organizations sought to recruit students to join their causes.

The signage for one particular organization stood out like a beacon. It was the lesbian, gay, bisexual, transgender group, better known as the LGBT Alliance. She readily signed up and listened to the enthusiastic spiel of the eager gay, white guy named Daniel, who extolled her about the virtues of joining. When the young transsexual college student met other transsexuals, lesbians and gays, she felt an immediate bond.

It was her first time meeting trannies who were political and serious about getting an education, not only to better themselves but to benefit the transgender community at large. After meeting and talking to so many wonderful people, she went to bed that night exhausted, but happy to be in college. Unlike most trannies who had to prostitute to get by, she was going to get her education and change the world for the better...or make a lot of money—hopefully both! She didn't want to end up like Princess, who was bitter and out-of-control for being thrown out the house at 16, when she started wearing makeup. Nor did she want to end up like Precious, who seemed to have it together on the outside, but seemed to lack any

empathy for her fellow man. No matter how well her neighbor seemed to have it together, in the end, she was just a prostitute. That wasn't going to be Monique's life, and getting an education would assure that she would never have to sell her body.

Monique hardly slept a wink that first night at college, and she awoke early, eager for the first day of classes to begin. She dressed conservatively in jeans and a blue blouse, accented by pink Nike tennis shoes. Being too nervous to eat, she drank a glass of orange juice instead of having cereal. Since milk gave her gas, the last thing Monique wanted to do was fart in class! After a quick inspection in the full-length mirror, the freshman grabbed her bookbag and headed out the door to class.

While walking to class among the throng of loud, chatty students, she realized her future was hers alone to mold and shape. The future was uncharted waters, and she was the lone explorer who would map the journey. And what a thrilling voyage it would be. Marcus, aka Monique Devereux, felt at home on that campus.

****

Eric couldn't believe that young bitch had come over to the crib, asking about a goddamn phone number that he had disconnected. Obviously, ol girl fell in love with his big dick and came back for more. Being a player, once he got the ass; he usually didn't want it again. But the real reason why the number was turned off was because of his HIV status. Since he fucked raw, the diseased whore knew that sooner or later, some angry ex-lovers would accuse him of giving them AIDS, and more than likely, they would be right. A disconnected number would probably discourage most from contacting him.

Many of the guys and trannies he fucked were young and dumb anyway—too stupid to make him use a rubber. And since they practiced unsafe sex regularly, how could they blame him for being HIV infected? Most people who caught the infection were too ashamed to confront anyone about it, publicly or privately. Only one guy had ever accused him of giving the deadly disease, and his name was Brian. He played college football for the Clark Atlanta Panthers and had the fattest ass ever. The gridiron warrior was 5'10" and 280 jiggly pounds, with suckable breasts that would put a woman to shame.

Eric's dick still got hard thinking about that football playing queen! Brian loved for Eric to ride his fat ass raw, begging for dick like a little girl begs for candy. After getting pumped with cum all day, dude would go to football practice and play with sticky cream leaking out of his anus! Brian confronted Eric at his apartment one day and wanted to kill the bastard, but the sneaky muthafucka convinced the upset fag that he was HIV free, so getting the disease from him was out of the question.

In an effort to calm the footballer down, they sat on the couch and smoked a blunt, while Brian laid his head in Eric's lap, crying like a little girl. While getting high, Eric fondled Brian's giant saggy tits, pinching his plump nipples until he was moaning with pleasure. In an instant, the fool had Eric's huge dick in his mouth, licking it like a big chocolate ice cream cone.

Knowing they were going to fuck, Brian told Eric to use a condom but Eric knew the horny, fat bitch wanted it raw, and that's how he gave it to the fag; hard and raw. That was three years earlier and they continued see each other, on and off, even though Brian still thought Eric gave him AIDS. His weakness for good dick made him come back for more and more, even if it was a diseased cock.

The night Monique left his apartment with an asshole full of cum, Eric went back to Traxxx and found Princess there, flirting as always. They chit-chatted a while before going out to the car to talk in private and suck each other's dicks. After taking turns cumming in each other's mouth, they made a date for the next evening, where she showed up right after her friend, Monique, left crying. Since that time, Eric hadn't seen either of them. He was getting enough ass already and didn't need two dizzy trannies jocking him. For the time being, he promised himself to stick with regular faggots and leave trannies alone. They acted too much like real females for his taste. Yuk!

Chapter 12
An Uneasy Alliance

It was 8:30 Tuesday evening as Precious sat in the BMW at Redan Park, waiting on her extortionist. The pissed tranny had just spent two hours at Wendy's, collecting her blackmail money, and now she had to turn around and give $1,000 of it to David. She detested the forced partnership with fat ugly-ass David, which wasn't a partnership at all.

It was humbling to be the target of a blackmailer as opposed to being the blackmailer. In the last three weeks, she'd given the fag $3,000, so the situation was seriously messing with the finances and nerves. God, she desperately wanted to get the dick-sucker to come over to the crib, but he was being careful. The fatso didn't want to be alone with her for fear of falling under the spell of her thick magic stick. After seeing what he saw, who could blame the guy?

It was disconcerting being intimate to someone and then burning their corpse. Reflection on that night made Precious tremble with fear, because sooner or later, David was going to tell somebody. Whether it was by choice or by accident, the hardened tranny knew the fat fag would crumble under pressure, and she couldn't afford that. He had to be stopped—one way or the other. But how? She thought about using another tranny as a lure, but the less people involved, the better.

More people involved increased the chances of the police knocking on the door. She had to give David the hard-earned money she made from blackmailing other suckers. She felt like a sap, getting played by a cocksucker! Unlike her other marks, there was no way to threaten him, because she had no leverage. While he had a career to lose, a conviction meant she would lose her life. The last thing Precious wanted to do was live her last days on death row in a concrete cell.

She cursed the day she picked up Deshawnte. With all the cute little boys in Atlanta, the horny pedophile had to pick him to fuck. If not for the boy's sexy bubble-butt, she wouldn't be in her current situation. No little 14-year-old boy should have had an ass so fat and sexy. The little faggot was just begging to get fucked! And like a good ho, she obliged the youngster, taking him to heights of pleasure never experienced in his short life. His death was tragic, but it was an

accident. But who would believe a transsexual prostitute who cruised the city, looking for little boys to fuck? Not even Jesus himself! So Precious did what had to be done by burning the body. Why ruin her life over an unavoidable accident?

What good would a confession and explanation do Deshawnte or his family? His crack-head mammy had already made a few bucks off his death, because like most ghetto families, they couldn't afford the funeral, so a fund was set up for the family at Bank of America. It was all water under the bridge.

Her new problem was David and how to get rid of him. God, she hated how her careful, comfortable life was slowly unraveling, like a ball of yarn between the paws of a cat. Precious wished she had a mom like Rosa Lee. If Precious' mom had been a mother instead of her pimp, then her life would have turned out differently. Maybe she would have gone to college, like Monique, instead of selling cock and ass to the highest bidder, like a slave for rent.

There she was, waiting to pay off a man who held her fate in his greedy, fat hands. Eight-thirty, and still no David. Precious was getting tired and frustrated. Not only was the nigga blackmailing her for a $1,000 a week, but dude had the unmitigated gall to be late for every damn pickup. The only reason the fat nigga came late was to irritate her, which made the tranny want to kill the down-low faggot even more. This muthafucka would rue the day he ever fucked with a pissed-off, motivated bitch from Detroit!

When 9:15 came, Precious called but got no answer, so she couldn't decide whether to stay or leave. The wrong decision could cost her life, which was already hanging by a thin thread, controlled by David. But what kind of life would she have if that nigga was alive? Precious thought carefully and made a tactical decision, started the car and sped away from the park, almost running over a gimpy old dog.

The angry tranny had no idea what would happen when David came and saw she had left. Would he have a hissy fit and snitch, or would he come by the house to collect? Precious was banking on the latter. David seemed to relish the power over a dominant big-cock tranny, and if he told on her, their relationship, such as it was, would end. The fag enjoyed humiliating and calling her names while collecting the blood money she earned with her famous dick. The fiercely proud she-male took the verbal abuse in stride and swallowed her pride, knowing one day the muthafucka would be sorry he ever

slurped on her cock. The dude didn't know it yet, but his days were numbered.

Why couldn't the fool be on time instead of being so smug and discourteous? Precious was starting to feel like the sociology professor was a pimp, which made her the streetwalking ho, who gets fucked all day then brings the money home to daddy.

She drove home, obeying the speed limit, thinking David would call and tell her to come back to the park, but he never did. By the time the anxious tranny closed her garage door, it was 11 p.m., and she was beginning to worry. Where the fuck was David? Precious smiled thinking maybe he had an accident, or better yet—he had a heart attack and died! Or maybe the bastard had dimed her out, and the police were on their way to arrest her ass!

At first, she thought about staying at a hotel, but realized that if they were after her, they would eventually catch her. Being a tall, black transsexual, or she-male, it wasn't easy to hide, especially in the daytime, and she had no desire on being a fucking fugitive. She decided that running was too much drama, and she shuddered at the thought of being featured on *Americas Most Wanted* as a murderous, perverted tranny pedophile.

Since running was out of the question, she rolled a fat blunt and tried to relax by watching TV, not knowing whether the next knock on her door will be David or the Decatur Police department. About an hour later, the phone rang and it was "you-know-who" explaining why he didn't meet her. When she recognized the number, a smile came over her worried face, because she knew he hadn't snitched.

Thankfully for her, greed and lust held more sway over him than weak pathetic morals ever did. If she only she could convince the fat, black, baldheaded dick-sucker to come over to the crib and get the money, instead of meeting at the park every damn week! The park was his turf, while the house was her home field advantage. Once he came over, she could answer the door butt-naked with her dick hard enough to do chin ups on it. She knew he wouldn't be able to resist a juicy cock pointing right at him, ready for action.

David intentionally failed to show up for his weekly rendezvous with Precious. He was torn between doing the right thing, which was reporting the crime, or keeping silent and continuing to collect the money. The professor loved the fact that he had complete control over the sexy transsexual who, like a wild stallion, refused to be

tamed. But like the cowboys tamed the stallion by throwing a saddle on its back, David's "saddle" was knowledge of her crime.

He realized the thrill of having control over her was going to be a burden on his chubby shoulders. What if the police find out she committed the murder on their own? What if they were secretly following her in order to gather more evidence? If that were the case and she got caught, would Precious dime him out for blackmailing her? Of course she would! It wasn't like the murderer had any empathy for anyone but herself. Hell, the bitch might even try to implicate him in the murder, just for the perverse pleasure of watching him suffer.

She'll tell on him just for spite, even though it wouldn't do any good in court, because it was definitely a death penalty situation. For a young black DA with political ambitions, like the one currently presiding in Decatur, hers would be a career-making case, so going for the death penalty was a no brainer. Sitting outside the tranny's house, David was torn between leaving and never calling the bitch again or getting his weekly stipend.

But dude was feeling weak, and he desperately wanted to wrap his fat black lips around Precious' long, thick cock. It had been almost a month since Derrick fucked him, so he was very horny. Though Derrick loved him, it was obvious his lover was seeing someone else. That became painfully apparent when he saw Derrick at Wal-Mart a week earlier with a boy that looked no more than 18 or 19 years old.

Watching his lover fawn over the young boy was embarrassing, and it made him sick with jealousy. Being curious, David followed them to Derrick's car, where as soon as they got in the Lexus, the old bastard tongue-kissed the boy like it was his last day on Earth. David couldn't believe that fucker was messing around on him and being so public about it. Not that he was faithful either, but it was disturbing to be played for a fool, even though he was doing the same thing to Tammy and Derrick. After giving it much thought, lust won out, and he dialed Precious' number, much to his chagrin.

"Why did you leave the park?" an exasperated David asked, trying to seem in control.

"Maybe because you were over an hour late, and it's scary sitting in an abandoned park all night," she told him. "We can meet tomorrow or you can come get it now if you like."

"Okay, I'm right outside your house now," he said nonchalantly.

"You are?" a surprised Precious exclaimed as she peeked out the window and saw his fat ass parked out front. "C'mon in, then! What you waitin on?" She was ecstatic to finally get the fat fucker to come over to the crib again.

"Okay, but all I want is my money. I'm not coming in," he managed to blurt, against his will. With nipples hard and his asshole puckered and ready for a hot cock, David fought, like a true warrior, against the sexual temptation.

"Damn! You can't stay and have a drink or something," she asked, disappointed as hell. "Or at least help me get rid of this raging hard on I got..."

"Nope—just want my money. Please have it ready. I'm not here to play games," David said again, this time more forcefully.

Precious saw him exit the car and waddle his fat ass up to her door. She unzipped her pants before opening the door and stood, with her long dick standing at attention.

"You can come on in, baby. I'm not gonna hurt you, boo. Stop acting like a lil fag," she said smiling and shaking her dick from side to side. David didn't seem to notice the snake hanging between her legs.

"Look, I'm gonna walk back to my car and we won't ever see each other again. But I *will* see you on TV tomorrow." Precious responded as he turned to leave.

"Here go yo money, fool," she said handing him an envelope through the open storm door, with her dick pointing directly at him, like a sword ready for battle. "I just thought you may wanna suck some of this cock, like old times."

"Nope, you thought wrong," David said after putting the money in his pocket and turning to leave. "I can meet you here next week if it's easier for you. By the way—you still sexy as hell." He got in the car and left Precious standing in the doorway with a hard dick and a stunned and disappointed look on her face.

The horny professor wanted to stay, but knew it would lead to groveling for her gorgeous dick and begging to be fucked. Being face-down, ass-up wasn't exactly a strong negotiating position. Then she would have complete control over him, like before. There was no way that could happen again, so he sped away, thankful to have gotten the money and kept it professional. He looked at his reflection in the rear-view mirror, smiling as he let out a sigh of relief.

The chubby fag had dodged a bullet this time, but would he be so strong next week? With a little more persuading, he was weakening to succumb to her magic wand, throwing caution to the wind. In the back of his mind, he knew the beautiful, big-dick tranny was a cold-blooded murderer. The bitch wouldn't hesitate to kill to keep the dastardly secret of the murder a secret. A cold sweat came over the professor as the fag realized the only thing standing between her and the electric chair was him.

If she could get rid of the only eyewitness that she knew to exist, there'd be no one who could pin the murder on her... unless the police found other evidence. Derrick knew, but he didn't know her, and he wasn't eager to talk for fear of his alternative lifestyle being made public. Luckily, Precious didn't know Derrick witnessed her at the body burning scene too, or he might be in danger from a desperate tranny.

Unless someone talked, the investigation, after three months, seemed to have gone cold, like most cases do. Feeling hungry, even after devouring four Big Macs less than an hour earlier, David stopped at one of the many cheap Chinese restaurants that dotted black communities across America. Food—any food, always put him in a better mood. He ordered his favorite Chink meal: sweet n sour chicken, smothered in rice, from the drive-thru. Sitting in the parking lot, fatso scarfed the vittles down like he was a starving refugee. The nigga didn't get to be fat as hell by eating like a supermodel! When there was nothing else in the cheap Styrofoam plate to consume, David drank the rest of the watery coke and headed home to his family.

His family was unaware of the secret and dangerous life their patriarch led. Even though he was in love with Derrick in particular and big black cocks in general, family still came first. After pulling into the garage, he thanked God for getting home safe. He wondered how much longer it would be before his world came crashing down, consuming everyone in its destructive wake?

The house was quiet. Tammy and the kids were asleep, so David went to the study to catch up on paperwork and grade papers, though after 15 minutes, he was snoring like a buzzsaw, courtesy of sleep apnea. He dreamt of hot Krispy Kreme donuts glazed with cum from Precious' cock, melting in his mouth! Maybe it wasn't a coincidence that the next morning on the way to work the professor stopped by the Krispy Kreme at the West End Mall. After buying a

dozen original glazed and a cup of coffee, he ate them on the way to the university.

He wolfed the hot pieces of sugar-coated delights down his throat in less than ten minutes. Since they were so warm, chewing was unnecessary. They melted in his mouth, leaving the essence of ecstasy on the tongue. He consumed the last donut while pulling into the parking space marked, Dr. David Morris. Still hungry, he ate all the yummy bits of dried glaze in the box that had dropped off the donuts. Checking his appearance in the sun visor mirror, the dried glaze around his thick black lips reminded him of Derrick's dry cum. Licking the glaze off his fingers, the professor imagined it was cum dripping from a big cock lover.

Precious was pissed that she couldn't reel the fat faggot inside the house. There was no way on Earth any nigga could withstand the power of her powerful cock, until David proved that weak, unsubstantiated theory wrong. At least he would be coming back in a week, which meant she would have another opportunity to persuade the professor to trust her. The conniving tranny had to make him believe there was nothing to fear. She figured that on next Tuesday, there was no way fatty wouldn't step into the house, *or why else would the guy change pickup locations?* Professor fatso had to have planned the change all along, which meant he wanted some dick after all.

Obviously, he was confident they could still be lovers, or better yet, fuck-buddies. Slowly, the stoic business persona was crumbling, replaced by lust and passion, which could prove fatal for both. Precious knew what had to be done: the low-down bitch had exactly a week to plan the murder of David.

Sitting on the couch, watching CNN report all the heartache and misery in the world, she realized no one would care about another dead nigga. As with Deshawnte, once the initial outrage subsided, nobody gave a fuck, because people were just glad it wasn't them lying dead in the ditch. Unlike the last killing, which was accidental, this murder had to be planned meticulously.

In this case, she would have to get rid of both a body also a car, and the plan had to be executed without any pesky witnesses to muck things up. If David hadn't been in the park that night, then there was a good chance the murder of Deshawnte would have gone unsolved forever, but the fat faggot had to stick his nose in where it didn't belong, and now would pay dearly for it. Now his kids would grow

up without a father, and wife would be a widow—all because he had the temerity to blackmail a streetwise hustling ho.

Dude was out of his league when it came to understanding human nature. He may have held a doctorate in sociology, but he was a dummy when it came to understanding how desperation could push someone to commit murder. His sexually-repressed appetite needed to be fed, and she was only too happy to feed the fool. What the over-confident professor didn't know—it would be his last time feeding on big black cock! But how many more people could say they died slurping on a juicy penis?

Planning a murder was mentally-draining for the fearsome tranny, so she fixed a drink, rolled a blunt and lay awake in bed, thinking what the future would bring. With the lights out and the house dark and silent, the tranny heard the faint sounds of the highway traffic that ran behind her yard. She enjoyed the early morning, two a.m. silence, because it allowed her to think more clearly, without the din of daytime clogging up the brain with fear and self-doubt.

She smiled between puffs of Jamaican Ganja, thinking how David would look when fatso realized he was about to die. Her dick got hard at the idea that her cum would literally be his last supper. The bitch had no idea how she would do it, but she knew in her hardened heart that she would. She didn't have the luxury of putting off the inevitable, because hesitation could mean incarceration and eventual lethal injection. Yet if she didn't get the death penalty, a life in prison, without the possibility of parole, was certain death anyway—either at the violent hands of another inmate, as with her brother, Tommy, or by suicide

David had to be stopped before the fool got a conscience and snitched to the police. At some point, he would grow tired of her, and when she knew anything, the police would come knocking. Before falling asleep, she vowed to call her prey everyday day, just to chat and for small talk. By calling him every day, she'd be able to chip away at the man's defenses and put his mind a little more at ease so that when he came over, his defenses would be weakened to the point where the fag would become an easy victim. Exhausted from the hectic day, the tired tranny fell asleep, and the only sound in the house was of her snoring.

When morning came, the first thing the tranny did was call David, who was on a sugar-high from eating a dozen donuts. Sitting

on the toilet, taking a shit, a smile overcame the professor when he saw the call was from Precious.

"Hello, Precious. Good morning," David cheerfully said, "what can I do for you?"

"Oh, hey boo! I was just calling to say 'hello,' that's all. You workin today?"

"Yes, my first class starts in 20 minutes," he answered. "I must say, you sure were looking *beautiful* last night."

The professor felt good while dropping turds as big as footballs into the hapless commode. Cheap Chinese food did that him, in addition to the two bowls of chili he ate before going to bed and the dozen donuts he consumed on the way to work. It wasn't a pleasant night for Tammy, who thought she needed a gas mask to get through the night.

"If I was looking so sexy, then why didn't you come in and get on your knees like a good bitch should? You know how I get when I'm horny, yet you left me there hanging, with my dick out hard as hell and nobody to put it in!" she said, pretending to be angry, teasing.

David's dick was getting hard listening to her talk so bold and filthy. Right then, the nigga remembered why he loved transsexuals so much, particularly Precious—because outwardly, the lady looked feminine, but on the real, she was still a vile lustful man. When that girl got horny, her insatiable manhood came out with a vengeance. It seemed her manliness was held in check by the high heels, weave and lipstick, revealed only when she was ready to fuck. Maybe that's why she fucked him like it was her last night on Earth.

"Well, you know I had to keep it about business, Mrs. Meat." He enjoyed calling her that because first, it was proper, and second, it was a cool name. "Believe me! As good as you looked, I wanted to stay but I didn't want to mix business and pleasure, but next week, maybe we can."

Those words were manna to the tranny's ears. She knew that Tuesday would be fatty's last night on Earth! Her mind whirled with dozens of ideas on how to kill and get rid of the obese piece of shit who was stealing the hard-earned money she made from blackmailing. A big smile came over the hustling scheming tranny's face, because David had no idea what was in store for him the next time he knocked on the door.

"Damn, baby—that's all I wanted to hear! I can't wait to slam my cock into your fat juicy asshole while you scream my name so loud the neighbors can hear!"

"You know what I was thinking, baby," David asked while dropping the final stinking turd from his cholesterol-filled body, "I was thinking that perhaps we could be partners. We could make plenty of money, because I know you blackmailing lots of guys, right?"

Precious knew fat-ass would eventually demand more money, so she played along, pretending to agree with this asinine proposal.

"Yes, baby—we can discuss that in person, but you have a good point, I need a partner to handle the loose ends for me," she lied. "Like some guys won't pay, but if they hear your deep, masculine voice on the phone, maybe they would." Precious was amused at the thought of the fat, feminine, big-breasted fucker being an enforcer.

David swelled with pride on hearing Precious agree to the proposal. He imagined making a boatload of money, but the better part was having Precious all to himself. The professor figured they could make $5,000 a week in their joint-venture. Finally, he finished shitting and used almost a whole roll of toilet tissue to wipe his massive ass.

"Okay, baby. I can do that. We'll talk in more detail when I come over. I have to go now, boo—my class starts in a few minutes.

"Take care of yourself, baby, and you can call and talk anytime you feel like it," she assured him before they hung up. She was ecstatic, because soon all her worries would be over. The unsuspecting prey was rushing into her spider web.

The professor couldn't believe his good luck. Thank God he was in the park that night, getting bent over and fucked by Derrick. If not, he wouldn't have seen Precious dump and burn the body. Now he was in position to profit from that knowledge that would ultimately double the $67,500-a-year salary he made teaching a bunch of bored students. After checking himself in the mirror one last time, the professor let out a long, loud fart before exiting the faculty bathroom. He waddled to class with two things occupying his thoughts: donuts and Precious. *Tuesday can't get here soon enough, damn it!*

After hanging up the phone, the tranny lay in bed, watching the ceiling fan go round and round while fondling her baseball-sized testicles. She turned on the TV to watch one of her many homemade movies, downloaded from the computer, starring some unsuspecting

down-low faggot. Within seconds, her cock was at its zenith, measuring a legitimate ten and one-half inches by six inches in all its glory.

She truly admired the baseball bat dangling between her legs and stroked it while watching the screen as she ferociously impaled one of the clients with the Louisville Slugger. She couldn't help but admire her strong fuck game. Once a nigga felt that big black cock penetrating them, they became helpless, begging for it, like crack-heads beg for dope, throwing aside all pretense of manhood.

When their voices lost their bass and the dudes started moaning and talking like little girls, then Precious felt she did her job. It was like a feather in the cap to turn a seemingly straight nigga out. Even though she called them faggots and shit, she didn't really see them as such. Most of her clients were married family men, with professional careers. Outwardly, they were conservative in their appearance and actions, but inside a lust lay dormant, like a volcano, waiting for someone or something to erupt the secret desires hidden just beneath the surface. After weighing the pros and cons of getting caught, the guys gave in to temptation and called her to satisfy their appetite for a thick juicy penis.

Reflecting on her clients' secrets and desires turned the tranny on, as her masturbating entered the point of no return. While watching herself ride a faggot doggy-style on the screen, the horny tranny timed the orgasm to coincide with her orgasm on the TV. She imagined cumming in a cute fresh-face 15-year-old boy's virgin ass as cum shot oozed out of her penis like an oil gusher. Feeling relaxed, she let out a sigh of relief, licking the cum from her fingers while reveling in its sweet salty taste. After a few puffs from the blunt, sleep overtook her, and soon the girl was dreaming about little boys, with fat asses.

As one day morphed into another, Tuesday finally arrived. After getting off the phone with David, she realized the next 24 to 48 hours would be the most important of her life. To Precious, the day meant her freedom. For David, it meant a better business opportunity and having a sexy tranny as a personal sex slave. The murderess had talked to her prey every day, so by that morning, the fool's guard was compromised, if obliterated.

She called every morning just to say hello, or chat about how his day was going. The professor enjoyed talking about the teaching profession, and Precious feigned interest, encouraging him. The fag

had to know, deep in his heart, that the bitch didn't give a fuck about his career or the state of education as it pertained to the black community. Dude would have been right, because her only concern was making him feel comfortable so she could carry out the scheme to kill him.

The plan was to have David pull into her garage and surprise him with a Smith & Wesson .38 revolver. Next, she would pull him out of the front seat, cuff his hands and feet and throw fatty in the backseat. After that, the hard-hearted tranny would turn on the ignition of both their cars and let the carbon monoxide do its work. Since he was fat as a cow and had trouble breathing anyway, death wouldn't take long. That was the plan, if nothing went awry. After watching hundreds of hours of the Investigative Discovery Channel, she realized that sometimes even the most minute element or clue would lead investigators to the perpetrator, no matter how much care had gone into planning the crime or how well the perpetrator had thought things through. So why would hers' be free of any mistakes, when it seemed like so many others weren't?

Precious pulled herself out of bed and went to take a shit. A good shit in the morning always relaxed her, especially when accompanied by a fat blunt. She sat on the porcelain throne contemplating over and over what could go wrong. What if David had a gun? What if he fought back and she had to shoot him? As the smoke permeated the brain cells, the cannabis always made her feel confident and in control. After getting off the toilet, she took a long cold shower to get ready for another hot Georgia day.

The big-dick bitch relaxed even more by jerking off, with visions of Deshawnte's plump ass riding her cock. It seemed the boy, or rather the boy's juicy anus, was haunting her, but in a good way. It was a shame the child was dead, because he had one of the most beautiful asses she'd ever seen. God must have been working overtime for a 14-year-old boy to have a booty that would make the average black woman envious! What a creation!

Precious had stopped feeling guilty about the boy, rationalizing that his death was the result of cocaine and crack use. The fact that she supplied it to him (though he'd never tried it before) didn't enter the equation. Why let facts get in the way of a good narrative? No one cared that the little nigga was dead and wasn't coming back. *Oh!* she smiled to herself, *the police care.* All that was ancient history now— today was what was important, yesterday irrelevant. If everything

went well that day, then Precious could erase the effects of the tragedy of Deshawnte's death… or eradicate her involvement in it.

It was 2 p.m. when she left the house to meet her clients at Wendy's. It might have been the last time she would see them if anything went wrong when David came over at 11 o'clock that night. She was certain they would be delighted to never see or hear from her again.

The blackmailing tranny arrived at Wendy's around 2:45 and ordered an apple pecan salad, along with a large coke from the drive-thru window. To be inconspicuous, she parked in the back of the restaurant to wait on the money. Her extortion victims, who presently numbered nine, wanted to be as discreet as possible when making their payments in public. For that reason, she changed the pickup day every few months, though she had chosen the place because it was so crowded. These pissed-off niggas wouldn't try anything there that they might in private.

A week earlier, the industrious tranny collected $3,000 from these foolish faggots, which would have been nice, except she had to give a thousand of it to David. Today would be the last time that happened—that is, if everything went right. It was a beautiful, sunny day, with temperatures reaching eighty degrees, which was still hot—but at least it wasn't muggy and humid. After an hour, the first client sauntered over to the BMW and handed over a Wendy's bag, filled with $400 cash. Without saying a word, he turned around and left, but not before looking back and calling her a bitch! Before getting back in the car, the mad fag gave her the finger and drove off with a disgusted look on his face. She just smiled and waved. After all, the fag just put four Ben Franklins in a bitch's hand.

That was Richard, aka dickhead, who was usually pissed off. But the tranny couldn't really blame her victims for being angry. She just didn't give a fuck. As long as the bastards paid, they could say anything fucking thing they wanted—as long as they don't put their hands on her. Asshole Richard was the first to show, followed in succession by Harrison, Michael, John, Charles, Milton, Douglass, or Dougie, as he liked to be called.

As usual, some of the muthafuckas called and said they were running late. By 7:30 all the extorted had paid, except for the same two who were always tardy: Calvin Hanson and Spencer Collins. Precious thought they were just testing her to see if she would follow through on the threat to expose them. That night was their lucky

night, because if David didn't have to be killed, then Mrs. Collins and Mrs. Hanson would be getting a special package from UPS in the morning. When eight o'clock rolled around, it was apparent they weren't coming, so she called and left them a message to meet there tomorrow night at six.

If they reneged again, their lives would be ruined, and she wouldn't have lost a minute of sleep over it. Rules were rules, and once a victim started thinking he could get away with something, then all the others would think they could too. It wouldn't have surprised her if the two fags were working together, but it didn't really matter because they had no leverage. Before leaving she purchased another salad then headed home to put her wicked plan in motion.

****

Tuesday had finally come, and David couldn't have been happier. After getting off the phone with Precious, he was giddy with excitement and couldn't wait for the cover of night. Down-low guys loved to creep and did their butt banging activities down-low, in the dark. It was as if the shadows shielded them from the mental anguish and guilt of leading a double-life.

The horny professor was scheduled to meet his reluctant business partner at eleven, which was too many hours away in his mind. At ten in the morning, he would have to wait 13 hours before gazing upon the beautiful Precious Meat. Feeling hungry, he did what all red-blooded humans did when he got up—he stunk up the bathroom.

Relieved, he fixed a hearty breakfast consisting of seven soft scrambled eggs with cheese, an entire 12-pack of Jimmy Dean sausage links, and huge bowl of grits, slathered with butter and sugar. With Tammy at work, and the kids in school, he enjoyed those rare moments of quiet in the ever-bustling household. No one was there to scold him about his weight or glancing with disapproval at the huge amounts of food piled on his plate. He sat butt-naked at the kitchen table and ate slowly, savoring every bite of the greasy heart attack-inducing fare. For 20 minutes, the dining area was filled with the sound of chewing and smacking of lips, followed by gulps of Diet 7up.

He put his plate in the sink and lumbered to the bedroom, farting and belching all the way. His little dick was almost hidden by his massive belly, and his sagging breasts jiggled from side to side, making him feel like a bitch. He loved the way Derrick sucked on his long, sensitive nipples when they made love, comparing them to chocolate chip cookies.

Thinking about the big-dick bastard brought a smile to his face. Tired after eating 5,000 calories and walking up the stairs, he collapsed onto the soft, king-sized bed. Still feeling horny, he played with his cock until it was a hard five inches, and then his squeezed his nipples until they doubled in size.

Imagining Precious' gigantic cock impaling him unmercifully, David moaned with pleasure as his testicles filled up with gooey semen. He nutted all over his massive belly after a few minutes and wiped the slime off with the bedspread. With his stomach full and cock empty, he felt content and sated. Like a beached walrus, he nodded off to sleep oblivious to the strange sounds and unpleasant smells emanating from both mouth and anus.

Tammy came home to the revolting sight of that obese man, lying in their bed, wheezing and snoring, like a damn freight train. What the hell happened to that sexy dark man she married years earlier? He had turned into a fat, overeating fart machine who liked pizza more than pussy. To think he used to rush home to fuck her brains out! but now he was too damn fat to screw longer than a few minutes at a time. She married a guy who could walk up a flight of stairs without stopping to catch his damn breath, but now he broke out into a sweat just looking at a staircase!

When they did make love, fatty could barely keep it up. Hell, besides being a lousy lover, that fat bastard had the nerve to be a selfish lover too. Once hubby got his nut, she was left unfulfilled and wanting more. When she would ask him to eat her pussy, the fat fucker wouldn't even do that. She hated the irony: she married a man who ate everything under the sun, but he wouldn't eat his wife. If not for Joanne, she wouldn't get any dick at all—if a double-sided vibrating dildo could be called a substitute for dick. It might not have been better than the real thing, but it was certainly better than nothing.

Tammy let him sleep while she undressed and took a shower. The crisp, clean water was soothing and relaxing as it washed the dirt and sweat resulting from the hot southern weather. After cleansing

the mind as well as the body, she put on her favorite outfit: a pair of white granny-panties, along with a tattered nightgown. After wearing tight-fitting clothes and heels all day at work, it felt good to let everything hang loose.

Tammy loved letting her size 36C breasts sag and swing from side to side, unrestricted by a bra. Inspecting herself in the mirror, she admitted she was getting fatter by the day. At barely 5' 3" and weighing in at over 180 pounds, the inevitable had happened. There was a thin line between thick and fat, and she was now on the other side of that imaginary line.

Hell, she couldn't remember the last time a guy flirted with her—not a sexy young guy as opposed to some old ass man on the prowl. At 38, she looked like a shapeless blob with boobs. Her stomach sagged almost as much as Hubby's did. It was little wonder why he hardly touched her anymore. Feeling and looking unattractive, she promised herself for the umpteenth time to go on a diet, *maybe tomorrow*. But the mind was willing, while the body was so very weak—especially when it came to fried foods.

David suddenly let out a roaring fart, turned over and resumed snoring, barely aware that anyone was in the room. Sometimes Tammy couldn't believe the atrocious smells her husband produced when farting. In need of a gas mask, she exited, leaving fatty to his funk.

The familiar smell of fried chicken woke David from the long calorie-induced nap just in time for dinner. He woke up like an angry hungry bear, sniffing the air for food and following the scent like a predator. After shitting out the big breakfast from the morning, the insatiable professor rushed down the stairs as fast as an overweight person with high blood pressure could. Dude was so excited that he had to run back and put on some pants, completely forgetting he was butt-naked—but not before his two beautiful children saw his flabby, jiggly nakedness in all its glory.

His son, nicknamed DD, laughed, while daughter, Tamika, blushed, embarrassed by her father's big breasts and ugly fat body. David came back down, dressed in a tee-shirt and red boxer shorts. Tammy looked at her husband with jaundiced eyes, but she knew better than to say anything. At least the shorts didn't have shit stains in them, which was a minor miracle with him.

As he sat for dinner, his eyes lit up with lustful delight at the feast on the kitchen table. It was a masterpiece, with fried chicken,

mashed potatoes, green beans and cornbread, *smellin good enough ta make ya slap God!* After saying the blessing fast as hell, David attacked the dinner with a slow but deliberate fury. He piled four pieces of chicken on his plate, followed by the potatoes, which he mixed with the green beans. Then he ate and ate and ate. The man didn't stop eating until he consumed a whole chicken by himself, but at least ate only two helpings of the side dishes, which would be the equivalent of six portions for a normal human being.

For dessert, Tammy had bought a family favorite, an apple pie from Publix. Half of it went to fatso, while she and the kids divided the rest. After dinner, David shuffled over to the couch to rest his weary, overworked heart. After having consumed over ten thousand calories that day it was a wonder that it was beating at all. Seeing that it was only 6:30—almost five hours before the meeting with Precious—a nap was in order, so he stretched out on the recliner. Within minutes, he was sleeping like a hibernating bear.

****

By the time Precious arrived home, it was a little after eight o'clock, which meant that in three hours, David would be pulling into the garage. She had gone over the plan a thousand times in her head, but she was still sure something would go wrong. Getting away with murder once was luck—doing it twice was pushing the envelope. The cops were corrupt and dumb, but even the dumbest squirrel finds a nut every once in a while. She didn't want them knocking on her door, looking for that nut.

If she was truly going to get away with murder, one person stood in the way, and that person would arrive in a few hours. If she got rid of him, everything would be cool, though if the fat faggot left her house alive, then her future remained in someone else's' hands.

After getting undressed, she sat naked on the couch, enjoying the air conditioner and playing with her balls. Rolling a blunt bigger than a cigar, the first tokes caused her to cough violently, which means it was some good-ass weed. Being buzzed gave the tranny tremendous confidence that was required in such times. Sitting there, high as fuck, mindlessly watching TV, a wonderful idea suddenly popped into her head. It was so utterly fantastic—while at the same time simple—that all she could do was smile and laugh out loud.

The new addition to the plan would make both murders foolproof: before David died of asphyxiation in the garage, he was going to write a letter to the police. The message would convey his deepest sympathies to the family of Deshawnte for having brutally-murdered their innocent loved one. Yes, the low-down bitch was going to make fatty take the fall for her murder! *How utterly brilliant!* the big dick bitch thought, smiling to herself.

But would the new wrinkle really work, or would it complicate the plan already in place? Would the cops believe the letter, or would they think it was a ruse to throw them off the scent of the real murderer? After weighing the pros and cons, Precious decided against the letter, favoring the original plan. Why complicate matters with more details, because the simpler the plot, the less chance of mistakes being made. The fewer the odds of something going wrong meant she could avoid the death penalty.

After David pulled into her garage, he couldn't leave there alive. That way, there would be no evidence of the victim being in the house. After disposing of Deshawntes' body, the house had to be thoroughly cleaned to eliminate any evidence of the child's presence. She didn't want to go through the ordeal of scrubbing blood stains again—the paranoid tranny still worried that some of Deshawnte's DNA was still lurking around the house, waiting to be discovered by a forensics team. No matter how well a murder scene was scoured and cleaned, forensic teams often still found evidence, no matter how miniscule, the way it happened on TV crime shows.

Simplicity, in this case, would bring her freedom. After that hiccup in her life was relieved, she could have peace of mind again. No more waiting in fear of being caught because that fag happened to be in the park that fucking night! The chubby fool was going to rue the day he blackmailed a bitch like her.

Precious sat back on the couch, massaging her massive dick until it was harder than a brick. For a minute, she thought about giving the fag some cock before murdering him, but it was an insane thought, nothing more. The idea of fucking him was arousing, but too many things could go wrong. *Keep it simple*, she thought to herself while jerking off, *keep it simple*. Precious stroked her gigantic cock until it exploded, spewing cum all over the carpet. She screamed, as thick cum oozed uncontrollably out her dick. Feeling relaxed, the bitch lay back on the sofa, patiently waiting on her prey to attend his demise.

David couldn't wait to get over to Precious' house. Waking up from his nap on the tattered but comfortable lazy boy recliner, he headed straight for the porcelain throne to shit out the heavy dinner. He didn't want Precious' dick getting shitty while she plowed his loose fat booty with her telephone pole of a cock.

After wiping a few times, he jumped in the shower to scrub away any remaining feces the toilet tissue failed to absorb. He washed every inch of his fat, black, flabby body, making sure to scrub the anus real good. Not only did his anus have to be clean, but it had to smell good too. There was no better feeling than having his asshole licked before getting fucked. Within hours, that bitch was going to lick and fuck the daylights out of him.

Exiting from the shower, he flossed and brushed his pearly whites. The professor was a stickler when it came to hygiene, and he knew Precious was too. Nothing could fuck up a romantic evening more than having a lover who didn't take hygiene seriously. Who the hell wanted to smell someone else's' funk? Next to follow, was lotion, with a generous splash of Hugo Boss cologne all over the chest and neck area. Looking for something comfortable to wear, fatso chose a blue jogging suit because it had an elastic waist band that seemed to stretch forever. Like many heavy-set men, David hated belts, with their restrictions, and preferred stretch pants so his belly could sag and move freely.

After checking himself out in the mirror, the image staring back had a look of lust and greed on its face along with a devilish smile. Before leaving, the adulterous husband told his unfaithful wife that he was going over to Derrick's house for a few beers. Although he sensed she knew it was a lie, she said nothing to that effect. Instead, they kissed like always and said their goodbyes.

David hated lying to his wife, but it was better than the alternative. Telling her he was going to go get fucked by a big-dick transsexual probably wouldn't have gone over well with the little lady. After promising not to be too late, he was ecstatic as he backed out of the driveway. The clock radio read 10:10, which meant that in less than an hour, a fat, ten-inch dick would be probing his eager asshole, unmercifully.

Tammy was watching TV in the den, drinking a glass of wine and eating Fig Newtons when David came in to say goodbye. She had known for over two years now that he was on the down-low. Derrick's wife, Joanne, had caught them in the basement, fucking up

a storm. She said her husband had David on the pool table, legs spread-eagled, humping him ferociously, like a wild animal. It was so intense that they didn't notice her watching from the stairs.

Joanne also conveyed to Tammy how passionate and powerful their fuck session was, while lamenting the lack of it when he made love to her. When Tammy found out about the man-affair, she was shocked, but what made it even more egregious was that this incident happened over a year before Joanne mentioned it. That meant her husband had been on the down-low for almost four years or longer.

Hell, who was she kidding? The man was obviously bisexual. It hadn't started recently, like some midlife crisis. Divorce was the first thing that popped into her mind after finding out, but after she calmed down and talked to Joanne, she decided against it. She had already invested ten years in the marriage, and she wasn't ready to throw it away. Reflecting on two beautiful kids and a nice 3,000 square-foot house, she liked the lifestyle that marriage to a college professor afforded her. It wasn't exactly the lifestyle of the rich and famous, but it was better than most.

That's why she never confronted David about his alternative lifestyle, because she believed that nothing she said or did could change things. Her Master's Degree in social work was rewarding and paid well, but two incomes were much better than one. She loved working with troubled youths at the Juvenile Justice Center in Decatur, but with an annual salary of a little over $53,000, it wasn't enough to leave her man over. The children would have suffered without their father, so she didn't want to put them through the unnecessary heartache.

Since Joanne's discovery, their friendship blossomed into a romance. It was her first lesbian experience, and she was grateful to have a thoughtful and gentle lover like Jo. Her dildo wasn't as good as the real thing, but she liked how she and Joanne cuddled for hours afterwards. Feeling groggy, from drinking too much, Tammy finished off the bottle of cheap Robert Mondavi red wine and went to bed. Before going to sleep, she noticed it was past 1 a.m., and David still hadn't come home, which probably meant Derrick must have been fucking the shit out of him.

****

As 11 p.m. drew nigh, Precious considered a better plan, and this time it was close to foolproof, or at least better than the one previously devised. She could get rid of David's' body by burning him in the big steel tub in the backyard. Without a body, it would be much more difficult to prove a murder had taken place at all. The tub was huge, and it had been used by the previous homeowner for burning trash. Still naked except for some flip flops, she ran outside to inspect the makeshift tomb.

Despite living in the house for over a year, she had hardly noticed the tub and considered the large black rusty bin as an eyesore. It was filled with debris and water that she hurriedly emptied. She turned it upside down to make sure there were no holes on the bottom. Except for the rust, the tub was in fine shape—definitely capable for what she had in mind, which was to burn the body until it had the consistency of ashes.

After emptying the debris, the next step was to fill it with the can of gasoline sitting in the garage. Then the clever deceitful whore took a dozen magazine and newspapers and threw them in as well. Feeling satisfied, she went back in the house and noticed it was five minutes before eleven. After a quick hand washing and donning a pair of shorts and tee-shirt and gloves, she fixed herself a drink and sat back on the sofa with the .38 revolver on the coffee table. When David arrived, 15 minutes later, she was ready for his fat ass.

The tranny hid the pistol in her waist, covered by the tee-shirt, and opened the garage door to wave David toward the garage. After the door was closed and before he had a chance to get out of the blue Volvo, she pointed the gun at him, scaring the shit out of the professor.

"Get the fuck outta the car you, fat muthafucka!" Precious snarled, with venom oozing from every syllable. David was so startled he just sat there with his hands up, too afraid to talk.

"But, but—but what did I do?" he managed to protest.

"Bitch! I said get out!"

She opened the door and pulled him out by the collar. Quickly, she handcuffed his hands and threw him in the backseat. Once he was in the rear, she cuffed his feet and instructed him to lie on his ample stomach and *shut the fuck up!*

"Why you doing this to me, Precious? I thought we had something special," he begged the heartless tranny, but Precious said nothing. She just turned on the ignition and slammed the door.

"Naw, fool—we never had a goddamn thing goin. You was just taking ma fuckin money. But that won't happen again," she told him through the driver's side window. That shit gonna stop tonight."

David was blubbering and begging for his life by appealing to her humanity, but it was hopeless. Finally, the professor realized in that dark moment how much he had underestimated her vindictiveness. She had been playing him all along, even though she made him think he was playing her. That evil, no-good big-dick bitch! *His arrogance and lust had led to this outcome!*

"Let me out you, fuckin bitch! Let me out!" David yelled at the top of his fluid-filled lungs. "Please! I won't blackmail you again! Just let me go home," he cried.

"Nigga please! You was gonna rat me out eventually, tell the truth. As soon as you didn't get yo way or you were tired of me, my ass was toast. I refuse to live with that over my fuckin head for the rest of my life. See nigga—if you hadn't been so nosey and greedy, ya wouldn't be in this situation. Well, at least ya got a full tank of gas," she joked.

"Oh God, Precious! If you let me go, I'll give you all the money in my checking account! It's over $10,000. I'll do anything you want! Please, please, please!" he sobbed uncontrollably.

"Muthafucka—it's too late for that now."

She remembered to grab his cell phone and wallet, along with all other ID. Then she rolled up the window and left David crying and blubbering like a child.

"Don't go! Please don't go! I love you," he pleaded, but tranny wasn't moved by the desperate begging. Instead she cut off the lights and exited the garage through the kitchen door to wait for death to come.

While sitting at the kitchen table, she took the battery out of his cell phone, in case anyone tried to call. That way, no one would be able to trace calls back to her house. She already knew there would be records of the victim calling, but with so many cell phones in Decatur, the calls would be difficult to trace.

She had two main phones—the typical landline, and a mobile phone. While she hardly talked on the landline, the other phone was for friends and legitimate business transactions, like paying bills. Since taking her website down, she didn't want tricks calling either of those numbers. So she purchased a burner phone for dick-sucking fags calls.

There was no contract for the burner phone, which would be hard to trace because the Subscriber Identity Module, or SIM card, can be purchased off the store shelf for cash. The beauty of that meant the owner didn't have to sign a contract or get a credit check. The SIM was a memory card that held the personal information of the account holder, such as phone number, texts and other data. Since she was in an illegal business, it made sense to be very cautious and change things up every other week. That way if her burner phone was confiscated by the police, it would only have data on it for one week at most.

She hoped she had taken enough precautions to conceal her identity, or at least to throw the authorities off her scent once the fat ass in the garage was reported missing. She fixed a vodka orange juice and went to check on David, who had already been in the closed garage for over 30 minutes. After she opened the car door and poked him, she could tell he was drowsy, but still alive, so to speed up the process, she took a garden hose, cut it in two, put one end in the exhaust pipe and inserted the other end through a crack in the car window. Then she sealed the window with duct tape.

Delirious, David thought he imagined somebody had been poking and prodding him, but was too sleepy to respond. How could this bitch do this to him? How would Tammy and the kids survive without a husband and father around? Who would give Tamika away at her wedding if he was dead? Would his death cause her to drop out of school and get pregnant like most fatherless black girls? And who would teach DD how to be a responsible man and not some ignorant thug if there was no role model in the house?

David wouldn't have been in that dangerous predicament if not for greed and an insatiable desire for large black cocks. He couldn't believe the bitch had him shackled like a fucking slave, and there was not a damn he could do about it but pray. A lot of good that did, because after praying fervently, nothing happened—no miracles or angels descending from heaven, like in the Bible stories.

The dying professor wondered who Tammy would remarry and whether or not the children would remember him as a loving father as they got older. Would they love their step-daddy more, once the shock of losing their father subsided. As things became bleaker, he struggled to keep the eyelids open.

In his final dying moment, he wondered what Derrick was doing just then. Was he at home, or was he in the park, fucking that young

redbone boy in the same dugout where they'd had rendezvous so many times over the years. David felt no shame thinking about his lover before closing the eyes at last. He imagined Derrick on top of him, slamming that long dick into his eager fat ass. Remembering the good times, a smile came to the condemned man's face, and then he took his last breath.

After another hour and two additional vodka and orange juices, Precious went out to check on the victim and was pleased with the results. David lay there motionless, dead as dead could be. She stood over the body with a smug smile, reveling at her awesome wicked intelligence. She turned off the car engine and dragged the heavy body by his feet from the car to the backyard, going through the kitchen and out the back door.

His heavy bald head made a distinctive bumping sound while being dragged through the house. So far so good—the easy part had been done. The hardest part would be putting this fatso inside the tub and barbequing him like a side of beef. Once outside, she dropped David and dragged the tub away from the house. The last thing she wanted to do was set the house on fire while getting rid of a dead body. Satisfied with the tub's new location, she dragged her prey over and dumped him inside, like a piece of trash.

The tub was only five feet in diameter, so she had to sit the corpse up, like he was in a bathtub, with his head bent down into his lap. Glancing around nervously, the tranny waited for a few minutes before lighting the gasoline soaked newspaper around the body. She walked around the perimeter of yard twice to see if anybody else was out so early Wednesday morning.

The neighborhood was quiet as usual, which was a major advantage when buying a house in an older community. When the coast was clear, she lit a piece of paper, and just as she was about to throw it on the victim, something scared the shit out of her. It scared the bitch so bad that she dropped the lighter and paper. David was still alive! but just barely! Suddenly, the fat fag let out a belch, followed by a fart, and he started breathing again. Just as quickly, he nodded off, still fucked-up by the carbon monoxide.

Precious could hear him taking quick shallow breaths, so without wasting any time, she lit the paper and threw it into the tub. The flames engulfed his lower body and quickly spread until he was a ball of flames. Though not completely dead, he had inhaled too much poison to fight. He let out a haunting scream as the flames melted his

ebony skin away. *Now, he definitely knew what Hell felt like!* He saw it as a preview of eternity.

Precious watched in horror as David burned alive, realizing that animal-like scream would haunt her for life. She sat on the back step, watching the fire until daylight, making sure it kept burning. By morning, David's fat body had been reduced to nothing but a skeleton. Everything else, including his clothes and the wood was gone, leaving only the burned bones and handcuffs.

After examining his still-intact skull, Precious realized she had underestimated how hot a fire had to be to burn a body. She retrieved a box of Hefty trash bags from the kitchen and meticulously put the bones and fragments into them. After putting everything, save the handcuffs, into three separate bags, the tired tranny went out to the garage to crush the bones with a hammer. To her surprise it was relatively easy to crush human bones through the plastic bags.

The fingers and hands, along with the feet, were the easiest to break. The skull was the hardest. To make sure no dental records could be used identify the body; she broke up the cranium, crushed the bones and put in separate bags. After bone breaking for a couple of hours, she scooped out the rest of the ashes in the tub with a spade and deposited the burned evidence into the trash bag.

With all the incriminating debris placed in ten separate Hefty bags, the next step was to get rid of it as soon as possible. Placing them on the curb for the garbage men was out of the question, naturally. After taking a shower to wash the soot and ashes off her ebony skin, the tired tranny threw the bags in the trunk of her BMW. The best way to get rid of David was to dump the smashed bones around town at various places. That way, he would just disappear, like dust in the wind.

As she backed out of the garage, she decided to dump the crushed bones in one of the numerous ghettos in Atlanta. She knew the perfect spot: her old stomping ground in the northwest part of the city, off Johnson Road. She smiled, remembering the cute little boys she used to take over there and fuck in the driveway of one of numerous abandoned houses. There was already a lot of illegal dumping going on, so emptying trash bags wouldn't even be noticed.

David's bones would be gone forever, lost in a sea of tires, wrecked cars, old appliances and other assorted garbage, dumped by the good citizens of Atlanta. It was a beautiful Wednesday morning, and traffic was heavy going down I-20 West.

She made the drive in silence, not bothering to turn on the radio—scared it might distract from the task at hand. And instead of speeding as usual, the sleek German car never went above 65 mph. The last thing the murderer needed was to get pulled over by the cops, with a dead body in the trunk. Exiting at Hamilton Holmes Drive, she drove south to her predetermined destination, oblivious to anything except getting rid of David.

When she turned onto Johnson Road, she made a left on a small side street named Lois Lane Drive, where big piles of garbage were everywhere. Looking around to see if anyone was watching, she popped the trunk and started dumping the contents out of the bags. She was satisfied that the bones were smashed sufficiently, and to the untrained eye, no one would be able to tell they were of human origin. After throwing the remains amidst the other junk, the bags were suddenly empty. Just like that, David was gone forever.

It was hard to believe that, less than 24 hours earlier, he was alive, and now the empty bags symbolized his departure from the cruel world. As a crack-head approached, Precious dropped the bags, got back in the car and drove away before the begging nigga could ask for money.

Soon, the wicked genius was back on the highway, headed home and trying to think of the best way to get rid of the victim's car. She turned the radio on V-103 to relax and jammed all the way home. The hard part was done. His body would never be found because it had been burned, bones smashed to smithereens, and scattered around a fucking dumping site. If only the car would be so easy to make disappear!

It was only 9 a.m. when she made it home, which meant the garbage men hadn't yet come. Adrenaline still pumping, she grabbed the tub and set it on the curb to be picked up. After it was there, she realized the container was too big for the sanitation trucks. If the big-dick tranny had read the pamphlet sent out by the DeKalb County Sanitation Department, she would have known they picked up big, bulky items by appointment only. Damn! Just what she needed—more fucking problems!

She would have to take the tub and dump or cut it up somehow. Since there were no tools in the house she could use to destroy it, she'd have to haul it away. By then, the tranny was exhausted, so she went inside to relax and collect her thoughts. After rolling a blunt, she searched online for scrap metal recyclers in DeKalb or Fulton

counties. Dozens of companies popped up on the screen, but the closest was the Allied Recycling Center on Lithonia Industrial Boulevard, about five miles away.

When she called the place to see if they'd take the tub, the receptionist assured her that the company recycled "any kind of metal." It was good news to the stressed tranny, who immediately hung up the phone without as much as a thank you. Even though fatigue was starting to envelope her body, she knew the tub had to go right away.

She wondered if taking it to a recycling center was the best solution—a recycling center—where they would surely ask for ID and shit? While fixing a bologna and cheese sandwich, slathered with mayonnaise, she decided to take the tub to some park and just leave it where it was. The cold-blooded murderer thought about dumping it on Johnson Road, but that was too far to drive with the tub tied down in the trunk.

There was no way she would get on the highway with a damn tub sticking out of the trunk, especially the way fools drove in Georgia. No, the best way was the simplest way. After washing down the sandwich with a Diet Coke, she stuffed the tub in the trunk of the BMW and tied it down with three bungees. She drove south on Wesley Chapel, made a right on River Road, where Gresham Park was located.

Gresham was a nice, large wooded, secluded park. Other than an old gray-headed black woman walking a feisty brown Chihuahua, the park was empty. Outside the car, Precious untied the bungee cords and dragged the tub over by the big garbage bin. She cursed under her breath, because the bulky tub had scratched the back bumper as she pulled it to the ground.

She sighed with relief when she got back to the car, amazed at how well things were going. With the exception of the four-inch scratch on the beautiful Beemer, her plan was moving forward, but there was still much work to be done.

While driving home, the devious murderer struggled to figure out the best way to get rid of David's' Volvo without it ever being discovered. The best options included taking the vehicle somewhere and burning it, or sinking it in a pond or lake. Burning the car meant someone would find out, and it would eventually be traced back to its owner. As for sinking it underwater—that was out of the question

for two good reasons: one, she couldn't swim; and two, there would be a problem if it didn't sink far enough in shallow water.

She had to act quickly, because the clock was ticking. There was no way that car could be in her garage another day. Selling it was out of the question, but parking it somewhere wasn't. Again, the simplest solution was always best. Why not park the vehicle near a junkyard entrance where some greedy operator would confiscate it, possibly off-the-books? That way, it wouldn't be traced back to Fat Ass.

She knew the perfect place: a junkyard off Constitution Road. It was far enough out, in an industrial area, but it was close enough to MARTA so that she would be able to catch the bus back home. It was a plan, but she wasn't exactly thrilled about it—too many loose ends. It would work only if the business owner was crooked enough to keep the car for himself and strip it for parts. If he was an honest bastard, then the car would be traced back to David. She dismissed the plan, because she couldn't involve the actions or will of anyone else. Testimony by witnesses or accomplices meant the death penalty.

As she pulled into her subdivision, everything seemed normal. Her neighbors would have never suspected that one of their own had suffocated and barbequed a man the night before! Since she been here a little over a year, only Rosa Lee and Monique had been neighborly, which was okay, because nosey neighbors were bad for business. Many of her neighbors were senior citizens, which limited interaction as well.

Sitting in the garage, she listened to the news in the Volvo, mesmerized by the happenings of the last 12 hours. After 15 minutes of deliberation, the tranny decided a blunt between the lips would induce better thinking, so she went to the bedroom to get high as she contemplated her next move. But the marijuana didn't seem to help, because no scheme came to mind that would get rid of the vehicle without it being discovered. Wherever the car was ditched, it had to be done in complete secrecy, because for potential witnesses, a tranny would be easy to remember.

She realized that whatever she would do would have to wait, again, for the cover of darkness. She was sure David hadn't been reported missing yet, but road violation, such as speeding or an accident, would bring the scheme to a screeching halt. If the cops stopped her for any reason, she would have to decide immediately how she wanted to die—by lethal injection or getting shot for

resisting arrest! All had to wait, because she was tired as hell. Within a few minutes of closing her eyes, the evil tranny slept like baby.

After ten hours of sleep, Precious woke refreshed and eager to get going. Noting it was dark outside, she was surprised to have slept so long, but glad for the much-needed rest. Still groggy, she went to take a piss, careful not to misfire and get urine all over the floor—a pet peeve of hers. There was nothing nastier than stepping in piss, even if it was her own.

While brushing her teeth, she let out a long, stinky fart that brought a smile to an otherwise worried face. After taking care of personal hygiene, her thoughts moved to the car. Cleaning the car was an important factor in getting away with the crime and could not be underestimated. Donning a pair of gloves and a towel, she carefully wiped the Volvo down, both the inside and outside. Then she retrieved all his paperwork and other identifying items from the vehicle, so when they eventually found the car, it would take a few days to match it to the owner.

Watching countless hours of the Investigative Discovery channel came in handy for the burgeoning serial killer. The two-time murderer didn't think of herself as a serial killer, which was the dominion of sexually perverted white men, not black people. She had only killed once… well twice, really, but the first was an accident, so it didn't really count.

When the car was clean and ready to go, Precious began to panic. What if the cops stopped her in the car? And how would she explain driving a dead man's car? The plan to ditch the car in downtown Atlanta involved too much driving, which increased the risk of getting caught. So instead of driving all over creation, she decided to park the car at Scores, a sports bar right around the corner, on Wesley Chapel Road. That way, she could walk back home instead of having to take MARTA or a cab. Simplest was best.

Smoking on a blunt to calm the nerves, Precious gave the car a quick inspection before entering. While backing out of the garage, something seemed like it was missing, but the nervous bitch couldn't figure out what it was. Yet as soon as she drove off, it dawned on the sexy murderer that she forgot her purse. Instead of pulling back in the garage, the tranny ran back into the house, leaving the car in the driveway since no one was outside. Purse in tow, she headed toward Wesley Chapel Road.

The sports bar was in a shopping plaza anchored by a Kroger's grocery and other assorted shops, which made it easy to park the car, unnoticed, and walk away. Since it was only a little after 9 p.m., the huge parking lot was crowded with shoppers. She parked nearer to the grocery than the bar—not that it mattered, since they shared the lot. She parked between a black Dodge Charger and a silver Ford Explorer and hurried from the vehicle. She left the keys in the ignition and driver's side window down before she walked away while peeling off the plastic gloves.

She discarded the gloves in the vast parking lot and hiked the four miles back to her subdivision on that beautiful Georgia night. The temperature was 75 degrees—wonderful weather for an evening stroll. While walking, a few guys hollered at her, some admiringly, and some in disgust when they saw she was a transsexual. Dressed in a pair of simple jean shorts, a white blouse and sneakers, she knew the niggas wanted some of her. The same niggas pretending not to like her in public today would be the muthafuckas who will be sucking her dick tomorrow.

A man in a red pickup truck stopped to offer her a ride as she turned down Snapfinger Woods Drive, but she declined. The driver was her perfect type, too: middle-aged, wedding ring and desperate for big black dick. Even though it was tempting to get in the truck, the horny bastard could have been a potential witness against her if she were ever caught. The old dude had no way of knowing the tranny he was begging to get in the vehicle was a murdering sociopath. Like most horny muthafuckas, his thinking was dictated by his dick, not his brain.

After getting repeated nays from Precious, the old dude scribbled his number on a piece of paper and begged her to take it, which she did. That seemed to make him happy, and when she promised to call, the lusty senior citizen waved and drove off, smiling. The walk took 45 minutes, so the first thing she did upon entering the crib was undress to free and cool her hot and sweaty testicles. After that, the bitch fixed a quadruple shot of peach Ciroc vodka in a big Mason jar.

She lay on her bed butt-naked, watching TV and getting high until she began to nod. With David out of the way, sleep came easier for the ruthless tranny. The thorn in her side had been reduced to ashes. Life was indeed good again!

****

It had been 24-hours since David was missing, and Tammy was beside herself with fear. At first, she thought he probably drank too much and crashed on Derrick's couch, but after talking to Joanne Wednesday morning, she found out he never came over in the first place. Her mind immediately started imagining that something horrible had happened. Her calls to his office later in the day revealed he hadn't shown up to teach any of his classes, which was unusual.

Tammy talked to his colleagues, but no one knew anything. She also realized that either he or someone else turned off his cell, which further added to the stress. She hardly slept all night, calling her husband's phone repeatedly, praying for someone to answer.

She went to make a missing persons' report with the police the next morning, after dropping the kids off at school The good-natured white cop who took the report assured her it was probably nothing and that over 90% of missing persons were found alive and well within a few days, but his words did little to comfort the grieving wife. After leaving the police station, she called her job told them the situation and went home to wait on David.

While sitting on the couch with a bottle of red wine for comfort, Tammy couldn't control the terrible thoughts running through her head. What if Derrick and David had a lover's quarrel and he killed her husband in a fit of jealous rage? That would mean Joanne was covering up the crime for her undercover faggot husband!

Or maybe David found another woman or man and had decided to leave her and the kids? Her mind returned to dark thoughts of murder, but who would kill a middle-aged college professor? It wasn't like he had any enemies or was a bad person. As far as she knew, he didn't hang around any thugs or lowlifes. He was a good person, even if he liked to get fucked in the ass on occasion. By the time she finished the bottle of wine, the kids were just getting off the school bus.

She braced herself for their questions about Daddy's absence. Like any good mother, she had a lie ready. Why tell a hurtful truth when a comforting lie would suffice? She acted preemptively, telling them even before they asked that their father was visiting relatives and would be back in a couple of days. The kids bought the story hook, line and sinker—partly because they didn't want to think anything bad had happened, and because they knew she wouldn't lie

to them. After fixing the kids a snack she went to bed and cried herself to sleep, thinking David would probably never lie beside her again.

Chapter 13
Precious' Prayers are Answered

Jamaal couldn't believe such good luck while walking around the parking lot of Kroger's. As usual, the ex-con meandered between vehicles to see if anyone had left their doors unlocked or windows down. That stroke of luck was much more than even the most optimistic muthafucka could have hoped for! There, before him, was a blue Volvo—not only with a window down, but the keys still in the ignition! After checking around to see if anyone was watching, he reached in, took the keys out and slipped them into his pocket.

Then the thieving nigga strolled inside the store to do some grocery shopping for grandma. While inside, he tried to figure out which one of the customers was stupid enough to leave their keys in the ignition. He thought it was a bitch's car, because in his feeble mind, "real" niggas don't drive faggot-ass Volvo's. No matter who owned it, they were going to be highly-disappointed when they come outside and see an empty space where they previously parked their vehicle.

The thief went up and down the aisles until every item on the grocery list was checked off. While the cute, chocolate-skinned cashier named Rasheedah rung him up, Jamaal was having second thoughts. It seemed too good to be true—like it had to be a setup or something. He remembered the TV show, *Bait Car*, where the muthafuckin crooked-ass cops put cars in the hood with the keys in them to entice young niggas to steal them.

He cautiously approached the Volvo, looking around to see if any undercover pigs were nearby. As an ex-con, he was adept at spotting the police, even if they tried to disguise themselves to look like regular brothas. Jamaal pretended to be on a cell phone call while slowly approaching the car. The nearer he got, though, the memories of jail doors clanging shut almost made him walk away from the new-found opportunity. But as a career criminal, the prospect was too good to pass up. After a final look around, he opened the door, slid in and started the engine.

So far so good! No police had swooped down on him, and whoever left the car hadn't come out, running and screaming. Jamaal pulled out fast as hell, almost hitting a pregnant woman in the process, and made a right on Wesley Chapel, and then a right on

Snapfinger Woods Drive, before turning left into Walden Springs subdivision. Even though his grandma stayed on the same street as Precious, they had never met.

Jamaal had seen her fine ass a couple of times when he came over to do yardwork for his cheap-ass grandparents, but the fool had no way of knowing it was the tranny who left the car for some sucker to steal. Driving past Precious' house, he wondered if anybody was fucking her or not. He secretly wanted to, but he had a woman and hadn't been with a nigga since getting got out of jail eight months earlier.

Not that he was a fag, but sometimes a nigga needed some booty-hole or dick as a change of pace from the monotonous pussy. Jamaal parked at the end of the long street in a cul-de-sac, about a quarter of a mile from the murderer's house. His grandparents were in their 70s and couldn't see or hear well, so he told them he was borrowing a friend's car. After putting the few grocery items away, he begged Granny for $50, but the tight old bitch only gave him a twenty-dollar bill. After mumbling a few curse words, he insincerely thanked her and said goodbye, mad as hell but grateful for not having to spend the night, now that he had a new car.

Before driving off, he checked the car for any papers, but the only thing found was a cell phone in the glove compartment. To him, it seemed odd that the car was devoid of any insurance papers or anything else people usually had in their cars when driving. Then it dawned on him why the windows were down and the keys were in it—somebody *wanted* it stolen! Suspicious, he checked the trunk to make sure no one, dead or alive, was back there.

Satisfied that everything was okay, he hightailed it back to Bankhead Courts in Atlanta. When he got home, the thief parked the car and told his girlfriend, Sophia, what happened. She went outside to inspect the vehicle and immediately started scheming on how to sell it. Jamaal didn't tell her about the phone for two reasons: because he was afraid she'd want to use it; and the police might have been able to trace it. As he went bed that night, feeling good from weed and liquor, Jamaal prayed to God that taking the car wouldn't get him in trouble. God did not answer his prayer, but he certainly answered that of Precious.

Jamaal Abraham Russell was born 30 years earlier to Avery and Brenda, the youngest of three boys. When he was five years old, his parents died in a car crash. From then on, the kids were raised by his

visions of fucking the whole family. Their mom, Juanita, was dark-skinned and on the chubby side, but she has a big bodonkadonk and a cute face. Latrice, the 13-year-old, was just starting to grow some titties and ass. The chubby teen was definitely ready to get fucked, if she hadn't been already.

He figured both those hos would be sucking on his cock in a few months, just like Porsha was. Though she hated it now, he knew the little bitch would be begging for his black snake in a few weeks. Her fear of him would be replaced by a lust that only a big dick can tame. Too bad Jamaal never got a chance to test that theory, because they were soon interrupted.

When the police busted down the door of Apt. 2208, Verbena Street. they were shocked to discover a little girl, sucking a big bloody dick. Jamaal got up to run, but a pissed-off Atlanta cop tackled him, with extreme prejudice. Porsha was bawling and screaming, complaining that he hurt her.

While Jamaal kept insisting the sex was consensual, two of the cops took turns slapping him in the face, until he started crying like a little bitch. They covered Porsha's naked body and called an ambulance. She waited inside a police car with another officer until the ambulance came to take her to Grady Hospital. The sight of blood running down Porsha's legs enraged Officer Marsha Burnett—so much that she took her nightstick and cracked the crying and cuffed rapist so hard across the back that it knocked him to his knees. After she landed a right hook to the jaw, the other officers pulled her away for fear she would go too far.

Jamaal lay on the ground, crumpled, like a naked baby, pleading with the police to stop beating him. After a half dozen or so more blows and kicks, they relented. While reading the low-down nigga his rights, they let him put some clothes on, as undercover detectives searched the apartment. Sitting at the kitchen table, nose bleeding and head aching from getting beat like a dog, he realized why the pigs was there.

Two weeks earlier, during the robbery of a liquor store on Martin Luther King Drive, one of his boys shot the owner. This wasn't the only robbery they interrogated him about, because he was suspected in at least three more. Like a good soldier, he kept his mouth shut and tried not to answer anything and asked for a lawyer.

As they walked him to the police car, the crowd outside was the typical black, ignorant ghetto throng. There were shouts of police

brutality and the usual Ebonics, but no one did anything. Jamaal was charged with rape, armed robbery, aggravated assault and auto theft. Jamaal tried looking hard and brave for the crowd, even though the boy was scared shitless of going to an adult jail. When they put him in the back seat, he put his head down and kept it there until they pulled up at Grady. Before being booked down at the jail, they got a sample of his DNA to match it to the sperm in Porsha's vagina, which was a formality.

After the sample was taken, officers took and booked Jamaal in the Atlanta Detention Center on Peachtree Street. He tried to be brave in the holding cell, but his act didn't fool the older niggas. They saw a scared little boy, trying to look and act tough, just like most of them did when they were younger. The holding cell was a 15x15 room that held 20 angry pissed off niggas, talking loud and saying nothing.

Although nobody bothered him, the boy felt lonely and afraid. At 5'4" and weighing 130 pounds, he was easily the smallest nigga in the cell. His diminutive size, along with his young age were a recipe for disaster. With the system crowded as hell, he stayed in the holding cell all night and didn't get processed in until early morning.

Processing an inmate consisted, among other things, of an embarrassing and painful anal probe by some big-ass, pissed-off security guard. The sadistic officer donned a pair of plastic gloves and squeezed lubricant on the gloved hand. Another guard forced the prisoner to bend over like a bitch, while the other painfully inspected the asshole for contraband. After the officer was finished probing with his fingers, the prisoner was then showered and doused with a powdered disinfectant to prevent disease. Then the inmate was given a jumpsuit—orange, in Jamaal's case—and sent to a two-man jail cell, where a roommate was waiting—hopefully not some crazy-ass motherfucker, looking at life behind bars!

Jamaal's cell mate was a 28-year-old black male, a career petty criminal named Darnell Stokes. He was brown-skinned with a medium build of 5' 8" with a sneaky smile and friendly manner. Stokes was sentenced for nine months on a conviction for forging bad checks, but he only had three months left when the guard opened the door and pushed the scared young boy inside.

Lying on the bottom bunk, he greeted the youngster and barely got an audible response in return. After putting his sheets on the bed, the boy climbed onto the top bunk and tried going to sleep. After his

arrest, 24 hours earlier, it felt good to be lying on a mattress instead of the metal benches in the holding cell. As soon as his eyes closed, Jamaal drifted off, but his peace was short-lived, because the noisy-ass breakfast cart came around, waking him up an hour later.

Then it dawned on him that he hadn't eaten since morning yesterday, so was grateful for the interruption. As the trustee slid the breakfast's through the slot in the door, Darnell handed the youngster his tray, and they ate in silence. Their meal consisted of cold scrambled eggs, cold grits and two stale cold sausage patties, along with two pieces of toast and a carton of warm milk. Jamaal was disgusted by the foul, tasteless fare, but Darnell ate like it was a five-star feast.

When breakfast was over the guards entered and got Jamaal to take him to court. All the prisoners who had to go before the judge were lined up outside the holding cell, shackled together by twos. For added security, guards ran a long chain down the middle and shackled all the prisoners to that chain. They marched the accused to the elevator and up to another holding cell, awaiting until the judge convenes the courtroom. When the judge arrived, all the prisoners were seated at the front of the room, and they remained shackled until the judge called them up, one by one.

On this particular day, there were 21 men seated before the judge. Except for the two wetbacks who pretended not to know English, all were black. There weren't any women prisoners that day, which was rare, though it had happened before. Jamaal looked around for Arthur and Rhonda, but didn't see them anywhere in the courtroom. They vowed that the next time he got in trouble, they wouldn't be there to bail him out. To Jamaal's deep disappointment, they kept their word.

Aretha Chiles, the judge, was a slim, dark-skinned, middle-aged black woman with a no-nonsense demeanor and an unusually big nose. Looking at the chained black defendants seated before her, the magistrate didn't try to hide her disappointment at the site of these young black thugs, shackled to one another like slaves.

If they were slaves, then they volunteered for the job, because nobody made them break the law. Deep in the recesses of her heart, the judge felt sad for them, but her compassion and pity would interfere with her sworn-duty to uphold the law. One by one, the shackled black prisoners stood in front of the judge at a podium with an overworked frazzled public defender by their side. As she read off

the charges Jamaal was facing, he tried looking as humble as possible, but the judge was unmoved.

She seemed delighted in telling the frightened tired teen that he faced a maximum of 80 years in prison for the crimes he committed. Jamaal felt his legs weaken as he leaned against the podium for support. While most pleaded guilty, a few, like Jamaal, asserted their innocence and pled the opposite. The boy was scared, but not enough to plead guilty.

A trial date was set for July 19th, which wouldn't have been bad if it wasn't two months away. It wasn't the only bad news for the little rapist, since the DA decided to try him as an adult. The astute, bald, black district attorney, Paul Hollins, also recommended no bond, but the public defender objected, and one was granted. The only problem: bail was set at $500,000. When Jamaal heard the money figure, he nearly fainted again. After signing court paperwork, he sat his little ass down, hardly looking up until it was time to leave. It was finally dawning on the black bastard that this wasn't juvenile anymore. *This was big boy jail!*

By the time July 19th arrived, Jamaal learned that two of the charges—auto theft and armed robbery—were dropped by the DA for lack of evidence, but the aggravated assault and rape charges weren't, so the public defender suggested a bench trial rather than a jury trial. A bench trial is held before the judge, sans jury. After reading the police report, Julie Winthrop, his Caucasian liberal lawyer, whom he had met only once, was horrified by the details. There was no way would she let her animal of a defendant stand before a jury, full of pissed-off women. Hell, even the black jurists would recommend he be thrown under the jail for brutally raping an innocent ten-year-old.

A bench trial was best, preferably with a male judge, though even a female judge was better than a jury. Judges were more jaded and heard lots of rape trials before, so another one—even one as heinous as Jamaal's, wouldn't rattle a female judge as much as it would civilians. The trick was to make this piece of scum look as human as possible, which wasn't going to be easy. His hair was in dreads, he looked angry and he had a damn orange jumpsuit on. Not exactly a presumption of innocence, when the client was already locked up and came to trial cuffed-up.

The little thug had no family support or anyone from the community to speak up for him. Julie implored the young fool to

plead guilty so Porsha wouldn't have to take the stand and testify against him. She made the boy realize that the three policemen who saw him sodomizing her were also ready to testify, and that was no way would the judge take his word over those of the victim and the officers. If that weren't bad enough, the DNA evidence matched the semen found in the child's mouth and vagina to one, Jamaal Abraham Russell.

After hearing all the evidence stacked against him, the 18-year-old knew he wasn't getting out anytime soon, but at least he wouldn't have to face Inshallah or Porsha in the courtroom, who were waiting to testify against him. That moment marked the first time he felt ashamed for raping the little girl. Or maybe he was confusing shame with the fear—of being locked away for a long time.

The courtroom was almost empty as Jamaal stood in front of Judge Marvin Lawrence, an African-American with a pleasant smile and deep booming voice. Winthrop was both pleased and disappointed at the sight of Judge Lawrence. She hoped the judge would identify with the young defendant as a black male, growing up in racist America, and take it easy on him. At the same time, she hoped the judge would not show the thug leniency for the horrific act. This animal hadn't shown any mercy to the little girl, and yet he was begging the judge for something he lacked: empathy.

After the judge listened to the testimony from the prosecuting attorney, who begged the judge to throw the book at Jamaal, it was Winthrop's turn. While she tried to match the fervor of her esteemed colleague on the other side, she fell short in both enthusiasm and zeal. To her, this young thug was just another bad "nigger" who should have been aborted so he couldn't contaminate the world with his seed.

Years of representing black scum like him had jaded her once sunny outlook on humanity. With so much evidence against him, including pics of the girl's bloodied and bruised vagina, Winthrop was satisfied that the little black bastard would be going away for a long time.

She was right. Judge Lawrence sentenced the boy to ten years without batting an eye. When Jamaal heard the sentence, he cried imploring the judge to reconsider, but the magistrate was unmoved by the little monster. After looking at the sad pictures of Porsha, Lawrence lost any sympathy he had for the perpetrator.

Winthrop felt a tinge of sorrow for her client as he wept, like a little girl, in her arms. Guard removed him from the courtroom, taking him to the holding cell as another dumb, ignorant nigger took his place beside Winthrop to face judgment from Lawrence.

Jamaal paced the small holding cell, raging at the world and discussing the case with the other losers who would also be sent away. He was amazed that everybody had answers to his case, but none for their own. Those motherfuckers were advising him on how he should have pleaded and how he should have asked for a jury trial. Yet those same jailhouse niggas playing lawyer—who had so much advice for him—they was all going to prison too.

When he got back to his regular jail cell that evening, Darnell was gone, having gotten out a month early due to good behavior and overcrowding. Jamaal liked Darnell and hated to see him go. His new roommate was a 22-year-old 6' 3" muscular thug named Mushawn Simmons, who was in for double-murder.

Jamaal instantly feared Mushawn, whose presence was imposing, and when he learned about his violent charges, he was overtaken by an ominous feeling. As they lay in their bunks talking that night, Jamaal could hear Mushawn playing with himself, which made Jamaal uncomfortable. At least when Darnell jerked off, he was quiet and discreet about it!

"I sho do miss pussy, my nigga. When the last time you had some?" Mushawn asked while fondling the hardening black pole between his legs.

"The day these muthafuckin pigs picked me up," Jamaal answered, not bothering to mention the girl's age.

"How long ago was that?" the alleged murderer wanted to know.

"Damn, man! That's been about three months! Shit, my dick stay hard up in this muthafucka. When the last time you had some pussy?"

"Man, just like you I was fucking my baby mama all day and just had to go get some damn cigarettes. I knew I had a warrant out on me, but I didn't know them mofos had tapped my mamas phone and shit. Anyway, when I came outside my girlfriend's house, them bastards jumped me and beat the fuck outta me. I laid a couple of them muthafuckas, out though—ya feel me, ma nigga?" Mushawn smiled, remembering how he knocked the teeth outta one of them cracker officers.

"So how long you been in here?" Jamaal asked, in order to gage this nigga's horniness.

"Six fuckin months! Ma lawya's delayin the trial as long as possible. That way, witnesses might die or move away—ya know what I mean," he sneered in a James Earl Jones-like voice.

As Mushawn let out a long, stinking fart, he realized he may have said too much. The last thing he needed was a jailhouse snitch, jeopardizing the already-slim chance of a nigga's freedom. He changed the subject.

"Damn them cheap-ass mashed potatoes at dinner! Got a nigga fartin like hell," he joked while Jamaal almost gagged on the odor. "Sorry bout that, ma nigga, but you know how it is."

"Yeah, they got my stomach fucked up too," the teen lied.

"Yo nigga—how old was that girl you was fuckin when them folks picked you up?" Mushawn already knew the answer because he had talked to a couple inmates, and one of the guards was his first cousin.

Jamaal was surprised by the question. Why the fuck would this dude want to know how old the bitch was? Even at his young age, he knew pedophiles weren't the most popular offenders in a prison. Although child rape wasn't as heinous as murder, most inmates saw it as cowardly and weak. While inmates bragged about murdering a nigga, no one bragged about raping a ten-year-old.

"Uhh, I dunno," Jamaal answered quietly, hoping his answer would satisfy the fool's curiosity.

"Ya know what I heard? I heard she was ten years old. I bet that pussy was tight as hell!"

Jamaal rose immediately. "Where you hear that bullshit from?" he scoffed, trying to sound believable.

"From one of the correctional officers who's my cousin. Yo, my nigga—if that's yo thang, then it's cool with me." Mushawn wanted to put the young boy's mind at ease and befriend him, because he could sense that the boy was vulnerable and afraid of him. "Did she have some good pussy?"

Jamaal realized that there were no secrets in that god-forsaken place and confessed.

"Yeah, that young pussy was good and tight—like a vise grip, my nigga! I was the first one to nut in her cute little ass. As long as she live, she ain't never gonna forget me! And that muthafuckin,

cowardly judge gave me ten fuckin years just for gettin some pussy," the boy said, shaking his head like he did little Porsha a favor.

"Damn, I bet it was good," Mushawn commented as he rose from the bottom bunk, butt-naked, to take a piss. His hard, veiny dick was almost 12-inches long and thick as a cucumber. Jamaal was astonished by its size and turned to face the wall to avoid staring at it. Mushawn knew the nigga was trying to dodge the inevitable by turning away. When he first laid eyes on the sexy little chocolate boy, the murderer knew he would soon impale the young'un with 12 inches of Georgia cock.

"Dude, you aint gotta turn around cuz I'm naked and shit. I mean, we both got the same thang, right? Only mine's a little bigger," he teased the youngster. After pissing he wiped his dick off, wanting Jamaal to turn around to watch instead of acting like a scared little bitch.

"Naw, my nigga—it's cool I was just sleepy, that's all," the boy lied, trying to sound drowsy.

Instead of lying back down, Mushawn stood beside the bed, talking to his new cell mate while stroking his cock and staring at Jamaal's butt. The scared teen was lying on his stomach in nothing but a pair of prison-issued boxers and sox. Leaning in, Mushawn began tickling Jamaal, and though the terrified boy fought it, he couldn't help laughing as he pleaded

"Stop! I'm trying to sleep," Jamaal begged to no avail—probably because he sounded like a whiney girl, which only encouraged the big-cock nigga.

"Nigga, stop lying—you ain't sleepy! Don't let me come up there!" he said while poking the boy in the ribs playfully, to gauge his reaction. "I didn't know you was ticklish," he said, while rubbing his hands along Jamaal's smooth dark back. "Ya know what I want don't cha?"

Jamaal turned over on his back and saw the biggest dick in the world staring back at him, attached to a depraved, muscular nigga with lust in his eyes.

The frightened teen's answer was meek, girlie.

"What do you want from me?" he asked, turning away from the huge cock—even though he knew it was obvious to Mushawn what he was trying to avoid.

Mushawn grinned and started rubbing Jamaal's chest as the boy lay back, both knowing Jamaal was helpless to stop what was going

to the touch. Both knew the question was rhetorical, because nothing was going to stop that horny nigga from fucking the boy's sweet virgin ass. Looking up at the rapist through tear-stained eyes, Jamaal just nodded and continued licking his master's sweaty balls. The teen had resigned himself to the reality that he was going to be raped, and there was nothing he could do about it but shut up and take it. He could resist and yell for the CO, but that would only result in getting his ass beat and still getting fucked by the big, ugly ape.

The murderer pulled the boy up, wrapping his sinewy arms around the tiny teen's waist, while Jamaal reluctantly put his scrawny arms on the rapists' broad, muscular shoulders. Mushawn licked his lips while looking into the frightened, but "oh so sexy" eyes of the scared little boy. Then he planted a gentle kiss on his forehead and started massaging Jamaal's erect cock.

Jamaal couldn't believe his dick was on hard during such a traumatic and shocking experience. He didn't like niggas, and he didn't like sucking big, pissy dicks. Yet if that was the case, then why wasn't his dick limp instead of hard? There he was being raped, and it was obvious it turned him on, because a hard cock doesn't lie. As Mushawn kissed his nipples, Jamaal felt like a dirty ho—turned on and ashamed at the same time.

"You like your dick sucked, boy," Mushawn whispered in his ear. Without waiting for an answer, he got on his knees and started slurping on Jamaal's' cock.

To the boy's surprise that nigga sucked dick better than Inshallah ever could. Try as he might, the boy couldn't stop himself from moaning and playing with his erect nipples. Damn! Why did it have to feel so fucking good? Watching the big, masculine nigga sucking on his dick made Jamaal feel things he had never felt before.

"Damn, my nigga, you can sho suck some dick!" the youngster said without thinking. "Yeah, suck that muthafucka! Suck it, ma nigga!"

The boy tried to imagine that it was Porsha and not a fucking man sucking his dick, but he had to admit the nigga had some serious tongue-skills. Neither Porsha nor her sister were anywhere near that damn good. In his first homosexual experience, the youngster was unaware of the extraordinary cock-sucking skills that gay and bisexual men possessed. After only a few minutes of Mushawns' talented tongue, Jamaal felt an explosion rising up in his loins. Soon the teen nutted in Mushawns' willing mouth, and like a pro, the big nigga

was consensual, but the boy's bloody, swollen anus told a different story. The victim was taken to Grady Hospital, where they tested him for AIDS and stitched up his bleeding anus. Mushawn was charged with rape, but with two murder charges against the nigga already, he didn't give a damn, especially since the accuser was a convicted rapist himself.

Jamaal's stayed in the hospital overnight, where they did a rape kit on him and asked embarrassing-ass questions. Unbeknownst to the lad, they were the same nurses that treated Porsha when she came in, bloody and traumatized after being violently raped.

The overnight stay in the hospital was like a vacation, with its soft mattress and fluffy pillows to sleep on, but the next morning, reality set in and he was escorted back to city jail, bloody asshole and all. This time though, instead of being in general population, the boy was put in solitary confinement for protection.

Since word had gotten around that he was a child rapist, the COs knew the small, fresh-face teen would be an easy target for the older stronger convicts. With their innocent looks and air of vulnerability, teenagers were a prized commodity in jail. Hell, sometimes they weren't even safe from the guards, who routinely raped prisoners they took a liking to. After dealing with older, hardened thugs most of the time, the COs knew how to befriend the young prisoner, who they sensed was terrified at being locked up with grown men for the first time.

There usual arrangement worked when a guard who wanted to fuck a young thug worked the situation to make the boy believe he was an ally. The CO could accomplish that easy feat in a number of ways: he could give the boy extra food during meal time, or let him work in the kitchen, or even put money on the inmate's account so he could buy items from the prison store.

Since most prisoners were from single-parent, poverty-ridden homes, an outside person would be surprised how much a measly five dollars and a shoulder to cry on could buy. So a young thug comes in completely heterosexual, but after a few weeks of loneliness, he needs a friend to lean on—be it another inmate or a CO.

Fucking these ignorant illiterate teenage boys was like taking candy from a baby for the savvy correctional officer. That's why, within a few weeks, the youngsters either found themselves on their knees with a fat cock staring them in the face, or getting their own

big cocks serviced by an older man. Of course they'd deny they were gay, chalking their behavior up to doing what they had to do to survive in jail or prison. All too many a man believed that once they get out, they would immediately revert back to 100% heterosexuality. That's what they wanted to believe, but it was easier said than done.

After years, or sometimes only months of looking at the same sex sexually—and having other men looking at them sexually, it was hard to turn the lust off, just like that. By the time they're released they'd seen men make passionate love to each other numerous times, and once back on the street, they find themselves checking out men's' asses, like they used to do women.

The first night in solitary confinement was lonely for Jamaal, but at least it was safer than general population. The teen cried all night, wishing his grandparents would come see about him. Naturally the boy would never tell them he had gotten raped. It was too embarrassing for any man to admit. Jamaal didn't want to be subjected to their judgmental stares and dumb-ass questions.

Lying on the stomach because his asshole hurt so much, the rape victim tried to make sense of what happened and wondered if the sexual assault was somehow his fault. Did he entice the big-dick nigga without knowing it, or was he really just a soft faggot who could be easily raped like a little girl? Finally, he realized what Porsha must have felt like afterwards—confused, ashamed and blaming herself for being the victim of a lustful, depraved monster.

He was also confused about why his penis was on hard during the terrifying ordeal. He tried to resist when Mushawn wrapped those big black lips around his cock, but it was futile. How was he to know that masculine ape was an expert cock sucker? Weary from the stress, he fell asleep, but he had nightmares of being passed around like the neighborhood ho, which explained the awful nightmare that ensued.

Jamaal was running down the hallway butt-naked while being chased by fellow inmates, who were also nude. The whole jail was in chaos. The prisoners rioted because they didn't get fried chicken for dinner. Instead, they got dog food, sent in from the local animal shelter. When the boy made it to one of the guard stations, he saw a fat redbone CO getting gangbanged by about ten niggas. Jamaal ran to one of the bathrooms, but what he saw there was worse, as numerous thugs were unmercifully raping a white guy who cried and begged for them to stop. In one of the stalls, an inmate was fucking a dead corpse while smoking crack and laughing. Unable to take such

madness, Jamaal fled from the latrine, appalled by the animalistic madness around him. All through the hallways and in the open cells, men were fucking everywhere, some voluntarily and others after some painful persuading.

The air was filled with the stench of shitty and bloody asses being ripped apart by malicious, lonely men, whose only concern was satisfying their degenerate sexual appetites. Before contemplating the next move, a vicious punch in the jaw sent Jamaal to the floor in pain. Lying there, he looked up and saw that it was Mushawn, nude and standing over him, grinning, fists balled. For good measure, he kicked Jamaal a couple of times in the ribs before picking him up and throwing over a muscular shoulder, like a sack of potatoes. The youngster was groggy and was hardly aware of being carried on someone's shoulders until Mushawn dropped him on the floor of the wardens' office.

There, seated in the wardens' chair and wearing a judge's robe, was none other than Porsha. Also in the room, sitting next to each other, and naked as jaybirds, were Inshallah, Latrice and Juanita. Mushawn pulled Jamaal up by the throat and slapped him on the ass for good measure. So there Jamaal stood, in front of Porsha, naked and dick on hard, pointing right at her. He waved at his girlfriend's family, but one by one, they walked over and spit in his face as Mushawn laughed outrageously.

"Order in the court! Order in the court!" Judge Porsha demanded. "Jamaal Abraham Russell is charged with raping me and taking my virginity at ten years old. How do you plead, nigga—I mean Mr. Russell?"

"But Porsha, I thought you wanted it!" Jamaal pleaded.

"You nasty muthafucka!" Juanita exploded. "How the hell you thought my little baby wanted a big-ass dick at ten years old? She was a virgin, you ignorant black bastard!"

"But, but, but—I just wanted some pussy, and Inshallah was pregnant! Please, I didn't mean no harm!"

"Nigga—pregnant pussy is the *best* pussy!" was Inshallah's response, complete with the customary hood neck-rolling.

"I love you, Inshallah. If your sister hadn't been coming on to me, I never would have fucked her little hot ass."

"That's a lie, nigga! I was watching TV, and you started tickling me," the judge reminder her rapist. "See—look at your horny ass!

Why your dick on hard? You wanna rape me again and have me bleeding all ova myself again?"

"No, Porsha. I said I was sorry."

Juanita chimed in, "Muthafucka you gonna be sorry alright, real soon," he was assured.

"Before I find you guilty, uh—I mean before I rule on this case, how do you plead, rapist?"

"I'm innocent! Please don't send me to jail! I wanna go home," Jamaal cried as tears ran down his face. "I don't like this place, and want my mommy. I want my mommy!"

Jamaal fell to his knees and crawled behind the desk, kissing Porsha's feet and blubbering like a little girl.

"You don't know what they been trying to do to me in here," he pleaded, crying on her feet. "They been trying to rape me! Please don't let them take my booty! Please don't let them take my booty!"

"Nigga, will you please stop getting snot all over my toes! Eeeww I just got them painted today. Besides, you weren't doing all that crying when you was sticking your dick up in me, was you, muthafucka? Now you ready for your sentence?"

Juanita and Mushawn laughed at Jamaal, while Inshallah felt sorry for her baby daddy. Latrice was indifferent as she texted friends.

"Sooner or later, we gonna make you pregnant," Mushawn reminded the boy while stroking his foot-long, smiling devilishly."

"See, I told you they trying to rape me! Please, please—please let me go back home to granddad and grandma. I promise not to get in anymore trouble and go to school."

"Yeah, fool—that's what they all say. Now you ready for your sentence? But first, get your ass up and get back on the other side of my desk, you blubberin bitch!" Whimpering, Jamaal obeyed as Porsha continued. "Now are you ready for your sentence, or do you got something else you want to say?"

"Do I have a choice in the matter?"

"Obviously not, you arrogant bitch. I was just trying to be nice with yo soon-ta-be-sissy ass, but I won't make that mistake again," the judge snapped. "You are hereby sentenced to get fucked by 100 big-dick niggas. And your punishment starts immediately."

The judge then pounded the gavel and Mushawn handcuffed Jamaal's hands in front of him and bent him over the desk so he is forced to look straight into the judge's eyes. Then the doors are

opened and, standing in line, are 100 black, horny prisoners, all naked with cocks standing at attention. When Jamaal sees this, he starts crying and pleading, but Porsha and her family laughs—even Inshallah is amused and smiling.

Mushawn then motions for the first big-dick thug in line to come in. Jamaal's eyes grow large looking at the guy's swollen, veiny meat, swaying side to side with low hanging testicles coming toward him. Porsha grinned, watching the fear in her rapists' eyes.

"Yeah, muthafucka—we gonna turn yo ass into a sissy today," she yelled, leaning back in her chair to view the show. "This big-dick nigga ready too," she laughed while admiring the prisoner's beautiful cock. "You got anything else smart to say before you get your virginity taken?"

The prisoner stood behind Jamaal's bent-over body, resting his diseased cock in between the boy's sweaty, trembling butt cheeks. Porsha was mesmerized by the fear in Jamaal's' eyes and the magnificent piece of meat that would soon deflower him.

"Please don't turn me into a faggot! I'm sorry for what I did to you," the boy sobbed.

"I bet you is sorry *now*, but you weren't sorry when *I* was begging for you to stop. You weren't *sorry* when my tight pussy was bleeding and you kept ramming your dick in me, like a dog in heat."

"I want you to fuck this little bitch until he starts bleeding," she told the prisoner. "You got that?"

The prisoner grinned and nodded. Jamaal braced for the worst and said a silent prayer to God. The desk was wet with his puddle of whiney tears. The last thing he remembered was the smile on Porsha's face as the thug was about to rape him. But just as the prisoner slammed his cock in, Jamaal awoke in a cold sweat.

The scared little boy lay awake, listening to the sounds of the crowded jail and feeling like a damn girl. After the weird nightmare, it was hard to go back to sleep. Jamaal wondered if he had the strength to endure being locked up for ten years and possibly being some nigga's bitch. One thing was for sure: *if the city jail was this bad, then Georgia State Prison in Reidsville must be a hell-hole!* In that place he'd be housed with lifers, doing time for triple-murders and shit. That was his future, but he was struggling to survive the present.

Solitary confinement was what it sounded like: solitary. Inmates are locked up alone and spent 23 hours in the cell, with one hour for exercise. All the meals were eaten in the cell, so contact with the

general population was kept at minimum, which was by design. Most of those in segregation were there because they didn't get along with other inmates. Some, like Jamaal, were there because they were at risk to get sexually-assaulted and were unable protect themselves from predators.

He liked solitary because it gave his body time to heal, mentally and physically. Three weeks after being put in isolation, the moment he most feared finally arrived; which was his transfer to Georgia State Prison. While his two brothers were in college, he had now graduated to the big house.

Reidsville is a little town about 200 miles southeast of Atlanta in Tattnall County, named after Robert Reid, a former congressman who represented the district from 1819 to 1823. With a population of about 2,500, the prison was by far the biggest employer of the tiny burg, which held approximately 1,550 inmates.

The morning of Jamaal's transfer was bittersweet for him. He had grown to be comfortable at city jail and hated leaving. At the same time, he was excited to embark on a new adventure, even if it was at a notorious prison. So, along with 14 other black male thugs, guards shackled the men from head to toe and led then to the waiting prison bus where, they were cuffed to their seats for added security. When every inmate was seated and secure, the bus rolled out, escorted by two police cars in front and two in the rear.

There were four officers on the bus, in addition to the driver, each armed with a pump shotgun. On the long, boring ride the guards did not allow bathroom breaks for the chained inmates. They forced the prisoners to sit and shut up. As much shit as the inmates talked back in jail, they knew that, on the road, the guards took no shit and wouldn't hesitate to blow one of them away. They all sat in silence as the concrete ribbon of I-75 S took them to their new home.

Most were wondering how they would fit in with the much rougher and violent inmates, which was akin to middle school student wondering how they will fare at the high school. Though they pretended not to worry, the number one thought on their minds was sexual assault and rape. That was the big elephant in the room, especially for the younger smaller prisoners, like Jamaal.

While a few of the nervous inmates gazed at the rolling countryside through the bars on the windows, some tried to get sleep. The nearer the bus got to their destination, though, the more

fidgety and scared the passengers got. Guards told them twice to *shut the fuck up*, just hoping one of the niggas would act ignorant, providing an excuse to use their shotguns.

To Jamaal, the prison looked like a big university or college campus, except for the 20-foot wall enclosing it. As he got off the bus, the teen tried his best to look tough, but at 5'4", that was kind of hard. Guards first led them to the reception center, where other guards made them strip naked and submit to medical checkups. Other guards forced them in the shower for delousing to rid them of lice and other bugs.

Intake guards gave the neophytes two pairs of white jumpsuits, the color signifying that they were newbies, aka freshman. Along with the jumpsuits, guards issued prison flip-flops, soap, deodorant, toothpaste and other toiletries.

From there they led the thugs to a big classroom, where numerous other guards went over the rules of the prison and what they expected from each inmate. Finally, after four hours, they marched the inmates to their assigned cells to begin their new life inside the most violent community in Georgia.

At Georgia State Prison, the new inmates weren't housed with the general population for at least a year. The prison housed the newbies in the transitional center initially, in order to get them acclimated with prison life. The program was started to cut down on the sexual assaults and violence new inmates often endured at the hands of more experienced and prison-savvy inmates in general population. The transitional center wasn't as violent as the rest of the prison, but it wasn't a bed of roses either.

As guards marched the newbies to their cells, the other prisoners—unlike it was portrayed in the movies—the other prisoners hardly paid any attention to them. The inmates in the occupied cells simply stared out, while a few asked where inmates were from and shit like that. Guards told the newbies to ignore any questions and keep walking.

Jamaal was nervous as hell, wondering if he would get a roommate like Mushawn again, but when the guard stopped in front of a cell with a short, slim redbone nigga, reading a comic book, Jamaal was greatly relieved. Neither knew it at the time, but they would become not only friends, but lovers as well. After getting acquainted with the new roommate, Jamaal wrote a long, four-page letter to Grandma and Grandpa to ask for their forgiveness.

With time off for good behavior, Jamaal stayed a total of seven years, eight months and twelve days in this manmade hellhole. He did not get raped once, but he did have numerous boyfriends and lovers over the years to ease the loneliness of incarceration. He also learned a valuable skill—baking, which he enjoyed very much.

Over the years, the only visitors were Grandma and Grandpa, along with AJ and Michael. They always came together and visited him over 21 times. Jamaal only heard from Inshallah once, and that was to blame him for miscarrying their baby, due to the stress he caused by raping Porsha. After eight years, the rape was a distant memory. Sitting in the rear seat of his grandparents Ford Explorer on the way back to Atlanta, Jamaal promised to walk the straight-and-narrow going forward, but that didn't last long.

After being fired from job after job, he drifted back to the ghetto thug life within a year of being released. He met some old acquaintances and started slanging rocks in Bankhead Courts. And now, three years after getting out of prison for rape and eight months after getting out of jail for shoplifting, the fool decided to steal a car, knowing that if he got caught, he would get charged as a Persistent Felony Offender or PFO. He didn't think selling the car would be much of a problem, because he was too seasoned and street-wise to get jammed.

Upon awakening the next morning, he peeked outside to see if the car was still there. Then took a piss and went back to bed beside the snoring, farting Sophia. Jamaal smiled to himself, thinking how much money a nice Volvo would bring. Yes, today would be a money-making day. While his girl was still, sleeping he couldn't resist taking the car out for a test drive.

Chapter 14
Sometimes Crime *Does* Pay

As soon as Precious woke up the next morning, she quickly dressed and drove up to the Kroger shopping center to see if somebody had taken the Volvo. When she saw the car wasn't there, the murderous tranny let out a big sigh of relief. It could only be better if the sucker who stole it would use David's' cell phone. Then the police could trace the number and have the unsuspecting fools arrested—not only for vehicular theft, but for murder as well. Whoever stole the car was going to get the surprise of his life when the police pulled up on them with lights flashing and guns drawn. Satisfied that her plan seemed to be working, Precious did a little grocery shopping.

****

Tammy woke up in a dazed and confused state resulting from tossing and turning all night. After watching the kids get on the school bus, she decided to take a sick day. With David missing, going to work was out of the question. As soon as the kids left, she started calling his cell again. But just like the more that 130 calls before, there was no answer.

Stressed and frantic, the grieving wife poured a glass of wine to calm her frazzled nerves. After finishing the glass in one gulp, she got dressed and went out looking for David. The amateur sleuth didn't know where to begin looking, so she headed toward Atlanta and his job at Clark Atlanta University. She talked to his colleagues, student assistants and even students on campus, but no one seemed to know anything.

Then she drove around the ghettos of Atlanta, hoping against hope to spot his car. It dawned on her that if she saw someone else driving his vehicle, it would mean he was probably dead. At noon, she felt hungry and pulled into the Checkers on Bankhead Highway in northwest Atlanta. Though not one to usually eat fast food, she hadn't eaten since yesterday so she was starving. She ordered the new Philly cheese steak sub and a large coke at the drive thru. Then she sat in the parking lot to rest and contemplate her next move.

Just as she was finishing the greasy, tasteless sandwich, a blue Volvo whizzed down the street. At first, she couldn't believe her puffy, sleepless eyes, so after taking a gulp of watered-down soda, she immediately followed the vehicle. The car was already a mile ahead, but after running two stop lights, she caught up with it at Bankhead and Mayson Turner Road. Nervous, she pulled up behind the vehicle, instantly recognizing it David's car from the license plate number.

Some ugly ass black nigga was driving the car, like his ass paid for it. At the next light, on the corner of Ashby Street, a cop was parked at the liquor store. Tammy tried desperately to get his attention by honking her horn and screeching into the parking lot. She jumped out of her car and ran over to the startled cop and pointed at the Volvo that was just turning down Ashby, thanks to the long light. Tammy told the cop that the car was stolen and her husband was missing.

Almost as soon as the words "stolen" were out of her mouth, the cop took off after the Volvo. Tammy followed, but at a much slower pace. In the distance, she could see the police car's flashing lights behind the speeding Volvo, and soon, both were out of sight as they sped through the busy traffic.

What she didn't see was that Jamaal Russell had slammed into a MARTA bus at the Ashby train station, wrecking the Volvo killing a little girl who happened to be crossing the street. While exiting the vehicle, he began shooting at the police, ran down into the station boarded a train with the cops right on his ass. Luckily, there weren't many passengers on the train car when the police ordered Jamaal to surrender. But the ones who were there started screaming and praying for neither side to start shooting.

Jamaal almost surrendered, but he knew a lifetime imprisonment awaited him if he did. So he took aim and emptied his glock in the direction of the two cracker policemen who had him cornered. Fortunate for the officers, Jamaal was a bad shot, but unlucky was the brotha who happened to be a victim of the car thief's' errant aim. One of Jamaal's bullets hit a male passenger as he wildly fired.

With the train still stopped and doors open, Jamaal tried to escape, but the brave officers gunned him down on the train platform, thus ended a thug's reign of terror.

When Tammy got close to the scene, she couldn't believe the carnage. A little girl was dead in the street, the Volvo was totaled, sitting haphazardly on the street after having lost its battle with the

bus. After identifying herself to one of the officers, she told him the stolen Volvo was her missing husband's car. Detectives quickly assumed that Jamaal had most like killed her husband and stolen the car.

Soon television cameras arrived, with reporters seeking to interview "the brave housewife who hunted this thug down"—at least that was the narrative that ran on all the local news stations that evening. With Jamaal dead, she worried that her husband's whereabouts might never be known.

Lying in bed that night with the DD and Tamika beside her, Tammy wondered if she did the right thing by going to the cops. What if she had decided to just follow the car to see where it was going? She felt responsible for the little black girl getting run over and killed. The little girl looked kind of like Tamika, or at least that's what the guilt told her. Tomorrow had to be better than today, she told herself just before nodding off. Today the kids had learned that their father was never coming home again.

****

Watching the news, Precious couldn't believe her good luck. Not only did she get away with murder, but the guy who everyone would think was the murderer was gunned down by the police. It couldn't have happened any better if it had been scripted by Hollywood writers.

Now, there was no way any of the murders could be traced back to her, and since the thug had a history of violence, the dumb-ass police would just close the case as "solved."

The big dick-tranny poured herself a double shot of vodka and orange juice and mockingly made a toast to some dumb nigga named Jamaal Russell. Since that this shit was taken care of, she'd start taking on new clients in the morning. Precious truly loved her job. After all, what could be better than selling cock and taking niggas' money?

THE END

ABOUT THE AUTHOR

My name is Miles Coleman. I was born in Hopkinsville, Ky. in 1963. After moving to Atlanta, I went from one dead end job to the next, and finally settled at Papa John's Pizza, where I became a delivery driver. In 1997, while on a delivery I was shot and paralyzed from the waist down. In 2008 I graduated from Georgia Perimeter College with a degree in journalism. After years of intense depression and anger, I decided to start writing and put my feelings down on paper. This is my first book.